THE THIEF WHO SAVED CHRISTMAS

ANGELA CASELLA

ALSO BY ANGELA CASELLA

Unlucky in Love

The Love Fixers

The Love Bandits

The Love Losers

The Love Destroyers (February 2025)

Spin-off Standalone

The Thief Who Saved Christmas

Finding You

You're so Extra

You're so Bad

You're so Basic

You're so Vain

You're so Phony (coming soon!)

Fairy Godmother Agency

A Borrowed Boyfriend

A Stolen Suit

A Brooding Bodyguard

A Reluctant Roommate

Bringing Down the House (Nicole and Damien's story)

Highland Hills

(co-written with Denise Grover Swank)

Matchmaking a Billionaire

Matchmaking a Single Dad

Matchmaking a Grump

Matchmaking a Roommate

Matchmaking a Player (novella) by Angela Casella (May)

Bad Luck Club

(co-written with Denise Grover Swank)

Love at First Hate

Jingle Bell Hell

Fraudulently Ever After

Matchmaking Mischief

Asheville Brewing

(co-written with Denise Grover Swank)

Any Luck at All

Better Luck Next Time

Getting Lucky

Bad Luck Club

Luck of the Draw (novella)

All the Luck You Need (prequel novella) by Angela Casella

To my parents—
I wrote this book partially in your basement. A million thanks for
giving us shelter after Hurricane Helene hit Asheville. Without your
support, this book wouldn't exist. Love you lots and lots.

CHAPTER ONE

RYAN

Let's be clear about one thing from the start: I'm an asshole. Always have been, probably always will be. If you're the type of person who's inclined to make excuses for assholes, I won't try to convince you otherwise. You can blame my parents if you'd like. My father took off before my twin brother, Jake, and I were born, and my mother abandoned us in a motel room for several days when we were four years old. She came back...eventually. But not until we'd already been picked up by Child Protective Services. When they made it clear she'd have to fight to get us back, she said she'd rather not.

The child psychologist New York State sent us to for a few months seemed to think that sort of thing could mess a kid up.

Maybe he had a point. To this day, Jake can't bear to be in a locked room, and I slipped into survival mode and stopped caring about anything but protecting my brother and myself.

So you can blame them, if you're inclined. Or you can blame Edmund Roark, the man who made us thieves.

To be fair, I only met the guy because I tried to pickpocket him in Central Park when I was thirteen years old. I had it in my head that I could steal enough money for Jake and I to pull a runner from our foster home and live alone, obviously dumb given the cost of rent in New York City. Even in former crack dens, it's expensive enough that no kid could afford it unless he stole the *Mona Lisa*.

I failed to pickpocket Roark, partly because he was a good half a foot taller than me and a faster runner. But also because he is a *very good* thief of *very fine* things. Given that he keeps a couple of goons on his bankroll at any given time, it could have been a painful lesson. But he asked me a few questions, which I answered because I was so scared I nearly pissed myself. Then he had his guys give me a few punches—fair's fair—and offered to teach Jake and me "the art."

At the time, I figured it was because he recognized the potential in me, like I could be the Captain America of thieves. No one had ever seen potential in me. My teachers all thought I was an idiot, and for my class superlative, I was voted Most Likely to End Up in Jail.

In eighth grade.

So it felt pretty damn good to have someone who was obviously successful see something in me. Jake felt the same way.

But as we got older, we figured out the score. We're identical twins—a gold mine for a man who's looking to con people out of their treasures. Get Twin One to turn on the charm, find out every damn thing he can about the treasure, like where it's kept and how it's guarded. Then send in Twin Two to make the grab.

Perfect alibi for Twin One, am I right?

I was Twin Two. Jake's a better actor, and I have poor impulse control but a better ability with locks.

You might think I'd get pissed about being used, but it wasn't a new feeling. From what I could tell, everyone on God's green earth used everyone else. It was a food chain, and you didn't want to be on the bottom, even if that meant climbing on a few heads to avoid it.

See? Asshole.

For years, Jake and I worked together for Roark, bringing in treasures for him. It was a challenge. A game. And I didn't mind much, because the people we robbed were wealthy, with plenty to spare.

But this story isn't about me being an asshole, or at least I hope it's not. It's about me deciding to do something decent for a change.

Of course, people don't just wake up one day and decide to be decent. You've got to fall really low for that message to sink in…

And that's exactly what happened to me.

RIGHT BEFORE CHRISTMAS LAST YEAR, my brother stopped talking to me. (If you're wondering why, let's just say it was my fault.)

On a related note, he told me he was going legit and probably leaving New York City. He made it clear that shit wouldn't be right between us until I turned over a new leaf too.

He seemed to really mean it this time, unlike the half a dozen other times he'd said things like: *I swear to God, Ryan, if you get me into any more messes, I'm done.* Or: *Why is there a groundhog in my apartment? You're not allowed up here without supervision.*

So when Roark called me the day before Christmas Eve and said he had a super important job for me, and if I didn't do it, he'd pull Jake back in, whether my brother liked it or not, I asked, "Where am I going and when?"

It just so happened that when he called, I was in the bathroom of my friend's bar, trying to scrub a cartoon dick off my face. Someone must have drawn it on me after I'd passed out in the back room. The air smelled like stale cigars and old vomit, the dick wasn't coming off my skin which suggested the involvement of a Sharpie. So, yeah, at that point I was down for anything that would get me the hell out of New York City for the holidays.

"You're going to steal Christmas," Roark said with a huff. He liked to amuse himself. Didn't matter to him whether anyone laughed at his jokes.

"That's not specific enough for me. I'm a simple guy," I said.

"You're going to The Crooked Quill bed and breakfast in Colonial Williamsburg, in Virginia, and you're going to steal an ornament for me."

Half the time, I wondered if the shit he sent us to grab was actually worth anything, or if he was just a rich dude who liked messing with people who'd pissed him off. Either way, he paid a finder's fee, and it was more than I could make working as a checkout clerk or a bartender. Unlike my brother, who at least had graphic design skills, I wasn't good at anything that lent itself to making money legally.

"You got a thing for Christmas suddenly?" I asked.

"I have a thing for money, Ryan. Javier will deliver your car and identity."

Javier was one of the guys who worked as Roark's hired muscle and errand boy. It wasn't a fancy gig, and he'd complained to me about it on a number of occasions. He was a good guy, Javier. We'd hung out at this particular bar several times, and he'd never once drawn a dick on my face.

"Who owns the B&B?" I asked, pushing my way out of the bathroom. The dick was still very much there, but I was too exhausted to care. No one was in the bar, so I walked toward the side exit, past the fake Christmas tree with its mini-alcohol-bottle ornaments... then swung back and checked to see if they were full. No dice. Holding the phone in place with my shoulder, I let myself out of the side door, which locked automatically when it was closed.

The first person I saw, of course, was a toddler girl with floppy blond hair and a headband with two bobbing Christmas trees on it. She pointed at the dick on my face and said, "What's that, Mommy?"

I grinned at her mother and saluted.

She gave me the finger.

God bless New York City.

Roark still hadn't answered—taking the whole dramatic pause thing too far, like usual—so I started walking toward my place, a railroad-style apartment I shared with a college kid named Billy.

"She's a little old lady," Roark finally said, amusement thrumming in his voice.

I cursed under my breath. "You want me to steal a Christmas ornament from a little old lady who runs a bed and breakfast?"

Sounded like a punishment, right?

"Good, you were listening," he said with a hoarse laugh. "It's a very valuable Christmas ornament."

Which only made it worse.

I darted across the street, not in the mood to wait for the light, and nearly got creamed by a yellow cab. The driver honked at me, making my headache an automatic ten times worse. "I don't like the sound of this, Roark."

"I don't care. If you don't do it, I'm going to make your brother—"

Make him pay, make him regret, make him dance like a puppet. Blah-dee-blah-blah-blah. I had a feeling I was going to be hearing a lot of threats involving Jake moving forward. Worse, I had a feeling they were going to work.

Sighing, I said, "Fine, whatever. It's not like I had any plans for the holiday."

"I knew you didn't, kid," he said, almost sounding sorry for me.

He should.

Normally, I'd spend the holiday with my brother. In fact, this would be the first Christmas we weren't spending together. But as I said, Jake wasn't talking to me, so I hadn't put up a single strand of twinkle lights. The little crappy plastic tree an ex-girlfriend had bought me was still packed up in one of the plastic crates next to my bed. Nowhere to store them. Billy wasn't much for Christmas either, so he hadn't done any decorating of his own.

"The information you need will be in a packet in the car. Do we understand each other?" Roark asked when I didn't say anything. He was always careful with what he said over the phone.

"Yeah," I told him, suddenly feeling my age. I was nearly thirty, and here I was, sharing a crappy apartment with a college kid, being exploited by a criminal five hundred times richer than me. Worse: it was all happening while I had a Sharpie dick on my face. It felt like a low moment.

I didn't know anything about low moments yet.

"Yeah," I agreed. "I'll do it."

CHAPTER TWO

RYAN

The next day I'd been rechristened Ryan Reynolds—Roark's idea of a cute joke—and was walking up to my room in The Crooked Quill with Edith Whitman, the owner. She looked like she'd been picked out of a casting call of hundreds to play the "sweet old grandma." Worse, she'd already insisted that *I* call her Grandma, as if she knew she was twisting the thumbscrews.

My conscience, which had been more or less asleep for most of my life, was prickling...especially since Grandma Edith didn't seem particularly well-off. The inn was nice enough, and I knew from the packet Roark had prepared for me that the building itself was worth a bundle, but the carpet wasn't much nicer than the one in my apartment building, which had probably seen its last update half a century ago, and some of the furniture in the lobby looked like it would collapse if a bird perched on it.

I'd only gotten a quick glance at the Christmas tree from the front window when I'd circled the place on foot. I hadn't gotten eyes on the ornament Roark wanted, but from the picture he'd provided, it didn't look like much—a smallish glass ball covered in spikes. Kind of like a ball from a sweetgum tree but red and white. The only way I could figure it was worth anything was if it was stuffed with something more valuable and probably illegal, but this little old lady sure didn't look like a drug peddler, and I'd never known Roark to mess with that stuff.

So maybe it was personal, although what this broad could have done to piss him off was anyone's guess.

"Grandma" led me up the stairs, stopping every three or four steps for a rest, taking so long I wanted to pick her up and carry her to the top for both of our sakes.

When we reached the landing, she led me to a door with a mini holiday wreath attached to it.

"This is it, dear," she said, breathing heavily.

I opened the door and saw a room like any other, with two beds —both of them too small—a bureau, a desk, and a small Christmas tree set up in the corner.

She was lingering in the doorway, though, like she wanted something, so I nodded toward it. "Nice tree."

Clearly, I'd read her right, because she glowed in response. "Oh, thank you. My granddaughter, Anabelle, decorated the inn for the holidays. She has a Christmas store, but online, you know. It's called It's Christmas Again. She repurposes old Christmas decorations no one wants anymore and makes them new again."

"Cool," I said, entering the room and depositing the duffel bag.

Still, the old lady hadn't budged, so I turned back to face her, feeling a weird prickle of guilt across my skin. Because she wasn't just little and old and kind of frail. She seemed lonely. I was liking this job less every minute.

"You know," she said slowly, as if she was about to deliver a chestnut of wisdom, "you have genitals drawn on your face."

Surprised laughter spilled from me. "Yeah. Someone drew it on my face when I was...asleep. It was in permanent marker, and I haven't been able to get it off."

"I'd wondered if you'd drawn it yourself," she remarked with a smile. The wrinkles around her mouth were deep and there were plenty of them, like she was a person who'd smiled a lot in her life. It made me like her more, and myself less.

"Nah." I shifted my weight between my legs. "I'm enough of a dickhead that I don't think I need to announce it with a picture." I cringed and tried to backpedal. "Sorry for the language, ma'am. Grandma."

Her smile grew wider. "I've been using adult language since before you could toddle on two feet, young man. And I also know a secret for removing permanent marker."

"No shit," I said, then gave her my best *oops* face.

"Come on down." She gave a weary sigh and glanced back at the staircase before taking a weak step toward it.

"Uh, is what you need down there?"

"Yes," she said with another sigh, "and I'll admit my legs aren't what they used to be. Anabelle keeps telling me I need to employ a helper, but I'm sorry to say business hasn't been brisk lately. My dear granddaughter helped me update the website, but it's not up and running yet. You're my only guest until after Christmas."

Dammit. This was further proof that Roark's story about the ornament was bullshit. He was just doing this to punish me. *Want to put Ryan in his place? Make him steal from a little old woman on Christmas. That'll teach him.*

"I'm going to carry you down the stairs," I say.

"Excuse me?"

"I'm going to carry—"

"My eyes may have given out, but there's nothing wrong with my ears. The last time a man offered to carry me on a staircase was just after I'd gotten married."

"I'll marry you if you insist. But I don't think carrying needs to come with a lifetime commitment."

She snorted. "I'm sure you're a lovely young man. But I have a firm rule against marrying men with genitals drawn on their faces."

"You're much too young for me," I tease, "but if you help me fix the problem with my face, I might stand a chance at charming someone else."

We left the room together, and I closed the door behind us and turned toward her. I didn't know shit about carrying people, so I picked her up under the armpits and started walking. She couldn't weigh much more than my duffel bag. It was cold outside, and not much warmer in here, yet I felt sweat beading at my temples. I couldn't take something from this woman...

"What on earth are you doing?" she asked, affronted, and the dozens of romance movies I'd been made to watch by a long stream of disappointed women came back to me. Feeling like an idiot, I picked her up like a princess and carried her down the stairs.

She seemed amused by the whole thing and chuckled softly as I set her down at the bottom. Reaching up, she patted me on the cheek. "You're a good boy."

It was like she knew she was twisting my heartstrings. I trailed after her like a lost little kid latching on to the first friendly face they see as she walked to her desk by the front door. She took out a few alcohol wipes and, giving me a stern look, started rubbing one of them across my cheek with as little self-consciousness as if she were my mother. Not that my mother would have given a shit about a thing like that. After she finished with one wipe, she assessed my face and then started in with another. "You shouldn't be drinking that much around friends who'd do a thing like that. Friends like that aren't much good at all."

"You've got that right," I muttered as I took the wipes from her.

It was probably time to go back upstairs. I could come down later to scope out the tree. But I found myself wondering what this nice old broad was doing alone on Christmas Eve. I didn't like it.

"Where's Anabelle tonight?" I asked.

"Why? Would you like to draw a phallus on her face?" she asked, completely straight-faced.

"No," I said, laughing. "Just wondering why you're working on

Christmas Eve. Especially if you've got a granddaughter who has a thing for Christmas."

Moving slowly, as if her whole body hurt, she edged out from behind the desk and motioned for me to join her. I followed her into the room with the Christmas tree, which she'd probably call the parlor.

It should've felt like a windfall—she was going to lead me straight to where I needed to go—but I didn't feel good about it at all.

There was a credenza just inside the door, with a thermos sitting on a shiny metal plate on top, next to a couple of Frosty the Snowman mugs. She uncapped the thermos and poured something into the mugs—hot chocolate, by the scent—while I scoped out the tree.

It was large enough that two guys must have had to haul it in, and densely decorated from top to bottom with lights, tinsel, and old-fashioned ornaments. Looking for the sweetgum ornament would be like trying to find one specific needle in a needle factory.

You're just looking for excuses to fail.

No one could call you out quite like the voice in your head.

Edith pressed one of the mugs into my hand, and I reflexively took a sip, lifting my eyebrows when I tasted the Baileys.

Edith shrugged. "We're both alone on Christmas Eve, son. I suppose we might as well make the most of it."

I could have pointed out that we weren't alone because we had each other. But she didn't seem like a woman who'd stand for bullshit, and truthfully, I would have been disappointed if she had. So instead, I touched my mug to hers and followed her to an old-fashioned, wooden-legged sofa facing the tree.

She lowered herself onto the gold-and-red-striped upholstery first, and I joined her.

For a moment, we sipped in silence, looking at the tree, my eyes moving over it slowly. But I couldn't focus. The question of why she was here alone kept bothering me. "Why'd you have the hot chocolate out if you weren't expecting company?"

"One never knows when a Christmas miracle will present itself." She said it seriously, and I didn't even feel like cracking a joke in response.

Another few seconds of silence passed, comfortably enough, and then she blurted, "My son is an idiot, and my daughter-in-law is no better. They *did* invite me to celebrate Christmas with them this evening, but I told them no. I don't hate myself. Keeping the inn open was a handy excuse."

Snorting, I raised my mug to hers for another tap.

But she wasn't smiling. She pointed to a framed photograph hanging on the wall opposite the tree, which I hadn't noticed because I'd been trying to look for the sweetgum ornament without appearing to look for it.

The photograph was of a woman about my age with long, wavy brown hair and eyes so big they made me think of a baby deer. I instantly wanted to protect her. The thought was ridiculous, because I'd never successfully protected anyone. I'd only accepted this job to protect Jake, and I couldn't even do that right, because I was getting the feeling I wouldn't be able to bring myself to steal from *Grandma*. Especially since she was this fawn-eyed woman's real grandmother.

I cleared my throat to make sure my voice came out right and said, "I'm guessing that's your granddaughter Anabelle?" I liked the musical sound of her name. It suited her. There was something elegant and sweet about her face.

She looked like she'd see right through me.

"Yes," Edith said warmly. "She isn't stupid at all, thank goodness. I'm grateful some traits skip a generation."

"Was your husband stupid?" I asked, because Jake wasn't around to tell me to stop running my mouth.

"Oh, yes. Terribly."

I laughed in delight, then felt a fresh rumble of guilt move through me like a garbage truck backing up and preparing to dump its load.

She sipped more from her mug, then said, "She's with a young man who's all wrong for her. That's where she is tonight. Nothing would do but to visit *his* family for the holiday. I'm worried he'll propose."

"What's wrong with him?"

"He's a hotelier."

I was unclear on how that would automatically make him an asshole, but I had a feeling I'd agree with Edith on this one. She was a solid, salt-of-the-earth sort—if she said someone was a prick, he was a prick.

"I never stay at hotels," I lied, lifting my hot chocolate for a sip. "Bed and breakfasts all the way."

She gave me a measured look. "You're a good liar, you know. And what are you doing here, all alone, *Ryan Reynolds*?"

She obviously knew the name was bullshit, and I didn't have it in me to try to convince her otherwise. "The only person I care about wants nothing to do with me, that's why. I figured why not come here? They say it's nice during the holidays. I could be anywhere, though, and it would be all the same to me."

Before checking in, I'd walked around Williamsburg some. Seen the big Christmas tree they'd hoisted up in Market Square and strolled around the college campus and the colonial area. Checked out the jokers walking around in their tri-cornered hats and stockings, pretending it was colonial times. Everything seemed to have a red bow on it, like the place itself thought it was a gift. And you know what? It was kind of nice. It felt like Christmas here in a way it hadn't at my apartment.

Still hadn't made me merry.

"Why does this person want nothing to do with you?" Edith asked, studying me with sharp eyes.

The question felt like a punch to the gut, but I was still half-heartedly planning on stealing Edith's prized possession. The least I could do was answer her truthfully.

"Because I ruined his life."

That was the conclusion I'd drawn from what little Jake had told me. I was the one who'd pulled him into our arrangement with Roark. If I hadn't tried to pickpocket the jerk, we never would have met him in the first place. We'd be...well, I wouldn't have made it as an accountant or a store manager or anything like that, but my brother might have.

"And is your lover the one who drew the genitals on your face?" Edith asked, giving my cheek a glance. Maybe a ghost of the dick was still there, outlined on my skin.

I snorted. "Jake's not my lover. He's my brother. I'm straight. But I haven't found a woman who's willing to put up with my bullshit either."

"Huh. You're a late bloomer, maybe," Edith said, turning away. I followed her gaze to the tree, and a red-and-white sunburst caught my eye. The damn sweetgum ornament.

Something strange happened in my chest as I watched it refract light from the white bulbs strung on the tree, but Edith didn't seem to notice anything was up with me.

After a moment's silence, she released a gust of air and said, "One thing's for sure. You've got time to change things. I envy you that."

I glanced at her sharply. There was something about the way she'd said it...

She nodded in acknowledgment, her bun grazing the top of the couch. "They gave me two years. Maybe three. I only hope I have time to convince Anabelle not to marry that fool. He'd never accept her for who she really is. I was in a marriage like that for half a century, Ryan, and I wouldn't wish it for her."

I felt the news more deeply than I would have thought possible, given that Edith was a complete stranger I'd known for an hour.

"Shit, I'm really sorry," I said.

She huffed and leaned back. "Try not to do anything you'll have to feel sorry for later. That's one thing I've learned."

"Then I'm definitely fucked," I said, and instantly apologized again, getting an amused look.

"I'm old enough to have heard it all, you know."

"You're not so old," I lied.

"I am, but I'm nothing compared to this house. You know, some of the things in here go back to the very start of this country. You wouldn't think it to look at them." She pointed directly at the sweetgum ball. "That ornament has been passed down in my family for years. My son brought it to that *Antiques Roadshow* thing this past fall. Didn't even ask me, of course. They told him it was worth hundreds of thousands of dollars."

Surprise kicked me in the balls. Hundreds of thousands for that puny little bit of glass. Some people had too much money to spare, money spilling out of their pockets and bank accounts. Money they didn't know what to do with. It was the only explanation I could think of for why a person would blow a wad of cash on something that was going to hang, barely noticed, on a Christmas tree.

Maybe this brings us back to my point about being an asshole, but I wouldn't feel so bad about taking money from a person like that. I would feel like shit on the bottom of Satan's horse foot if I took something from *her*.

"Who'd pony up that much for an ornament?" I asked.

"Someone stupid," she said, hoisting her mug. I tapped it with mine yet again, sensing a deep thrum of understanding between us. It had been a while since I'd gotten along with someone like this. Other than Jake, most of my friendships and relationships were transactional and brief. Getting drinks. Having a laugh. Hooking up. Getting into trouble together.

"Someone stupid," I agreed after a moment. "You made him give it back?"

"I did. He wanted to sell it and share the profits. I told him I'd turn him in for theft if he didn't bring it home to the inn, where it belongs."

"Which is why you're not spending Christmas with your son and his wife," I said with a half-smile.

"Oh, there are dozens of reasons. Maybe a hundred. Now, tell me about your brother."

The last couple of months of being a stranger to my brother— the one person I told everything—must have screwed me up more than I'd realized, because I did exactly as she asked. I told her about growing up in crappy foster homes, where we were treated like we were only worth the extra dollars we brought in each month, only to fall into an adult life that wasn't much better. I didn't cop to doing anything illegal, for obvious reasons, but I shared a lot of the truth with her nonetheless.

And she told me more about Anabelle, who was, of course, an absolute angel who was much too good for the hotelier. As I sat there listening, my gaze kept darting back to that photo. To the determined tilt of Anabelle's chin and those big eyes. I decided that while she looked sweet, for certain, she also looked tough.

It was late afternoon by then, and Edith announced she was making me Christmas dinner. I didn't say no, because I'd already decided I was going to leave in the night and never come back. Maybe it would get Jake in trouble, maybe not. But I wouldn't steal from this woman. I couldn't.

I understood now why he'd struggled so much with being Twin One. Getting to know the people you intended to screw over made it twice as hard. Thrice.

A couple of hours later, Edith and I ate Christmas dinner together—a real dinner, with roasted potatoes and broccoli and an honest-to-God ham. Afterward, at her insistence, we bundled up and went for a walk on Duke of Gloucester Street. It was cold, but not as cold as it would have been in New York, and the whole street was lined with glowing twinkle lights and those big red bows. Other people were milling around, singing Christmas carols and drinking hot chocolate, generally making merry. I have to say it was pleasant. The best Christmas Eve I could remember having.

I'd never had any family other than Jake. None of our blood relations had offered to take us in when we were little. No grand-mothers, aunts, or uncles had come forward. Not a single one. We'd only had our various foster parents, who'd seen us as a job, and Roark, who'd seen us as a paycheck.

Edith was like the two grandmas I'd never had.

After we returned from our walk, we said goodnight to each other and she kissed me on the cheek.

"You'll grow up just fine, Ryan," she told me, as if I weren't already fully grown.

I waited until two in the morning to head downstairs with my pack. The Christmas lights were still glowing in the parlor, the soft white light spilling into the hall. I wasn't going to take the ornament. But I wanted to say goodbye to the little ball of glass that was about to screw up my life.

I entered the room and approached the tree, coming to a stop a few feet away. My gaze narrowed on the red-and-white sweetgum ball. A pretty little thing, to be sure, but I didn't think much of anyone who'd waste their money on it. I *did* think a lot of Edith, however.

Satisfied with my decision, I turned to go—and stopped cold, because Edith was standing in the doorway. She was wearing an old-fashioned dressing gown, complete with a satin hair net. Her huge glasses were perched on her nose as she watched me, making me feel like the green grump in that Dr. Seuss story.

My heart lurched, but I hadn't been caught doing anything wrong.

"You move like a cat," I commented.

"My bones disagree with you. Are you planning on leaving?"

I adjusted the strap of the duffel bag on my shoulder, needing something to do with my hands. "Yes."

Her gaze still on me, she said, "You came here for the starburst ornament. I'd wondered if someone would come after that program aired. I told my fool boy he'd set me up for it."

"You should have an alarm system," I said.

"Would it matter? Any worthwhile thief would be able to disable it."

"But it would make it harder."

I took a step toward her—because the exit was that way, and I was guessing she'd prefer me to leave—and she instantly recoiled.

Something twisted in my chest. She thought I was going to hurt her. This little old woman who'd treated me like family all night thought I was going to hurt her.

It was a low moment, is what I'm saying.

"I'd never hurt you, Edith," I said, my voice as urgent as my racing pulse. "I don't hurt people."

"But you *do* steal from them."

I could have lied. I wasn't Twin One, but I had plenty of experience with lying when the situation called for it. But this day had split me open in ways I didn't understand. Or maybe it had just deepened the wound from my brother turning his back on me.

"I work for a man who hires me to take things, yeah, and he sent me here. But I'm not going to do it. That's why I'm leaving. I just..." I scratched my head. "I wanted to take one last look at the damn thing."

"What will happen to you if you don't bring it to him?" she said pointedly, her eyes taking my measure from behind her big glasses. Or maybe they weren't. I remembered what she'd said about being nearly blind.

"I don't know," I said honestly. "He threatened my brother. But my brother wouldn't want me to do this either. He's better than me. Always has been."

She was quiet for a long moment, studying me in the glow of the tree lights. Finally, she said, "You really will grow up to be a fine man someday. I can tell."

I huffed a bitter laugh. "I wish I shared your confidence."

"Take the starburst ornament. Take it, but I expect you to come back next Christmas. Come back, and tell me you've changed your life and made up with your brother. I'll be waiting to hear it."

Disbelief swallowed me like a black hole. This woman had threatened to turn her son in for taking the little ornament onto *Antiques Roadshow*, and she was just going to *give* it to me?

It would solve a major problem for me, no doubt, but I couldn't accept it. I'd already decided I was going to do something decent, dammit.

She stuck her hand out, her wrinkled chin held high, and I felt powerless to do anything but step forward and take the ornament, careful not to hold on too tightly. She squeezed my hand and then released it, nodding to herself as if she'd come to some conclusion she agreed with.

"I'll wrap it up for you."

"You're going to wrap it up for me?" I asked in shock as my whole world ripped open. This wasn't what experience had taught me to be true. People didn't just give you valuable things, ever. You had to take them. You had to trick your way to success.

Her sidelong glance held surprising humor. "I said you could take it, not break it."

"I can't possibly go along with this."

"It's a Christmas gift, Ryan. But there are strings. I meant what I said. You'll come back here next December and tell me what you did to turn your life around." She gave me that same creased-cheek smile as earlier. "And I hope to tell you that I succeeded in vanquishing that hotelier."

Thank you felt too small.

Thank you felt like nothing.

So I nodded, and tried to swallow the blockage in my throat. "I promise you, Edith Whitman, I'll be back next year."

"And I'll hold you to it," she said. "December 1ˢᵗ." She said it so assuredly, even though she didn't know my real name or where I lived, or have any meaningful way of pulling me back except my word. She was treating my promise like it meant something, which made me want it to mean something.

"Merry Christmas, Ryan," she added.

Then she wrapped up the ornament and sent me off into the night.

Something inside of me was broken and reborn, and I knew I'd be back. I *knew* it. Because Edith Whitman had changed my life.

CHAPTER THREE

ANABELLE

Eleven months later

Tuesday, December 2, 23 days until Christmas

> *Santas sold today: 5*
> *Santas made or purchased today: 7*

It's Tuesday afternoon on December 2nd.

Ryan Reynolds is officially late.

"He's already one day late," I whisper to my cat, Saint Nick, as he circles the claw-footed wooden legs of my chair. "I trusted Grandma Edith implicitly, but I don't think much of a man who can't be bothered to keep his commitments."

He meows in agreement, and I glance back at my laptop screen. I've gotten carried away at estate sales lately, hence my Santa-overflow problem.

The thing is...after my grandmother died, I've had a hard time saying no to elderly dead women.

That probably came out wrong. What I mean is that I feel a gush of emotion whenever I go to an estate sale and see a woman's holiday treasures collected into plastic bins or falling-apart boxes, unwanted by her survivors.

This creates an irrepressible need in me to rescue them.

The problem is that most of this stuff really is junk—plastic Santas without the correct number of fingers and toes, Santas dressed in hula skirts, or Santas who dance drunkenly to music if a sticky button is pressed. Ornaments that are cracked or should be. Sometimes I can reuse the parts to make a better whole, and sometimes I have to admit that I have trash on my hands.

Which doesn't make it easier to let it go, because each of these things was treasured by some little old lady, who would pack it lovingly into its box every holiday—only for one of those holidays to end up being her last.

It's been a month, today, since my grandmother died of heart failure. *Of course* it was heart failure. If she'd needed a kidney, I would have given her one. Bone marrow, too. I'd have given her half my heart if it would have done any good, but much to my disappointment, science and medicine have not progressed that far.

Grandma Edith died on a mild day—a high of 60 degrees, even in November. After we left the hospital, my parents offered to buy me lunch, but I turned them down. Instead, I parked in Colonial Williamsburg and walked down Duke of Gloucester Street, fondly nicknamed DoG Street, in a haze. Everywhere I looked, there were people outside going on strolls and kids playing with those purposeless hoops and sticks the stores market to tourists who feel obligated to buy them.

My grandmother, who'd had a love for efficiency, would probably have approved of life moving on so quickly, but it had felt like an affront to see such normalcy. So much so that I asked one woman, who was drinking boba tea from a disposable plastic container, "What's wrong with you?" in a shaking voice.

She dropped the boba tea, the little tapioca pearls bouncing slightly on the cobblestones. But either she hadn't been taught to clean up after herself or she thought I was mentally imbalanced, because she hurried away, leaving the mess.

I cleaned it up as best I could, because Grandma Edith had always believed in leaving a place better than you found it. I'd started crying while I was doing it, which had felt like a relief—*yes, you have emotions, Anabelle, and someone just gave Sadness the wheel.*

"Oh, it's only spilled tea," said a woman with puffy curled hair and an overpowering scent of pumpkin spice. "No use crying over spilled tea, sweetie." She clucked her tongue as she hovered a couple of steps from where I was trying to collect the tapioca pearls.

"My grandmother died," I said through a sudden torrent of tears. "She died, and now I'm alone."

The sliminess of the tapioca added to my grief, because what in the world was I doing, anyway? I *hated* touching slimy things, and that woman's saliva was probably all over it, and everything was a mess.

I cried harder.

In response, the stranger moved closer as if she was about to hug me, which was enough to jolt me out of my meltdown. I backed up several paces, clutching the cup to my chest. "Oh, please don't do that."

"Are you okay, dear?"

"No, I can't possibly hug a stranger."

She gaped at me. I was used to people gaping, though. That's what happened when you are a weird person who says weird things —a revelation I'd had years ago, which had made life a lot simpler for me. So I walked off, barely aware of my surroundings until I found myself at the door of The Crooked Quill. Using the key she'd given me years ago, I let myself in. Went to her desk. Sat in her chair and breathed in the smell of her. Lavender and a hint of vanilla. I had the aching awareness that it would fade soon and then *she* would fade—only in my own memory would she remain sharp, because I was Anabelle Whitman, and I never forgot anything that had ever happened to me.

Ask Rob Mertz, who'd pushed me into a pile of horse poop on our third-grade field trip to Colonial Williamsburg.

I know. How wildly exciting for a class of kids who live in Williamsburg to go to Colonial Williamsburg. But I digress...

I'm fairly sure adult Rob regrets his behavior on that fateful day, but only because he had the audacity to ask me out a few years ago, as if a woman could forget and forgive such a thing.

Sitting in my grandma's chair, I tried to catch my breath, slow inhales, slow exhales, but then I noticed the envelope lined up with the corner of the desk. My name was on the front in her hand-writing:

Anabelle Edith Whitman

"Oh, I don't think I'm ready for this," I said to no one in particular, rapping my fingers against the desk's surface.

Sucking in a breath, I opened the letter. It was thick, and there was another, smaller, envelope inside of it.

Anabelle,

Everyone will know soon enough, but the inn is yours.

So is everything else I have left.

It's not a lot.

You know, of course, that I gave the sunburst orna-ment away, and I'd do it again to keep your father from selling it the instant my body turned cold. There are a few other things you might be able to sell online to raise money, should you decide to keep the inn open. The armoire in my bedroom is an original, and so is the drinks cabinet in the parlor. Some of my jewelry has also been passed down and might be worth a penny or two.

It's all yours, my dear. Do what you like with it. I only want you to be happy.

The one thing I will ask is that you never, ever give or sell the inn to Weston. The Crooked Quill is and always has been a family place. For it to be owned by a corporation that buys paper-thin sheets and doesn't believe in deep cleaning or unprocessed breakfast foods is <u>unthinkable</u>.

I also ask that you reserve the enclosed envelope for a man who's calling himself Ryan Reynolds. You can expect him to arrive on December 1st of this year. He will likely want to book a room. I put him in Room B last time. But if you decide to close the inn, you can refer him to The Peddler and the Pig across the way. The boy may be upset, so try to be a friend to him, Anabelle. He will need one. YOU will need one.

He'll probably want to pay you in cash. Accept it, if you will.

Most of all, I hope you will be a friend to yourself, my dear. Your light shines brighter than you know.

With all my love,
Grandma Edith

Did this send me down a fruitless research black hole to try to find out who Ryan Reynolds could be?

Absolutely.

I learned more about *Two Guys, A Girl, and a Pizza Place* than I ever wanted to know, and it turns out there are many people named

Ryan Reynolds. There's probably one in every town in the United States. Five in every town in Canada.

I could have opened the mysterious letter, of course, but it would have felt like an affront. Possibly also a federal crime. She wrote his name on it, after all, and asked me to deliver it.

In any case, despite Grandma Edith's assurance that I could sell the B&B if I wanted to, I've kept it open. I had to. Closing it would have been like kicking those boxes full of other people's beloved treasures. Never. Not on my watch.

To be frank, I'm not very good at running an inn, a fact my parents enjoy pointing out to me every time they see me. I like most people individually, but in groups they can be overwhelming. Loud, demanding, pushy.

My boyfriend, Weston, also enjoys pointing out my inadequacies to me, and has made eleven and a half offers to buy the inn and absorb it into his hotel group, Comfort Zone.

The one-half offer is due to me cutting him off and telling him that I would never kiss him again, ever, if he let the rest of his sales pitch leave his mouth.

There are only two people who support me. One is Cynthia, who worked part-time for my grandmother and now does the same for me. I'm grateful that she makes breakfast for my guests, since I am an appallingly bad cook.

I've never understood why. I'm good at following instructions, and do it to the letter, but what I make never turns out the way it's supposed to. It's like there's a magic to cooking that I just don't possess.

Sometimes I think there's a magic to life that I just don't possess, which is why I've chosen to find it in Christmas.

The other person who supports me is my good friend Jo, who runs an online Christmas shop for vintage holiday finds: Santa Knows. We met while bidding against each other in an auction, and now we talk multiple times a day, every day. Of course, Weston would say we don't actually talk every day—we write. But for someone who thinks best in written words, it's the ideal friendship.

Thinking of Jo makes me think of my little workshop upstairs in my room. A couple of hours of crafting might be exactly what I need. I'm about to get up when the front door creaks and then opens with a gust of cold air, the bell above it ringing.

The man who just stepped inside is objectively handsome, with wavy light-brown hair, hazel eyes that look like sunbursts, and a leather jacket that is...well, cool (although my friend Jo says that calling something cool immediately makes you less cool). He's carrying a leather duffel bag.

There's a something look in his eyes as they move over me.

I know it's Ryan Reynolds.

I know it instantly, in my gut.

CHAPTER FOUR

ANABELLE

Guests with fake names: 1

I feel a wave of sympathy for this tardy stranger. Late or not, he must have cared for my grandmother. I'll have to share the news with him—a thought that fills my stomach with sick dread.

"Are you Ryan?" I ask.

There's a look of abject shock on his face, as if he can't quite believe what's happening.

Right. I may know who he is, but he has no idea who I am.

I set down Saint Nick and rise from my chair.

"My grandmother told me someone would be coming," I explain, stepping out from behind the desk. "I'd assumed it wouldn't be Ryan Reynolds the celebrity."

Saint Nick gets to our guest first, and to my surprise, he hisses at Ryan, his stripy orange fur puffing up like he's seen his arch-nemesis cat, Fiddlesticks, from three houses down. "Oh goodness...he's never like this with anyone."

Saint Nick bats at Ryan with claws extended, getting in a few good swipes, much to my horror. Those claws of doom hurt, but he usually only whips them out at bathtime.

"Lucky me," Ryan mutters, retreating a step toward the door.

His voice is a bit rough but still smooth—like the fine-grade sandpaper I use on some of the old things I make new.

I swoop down and grab my cat, who yowls in protest, his fur standing up like he's a puffer fish.

A line appears between Ryan's eyebrows. "Where's your grandmother?"

I take a deep breath. "Let's go sit in the parlor for a moment."

Something hardens in his gaze, and I know he knows. A gasp of air escapes me, because *I understand* the pain he's feeling. It's been sitting on my shoulders for weeks, making itself at home in my stiff muscles and dry eyes.

"Behave," I whisper into Saint Nick's furry ear and then set him down again.

He slinks away and then dashes behind the human-sized wooden nutcracker doll that stands guard behind my desk, but not before glaring at Ryan over his shoulder.

I slip the sealed envelope from the top of Grandma Edith's desk into the pocket of my cardigan and lead Ryan into the parlor. He brings his bag with him.

I've tried to create an inviting and fun atmosphere, but I've only had a couple of guests come down to Hot Chocolate Happy Hour, held each day at 5 p.m., to enjoy hot chocolate from the carafe on the credenza, seasoned with some of the liqueurs stored beneath it. My grandmother always kept hot chocolate for guests at this time of year. *It's the little things, Belle,* she'd say with a grin.

In the summer, she served sweet tea. Hot chocolate in the winter. Sometimes warm spiced cider in the fall. My memories of my childhood all seem to be organized around which drink was being served at the inn, a thought that makes me smile.

"Wow," Ryan says as we walk in, his head swiveling as if it's on one of those selfie sticks. "You've...made some changes."

I can't read the expression on his face, but his tone suggests he finds the changes off-putting. My personal Santa collection now lives in the parlor. All one hundred and seven of my merry men, an army of stuffed, stone, wood, plastic, and otherwise crafted Santas. Many of them are vintage, rescued from estate sales or bargain bins. Several of them are worth quite a bit of money, although none, of course, are as valuable as the starburst ornament that Grandma Edith gave away to a fellow collector to "spite" my father. Dad's word.

Grandma Edith informed him about her dispensation of the ornament at the end of February, after she told everyone about her terminal diagnosis. Because, of course, my father being my father, the ornament was the first thing he asked about. He now goes to every advertised estate sale in the hope that he'll find it and whoever took it has no idea of its true worth.

I try not to get offended by Ryan's reaction to my Santas. He's hardly the only one to have a knee-jerk reaction to my collection. But there's no denying the cards are stacking up against this mysterious Ryan Reynolds. First, he's a day late. Second, my sweet cat hates him. This is the third strike against him.

I give an aggrieved sniff. "It's a renowned collection. They've been written up in *House & Garden.*"

He angles his head, checking out the full magnitude of the collection. "No shit."

"Excuse me?"

He clears his throat. "Sorry. That's...uh...great. Not really much of a magazine guy, but I've heard of that one before."

He's probably thinking of *Better Homes & Gardens*, but I won't correct him. That *would* be impressive. "Some of my Santas date back to colonial days."

His gaze sweeps around the room again, lingering on one of my wooden Santas, whose face has been worn down by time. "Yeah, I can tell."

Now, that's just rude.

Grandma Edith asked you to be his friend, I remind myself.

So I take another big breath and turn toward him. How do I do this? Do I take his hands?

At a loss, I decide the best path forward is honesty. "I have some bad news, and I can't think of a nice way to say it."

"There probably isn't a nice way," he says, his mouth flat.

He already knows.

I gulp, then blurt out, "My grandmother passed away last month."

The words tie a knot in my stomach. *Passed away*, like she was a carton of milk we had to throw out because it soured. But he's right —there's no good way to say someone has died. No good way of sharing the way I felt that day, when I found myself cleaning up a complete stranger's spilled tapioca pearls.

Ryan works his jaw, and I don't have to be good at reading people to know this news is hurtful to him. Maybe even devastating. That makes me like him more. The castle of cards I've been building against him sways as if in a breeze, wanting to collapse.

"She's really dead?" he asks in an undertone.

"Yes," I say, gripping the edge of the striped upholstery to ground myself. "I was just thinking 'passed away' is a terrible euphemism."

He rubs his stubbled jaw. "I'm damn sorry to hear it. I thought very highly of her."

His gaze lifts to the Christmas tree, then stretches beyond it, to a framed photo of Grandma Edith I hung up last week. Gesturing to it, he says, "That used to be a photo of you."

I startle a little, thrown by the thought that he must have sat here with my grandmother at some point, the two of them looking at that photo of me together. What had she said to him?

I know what my parents would have said. *That's Anabelle. She looks normal, but don't let appearances deceive you.*

I rub the tips of my fingers against my thumb to release some anxiety. "Well, it would have felt a little conceited to keep a photo of myself hanging on the wall."

"I liked it. I like this one too." His gaze finds it again and clings. "Maybe you should both be up there. The ladies of The Crooked Quill."

I smile for a second, but it droops. I guess I'm the only lady of The Crooked Quill now, a depressing thought for everyone.

"Why'd she name it that, anyway?" he asks, shifting his attention to me.

"Would you like to hear the story Grandma Edith used to tell?"

"Please."

"She said it was about one of our ancestors who had a...well...a crooked quill. You know. Not the writing kind. But my father says it's because this place started as a print shop."

"I like her story better."

Sighing, I say, "I should mention now that Grandma Edith left a note for you. I haven't opened it, of course."

I tug it out of my pocket and hand it to him. He takes it from me, his hand glancing off mine—and an unexpected sensation ripples through me. Not disgust, but awareness. Probably because his hands are a bit rough, reminding me again of that soft-grade sandpaper. Voice like it, hands like it. He's a man who's all rough edges. I'm not used to that. Weston sees a manicurist once every two weeks.

Ryan sucks on his bottom lip, appearing to hesitate. It occurs to me that he might prefer to read his note alone, privately, so I smile at him and say, "Why don't you make yourself comfortable? You can have some hot chocolate while you read it. I'll be at my desk."

He nods, but before I can get up, he reaches over and captures my hand. Shock spirals through me as he gazes into my eyes. His focus is intense, and normally I'd look away, but I'm transfixed, frozen as surely as if I'd been turned into an ice sculpture.

"I'm so sorry for your loss, Anabelle. She told me how close you were. I'd thought..." He runs his other hand through his mussed hair. "I'd hoped I'd be able to see her again. Both of you. In fact, I've been thinking about it all year."

"How did you know her?" I say, then realize with a jolt that I'm still holding his hand. Worse, my fingers have started to slide across his skin, seeking out the different texture. I drop my grip and shift my gaze to his shirt—black, like the coat.

"It's a long story," Ryan says gruffly as he finally lowers the duffel bag to the floor. It lands with a heavy plop. He sits down on the striped sofa.

"And you don't want to share it," I deduce, nodding. I'm disappointed but not really surprised. He may have known Grandma Edith, but he doesn't know me. "That's okay."

It's not, but I get the sense it will have to be.

"Another day, maybe."

"That sounds like a nice way of saying never," I observe. It's one of those truths I should have left unsaid, but as usual, I don't realize my error until it's already left my mouth.

I nod again and start to retreat from the room, giving him space. But I glance back at him from the doorway, taking in his head bent over my grandmother's last words, his lips moving slightly as if he's reading it aloud. His eyelashes are a deep black, a pleasing contrast to his lighter hair. It makes a person want to trace them with a fingertip to see if any ink comes off.

Weston's eyelashes are short and stubby—a thought that instantly feels unfair, even though an observation cannot, by nature, be fair or unfair.

I find myself wanting to do something for Ryan, to help him, so I go to the credenza and pour him a cup of hot chocolate and tip some Baileys into it, the way Grandma Edith always did.

I bring it over, and only then realize you shouldn't make assumptions about things like alcohol consumption. Something I should probably know as an innkeeper.

"You're not an alcoholic are you?"

He nearly drops the letter as he glances up, his eyes wide before they settle on the mug. His lips edge up. "I don't think so, but I guess it depends on who you ask."

It's not a no. I hang on to the mug.

He gives a low laugh. "I'm not an alcoholic, Anabelle. Although I may be by the time I finish reading this letter."

I hand over the mug, and his fingers brush mine again. Suddenly, I feel embarrassed and hot behind the ears. Maybe because he's watching me with that slightly amused expression. Still, I don't turn away until he lifts the mug to his mouth for a sip, his lips pressing to the place where mine usually do.

He's still smiling as he lowers the mug. "Just like your grandmother made it."

Emotion presses through me.

I'm tempted to stay in the parlor. To peer over Ryan's shoulder as he reads the note so I can experience, through him, the last words my grandmother will ever say.

But I nod and say, "She knew best," before turning back toward the door.

It's been an intense afternoon, though, so I stop to pour myself some hot chocolate with Baileys too before I return to my desk and give him his privacy.

Saint Nick is roaming around my chair in agitation.

"You don't like him, huh?" I say as I set my mug down on the desktop and stoop to pick him up. He swats at my hand, giving me an affronted look that suggests he's doing some very important work, thank you very much, and doesn't need the interruption.

I wake my laptop from sleep and try to work, slowly sipping on the cocoa to calm my nerves. It doesn't work. I'm very aware of Ryan Reynolds sitting in the other room, reading that note.

I'm deeply curious about what it says.

I'm deeply curious about *him*.

About fifteen minutes later, which seems like a very long time to read a letter, Ryan approaches the desk again, his duffel bag once again slung over his shoulder. His eyes are slightly red, and I feel a fresh surge of sympathy.

"Hey, Anabelle," he says, planting a hand on the desk. I watch, a little mesmerized, until he pulls it away with a knowing smile. "Thanks for the hot chocolate."

"You're welcome."

I struggle with my brain. I don't want to ask what a private note said, but the need to do so keeps repeating itself in my brain.

"I'd like a room, if you have one available."

His request piques my curiosity more. My grandmother had warned me that he'd want to stay. But why?

The questions are surging through my head with such intensity that one tumbles out: "Why?"

The corner of his mouth tips up, his eyes crinkle at the edges, and suddenly his face is too much for me to look at. I glance away. "Sorry, that came out wrong. I—"

"I wish I could tell you what was in the note," he says, his voice low, pitched just for me. "I know you must be wondering. Hell, if I were you, I would have opened it last month, but I've never been good with self-restraint."

"You're still not going to tell me?" I sneak a glance at him. Those dark eyebrows of his are beautifully arched, I notice. Perfectly symmetrical.

"Not yet." He lifts a hand to his mouth as he glances around the lobby again. I notice a small scar under his lip, maybe half an inch long. "It's strange being here. Having everything look different."

"It's perfectly appropriate to have Christmas decorations at this time of year," I say stiffly. Because this is a comment that's shown up a couple of times in the guest book since I reopened last week.

Strange décor.

> *Trying too hard.*
> *One Christmas tree is plenty.*

Others have been more appreciative of the décor and less so of me—

> *Delightful holiday atmosphere, except for the stiff owner.*
> *Owner is rude; decorations are lovely.*

As usual, I have failed to please anyone.

"No," Ryan says quickly. "It's just...this was an important place for me. Your grandma and I spent last Christmas together. Well. Sort of."

"You did?" I ask in disbelief as Saint Nick sits directly on top of my foot.

Grandma Edith had told me she'd spent Christmas with a friend, but I'd assumed she meant Cynthia, and she'd never corrected me.

Ryan's jaw stiffens, but he nods at me. "I stayed at the B&B last Christmas Eve. Your grandma and I got to talking. She was quite the lady." He angles his head slightly, his eyes scanning my face. "You were at your ex-boyfriend's, I think."

"Current boyfriend."

"Ah, okay. Congratulations."

I rub my nose, feeling a pinch of self-consciousness. Being in a relationship with Weston doesn't feel like a cause for celebration. He's just...Weston.

Jo tells me this is not the way a person is supposed to feel about their significant other. I've argued it's natural for some apathy to slip in after over a year of dating. She contends that it *is* natural...in the twilight of a relationship.

I suspect she has a point, but everything in my life has changed over the past few months, and the thought of altering my life further makes me want to curl into a ball.

"You must've been together awhile now, huh?" Ryan says as if he can read my thoughts. Or maybe it's my face he's reading.

Grandma Edith was great at reading faces. She'd know if someone was hungry or hangry or just mean, all by looking at their expression. It seems like an impossible art to me—a face is only a collection of shapes, after all—but her guesses were almost unfailingly accurate.

"Yes, for over a year."

"And is he good to you, Anabelle?" he asks, leaning slightly over the desk, his tone low and intimate. His eyes are tawny, almost like the coloring of Saint Nick's, and for half a second, I feel myself leaning in toward him.

Which infuriates me even more than the impertinent question. My spine stiffens. "That, *Mr. Reynolds*, is none of your business."

I pick up a pen so I have something to do with my hands—and somewhere else to put my eyes. "I've reserved Room B for you. Grandma Edith said that's where she put you last time. How long would you like to stay?"

"Indefinitely."

I drop the pen and look into his golden eyes.

"Don't you have something to get back to? A job? Family?"

He flinches. "No. I've got nothing."

"Do you have the money to pay?" I ask, then immediately regret it. It was an impertinent question. It's just...people come here on vacation. They don't stay *indefinitely*. They definitely don't stay forever. "Uh...my grandmother said you might want to pay with cash when you leave."

He chuckles deep in his throat. "I do, yeah. I'm taking...a sabbatical, I guess you could call it, from my regularly scheduled life."

Frustratingly, he doesn't offer an explanation for the strange arrangement. A weeks' long stay would mean a lot of cash.

I take in a slow breath and blow it out. "I feel morally obligated to point out that there are cheaper lodgings if you're staying for an extended period of time. No one ever stays here for longer than a week."

"So maybe I'll be the first."

I study him for a second, smiling without really knowing why, before saying, "Well, you don't have nothing anymore. You have Room B, *indefinitely*. That's something."

His eyes twinkle beneath those long lashes. "Lucky me."

I retrieve Ryan's key and give it to him, trying not to notice the brush of his skin against mine as he takes it. "Here's your key."

"My question about your boyfriend pissed you off," he observes, studying my face.

"Yes," I reply, surprised that he's bringing it up. I'd decided to be a good sport and sweep it under the rug, but I won't lie in response to a direct question.

"I'm sorry. I'm not very good at saying what I should say when I should say it."

His honesty startles me into laughter. "That makes two of us, Ryan Reynolds."

It occurs to me that he's here under an assumed name and has said he's staying indefinitely. Is he famous? He's not *the* Ryan Reynolds, obviously, but he could be someone else I should recognize.

But I'm bad at recognizing people. So even if the real Ryan Reynolds stepped through my door, I probably wouldn't know it.

I realize I've been staring again, absorbing the shape of his nose, including a little bump which might have been a break at some point, the small scar beneath his mouth, and the cluster of gold around his pupils. At some point, Saint Nick must have freed himself from my foot, but I don't have any idea where he went.

I absentmindedly reach for my hot chocolate and lift it for a sip—and spill it all over the front of my emerald-green blouse, purchased for me by Weston's mother. The drink's not hot, thankfully, but it will stain.

"Oh cripes," I say, just as Ryan says, "Oh, fuck."

He looks around, as if he thinks an absorbent towel might be waiting on my desk, and then unzips his bag and tugs out a huge blue sweater and presses it into my hand.

I don't know what I'm supposed to do with the sweater, so I stand there like a deer caught in the headlights, clutching Ryan's remarkably soft sweater to my belly while the soaked blouse clings to my skin. The air is full of the scent of chocolate and Baileys. It's like someone pressed pause on the moment, because I feel incapacitated by the sensation of the wet fabric slicked against me.

"You can use it to wipe off your chest," Ryan says, his voice a bit lower than before. He's averting his gaze, staring at the little Christmas elf that sits on the corner of my desk. Which is when I realize my blouse is clinging to my chest in a suggestive way, plastered to the front of my bra. It's obscene. "Please," he adds.

"I can't do that to your sweater!" I sound offended on the sweater's behalf.

His lips twitch, but he doesn't look at me. "The color won't matter. It's already dark. Or you can put it on over the shirt."

Suddenly flushed, I insist, "I won't ruin your sweater."

"I want you to." His lips curl into a nearly there smile. "I don't like the person who gave it to me, so you'd be doing me a favor. You can keep it."

He's obviously in no hurry to leave, and it would be rude to give him a flat-out no, and I really, really want to get out of my wet shirt. I need to, to be honest.

"Thank you," I say. "Of course I won't keep it, but I would appreciate borrowing it."

I pull his sweater over my head and down my waist, keeping my arms inside so I can quickly unbutton the sopping wet shirt. I start to pull the blouse off through the neckline, which is loose. The whole thing is loose, because Ryan's a broad man with big shoulders. And his sweater smells *amazing*—like Smokey the Bear threw some cloves into a forest fire in an effort to stifle them.

I hear the bell over the entry door chiming just as I finish pulling the original shirt loose.

Oh no, oh no, oh no.

If guests thought I was unprofessional before, what will they think now that I'm performing a soaked-shirt striptease in the lobby?

I don't know what to do with the dirty blouse, so I keep it in my hand as I turn to face the newcomer.

"Anabelle?" Weston says, his tone shocked.

CHAPTER FIVE

RYAN

I should be sainted for looking away from Anabelle Whitman's tits. I got a enough of an eyeful to decide they're perfect—Goldilocks would be blissed out, because they're not too big, not too small, but exactly the right size for a handful of heaven. But I showed the restraint of a much stronger man and looked away from her as I all but shoved the sweater at her, a Christmas gift from an ex-girlfriend who'd told me I dressed like a high school dropout and needed all the help I could get. I'd pointed out that I *was* a high school dropout, something she hadn't known, I guess, and she'd walked out on me. Left me with the sweater, though, and suddenly I have a new appreciation for it.

Anabelle looks softer in the big, oversized sweater, her eyes still those same baby-deer eyes I admired a year ago.

God, she's pretty.

A *can't be touched* kind of pretty, which, let's be honest, makes her even prettier.

Some guy just came through the door—someone she knows, clearly—but now that I don't need to look away from her anymore, it's hard to want to. Especially when she's wearing something that's mine.

My first impression of Anabelle was that she's a bit uptight. Nothing that's happened in the last half hour has made me think otherwise, but that side of her is balanced by sweetness, like the cherry in an old-fashioned. That sweetness is reflected in those lovely light-brown eyes of hers and the satisfaction she takes in her Christmas decorations. And when she talks about her grandmother, it's all around her, dancing on her skin and in her eyes, and in the slight curl of her hair—more than a wave but barely.

I'll bet she was the valedictorian of her class, and made a heart-felt speech that pleased the adults in the audience and made the kids roll their eyes. I wouldn't know what a speech like that would sound like, on account of the whole high-school-dropout thing, but I wish I could listen to Anabelle recite hers.

"Anabelle?" the newcomer repeats, and I finally turn to look at him.

The guy is a couple of inches taller than me but skinny, with blond hair that forms a widow's peak at his forehead, shoes so shiny I could probably see my face in them, and a black overcoat. A peacoat, they call them.

He looks like he should speak with a British accent.

"Weston," Anabelle says, her tone worried. She lets her sopping-wet blouse fall to the ground, and the cat rushes forward from behind the giant nutcracker in the corner and snatches it with his mouth.

"*Saint Nick,*" she hisses, and again, I feel a stab of protectiveness. She's twisted into knots, overwhelmed. I can see it in the way her eyes are bouncing between the cat, who's licking the chocolate-stained shirt like it's catnip, and the guy in the peacoat, who's watching her with horror. Like he thinks she just broke some iron-clad law of manners.

"What on earth is going on?" he asks, with plenty of bite in his voice.

I make the split-second decision that I don't like this guy one bit.

Take Edith's impression of him and add in his holier-than-thou attitude, and you get an asshole.

I stoop to grab the shirt from the cat. Dogs can't eat chocolate. I know dick-all about cats, so it could be a four-legged-creature thing. But now I'm holding Anabelle's soaked shirt, she's in my sweater, and Weston is starting to look pissed off.

"Here," I say, handing him her soaked shirt.

Better for him to be holding it, I guess.

He accepts it reflexively—and then drops it with an expression of distaste. The cat makes another go at it, so I pick it up again.

"Oh, for goodness' sake," Anabelle says, swiping the soaked shirt from me.

"Were you *drinking*, Anabelle?" Weston's gaze swings from me, to her, to the mug she'd promptly deposited back onto the desk. "It smells like Baileys in here."

"Only a little." She straightens the sweater self-consciously. "I spilled my hot chocolate all over the front of my blouse, and Ryan was kind enough to give me one of his sweaters so I didn't have to walk up to my room sopping wet."

He shifts his weight on his feet, his mouth turning down in disapproval. "You were drinking in front of guests?"

"She was drinking *with* me," I say, because I don't like the way he's talking to her. Like she's irresponsible and dumb, when anyone who's met this woman must know she's smarter than them, their smartest friend, and *their* smartest friend. "I'm a friend of Edith's, and Anabelle just shared the bad news with me. It only felt natural to raise a toast to a great woman."

Weston's eyes narrow, and he shifts his feet again, drawing attention to his shiny shoes, which seem completely inappropriate for winter weather. "I take it you're Ryan Reynolds."

I lift my brow and glance at Anabelle. "My reputation precedes me."

She's worrying at the sleeves of my sweater, and I have to smile at the sight of her dressed in something of mine while her asshole boyfriend glowers at us.

"I told you I'd been expecting you," she explains, her gaze apologetic, as if she thinks this guy's poor attitude is anyone's fault but his own. "Grandma wrote about you in her last letter to me. It was a mystery, and I like solving mysteries. So I told Weston and my friend Jo."

I could point out that all she'd needed to do to solve the mystery was open the note, but this is another sweet thing about Anabelle: she clearly wouldn't have. I'll bet she would have kept it safe and sealed even if the world had been on the brink of ending.

"Well, mystery solved," Weston says flatly. "Why don't you get changed, Belle? I'll wait down here."

"Where are we going?" she asks.

"It's a surprise." His tone is terse, his jaw tense. I'll bet she's in for a barrel of fun.

"I'm working," she objects. "Hot Chocolate Happy Hour is at five."

His lips thin. "It seems to me you've already had it."

Dick.

"And you told me that no one showed up for it yesterday."

Double dick.

"I'll be going to Hot Chocolate Happy Hour today," I say. "And for the foreseeable future."

Weston glares at me like I'm a bug he'd like to grind slowly to death beneath his shoe. As if I give a shit. He's more important than me, obviously. He's richer than me, no question. But if it came down to a battle of wills, of man versus man, I know I'm the one who'd crush him.

We have a stare-off for an enjoyable minute, before Anabelle surprises me by glancing her fingertips off my arm. "Tomorrow," she says, her voice pitched low. "We'll have it tomorrow. Weston's right. We already had our happy hour today."

I don't like it. I don't want to send her off with this dick, but then again, he is her boyfriend, and I'm just the man who lent her a sweater and made her feel sad about her grandmother.

"Sounds good," I tell her before nodding to him. "Lovely to meet you, Weston. Or do you go by Westie?"

"Weston," he replies in a pissed-off tone.

Fair enough.

"I imagine we'll be seeing a lot of each other. I'm going to be staying at the inn indefinitely."

His jaw tightens further, to the point where the muscle probably wants to pop and crackle. "Oh? What do you do?"

"I don't think people should be defined by what they do for a living," I tell him. "I'll be seeing you around."

A bullshit answer, to be sure, but he's not the kind of man I want knowing I'm a former criminal. I head up the stairs, and to my surprise Anabelle walks beside me while Weston waits below.

When I give her a sidelong glance on the stairs, she explains, "My room. It's next to yours."

Well, mother of God. The possibility hadn't even occurred to me. I'm not sure if it's good news or bad, but it's definitely something.

I look at her one last time before entering my room. She's swimming in my sweater, the bottom hem covering her ass, and something twists inside of my chest.

The power of suggestion, I'm guessing.

I shake it off and say, "I'll be seeing you, Anabelle."

She nods and thankfully doesn't seem displeased.

When I get inside the room and close the door, I smile at the tinsel tree in the corner, decorated with Santa hats and jingle bells. The Anabelle Effect doesn't last long, though, because the news she gave me in the parlor was like a kick right to the 'nads. I sit down hard on the closest of the two beds, my elbows finding my knees, my hands finding my hair.

Fuck. Fucking fuckity shit balls fucky-fucker.

I can't *believe* Grandma Edith is gone.

In none of the thousands of times I'd imagined how my return to The Crooked Quill would go down had this possibility entered into it.

Which is dumb considering she flat-out told me she had three years at most.

You believe what you want to believe, Ryan, I can almost hear Jake telling me. *Always have.*

I'd cared about that old woman.

Maybe it sounds impossible for her to have mattered so much to me after one night, but she did. She made me feel like I could be more than what I was.

I pull my hair with my hands, resisting the urge to let out a primal shout that would probably freak out Anabelle, her cat, her prick of a boyfriend, and every Christmas-loving tourist burrowed into the inn.

Shrugging off my leather bag, I unzip it and withdraw the hard case nestled inside. Then I open it, revealing the ornament. The overhead light plays with the crystals embedded in the glass, as if the damn thing's happy to be home.

Grandma Edith will never get to see it now. She'll never know what I did to get it back to her...

Truth is, I've spent the last year trying to be the man Edith Whitman thought I could be. Most of the time, I've failed spectacularly. But I can be like a bulldog when I latch on to an idea, and I'd latched on to the idea of becoming a man she would be proud to call her friend and Jake would again be proud to call his brother.

The result?

It's been a bumpy road, but I finally broken ties with my boss, Roark, a couple of months ago. I convinced Javier and his buddy, Roark's other muscle, to do the same, and together we'd stolen back some of the valuable things he'd taken from other people.

Javier and his friend, the unfortunately nicknamed Bad Mike, took most of the haul to sell, but first I rescued two things: the watch that led to my falling-out with my brother and the ornament that rightfully belonged to Grandma Edith.

Is Roark feeling vengeful?

Probably.

But without his muscle or Jake and me, he's just an old man. Too old for the game he was playing. Besides, while he might want to stab me in the back, he'd have to find me first, and he would never look for me here. Only an idiot would return to the scene of a crime.

It's a well-known fact that I *am* an idiot, but my former boss thinks everyone is as mercenary as he is. He'd never dream of giving away what could be sold. So he'll assume I want to sell, same as Javier and Bad Mike are doing.

So if he's looking for us, it'll be on the dark web.

I get the sense that, like Bad Mike, Javier isn't looking to go clean, but I don't hold it against him. He's a buddy of many years' standing, which he's proven many times over. Like when he helped me track down my brother, who had indeed left New York City.

Jake is living near Asheville, North Carolina now, and he's got himself a girlfriend and a job.

He has a whole life that doesn't involve me, and for all I know, he'd like to keep it that way.

Maybe I should let him.

I have his phone number, but I haven't dialed it yet. He doesn't have mine, because all I have with me is my junk phone. I guess he could email me, and maybe he has, but I haven't checked the account. Can't bring myself to, in case there's nothing there.

I've changed, but a voice in my head suggests it's not enough.

I pick up the box and run my fingers gently over the spikes of the sweetgum ornament. They bite.

Part of me wants to head downstairs, hang the ornament on

Anabelle's tree beneath the flat stares of over a hundred Santas, and be done with this place.

I'd promised to return, and I did. With the ornament, no less. Most people would agree that I've fulfilled my duty, done and dusted. I can leave Williamsburg so I can start figuring out what the hell a retired criminal with zero skills at anything else can do with his life.

I can get over myself and visit my brother.

But then there's the letter...

Setting the ornament aside, I tug the note out of my pocket again, my gaze running over Edith's perfect penmanship.

> *Dear Ryan,*
>
> *Unfortunately, if you're reading this, I didn't make it. Believe me, I tried. I wanted to greet you here with some hot chocolate and hear your story. I imagine it would be an entertaining one. But our plans mean little to the universe, and mine, alas, will not come to pass.*
>
> *I know you came back, Ryan. I have faith that you're sitting in my parlor, reading this note. Inside of you, there's a man of honor, of integrity. I might not have been able to see clearly through my eyes, but I've always counted myself an excellent judge of a person's character.*
>
> *Which brings me to my next point.*
>
> *You have your own life, your own plans, I am sure. But I'm asking you for a favor, dear boy.*
>
> *Anabelle is in trouble. She's still with Weston, the heel, and I'm worried she'll stay with him. I'm also concerned she'll be in over her head with running the inn alone, if she has chosen to keep it open.*

I'm begging you, boy. Stay until Christmas. I believe you two can help each other. I'm praying for it.

Until we meet again.

Yours,

Grandma Edith

It's a hard thing to toss away someone's dying wish.

I tell myself that's why I'm going to stay, not because I have a crush on Anabelle Whitman.

Romancing Edith's lovely granddaughter would be a shitty way of repaying her kindness. I'm tempted anyway, which is probably why I don't think I've changed enough to present myself to my brother.

CHAPTER SIX

ANABELLE

Nothing is the way it's supposed to be. I need a reset, a couple of hours to pour myself into crafting, but Weston wouldn't understand. He knows about my diagnosis, but he's one of those people who says things like "all people are a little autistic," and "there's no real way of diagnosing it, Belle." He thinks I'm making excuses, when I'm only trying to explain myself.

Saint Nick bats at my ankle as I arrive at the door to my room. I reach down to pet his head, keeping the chocolate shirt out of reach. Then I let him in and close my door behind us, taking in the room I've repurposed for myself.

After I inherited the inn, I moved out of the single-room apartment I'd been renting in a complex full of college students and moved in here. Weston didn't approve, and neither did my parents. But I *love* this building—from the way the old wooden floors creak under my feet to the rasp of the brick under my fingers. I even love the smell, which reminds me of opening an old book and sniffing along the spine. Every last inch of this place reminds me of my grandmother.

There's a queen-sized bed with an old-fashioned canopy—an antique—a washstand, an old rolltop desk and chair, and of course, one of my Christmas trees in the corner. There's a workbench between the bed and the desk, precisely in the middle of the thick red carpet, and my fingers itch to go to it, to create. I found two ruined Santa Clauses at thrift stores last week, metal and wood, and I'm combining them into what Jo calls one of my Franken-Santas. They're what my business is most known for—Santas created from the ruined remains of other Santas.

But Weston is cross with me, and he's been so impatient lately. So have I, to be honest.

When Weston and I first met, I could barely believe that a man like him would be interested in *me*. He seemed so accomplished and put-together. He uses an accountant to prepare his taxes and employs a maid and a gardener even though his house isn't terribly large. I was drawn to his organized life. It felt *safe* and comforting, and I was charmed by the way he'd tell everyone we met about It's Christmas Again. He's the one who insisted I get business cards, and he's passed out more of them than I have.

But he's always seen my Christmas business as an eccentric hobby, and he's made it very clear that my decision to run the B&B myself is "misguided." Lately, every time he's around, I feel stifled, and my skin seems to revolt from his touch. I want to enjoy having his arm around me, the way I used to, but it's begun to feel like he's restraining me, not comforting me.

I throw the ruined green blouse in the trash, and then I tug off Ryan's warm, soft sweater, sighing slightly because I like the way it feels against my skin, and change into a fresh blouse. As I finish straightening the blouse, I hear a creak from the next room over, and suddenly I'm deeply attuned to the fact that Ryan's in there. What's he doing?

What's he *thinking*?

It's never been easy for me to guess.

I find myself pressing my palm to the cool wall dividing our rooms as if it were a beating heart and not made of plaster and wood. I feel a slight vibration against it, as if he's leaning on it from the other side, his hand pressed to the same spot where mine rests, and my pulse starts to race.

Coming to my senses, I recoil from the wall as if it stung me. It was kind of Ryan to lend me his sweater, and kinder of him to stand up for me, but I don't know him. He's a stranger. A stranger who swears and keeps secrets and does God only knows what.

Grandma Edith asked me to be good to him, and I will be, but I should keep my distance. He's unpredictable, and unpredictable things are inherently dangerous.

I fold the sweater up primly, meaning to set it outside of his door, but I can't bring myself to do it. Not yet. It's just so soft, so blue. Exactly the sort of thing I'd like to wear to bed.

You can't keep it, a voice in my head insists.

Ryan told me I could, but if I keep it, then it would mean something. That we're friends, maybe, and I'm far from sure it's a good idea to be his friend. So I promise myself I'll launder it and return it. Sometime.

Giving the sweater a final, wistful glance, I grab my coat from my closet and head downstairs. Weston is sitting at my desk, his head bent over my computer, and a strange feeling of *something's wrong* comes over me.

I hurry down the rest of the steps, but by the time I reach the desk, he's already shut the laptop.

"What were you doing?" I ask, hearing the accusatory thread in my voice. Feeling my heart pound.

You trust Weston, I remind myself. *It's okay if he uses your things.*

But my laptop is more than just a thing.

Everything for It's Christmas Again is on there.

All of the spreadsheets for the B&B, too.

My spreadsheet of Christmas presents is on there, for goodness' sake. It feels like a violation. My heart screams that it *is* one.

Weston glances up with a slight smile on his lips. "Shutting down your laptop," he says. "We're going to be gone for a while. You don't have anyone checking in today, do you?" His gaze shifts up the stairs, his mouth firming. "That guy must have taken the last room."

"I don't," I admit, "but you should have asked." Everything inside of me is screaming red alert. Weston knows I don't like people using my laptop, scrolling through my documents. It's hard not to wonder if he did it on purpose. Maybe as revenge for borrowing Ryan's sweater.

"Sorry, Belle," he says as he gets up and puts an arm around my shoulders. My gut reaction is to shrug him off, but that's not what a normal girlfriend would do. "But you need a real break. You've been working too hard. I've barely seen you for weeks."

A sliver of guilt slips into my heart. He's right. I haven't made time for him. I've been completely focused on taking over the inn and meeting the Christmas rush for It's Christmas Again. Everything else has slipped away. *Again.* I wish I had the ability to focus on more than one thing at a time, to pause and reflect and then resume, but my brain has always been monomaniacal.

And there's another reason I've pulled away...

My grandmother didn't like Weston.

She thought he belittled me and treated me like a child because of my differences, and now that she's gone, it's all I can see whenever I'm with him.

You know you're not good at this.

This is too hard, Belle. Let me do what I do best, while you do what you do best.

Maybe he's right, and I can't successfully run the B&B. Certainly, I'm not naturally suited for customer service work. Talking to strangers exhausts me. But I love this place more than any other place on earth, and the thought of handing it off to someone else makes me want to weep.

It would be like reliving the horror of losing Grandma Edith.

"Let's go," Weston says, shuttling me toward the door. I feel like I'm a Band-Aid he's pulling off someone's knee. But I go with him, because he's familiar, he's stood by me, and because I don't know what else to do. I can feel emotions stirring deep inside of me, but I can't identify them yet.

Just before we walk out the door, Weston turns to me with a huge grin on his face. "Are you ready for an adventure?"

No, absolutely not. What I'd like to do, if I'm being honest with myself, is go inside and slip on the cozy borrowed sweater and work on my Franken-Santa.

But I force a smile and say, "Yes, of course."

He opens the door with a flourish and practically pushes me outside.

A horse-drawn carriage has pulled up outside of my bed and breakfast. The attendant is standing beside it, wearing a red overcoat, breeches, and a black tri-cornered hat.

"We're going on a carriage ride," Weston announces with an expectant grin.

I can't think straight. The carriages pass the B&B several times of day, but they only ever stop here to pick up guests, never me. I *love* the horses—they're adorable and majestic—which I guess I must have mentioned to Weston at some point. But it's always seemed cruel to me that their lot in life is to walk back and forth down the same cobbled road with blinders on. It feels like torment.

I'd like to say *no, thank you,* or maybe *I'd rather not*, but those don't seem like options anymore now that he's gone and done it. The carriage rides are expensive.

The next thing I know I'm being helped into the painted wooden carriage by the attendant. As soon as we're seated on the bench, Weston grabs a gray blanket from beneath the seat and spreads it over my lap. It's scratchy, but I'm too stunned to push it off. Especially when he unearths a thermos.

"Hot chocolate," he says, and even though reading people isn't my specialty, I can tell he feels wounded. Maybe he's even hoping for an apology, but I can't bring myself to feel sorry for drinking a cup of hot chocolate with Ryan—or to pretend I do and apologize for it.

"No, thanks," I say, feeling annoyed. Angry. "As you pointed out, I already had some."

He tucks the thermos away, watching me as if he's expecting something he's not getting, and if he stares at me for long enough, I might give it to him.

The poor horses begin walking, clopping down the same route they can literally retrace with their eyes shut—since they can't see a thing—and the cart moves in a discordant rhythm over the cobbles. There are plenty of people out on the street—tourists dressed in heavy coats and hats, plus people who work here, some in colonial costume, some not, and college students. The air smells crisp with an earthy undertone that suggests our horses, or their equine friends, have deposited manure along the way.

"Isn't this romantic?" Weston asks, his blue-eyed gaze digging into me. Again, there's an edge of aggression to what he's saying, as if he's daring me to disagree with him.

He must resent the distance I've put between us. I can count on one hand the number of dates we've been on this past month. And I've barely even kissed him since the funeral.

"I'm sorry I've been preoccupied," I say, trying to meet his eyes.

He stares back at me for a long moment and then says, "You're forgiven."

Silence falls between us as the carriage clops along. What am I supposed to do? Glance out the window? Hold Weston's hand and look into his eyes? The thought makes me squeamish, and I find myself remembering the way he looked at me earlier, when I was wearing Ryan's sweater—as if I were a mess he had to clean up. It's a look I've gotten from him before.

And then the sight of him at my computer...

I feel jumbled up inside, and with so many sensations overlapping—the chill air, the scratchy blanket against my leg, Weston's heat beside me but not around me, and the horses huffing air in steamy breaths—it's hard for me to stop and untangle myself. Most of the time I can manage it, but it's a practice that requires either quiet or crafting. Because my brain is most at peace when it's doing something it loves.

Weston is still looking at me, and it occurs to me that I should probably say something. Am I supposed to be making small talk? Asking about his work?

We've fallen out of rhythm with each other. I used to be able to read his silences better, and he used to act like he cared about my preferences.

I squirm against the bench, my gaze flitting out the front window to see the poor horses as they continue on their thankless journey.

"You should have used the bathroom before we left the inn," Weston says, his tone that of a parent speaking to a child.

"I don't have to."

My response sounds more hostile than I'd intended, and he angles his head sharply and gives me a disapproving look. He probably has something he'd like to say, but the carriage comes to a stop.

Apparently it was intentional, not because of a carriage traffic jam, because the driver comes around to the back with an eager smile on his face and helps Weston down first and then me.

We're in front of the governor's mansion.

Weston thanks the man and hands him some cash before hustling me toward the square. Then, to my shock, he lets me go and hurries forward, taking the bell from a waiting town crier.

An uncomfortable feeling of impending doom takes hold of me as he rings the bell with a hideous clang. Tourists passing by pause in their tracks, and several people start to cluster around Weston. A trumpeter with a red-tasseled trumpet steps forward and starts playing the wedding march, the sound making my ears ring and my whole body shudder in horror even as I'm frozen in place, incapable of movement.

Weston looks handsome, standing there with that bell, his blond hair tousled by the wind and his cheeks pink from the cold. His ice-blue eyes are on me as he calls out, "Hear ye, hear ye!" at the top of his lungs.

More people gather around, drawn by the fuss, and I feel myself shrinking within my coat. Maybe if I shrink fast enough I can miss the scene he's creating.

Still speaking loudly, Weston says, "Anabelle, come here."

I'm swallowed by the urge to turn and run back to the inn.

Literally. Just turn and run. There is nothing, nothing, I hate more than being the center of attention for a bunch of strangers. I can handle strangers one or two at a time, but put me in front of a crowd of them, and I stop functioning.

Weston knows this. *He knows.*

I feel frozen and immovable. Stuck.

I'm Lot's wife, turned to salt.

I'm a woman made of stone.

He smiles at me. "There she is," he says, pointing directly at me. "That's my beautiful girl."

He walks toward me, drawing all of those staring eyes with him. Something cracks inside of me as Weston pulls a little velvet box from his pocket and pops the lid open, to a series of gasps and cheers from the crowd. In my peripheral vision, I can see people lifting their phones to take photos of us, videos maybe. A few of them are carrying backpacks, probably students from my alma mater William & Mary, the college that's a stone's throw away, but most are tourists. One person has an honest-to-goodness camera. The thought of this moment living on in the memories of strangers is horrifying.

I barely even see the diamond ring through the pressure pressing in on me from all sides.

Glancing around with a grin on his face, Weston says, "Anabelle, will you do me the honor of being my wife?"

I meet his eyes for a second, horror spiking through me. I want to ask him why. Why now, why like this?

He'd have to know this would be excruciatingly painful for me and not at all the way I'd like to discuss something so important...

He'd have to know I'd be horrified by every single detail of this experience.

I can practically hear my grandmother saying, *But it's gratifying for* him, *Anabelle. The man likes to put on a show.*

For some reason, I flash to Ryan's face, smiling at me.

Ryan, standing up for me.

He's a stranger with many objectionable qualities, yet even *he* cares more about my safety and well-being than my boyfriend.

I say one word clearly, and as loudly as that bell.

"No."

Apparently, not clearly or loudly enough, because Weston shoves the ring box at me again and says, "What? Did you say—"

"No." I jerk away from the box. "It's over, Weston."

And then I run.

CHAPTER SEVEN

RYAN

For the past hour, I've been sitting on my bed googling local jobs, because if I'm going to potentially be here for weeks, I can't sit on my ass the whole time. My body is already thrumming, wanting to move, to do, to see, to make. I might not have many talents, but I have energy to spare. I've always been like that, like an overcharged battery waiting to explode if I don't move enough. So far I've applied for a bartending job, two waiter jobs, a Christmas-tree-cutting gig, and a Santa job at a local toy store.

I'm looking up local gyms when the sound of a door slamming echoes through the whole building. Even the floors seem to tremble. Seconds later, the door to the room next to mine closes forcefully, and my jaw tightens with anger. Especially when I hear a second set of footsteps moving up the stairs seconds later.

That asshole.

I knew I didn't like Weston. He's a man who talks down to people and expects them to look up.

I step out of my room just as he makes it to the top stair. His cheeks are red. I'm pleased to see his hair is a mess and he looks pissed off.

He's about to be more pissed off.

I step in front of Anabelle's door.

"What the fuck do you think you're doing?" Weston demands, his face getting redder. He sweeps bright blond hair out of his face as he stops several steps away.

"She just stormed up here and slammed the door." I lift my eyebrows. "Does that sound like the behavior of someone who'd like to be bothered?"

"This is between me and my girlfriend," he snarls. There's a wild look in his eyes, like he's on the edge, and I won't lie—I'd like to push him off it. But I settle for standing my ground and nonverbally pointing out the obvious. He may be taller, but I'm a hell of a lot fitter. If I don't want to let him past me, he's not getting past.

I want to ask him what he did to her.

But if he tells me, I might be tempted to punch him. Punching could lead to an arrest, and I don't know anyone in town who could bail me out.

"You're out of line," he says, pointing a finger at me.

I reach up and swat it away, putting enough muscle behind it that he'll recognize what he's dealing with. "Probably," I agree. "But so are you. Go home and cool off."

He gives me a look that he probably hopes will kill me, but lucky me, he's no superhero.

"We'll talk about this later, Anabelle," he says, peering past me. "This isn't over."

The door doesn't open, and there's no noise from the other side. It's as if she's climbed out the window. Hell, maybe she did.

Giving me another death glare, he says, "You should mind your own business. You have no place here."

The joke's on him. I have no place anywhere.

I stare at him evenly, and he turns and stalks off down the stairs, straightening the collar of his coat. His posture is as ramrod straight as if someone stuck a broom up his ass. No one's ever accused me of maturity, so of course I give his back the bird. Then I stand there and wait, watching until he leaves and the front door shuts behind him.

Turning, I face Anabelle's door. I find myself flattening my palm against the wood as if my hand could send a silent message. Maybe I'm truly losing it, because I can almost feel her smaller hand pressing back from the other side.

"He's gone now," I say.

It's completely quiet in the room, and for a minute, I think she really did sneak out through the back. Either that or she has no more interest in talking to me right now than she did in talking to him.

But then she whispers, "Thank you," her voice so soft I can barely hear it.

"He didn't hurt you, did he?" I ask, because if he did, there's still time for me to run him down and lay into him. I'd do it too, despite knowing I'd probably get thrown into the can for it.

"No, nothing like that," she says softly. "But I think I need to be alone now."

Her voice is sad, too sad.

"Can I help you, Anabelle? Anything you need. Your grandmother..." I swallow, unable to finish. I'm talking to a damn door, and I'm getting choked up. *Get it together.* "She helped me out when I was in a low place. Let me do something for you. *Please.*"

She's quiet for a long moment, and then the door creaks open.

I'm stunned to see she's wearing *my* sweater.

Something primal in me is pleased.

Her hair hangs down around her shoulders in honeyed brown waves. There's a glassy look in her eyes, but she seems unharmed, thank God.

"Would you..." She looks away. "I'm sorry, Ryan. This is totally inappropriate."

"I told you I'd do anything."

"I forgot to officially cancel Hot Chocolate Happy Hour. I... Weston's right. No one will probably come, but if you could sit down there at five for an hour or so... And top up the hot chocolate. There are supplies in the kitchen. It's—"

"I remember. And it's no problem. It would be my pleasure."

"Thank you," she says again, her voice stronger. "That's very good of you. All the rooms are full, so there won't be anyone checking in or out. If any of the guests need anything, they have my phone number. I keep it in all the rooms."

I'm dying to know what happened, but I don't want to be one more burden for her. I won't be.

So I just watch as she softly closes the door, her body engulfed in my blue sweater, and I vow to myself that while I might not know what I'm doing here, or what I'm going to be doing here for the indefinite future, I am going to pull off one hell of a Hot Chocolate Happy Hour.

THERE'S only Baileys in the cabinet, which feels insufficient for a happy hour. So I run to the store to pick up some cinnamon whiskey and peppermint schnapps, some big-ass marshmallows shaped like Christmas trees, and a couple of packages of cookies. When I get back, I top off the hot chocolate and head into the scary Santa parlor with the goods. No one's there yet, and according to Anabelle, there's a pretty good chance no one's going to be there, period, so I pour myself some of the whiskey, sit down on the couch, and continue the job search on my phone.

Maybe I should be panicking—I don't have a job, a high school degree, or any bankable abilities, I'm still at odds with my brother, and I'm in a place where I don't know anyone. Hell, maybe I am panicking, deep inside, but a part of me feels *relieved*. I've got a clean slate, and even if I don't know what to fill it with, it's better than having a slate full of bullshit.

I set down the phone after a few minutes and pace around the room, taking in the changes since last Christmas. The Santa Clauses have moved in, of course, and the tree is bigger this year—a seven footer. It's like Christmas vomited all over the room. What I'm saying is it's too much—*much* too much—and yet it's not without charm.

I hear the creak of floorboards. Excitement leaps inside me, and when I look outside the double doors, I see a middle-aged woman beelining for the stairs.

"Care for some hot chocolate?" I ask, and she flinches in surprise and nearly trips over her feet before turning to face me.

"Who are *you*?"

"I'm Anabelle's friend, Ryan. I'm running happy hour for her."

She glances at the credenza with something like longing, but then her gaze pings to the Santa Clauses and her lips firm into a line of distaste. "No, thank you. Those dolls will be haunting my dreams. I see no reason why I should let them haunt my daylight hours too."

I don't deny the point. I'm none too fond of staring eyes watching me either.

I'd offer the woman a hot chocolate to go, but before I can say anything else, she's hurrying up the stairs like a fleet of Santa Clauses are chasing her.

Maybe someone should talk to Anabelle about the Santa Clauses. It may be an award-winning collection, but that doesn't mean they're not scary, grouped in here like a gang.

No one else comes by, so I return to my drink and my phone. The only other people who have this number are Javier and his buddy Bad Mike, so I'm not surprised to see a text from Javier:

You get in okay?

He knows where I am and why, just like I know he and his buddy are cooling their heels in New Jersey.

I respond by sending him a few photos of the room.

> You get fucked by Santa yet?

Other than my brother, Javier may be the only friend I've got who wouldn't take me being blackout drunk as an invitation to draw a dick on my face, but that doesn't mean he wouldn't be tempted.

> Not yet, brother, but give me time. All good on your end?

> No sign of snow.

Meaning no movement from Roark. Good.

After an hour, I leave the inn to wander up Duke of Gloucester Street. The air is chilly but not freezing. The shops are bustling, and all of the buildings have fake candles lit in the windows. I feel good. I could dig deeper under that feeling and find all kinds of not-so-good feelings, but I can't think why I'd want to.

When I get back up to my room, a note has been slipped under my door—

> *Thank you for helping, Ryan. Seriously. Thank you.*
> *Would you like to go to an estate sale with me*
> *tomorrow morning? I'll be leaving just after we clean up*
> *from breakfast, at nine thirty.*
> *Regards,*
> *Anabelle*

Smiling, I create a little checkbox at the bottom of the note, check it, and scrawl *hell yes* next to it. Then I go slide it under her door—and wait until I hear the rasp of her pulling the paper to her.

I'm grinning as I head back to my room, although I don't have the boner for estate sales my former boss used to. He had a talent for looking at objects and knowing their worth. I never have. But I already know what *she's* worth.

CHAPTER EIGHT

ANABELLE

Wednesday, December 3, 22 days until Christmas

> *Santas sold today: 5*
> *Santas made or purchased today: TBD, but I've seen*
> *the photos for this estate sale and fear the worst*

I figured I was being kind, inviting Ryan to the estate sale with me. Grandma Edith wanted me to befriend him, and so far he's been yelled at by my ex-boyfriend, maimed by my cat, and I topped it all off by stealing his sweater. Not an encouraging start. I *love* estate sales, however, and you're supposed to share the things you love with people you're trying to befriend, so I figured I was finally doing right by him.

Now, as Cynthia and I finish loading up the dishwasher with the breakfast dishes, I'm less certain.

Ryan hasn't come down at all, which feels like a slap in the face to Cynthia, who really is the power performer in our bed and breakfast team. She prepared biscuits and scrambled eggs and bacon, and even though I only eat biscuits out of that list, I must say she outdid herself. But Ryan wouldn't know, because it's nine thirty-one, and he still has not come downstairs.

Tardy, I decide, agreeing with my past self.

Of course, there are worse things in life than being tardy, but being off schedule is going to propel my day down the wrong path. I can feel it happening, like little prickles dancing across my skin. Everything's already off-kilter because I still haven't talked with Weston after he left yesterday. I texted an apology and an offer to discuss what happened, but he didn't respond. So even though I feel confident in my choice, it feels like we've drifted into a gray area. Not together, not officially broken up.

I'm ready for black-and-white.

Listening to Weston's proposal was like biting into an apple and only realizing it's rotten after a piece of it is sitting in your mouth. Our relationship has been rotten for a long time, and it's only because I've been so distracted by Grandma Edith's illness and death that I didn't realize it.

Worse, I can't banish the feeling that he proposed to me that way because he wanted to see me melt down, maybe so he could be the person who puts me back together like he has in the past.

"Tell me more about Edith's fella," Cynthia says, jolting me out of my head. She's been giving me pointed looks all morning, although I have no idea why. Maybe she noticed the circles under my eyes. "He's handsome, isn't he?"

"I suppose," I tell her resentfully, even though there's no disputing the fact. "He's very physically fit."

She waggles her eyebrows. "Did he do push-ups in front of you?"

I close the dishwasher, beyond grateful that one of my least favorite homemaking tasks is done for the morning. I can't stand the remnants of half-finished meals. It makes me queasy, even when the food's still mostly fresh.

"Yes, Cynthia," I say, turning toward her. She's wearing an old-fashioned blue dress with a frilly apron over it, and her curly brown hair is gathered beneath a bonnet. Her other job is as a historical interpreter, which means she pretends to be a colonial American for tourists. Cynthia is in her late thirties—I'm not entirely sure *how* late, and I don't want to risk insulting her by asking. "He told me hello, checked in, and then immediately dropped and gave me twenty. I thought it was a little strange, but it *was* impressive. Especially when he started doing them one-handed."

She kisses her fingers and lifts them. "From your lips to God's ears, honey. What I wouldn't give to sit on a man's back while he does push-ups. Someone's gotta get lucky."

"Well, it certainly won't be me."

Her eyes widen, and she puts a hand on her ample hip. "Anabelle Whitman, does this mean you're finally going to tell me what in God's name happened yesterday?"

Oh God. *Of course* she knows. The trumpeter probably told her. Based on what she's told me, the historical reenactor community is a hotbed of alcohol, sex, and sin. Shame wraps around me like plastic wrap. "I'd rather not talk about it."

"And I'd rather you did."

Sighing, I say, "What do you already know?"

"Well..." She lifts her eyebrows dramatically. "I met up with a few friends at the Green Leafe last night, and Jeremy Jacobs said he got paid an *obscene* amount of money to play the wedding march so some guy with more money than sense could propose to his girl in front of the governor's mansion."

"That was Jeremy?" I ask, my voice shaky. She's spoken about him before, usually to talk about what a dumbass he is, but his name comes up often enough that I guess she must like or at least tolerate him.

"Yeah. His buddy Phil gave up his bell too. But the woman shot him down and took off. The guy tried to shake it off and pretend it was performance art, but we're paid performers. We know when someone's pretending." She pauses, giving me a sympathetic look. "People got it on video, Anabelle. Maybe a lot of people. Jeremy got footage of it, too, because he'd asked his friend to record it for his portfolio."

"You watched it happen, and this is the first you're saying anything?" I ask in a shaky voice.

"Well, of course I watched it," she says, her hand still firmly on her hip. "And I've been trying to bring it up all morning, but you treat hints like they're mosquitos."

"Subtlety flies right by me," I say with a sigh. "Next time try writing it on your forehead."

She snaps her fingers and points at me. "Will do. But don't worry too much. I made Jeremy delete the video he had as soon as I realized it was you."

Sure, but after they'd shown how many people? What if it found its way onto social media? The thought of all those people watching me, making speculations about me, feels like ants crawling across my skin.

Over a year, and Weston never knew me at all...

It feels like a cautionary tale, but I'm not sure what it's cautioning me against. Opening up to people? Letting them in?

Still, there's a voice in my head that says I never let him in, that I always felt like I needed to be on my best behavior with him. Putting on an act.

I clear my throat, trying for a reset. "So everyone's gossiping about it?"

She shakes her head so adamantly her bonnet nearly comes off. "No, only the performers and probably some tourists. No one else knows."

"So just dozens of people and a couple of horses," I deadpan, feeling the truth choking me.

"Exactly. But now that we're putting it all out there, can I be honest and tell you that I'm *relieved*?"

"You didn't like Weston?" I ask, marveling. Most people *do* like him—it's as if it's written into their DNA that they have to.

She gives me a sympathetic smile. "If you take him back, I hope you'll forgive me for saying that I think he's a sanctimonious prick who doesn't respect you the way you deserve."

For a second, it feels like she just peeled a Band-Aid off my soul and shoved her fist inside. Then confusing feelings burst inside of me—I'm happy that Cynthia's my friend and is taking my side, but what does it say about me that I dated someone like him for so long?

"Sorry," she says, touching my arm lightly. "But you know me. I can't keep my mouth shut."

"I like that about you." Too many people lie or demur or pretend. I value her honesty, even if it hurts.

There's a knock on the kitchen door.

Cynthia turns toward it, cinching her apron so it better show-cases her very ample breasts. "Come in," she says in a sultry voice she usually reserves for rich-looking businessmen.

I guess she likes what I told her about Ryan.

I feel a blip of annoyance toward her, but it passes as Ryan steps into the room. He's wearing a dark green thermal shirt that accentu-ates his muscles and the green flecks in his irises. His hair is damp from a shower.

"Oh, damn," he says, sniffing the air, "that smells divine. I'm guessing this lovely lady must be Cynthia." He gestures toward her, and she grins.

"It is," I say curtly.

"I'm sorry I'm late, Anabelle," he tells me, his eyes like a shamed puppy's, "and even sorrier that I missed breakfast. I figured I could get in an early run and still have time, but I didn't factor in the sweat. I thought I'd do everyone a favor and shower."

"Not to worry." Cynthia beams at him. "I'll make you a break-fast sandwich, hon. We have leftover biscuits."

"I wouldn't want to put you out," Ryan insists, shaking his head.

His hair looks longer when it's wet. Wavier, too. "If you have the ingredients, I'll do it myself."

I fully expect Cynthia to object. If it were me, *I* certainly would. Jobs that are mine must be done by me. But Cynthia's smile spreads even wider. "Be my guest."

She shows him where everything is, then stands back against the cabinets while he expertly cracks eggs into a bowl, stirs them, then adds a little cream. He catches me watching and winks. I immediately look away, but he asks, "Want one, Anabelle?"

"No, thank you. I already ate," I say stiffly. Probably because it feels a little untoward, seeing a man wink at me after he poured cream into a bowl.

"Cynthia, what about you? Are you up for round two?"

Now, that *definitely* sounded like innuendo. I scowl at him, and then scowl harder when I see the hint of amusement in his grin. He's *teasing* us. People are constantly teasing me, because, Weston has told me, I'm too literal and earnest.

"Oh, I'm happy just to watch you, sugar," Cynthia says.

I'll admit, neither of us can look away as he prepares the pan with butter and then pours the eggs in with a sizzle that fills the kitchen. He flips them at the perfect moment, then splits a biscuit— the motion of his hands as they part the two halves impossible to look away from—and slides the egg on, before topping it with a slice of cheese.

Cynthia gives me a wicked look and fans herself with one hand. "It's hot in here. I think I'd better go get myself a cool drink. You kids have fun."

I watch, mouth agape, as she walks away.

Ryan doesn't seem to notice. He wraps up his sandwich in a piece of tinfoil, then puts the dirty dishes in the dishwasher.

I swallow against the dryness in my mouth. "There's coffee in the parlor, if you need some to feel human."

"I do indeed," he says, his eyes twinkling.

We head into the parlor, and he pours himself some coffee and grabs a few of the creamers. Sweet ones. I like the thought of such a strong, manly man enjoying sweet things.

"Would you like me to drive?" he asks. "I'd be happy to."

"You're going to drive while you eat your sandwich and drink your coffee?"

"That sounds an awful lot like a challenge, Anabelle," he says with amusement. "I'm not a man who backs down from challenges."

"I'm sorry," I blurt quickly, embarrassed without fully knowing why. "I'm being prickly. It's...I guess I'm still feeling off after what happened yesterday, but that's no excuse."

"Speaking of..." He bites his knuckle, hesitating, then says, "I know you have no reason to tell me, but what *did* happen yesterday? What did that asshole do to upset you?"

I laugh, and his brow furrows, which makes me laugh harder. It feels shockingly good. "You mean you didn't see the video? Cynthia informed me that I'm famous."

"I haven't had that pleasure."

"Sorry. I have a weird sense of humor. He...it's just...he *proposed* to me. That's the awful thing that ran me off."

"Oh," Ryan says, surprised. His mouth curling, he shifts his weight and says, "That *asshole*."

I laugh harder this time, and once I've laughed myself dry, I say, "Most people would say *I'm* the asshole. He'd gathered a crowd of people, hired a trumpeter, and I said no to him in front of all of them. People captured it on film. Hence my potential infamy."

His grin hitches higher, displaying a profound lack of symmetry that's more appealing rather than less. "There was his mistake. Never ask a yes-or-no question if you can't handle 'no.' And definitely don't do it in front of a crowd."

He pauses, studying me, and I'm struck by his physical presence. He's tall but not overly so and very strong, with thick, muscular arms and legs. Usually, people who are strong are intimidating, but I don't feel nervous around him. Possibly because he blocked my door to protect me yesterday. His stare lingers for a moment before he says, "You don't strike me as a woman who likes to be on display."

"I'm not," I agree. "After I said no, I ran away." I release a groan and rub my forehead. "Literally. It wasn't the least bit dignified."

His forehead furrows slightly. My gaze drifts down his face, taking in his nose, his nicely formed lips, that scar... When he speaks, it almost makes me flinch. "Did you step in horse manure? Or trip? I saw a video once of a woman who tripped while she was running away from the altar."

"No," I say, laughing. Then I feel bad for laughing, because there's nothing funny about the worst day of someone's life. "That's awful."

"Agreed. Which means your situation could have been much worse. And I'm guessing this guy knows you don't like being on display?"

"Oh, he definitely does. Crowds have always made my skin itch. Loud noises too. The trumpet made me feel like my head was splitting in half. Still...I didn't handle it well."

"Doesn't matter. He's the asshole. I'm officially clearing you of wrongdoing." He watches me for a second before adding, "Do you want to make up with him?"

I must reflexively make a face, because he laughs. But an unintentional grimace is not an answer, and for some reason, I want to give him one. "No. It doesn't feel right anymore. It hasn't for a while now." I draw in a slow, calming breath and let it seep out. "But I still feel awful for running off on him like that. I just...had to. And I'm sorry if I've been unpleasant to you."

He puffs out a breath. "I'm probably going to do something stupid within the next half hour, so let's agree to let our apologies cancel each other out."

I give him a sidelong look, smiling as I lead the way to the door. "Does that mean I get to revoke my apology?"

"Revoke away," he says with a grin as we exit the inn together.

"I hereby un-apologize to you, Ryan Reynolds," I say, tapping his hand as if mine were turned into a magical wand.

He grabs his heart with his egg sandwich hand, acting as if he's been mortally wounded, and I laugh so hard my eyes start watering as I lead the way to my car. It's parked behind the inn because there's no driving on this part of Duke of Gloucester Street.

I'm both horrified and fascinated when Ryan eats his sandwich on the way there, then tosses the wrapper into the public trashcan closest to the car.

Once we're loaded up, I check my phone and find a message from Cynthia:

> Please make this your rebound. I'm asking you kindly.

I ignore it, but a blush burns my cheeks as I plug the address into the maps app.

"Do you go to estate sales a lot?" Ryan asks.

"Oh, I *love* them," I say, immediately warming to the subject as I maneuver the car out of Colonial Williamsburg. The estate sale we're going to is in Newport News, and the listing mentioned four boxes of vintage Christmas decorations. "You never know what you're going to find, but I can always tell when something was loved by someone. It's like in that book *The Velveteen Rabbit*—sometimes the nose is worn off, or there's damage, but the object has been loved *real* in a way that changes it." I shrug self-consciously, aware that I've let myself sink into the conversation in a way that might feel like too much to him. "Anyway...it feels good to give things like that a new life. A new purpose. It's like I'm honoring the person who loved them."

"Will you show me?" he asks, turning a bit so he has a direct view of me. "I want to know how you can tell."

My heart warms to him, because I can tell he means it. He wants to understand my silly fancies and walk into my imagination with me. I should warn him that it's a place where I get lost. Instead, I swallow and say, "I will."

"You know," he says thoughtfully, "I never really had anything like that. Any belongings that were special to me, but I've known other people who've felt that way."

"Didn't you have a teddy bear or something when you were a kid?"

He smiles and looks off. "There was one. Only one. My brother and I shared it, but it meant more to him than it did to me, so I let him keep it."

I feel a grasping sensation in my chest, like a spectral hand trying to reach out to him in comfort. My parents are cold and usually disappointed in me—*grow up, Anabelle*—but they always provided for me. I had plenty of stuffed animals, an abundance of them. "Well...maybe we'll find something special for you today."

I promise myself it's true. Grandma Edith would have wanted me to do at least that much for him.

CHAPTER NINE

RYAN

Watching Anabelle in her element is something else. It's hard to look away.

Something awakened inside of her the second we got to the house, a big old colonial with skinny spindles on the porch that look like they'd snap like toothpicks if someone gave them a shove.

She asks a uniformed woman where the Christmas things are being kept, and we're led into a large, drafty room where several objects sit out on folding plastic tables. There are larger bins beneath them with cardboard labels reading $5.

I watch with fascination as Anabelle starts to methodically go through the items laid out on the first table. She touches each thing worshipfully, sweeping the soft pads of her fingers over it to take in the wear. Her whole being lights up when she picks up a carved wooden Santa Claus that looks no different from at least five others in her collection at the inn. The glow inside of her isn't like a match but a firework.

She motions me over and, in a hushed undertone that's so adorable I'm surprised complete strangers aren't drawn to her, says, "This is one of the real ones, Ryan. What do you notice about it?"

I take a closer look and still find it unremarkable, but I know better than to say so. My gaze catches on the worn paint on the belly, and I remember what she said in the car. "Someone's been rubbing his bowlful of jelly," I say.

She grins at me. "With love."

"Or maybe they just liked the way it felt. I used to have a rabbit's foot when I was a kid—"

Her nose wrinkles. "Gross."

"Disgusting," I agree. "But I loved the way it felt so much that I wore off all the fur."

"Exactly." She's beaming now, approval coming off her in waves, and I feel like I aced a test for the first time in my life. Then she runs her finger across the Santa's worn belly with that same big smile on her face, and I can almost see the old knickknack through her eyes—the something beautiful seeping out from the wood.

"Can't you imagine it?" Her voice is low, her words meant just for me. "The little kids rubbing his belly, discussing which cookies they should leave out for him on Christmas?"

I swallow through a dry throat. This woman is something else. Everything about her is unexpected. *Special*, a voice in my head whispers. But Anabelle can't be special to me. She may have broken up with her dickwad boyfriend, or close enough, but she's off-limits. Her grandmother didn't ask me to get rid of him so I could take his place.

"Do you notice anything about this Santa's face?" Anabelle asks, glancing at me over her treasure.

I take a closer look. Again, it looks like any other Santa Claus, until I see what she spotted immediately. Grinning, I say, "Looks like he got a nail polish makeover."

"He was *loved*," she says sadly, and those big deer eyes hook onto something inside of me. When this woman's looking at me, it's damn hard to look away.

"Are you going to buy it?"

"I don't have any other choice," she says firmly. "Let's look for other finds."

She explains that she chooses some things because they're valuable, others because they were loved, and still others because they can be repurposed into different pieces or used to decorate old trees.

"You're staring at me. Have I been talking too much?" she asks. Then her eyes widen. "Do I have something on my face?"

I shake my head. "No. No one's given you a nail polish makeover. It's just...you're so into this stuff. I've never had anything like that."

Her mouth parts, then firms. "Don't worry. You're going to find your shade of nail polish."

I laugh. "All right."

"And I'm going to help you find something real here. Because it's special to own something someone else loved." Her gaze turns far-off and dreamy, her eyes as shiny as copper pennies as she adds, "When you love something someone else loved, someone who's gone or has moved on, it's like having a beautiful connection with a stranger. You're doing your part to keep love alive." She shakes her head as if she thinks she's just said something stupid, and not the most profound thing I've ever heard. "I'm being—"

I catch her hand, feeling a spark blaze into a bonfire in my chest, and her eyes widen. "I truly hope you were about to say something like 'brilliant,' 'amazing,' or 'fantastic.'"

She laughs and then presses her small hand to her throat, as if she can't believe the laughter is coming from her. More heat fills me. I'd like to layer my hand over hers so I can feel her laughter too, so I can feel the vibration in the palm of my hand.

The laughter fades, and she looks at me like she's seeing down to my soul. "What do you need, Ryan? Where should we start looking?"

Damn, isn't that the question, though. What *do* I need? I need my brother to think I'm worth a damn, because it's the only way I'll feel like I am.

A sense of purpose would be nice.

But right now, looking at her, my gut is giving me a different answer.

I gulp. "A watch," I say, my voice sounding strangled. "I need a new watch."

"What happened to your old one?" she asks, giving me a look that suggests she knows that something did indeed happen to it.

The only object I've ever cared much about was the watch Roark gave me for my eighteenth birthday—the same watch I'd tried to pickpocket from him when I was thirteen. But I'd stuffed it into the back of my drawer years ago, after realizing that I wasn't as important to him as he was to me. And after Jake turned his back on me, I threw it away.

Of course, I felt like a dumbass for tossing it. It had to be worth at least two large. Still, I don't regret it. I haven't even thought about getting a new one until right this very minute.

Pulling myself from my thoughts, I finally reply, "I threw it away."

"But you loved it." She shakes her head at herself with a half-smile on her face. "I'm projecting. I can never tell what people are going to say before they say it."

"You're right, though." A knot forms in my throat. "But sometimes the things we love aren't good for us."

"So let's find you something that is."

She guides me out of the room, her reusable shopping bag full of Christmas goodies, and finds the attendant. She asks about watches, and we're directed into another drafty room. The jewelry is displayed on a saggy old table in the center, spotlit by sun streaming in through the window. A guard stands at the door, because while people might not be tempted to steal nail-polish-decorated Santas, they might want some old jewelry.

We walk over to the part of the table where a few watches are displayed. There's one with a leather band and two with metal bands, like the one I threw away. The two with the metal bands are objectively nicer.

I glance at Anabelle, feeling out of my element. "Which one should I get?"

"Which one feels *real*?" she asks.

It sounds like some woo-woo nonsense, or it would if anyone else were saying it, but I find myself drifting my fingers over the watches laid out in front of me. Trying to look through her eyes, I notice the wear on the leather strap and imagine someone putting it on every day, their fingers brushing over the leather.

My fingers drift over it too, and I feel a strange jolt. My eyes fly to Anabelle's, and she's already smiling at me. "That's the one, isn't it? It's meant to be yours."

"You're a witch, aren't you?" I ask, smiling back because I have to. It would be impossible not to. "A Christmas witch."

Her smile brightens as she adjusts her shopping bag over her shoulder. I want to carry it for her, but she might read into an offer like that. She probably should, which gives me an even better reason not to make it. I like her more than I should. More than is healthy for either of us.

"Oddly enough, I consider that a compliment," she says.

I swallow thickly. "Oddly enough, I meant it as one."

I check the price tag on the watch and find it acceptable, even though the money I have saved up won't last forever, and I will eventually need to find a real job.

"Screw it. I'm going to get it," I say, meeting her gaze. Looking for her approval, to be honest.

She beams at me, and I feel like a prize pupil for the first time in my whole life.

We're heading toward the front of the house, where we were told to check out, when someone calls Anabelle's name from the hallway behind us. We turn to face an older bald man wearing an expensive suit that feels overkill for what's basically a high-ticket yard sale. His hair is combed forward, including a few long, wispy tendrils on the top of his head. The moment Anabelle sees him, she nearly drops the shopping bag, so I silently take it from her. Her gaze meets mine for half a second, her eyes full of gratitude and... fear.

Oh, I don't like that one fucking bit.

Suit Guy keeps coming, strutting more than walking. There's a broad grin on his face as he stops a few steps away. "Do you have some good news for me, sweetheart?"

His gaze dips to her left hand, which she shoves into her pocket. "Dad..."

For the first time, the guy turns toward me, giving me a look that speaks a thousand words—*go away* being the first and second.

"I'm Ryan," I say, forcing a grin. "Pleased to meet you, sir. Are you the one who got Anabelle into estate sales?"

I hold my hand out for a shake, and he ignores it. A man and a woman squeeze by us, giving us annoyed looks. But as soon as they get past, the man turns to check out Anabelle's ass—so I reach out and wave my unshaken hand at him. He snaps to so quickly he probably cracked his spine.

When I turn back, Anabelle's dad is still staring at me. "You're the one my mother left that note for."

"That'd be me," I confirm. "She was quite a lady."

"Yeah," he says tightly, his jaw flexing. "*Quite.*"

Oh, hell no. Grandma Edith doesn't deserve that. I glare at him, but he doesn't seem to notice. He's already shifted his disapproving frown to Anabelle. "You shouldn't be personally giving guests tours," he says. "Your job is at the B&B. You insisted you wanted the job, so do it."

Her expression is frozen, almost like she's gone somewhere else and left behind her body.

Nope. Not standing silently by and letting this asshole go on a rampage of assholery. He started something by talking shit about Grandma Edith. I won't let him get away with putting Anabelle down too.

"Actually, *sir*," I say. "It's called customer service. I'm guessing it's a good thing Edith left the B&B to someone who appreciates what that means."

He looks like he just went on the show *Hot Ones* and swallowed a whole mouthful of ghost pepper hot sauce.

Anabelle tugs my arm, her eyes wide but no longer frozen. "You're right, Dad. I need to get back to the inn. We'll talk later."

A man with a long beard squeezes past us, headed for the Christmas room, and I catch Anabelle's eye and mouth, "Santa."

She smiles, which seems to piss off her father.

"You're going to let your friend disrespect me?" he says in a rumbling voice.

"You started it," she replies firmly.

He holds her gaze, ignoring me as if I'm part of the scenery. "If you rejected Weston, then you're a fool."

Her bottom lip trembles, but she keeps her backbone steady, and my God, I've never wanted to punch a man in the face this much before. But we're in the middle of a dead person's house, and he's Anabelle's *father*. Still, I can't do nothing. I think I'd implode if I did nothing.

"You're the fool for talking to your daughter like that," I say, letting myself shift one step toward him. He slinks back like I thought he would, and to my delight, his calves hit a wooden bench that someone set up in the front hall. His legs buckle, bucketing him onto the seat, and he makes a little *oomph* of surprise.

Anabelle stifles a surprised laugh, and I grin at him as I say, "Anabelle deserves to live her life exactly the way she wants to live it."

Though his face is the shade of homemade tomato soup now, he recovers more quickly than I would have liked. "Don't you get it? She's not normal. She'll never be normal."

"Thank God," I say, thinking of the way she brushed her fingers over the Christmas table earlier. Wishing he'd try to get up so I could at least have the pleasure of shoving him back down.

I turn to look at Anabelle, because if she looks pissed off, I'm going to take that as a go-ahead to deck this guy, but she's gone.

CHAPTER TEN

RYAN

I hesitate for a second, because this guy really needs to be taken to task, but Anabelle needs me more. I choose her. Easy.

I run out to find her, but Anabelle is out of sight. All I see is the table set up out front between two big ornamental bushes. The attendant sitting behind it is so interested in her own phone, she doesn't even look up to see if I'm a shoplifter. It's only as I barrel past that I realize I *am* a shoplifter. The reusable shopping bag is still slung over my shoulder.

I pause.

I consider.

I retreat to the table and clear my throat.

The attendant looks up at me with wide eyes. "Yes?"

I set the bag down in front of her.

"Did you see my friend go past? A gorgeous brunette with long, wavy hair and big brown eyes? About yay tall?" I say, lifting my hand up.

A throat is cleared.

Anabelle steps out from behind one of the large bushes.

The attendant points to her. "I think I found her."

"Yeah, thanks," I say, my gaze stuck on Anabelle. "I'll be sure to share the reward money."

"I need to go back to the B&B *now*," Anabelle tells me in a small voice.

I grab the keys from my pocket and give them to her, giving her small hand a squeeze before I release it. This is me being restrained. What I'd really like to do is lift her off her feet and carry her to the car. See, Jake, I can act like a grown up. "I'm not gonna let you leave without your real Santa."

"Thank you," she says.

I pay for the things with a cash app and then head to the car. Anabelle's father doesn't come out; I don't go in looking for him.

I halfway expect the car will be gone, and I wouldn't be too sore about it if Anabelle had left after the scene inside. But she's waiting in the passenger side, her eyes closed, rocking slightly in her seat. Alarm pounds through me, and I open the driver's side door so quickly I nearly slam it into my body.

"What do you need?" I say, ditching the bag on the driver's seat. Then I reconsider and pull out the real Santa, handing it to her. "Come on, Anabelle, give his belly a rub. You know you want to."

Thank all that's above and below, she laughs and takes it from me, her finger rubbing small circles over the worn spot. "You know, it really works."

"Christmas witch."

She gives me a soft smile, her eyes a little less glassy. "*Thank you*, Ryan. I didn't know he'd be there."

"You don't need to thank me." I put the bag in the back and then lower into the driver's seat and shut the door. "I'm damn sorry. At times like this, I figure I'm lucky that I never knew who my father was."

"You don't know?" she asks, looking up from the figure.

I grin at her. "Our mother used to say our father was Santa. I think she was hoping we'd stop asking questions, but that obviously led to more questions."

She smiles again. "So I'm in the presence of greatness?"

"You didn't already know that?"

Her gaze holds mine for a few seconds, and awareness zips through me, filling every cell in my body with a buzzing sensation. "Yeah," she finally says. "I knew."

A heavy pause hangs between us, and my gaze falls to her pink lips, which I'm not supposed to notice. They tilt into a mischievous grin.

"You put in a *remarkable* performance in *The Proposal*."

Surprised laughter bursts from me. "I fucking did, didn't I?"

Grinning, she leans toward me a little, her seatbelt biting into her. I hadn't even noticed her putting it on, not that I'm surprised—it's a reminder of how differently we approach life. Anabelle, cautious and careful; me, as if it'll all catch up with me if I don't move fast enough.

"Why'd you come to the B&B under an alias?" she asks.

I can't tell her yet.

I can't tell her ever, probably.

Her lips are parted, and they're glistening slightly, from the moment she licked them approximately thirty-five seconds ago—and if you're wondering whether I watched her do it, then you're damn straight I did.

I clear my throat. "I already told you my father's Santa. I can't share all my secrets."

She looks down at the Santa in her hands. "My father was right. I should be doing a better job at the B&B. And I have to talk to Weston. That wasn't a good way to end things."

"Look, if you ask me, you shouldn't rush into doing anything you're not ready to do. Why don't you let me handle Hot Chocolate Happy Hour again? When we get back, you can get some rest."

"I should be doing my job, Ryan," she says, straightening in her seat. "I should be able to do my job."

"My old boss told me delegating was what bosses did." Usually before he sent me to do something he didn't want to do, but best not to mention that.

She rubs the Santa's belly as if it were a genie's lamp, then looks at me again. "Why are you helping me?"

Because I want to.

Because I enjoy being around her.

Because she's gorgeous and funny and smart and interesting, and the only sensible thing to do is worship her.

But that doesn't make her any less off-limits...

I rub the back of my neck. "I have my reasons. Can we leave it at that for now?"

She sighs. "You could have said nothing and it would have meant as much."

Story of my life.

I INSIST on bringing Anabelle through a drive-through to get lunch, since she doesn't seem up for the restaurant experience. We park on the side of the road within view of the College of William & Mary's campus and scarf down our food. Her phone buzzes about half a dozen times with incoming texts and calls before she turns it off without checking the screen.

She tells me she attended William & Mary, which isn't surprising. It's a good school, probably only a mile from her grandmother's B&B, and she's both scary smart and not the sort of person who'd want to go far from home.

Besides...it looks like a place that would suit her, the same way the inn does. The buildings are old, brick, and covered in vines.

Old places, old things.

I'm a man who's stolen old things from wealthy people. I didn't do it for myself, but that doesn't make it better. If this law-abiding woman knew the truth, she'd want nothing to do with me. I should remember that.

"Where'd you go to school?" she asks offhandedly, her gaze on one of the buildings. Maybe she answered questions about Shakespeare in there.

"I didn't. I didn't even graduate high school."

She drops what's left of her veggie burger just as I'm taking a sip of Pepsi. Judging by the look of shock on her face, she did it in reaction to what I said, and I start laughing so hard the drink snorts up my nose. Which makes me laugh harder.

"I'm sorry," she says, reaching for her scattered burger and throwing the bits and pieces into the fast food bag. There's a look of disgust on her face, as if she's collecting worms and not a sandwich that was making its way into her mouth thirty seconds ago, but she doesn't give up. "I'm clumsy."

"And unimpressed by the uneducated. That's okay. Smart people usually are. I was no good in school. I hated sitting in one place for too long. It drove me crazy. Eventually, I decided to do everyone a favor and stop going."

She meets my gaze, her eyes wide. "Someone failed you."

I laugh again. "I like your interpretation. If you ask any of my old teachers, they'd tell you I'm the one who failed."

"Not everybody learns the same way. I didn't learn to talk until I was three. My parents thought I was mute, but then I started answering them in full sentences."

"Admit it," I say, stuffing my drink into the cup well by the seat. "You didn't want to talk because your dad's kind of a dick."

She shrugs. "It certainly didn't help."

I smile at her, feeling drawn in. Wanting more. But I can tell how exhausted she is—she wears it in the slump of her shoulders and the far-off look that keeps surfacing in her eyes, like she's fading in and out.

I pull out of the space and drive toward the B&B. When I park in Anabelle's usual spot, I give her a sidelong glance. "I can tell you were a straight-A student."

"You're mistaken," she says. "I got a C– in chemistry."

"A C– for me would have been like getting on the honor roll."

I don't know why I'm trying to be unimpressive, other than that I need to stay away from her, and my own willpower has been compared to Swiss cheese.

"Your parents didn't help you study?"

I laugh as I get out of the car, grabbing the shopping bag on the way out. On a whim, I go around to open her door, but she gets to it first, not that I'm surprised.

"Oh, do you want me to get back in?" she asks dryly as a breeze whips her hair around, a few silky locks getting me in the face.

I reach over and tuck the loose strands behind her ear. To my amazement, she leans her head into my hand. My dick responds with enthusiasm, but I know her better than to think it's some kind of sensual invitation.

I tuck my hand into my pocket. "Don't get back in on my account."

"Didn't your parents help you study?" she asks, returning to her earlier question as she inches away from me and closes the door. We start walking toward the inn, Anabelle reaching up to tuck her red and gold scarf more tightly around her neck.

I have to grin at her. "You don't forget anything."

"Never. It's exhausting."

"I'll bet. I try to forget every few years. Get a clean slate."

I'm joking, but there's some truth to it. There are plenty of things I'd like to wipe away. My mother giving up on me. Jake giving up on me. Countless disappointed girlfriends giving up on me.

Anabelle's gaze finds me over her shoulder, holding for a second before flitting away. "Something inside of you always remembers, even if you can convince the thoughts to stay hidden."

A heavy feeling presses on me, as if her words are tugging those old memories up through all the bullshit inside of me.

I rub my chest, telling the memories to stay put. "Let's hope you're wrong about that."

She pauses, turning toward me, and shocks me by taking my hand—shocks herself too, judging by how quickly she drops it. My breath feels heavy, and so do my lungs. My body. I watch her, waiting. People pass on either side of us.

"It's good to remember, Ryan. That's what I'm doing with these." She points to the shopping bag. "I'm remembering for other people, people who can't do it anymore themselves."

I nod, working my jaw. "But what if you have memories that aren't any good?"

"The good and the bad are always mixed up together," she says with a sad smile as another gust of wind whips her hair around. *Christmas witch.* "So if you gave up all of them, you'd be missing out on the good things too. You don't have any positive memories from those times?"

I think about making dinner for Jake. Shooting the shit with Javier at the bar, both of us complaining about our pain-in-the-ass boss. I think about Grandma Edith and how her bones felt like a bird's when I carried her down the stairs.

"Yeah, I guess I do," I say, swallowing.

People continue to step around us, one man grumbling under his breath, but it feels like we're in a bubble, a small world where there's only the two of us.

"It's like that for me too," she says. "Even with Christmas. The day I found out Santa Claus wasn't real, I cried for two hours. My father was the one who told me, and he wasn't kind about it. I was nine, and he told me I was much too old to still believe in children's stories."

"That doesn't make me want to punch him less."

She shakes her head slightly. "You don't have to punch him on my account. I don't see my parents much, but they're not all bad. When I was four, my dad brought me to the Christmas tree lighting and lifted me up on his shoulders. He said I was the star in his tree."

I cock my head. "You're how old?"

"Twenty-eight."

"And you had to go back twenty-four years to find something nice he did for you? I'm gonna hold onto my bad impression."

She smiles, her eyes twinkling. "Still. It was really nice."

"*You're* really nice," I blurt before I can think better of it.

Then again, that's my way—rushing in with both feet. And this woman in front of me, with her big brown eyes and perfect tits and infectious love for Christmas, is impossible to resist.

"Despite your chronic tardiness, I think you might be really nice too," she says. She's watching me, her hair a mess now, her lips so pink and soft, and...

And I know who I am, and what I can offer someone like Anabelle: nothing.

I don't even know what I'm going to do to make a living.

Resigned, I hand her the shopping bag. "Let's get you inside."

She gives me a sad smile. "I do have approximately twenty-five text messages to answer. Then I'm baking Christmas cookies for Hot Chocolate Happy Hour. Cynthia already made the dough for me."

"You're not going to cut me out of your baking plans, are you?" I tease. "I bake a mean cookie."

"Nope, sorry." She hitches the shopping bag more securely over her shoulder. "I only consume kind gingerbread men."

As if she needed to be any cuter.

CHAPTER ELEVEN

ANABELLE

Thursday, December 4, 21 days until Christmas

> *Santas sold: 2*
> *Santas bought: 0, but it's early yet*

Chatroom conversation with Jo

Jo-Ho-Ho: I need proof of life.

Ana-bell: [Selfie drinking hot chocolate.]

Jo-Ho-Ho: Oh, thank God. I was so worried about you. You didn't respond to the auction link I sent you. I figured you'd need that Rudolph bell. Did you see the fine detailing?

Ana-bell: I did. My checking account says I don't need it.

Jo-Ho-Ho: I'm dealing with something personal right now. Do you have time to talk?

Ana-bell: Oh my goodness, me too! That's why
I've been away from my phone. I'd love that. Can
we catch up this afternoon?

Jo-Ho-Ho: Yes.

Jo-Ho-Ho: There's something I need to tell you.
Something big.

My hand lingers over my phone.

I'm not sure I can handle another "big" thing right now. After
Ryan and I got back to the inn yesterday afternoon, I really did have
over twenty texts on my phone. Several of them were from Weston,
all sent after I encountered my father at the estate sale.

I may not be much of a mind reader, but I can certainly identify
the causality between events—my father left the estate sale and
immediately phoned my ex-boyfriend.

I've agreed to get lunch with Weston today, and I'm certain it
will *not* be a pleasant outing. Because the other texts I received
were from my college roommate, my hairdresser, and the owner of
one of the stores that stocks my Franken-Santas.

They'd all seen video footage of me refusing Weston's marriage
proposal and running from him.

They'd all recognized me.

Jeremy Jacobs was definitely not the only person who'd gotten
footage, and a couple of people had posted the video on social
media, where it got tons of views because A) it's a proposal-gone-
wrong video, and B) Jeremy's pants are too tight, and his sizable
attributes (Cynthia's words) were on display in his costumes tights.
When I saw her this morning, she said he wouldn't shut up about all
of the DMs he's been getting on social media as a result.

I know very few people; Weston is much more socially
connected and thus has probably received dozens more messages
about the incident. He is a man who abhors being laughed at, and

now several strangers on the internet have seen me reject him in front of a horse.

I'm guessing he's furious.

I'm guessing he wants to say hurtful things to me.

But I still agreed to meet him. I feel like I owe him that much. I've already publicly refused his marriage proposal—I can't also make our breakup official over text message.

Instead, I'm going to do it over a sandwich at The Bread Shop.

I almost laugh at the thought, but I'm too keyed up. It's eleven forty-five, and I have to leave by eleven fifty to get to The Bread Shop on time. I can't focus on anything else, so I've been pacing the room. Saint Nick is my little orange shadow, following me everywhere.

I pause, peering at the wall separating my room from Ryan's, and press my palm to it. I imagine I can feel a heartbeat behind it, but it's only my mind playing games. Making something of nothing. The wall is plaster and cement and wood, nothing more.

Last night, Ryan took care of Hot Chocolate Happy Hour again, then he placed a tray of food outside my door. He knocked and walked away before I could thank him, the same way he did the first night. Dinner was a bowl of delicious vegetable barley soup with a yeasty roll, and I have no idea how he acquired it. As an adult who does not cook, I'm quite familiar with the takeout offerings around the B&B, and I can't think of a single local place it could be from. Did he make it himself?

Either way, it was kind.

So kind it nearly made me cry, so I wrote a thank-you message and tucked it under his door, even though it felt much too inadequate. Everything he did for me yesterday was so...*kind*. There really is no better word for it. It's like he understands me, or wants to, and it made me realize how little of that I've gotten from Weston and my parents. And how much I've been missing my grandmother.

Ryan is tardy and confusing, and he missed breakfast *again* this morning, but he's definitely a caring person.

He is also good-looking.

Very good-looking.

Last night, I stayed up late working on my Franken-Santa only to discover I'd unintentionally made it look like him. As soon as I realized it, I changed its nose and started adding the beard, but it'll probably always be my Ryan Santa.

I glance at the clock sitting on the nightstand and sigh, then tug on my coat and grab my purse.

"Be good," I whisper to Saint Nick, whose response is to stalk toward the wall separating me from Ryan and start scratching it. I should probably put him in the bathroom or his pen, but I hate the feeling of being trapped, and I can't bring myself to do it to him.

I leave the B&B, feeling my dread mount with every step. When I arrive at The Bread Shop, Weston is waiting for me out front, a broody look on his face. He taps his watch officiously, even though I'm two minutes early.

"I already got our food," he says in an irritated tone when I'm close enough to hear.

"What did I get?" I ask, even though it hardly matters. My stomach is so topsy-turvy I probably won't be able to eat anything for a week.

"Ham and cheese."

I'm a vegetarian. Surely he should know that by now.

I look away. "Well, shall we go sit?"

There's a covered patio in the back with heaters. We walk in strained silence around the side of the restaurant, where there's an entrance to the patio, marked with a very strict sign saying only food purchased in the restaurant can be consumed in there. We step inside. It's early, but several tables have already been claimed. Weston chooses an empty one directly by the door and sits first, so I circle around to sit opposite him—and gasp.

Ryan is sitting at a table near the interior door to the restaurant with Cynthia and a few other colonial performers dressed in their "day clothes." I recognize one of them as none other than Jeremy Jacobs of the sizable penis. They're a few tables away, behind a group of elderly ladies who look to be having a crossword puzzle party.

Ryan glances up and startles at the sight of me. He opens his mouth to say something, but then his eyes catch on Weston.

"You won't even look at me?" Weston sneers, snapping his fingers in my face.

I flinch, shifting my gaze to him. His blue eyes are icy as he watches me, his mouth curled slightly at the corner but not in a smile. He's still wearing his peacoat. "Sorry. I just saw—"

"I was waiting for an apology," Weston snaps. "But I guess I'll be waiting for the rest of my life."

He takes the two sandwiches out of the bag he's been carrying and plunks the ham and cheese one in front of me. I push it two inches away.

"What, my sandwich isn't good enough for you either?"

"I'm a vegetarian," I say hotly, anger burning through some of my nerves. "I've been a vegetarian since I was five years old."

"You like making trouble for other people, that's all."

I gape at him. I'd expected him to be ugly, but he's never spoken to me like this before.

"You made a public spectacle of us," he says, sliding his chair in closer and leaning across the table so he doesn't need to raise his voice. "Several clients emailed me about it yesterday, and even more this morning. I heard from my high school girlfriend. Do you know how embarrassing that is, Belle?"

I sit back. "Then you shouldn't have made a public proposal." My throat tightens. "We hadn't even talked about moving in together, let alone getting married, and you know I hate being the center of attention. This has been a nightmare for me too."

"Always about you," he says, shaking his head. "Always about poor little Anabelle. So sensitive. So delicate."

"You're being mean."

He snorts. "And you're a child."

"You're the one who wanted to marry me."

He narrows his gaze at me. "I'll give you one chance to fix your mistake, Belle. If you apologize to me, I'll consider taking you back. But you're going to need to sell me the B&B."

"*Excuse* me?" I say, getting up.

"You heard me." He doesn't rise to his feet, doesn't move. Just looks at me like I'm a misbehaving child and he's the parent who's unlucky enough to have to deal with me.

He's never been this cruel, but he's looked at me this way before. Every time I can't do something he thinks I should be able to.

"No," I say. "Absolutely not."

I don't understand why he wants it—it's like a fixation for him. He's asked me dozens of times over the past few weeks. At first, I figured it was because he didn't think I can handle it by myself. Now, I *know* he thinks that. But that doesn't explain why he's so doggedly interested. He told me Comfort Zone is trying to buy up smaller properties to compete with B&Bs like mine, but why does my one little inn matter?

"Why do you want my B&B so badly?" I ask. "You don't even like it."

He finally gets to his feet and shoves his sandwich back into the bag. Then he makes a show of grabbing the ham and cheese one and throwing it into the trash can next to him.

"Because you're mishandling it," he says tightly. "It looks like a damn tag sale in there. I've been trying to tell you nicely that it's time to clear out your junk."

I think of my Santa collection, and tears finally begin to well behind my eyes. I wanted to take ownership of the inn, but maybe I was wrong to try. Grandma Edith knew what she was doing, and even though Weston's a jerk, he's also right—I don't.

I'm so focused on not-crying that it takes me a second to see them—Ryan and Cynthia and Jeremy Jacobs approaching Weston.

"Fancy seeing you again," Ryan says tightly. "I think it's time for you to leave."

Weston flinches and swivels around, his face flushing as soon as he sees Ryan. To me, he says, "You invited your fucking boyfriend to our lunch? Classy, Anabelle."

"I'm not her boyfriend," Ryan says, then winks at him. "But thanks for clearing out of the way and giving me a shot."

A gasp escapes me. I know he probably doesn't mean it, though. He's trying to be supportive.

More people have filtered into the patio, and they're all watching us, even the crossword puzzle ladies. I hear a low murmuring, and my skin prickles from the feeling of their eyes on me. Maybe they've seen the video. Maybe they think I'm an awful person...

I take a step toward the door, but Weston grabs my arm. It doesn't hurt, but it's deeply, bone-achingly uncomfortable to feel his hand on me after everything he's done and said.

"If you don't let me take over that inn, I'm going to help you destroy it," he hisses.

Ryan firmly pries his hand from me—the relief so profound I almost stagger—and says, *"Get out."*

Cynthia, who has been whispering to Jeremy Jacobs, gives me an encouraging smile as Weston sneers, "Gladly," before he stomps out through the door.

As soon as it closes behind him, Jeremy grins at me and says, "Duty calls," then dashes over to the table where they left their friends and grabs a carrying case from the floor under the table. My mouth parts in surprise as he pulls out his trumpet and runs out after Weston. Seconds later, I hear "Revenge of the Sith" being trumpeted in the street. The sound isn't quite as overbearing from a distance.

"We've got to see this," Cynthia says, her eyes shining. She opens the door, gesturing for us to follow. I can feel Ryan's eyes on me as I numbly do as I'm told. Maybe he can tell that I'm not really there, that I've dissociated because this is all too much.

Sure enough, Jeremy Jacobs is following Weston at a short distance, playing "Revenge of the Sith." A few people start laughing and filming the performance, probably assuming it's some kind of skit.

"Look at Jeremy getting too big for his britches," Cynthia says with a laugh. "He won't stop until Broadway producers are knocking on his door."

Weston halts in his tracks, swiveling around. But Jeremy steps behind a tree, stowing his trumpet behind his back.

"*Who's doing that?*" Weston bellows.

More chuckles break out from all around him.

The second he turns back around and starts walking, Jeremy resumes his dirge.

I glance at Ryan, biting my lip. "Weston's going to be even more upset after this."

He takes my hand and gives it a light squeeze, his thumb pressing into a pressure point on my palm, before dropping it.

"We won't let him hurt you or the B&B," he vows with purpose. The way people have made sweeping declarations for hundreds or thousands of years.

I want to believe him.

I want to let myself trust him and accept his help.

I also want to take care of the inn myself.

But if I've been doing it all wrong, how do I do it right?

CHAPTER TWELVE

RYAN

"Why were you having lunch together?" Anabelle asks, gesturing between me and Cynthia. We're in the inn, sitting on the sofa in the Santa room. Anabelle's on one side of me, and Cynthia is on the other. It's hours before Hot Chocolate Happy Hour, but Anabelle's sipping some cinnamon whiskey, which Cynthia insists is medicinal. She's supposed to be back at work, but she told her boss she needed an extra hour or two off to deal with a family emergency.

I run a hand through my hair, feeling a bit like a live wire next to a spark plug. Not just because I want to touch Anabelle. I'm still fantasizing about beating the shit out of Weston for talking to her like that. So I get to my feet and start pacing.

Anabelle tilts her head, studying me as if I'm a fascinating animal at the zoo. I walk faster.

"I interviewed for a historical interpreter job," I finally answered.

"You *did?*"

"Yeah," I say with a laugh. "They kind of felt the way you do."

"Your accent *was* abysmal." Cynthia grins at me. "It was the most entertaining thing that's happened at work since the guys circulated that video of Weston getting his ass handed to him."

"Too soon," Anabelle mutters. "And I didn't mean it like that, Ryan. I just didn't realize you were looking for a job here."

I shrug. "I applied for a lot of odd jobs. I need to keep busy. I'm no good at sitting around."

Cynthia points at the tumbler clutched in Anabelle's hand. "Bottoms up."

Anabelle takes a sip, her eyes finding me again. "So you applied for a job, and it didn't go well?"

"That's a nice way of putting it," I say with amusement. "A not-so-nice way of putting it would be that I got rejected from a job sweeping up horse shit, so Cynthia and that guy Jeremy took pity on me and offered to take me out to lunch."

"It seemed like the only kind thing to do," Cynthia says, giving me a wink.

I laugh, mostly because Cynthia's full of shit. Not in a bad way, but she's the kind of woman who flirts with everyone and only means it about two percent of the time. You ask me, she's interested in getting her hands on Jeremy Jacobs's trumpet. Unfortunately, based on what she's told me, he's *also* the kind of person who flirts with everyone, only he means it more like eighty to ninety percent of the time.

I reach the Christmas tree and turn around, pacing back toward the couch, but I stop when I see Anabelle's pale face. Her mind is clearly elsewhere, and I have an idea of where...

"What did Weston say to you?" I ask, trying not to growl. "We didn't hear it all."

She worries her hands, and I grind my molars together as I wait for her to tell me something that's guaranteed to piss me off.

"I think he threatened me," she says, her eyes widening. "He wants me to sell him the B&B, and when I told him it was never going to happen, he said he was going to help me run it into the ground."

Rage charges through me. "I'd like to run him into the ground."

"Yes, you're very strong," Cynthia remarks. "Your accent might have sucked, but you did shovel an impressive quantity of horse shit."

I sigh and close the distance to the couch, slumping back onto it next to Anabelle. My feet still feel like they have springs in them, but I want to comfort her, and I've been told there's nothing comforting about someone who gives off caged-predator vibes.

Anabelle turns toward me, her arm brushing mine, and I'm suddenly deeply aware of how close she is, how warm. How *single*.

I clear my throat. "You okay?"

"Oh no, not at all." She laughs, then hiccups, then says, "But I think I will be. I guess that's something, isn't it?"

"It's everything. Don't worry about Weston. I meant what I said. We're not going to let him hurt you."

"No way," Cynthia agrees, "and if he tries, I'll hire Jeremy to follow him around everywhere and play a soundtrack to his life."

"Maybe we should do that anyway," I joke. Well. Sort of joke. Let's be honest, it would be epic to have that douchebag followed around everywhere with a trumpet.

"Jeremy could play the sad violin song every time something bad happens to Weston," Anabelle says, "and 'Celebration' whenever he goes on a date or makes a business deal. The possibilities are endless." She's joking around, but I can tell her heart isn't in it. Hopefully not because part of it still belongs to Weston. I said it myself—sometimes people want what's not good for them, so I know better than to assume she doesn't have any remaining feelings for him. Hell, I've slept with plenty of women who treated me like a dirty secret, and it didn't stop me from going back for seconds.

Anabelle shakes her head. "Actually, no, it's possible he would enjoy the attention."

"That would make it less fun," Cynthia agrees, then makes a drinking motion to Anabelle, who smiles as she takes another sip of her whiskey.

"What can we do?" I ask.

Anabelle thinks about it for a second, and I remember that no one has successfully relied on me for anything...

Until I look up and see Grandma Edith's portrait hanging on the wall. I haven't let her down, not yet. I may have showed up one day late, but I came. And I brought the ornament back. That's something I can build on, isn't it?

"There is something..." She glances between Cynthia and me, and too late, I get the sense that she's going to ask a question I'll have a hard time answering. "Do you think the changes I've made to the inn are a problem? Please be honest."

I crack my knuckles, feeling all of the Santas staring at me in accusation. "Yes."

"Ryan," Cynthia warns, giving me a look that says I've failed in my assigned mission to be cool and agreeable.

"I'm not saying you should get rid of the Santas." I lift my hands in submission, meeting Anabelle's eyes. "But it's confusing. The inn's called The Crooked Quill, and you don't mention your Christmas collection in any of the advertising. Maybe you need to go all in. Change the name. The décor. Offer Christmas-themed tours of Williamsburg. Make it a whole thing. Hell, you could even crowdsource the name." I twist my mouth to the side. "And, you know, maybe spread the Santas out a little so it doesn't feel like the people who come in here are facing down an army of little red men."

Cynthia frowns. "I don't know. I mean, a Christmas B&B at Christmas makes sense, but what about in March when everyone wants to get wasted on green beer?"

"Look at all those Disney adults. They want to live there all the time. There are adults who are like that with Christmas. Like you, Anabelle."

Her gaze lifts, and I follow it to the portrait of Grandma Edith, feeling a pulse of sympathy in my chest. Shit. She doesn't want to change what her grandma built, I get it. Well, I don't really get it. As previously established, the only father figure I ever had was a man who taught me to lean into my worse impulses. So I don't know what it would be like to have a sweet grandmother who bakes you cookies and tells you you're a good person.

"I'll need to give it some thought," she finally says, wringing her hands. I have the desperate urge to take her hand and start massaging it, but that's probably me being dumb again.

"Why don't you go on upstairs," I say. "I'll bet that hellcat is looking for you."

She smiles at me, and it reaches her eyes, thank God. She's pulling out of the funk Westie put her in.

"Are you sure Saint Nick isn't looking for *you*?" she asks. "He seems fixed on digging a hole through the wall."

"Then I hope you'll climb through after him and save me," I say, then immediately imagine her being in that small room with me.

And the damn cat, a voice whispers, waking me up to reality. Reality being that Anabelle might be single, but I'm still a former criminal.

"I'll make you some dinner like last night," I say, changing the subject.

Her hand lifts to her throat. "You really made that?"

"The soup, not the rolls. Cynthia had some in the pantry." Her hand is still cupped around her throat, and I have to smile. "I didn't poison you, you know."

"It was *really* good," she says. "And your breakfast sandwich looked delicious yesterday morning too. You like to cook."

There's something in her eyes—a sparkle. The kind she gets for anything related to Christmas.

"Why don't you interview for a job in a kitchen?" she presses.

Cynthia snorts. "You'd be better off shoveling horse shit than being a line cook."

Anabelle shakes her head in response, watching me with a

hopeful look. "You have trouble sitting still. As a line cook, you'd never be sitting still."

"Well, that's true enough," Cynthia agrees. Tilting her head, she asks, "What if you film yourself cooking naked? You could be an online sensation."

"*Cynthia*," Anabelle snaps. "He doesn't need to demean himself for other people's entertainment. We'll leave that to Jeremy Jacobs."

"Nothing demeaning about having a tight body and wanting to show it off."

"Ryan isn't Jeremy."

"Nope," I agree, "but I'd have just as much of a bulge in my tights. Scout's honor."

Anabelle looks like she's fighting a smile as she shakes her head at me. The tip of her nose is pink from the cold outside, and her hair has settled into wild waves around her shoulders. She's beautiful in a way that's a gut punch. I've never known anyone like her. So passionate but prim, so funny but literal, so *herself*.

"There's no way you were a boy scout," she says.

Laughter escapes me. I lean over to gently shove my shoulder against hers, probably just for an excuse to touch her. "I'll have you know that I was kicked out of the scouts after two weeks, but for those two weeks, I was one hell of a boy scout."

"What'd you do to get kicked out?"

"We were on a camping trip, and the troop leader had this cooler of food that was just for him, while we were stuck eating canned green beans. So my brother and I stole his stash and held a party in our tent, but we got caught and were kicked out."

"So you led a revolt," Anabelle says with amusement in her eyes. "You're in the right place. Williamsburg played a significant role in the American Revolution. But I have to say you and I probably wouldn't have gotten along very well as kids. I had very strict views about following the rules when I was younger."

"And you don't still?" I ask with a grin, but inside, my heart starts thumping faster.

"That depends on whether they're sensible rules. Some aren't. Do you know that it's illegal to flip a coin to decide who pays for coffee in Richmond? And in Norfolk, you can't spit on a seagull."

"Who would spit on a seagull?" I ask.

"You haven't spent much time on the beach, have you?" Cynthia says with a snort. Her comment comes as a surprise, to be honest, because I sort of forgot she was in the room with us.

"Not really, no," I admit.

"Will you apply for line cook jobs?" Anabelle asks, reminding me that she's not a person who forgets.

I find myself nodding, my gaze still transfixed on her. "Sure, might as well add some restaurants to the list of places that won't call me back."

"You'll get a job if you want one," she insists. "People *like* you. You know how to talk to them. That's a valuable skill."

"Thank you, Anabelle," I say, my voice coming out hoarse. No one's ever told me I'm good at much of anything.

"I guess I'll go upstairs if you two are okay with holding Hot Chocolate Happy Hour."

No one's come for the past two days, so I nod. What's one more day of sitting in here for an hour and getting eyed by the Santas while I send off job applications?

"Of course. I've got it covered," I say.

CYNTHIA WENT BACK TO WORK, and Anabelle said she was going to her favorite spot for thinking, which is apparently in her bedroom with her yowling cat.

I'm not expecting anyone to show up for happy hour, so I get excited for approximately thirty seconds when a big, bearded dude wearing a utility jacket and jeans shows up at the front door.

"Are you here for hot chocolate?" I ask, eager for something to happen, even if it's a conversation with a stranger who has a thing for women wearing bonnets. I mean...why else would a dude travel to Colonial Williamsburg by himself other than to fulfill a promise to a dead woman?

But the guy gives me a hard look and says, "I don't take bribes."

"Wasn't offering one. Who are you, if you're not one of Anabelle's guests?"

I've never seen the guy before, and I've been hanging out in and around the inn for the last few days.

"I'm a building inspector. It's been reported that several areas of this building aren't up to code."

Goddamn, the trumpet thing must have really pissed Westie off.

"I'm guessing this report was anonymous?" I ask, still standing in the doorway.

"I'm not at liberty to say." He shifts on his feet, looking nervous suddenly.

"Can I see your credentials?"

He hands over a business card, and I look it over. His name is Sam Jones. It looks straightforward enough, but I have reason to be suspicious. I was always given identities that looked legit before Roark sent me on a job.

"The owner isn't around," I lie. "It would be more appropriate for you to come back when she's here to accompany you. Making an appointment would help."

"You're here," he says gruffly.

"Yes, but she's the owner."

The guy looks like he'd love nothing better than to shove his way past me, but the rule of law is on my side for once. Well, I'm guessing. I actually don't know shit about property law.

He pulls out his phone and messes with the screen, then looks up. "Friday at noon."

"You can ask the property owner," I say with emphasis. "Her contact information is available on the inn's website. I'm sure she'll get back to you promptly."

"You don't want to make this any harder than it needs to be, friend." His tone is hostile, and he shuffles on his feet again, as if he needs to take a piss and is anxious to get inside so he can use the bathroom. If there was any truth to that, I'd probably let him, but I have a feeling old Westie is behind this sudden visit. I suspect he's planning to hit Anabelle with an avalanche of code violations before he makes her a lowball offer to "save" the business.

I tilt my head and crack my knuckles, feeling like this guy deserves some intimidation in exchange for intimidation. "You wouldn't be implying you're not going to do your job properly, are you, *friend*? There might be people you work with who'd care about that. Obviously not whoever sent you over here, but if I dig deep enough, I'm sure I'll find someone who's honest. The woman who owns this building is. If there's a genuine problem, she'll fix it."

"She'd better." He glares at me in silence for a full ten seconds, but I don't budge. Recognizing defeat, he turns to leave in a huff.

CHAPTER THIRTEEN

ANABELLE

Santas sold: 3
Santas bought: 0
B&Bs in peril: 1

Chatroom conversation with Jo

Jo-Ho-Ho: I missed you last night.

Ana-bell: Oh, no. I'm so sorry, Jo. It's been nuts over here. Weston and I broke up, and I'm trying to turn things around for the inn.

Jo-Ho-Ho: You broke up??? Are you okay? Honestly, I thought it was coming, but I figured you'd wait until after the busy season. You're the one who broke up with him, right? Tell me you're the one who broke up with him.

Ana-bell: I am. He hasn't been very gracious about it, and to be honest, it was a bit of a scene. I'll tell you more about it later.

Jo-Ho-Ho: Of course he wasn't gracious about it.

Ana-bell: You just don't like him because he thinks my Christmas fixation is unhealthy.

Jo-Ho-Ho: If yours is unhealthy, then so is mine.

Jo-Ho-Ho: I'm having problems with Craig too. That's the personal problem I mentioned.

Ana-bell: Oh no! Didn't he invite you to spend Christmas with his family this year? We thought that was a big step forward.

Jo-Ho-Ho: Yeah, but now he's saying he might need to work.

Ana-bell: Isn't he the manager of the store?

Jo-Ho-Ho: Precisely. Which is why I think it might be code for him wanting to sleep with his co-worker. They've been spending all this time together lately. He says it's because they needed to do a full restock after all the Cream of Wheat got weevils. Maybe I'm panicking—you know how I spiral—but I'm worried he's cheating on me.

Ana-bell: If he is, he's an idiot. Did you talk to him about it?

Jo-Ho-Ho: He says I'm crazy.

Ana-bell: You are NOT crazy. Don't let him gaslight you. I've realized I let way too many things go with Weston.

Ana-bell: I don't want you to make the same mistakes.

Ana-bell: Normally, I wouldn't condone this, but maybe you should look through his phone.

Jo-Ho-Ho: Maybe I will. Thanks, Anabelle.

> Ana-bell: I'm thinking of changing the inn into a Christmas B&B. Would you be interested in helping me?

> Jo-Ho-Ho: OMG, yes. I was born for this. Does this mean you're ready to meet in person?

I start to respond, then stop. Jo is the person I probably share the most with, or she was before this week. Meeting her in person would be a big deal. Huge. I've already taken over the B&B, dumped my boyfriend, and befriended Ryan...

I take in a deep breath, hold it, then let it slowly gush out.

> Ana-bell: Yes. Of course. I can't wait to meet you.

It's Thursday morning, and it's the first day that *I* have missed breakfast since reopening the B&B.

I slept for only an hour at a time last night—something I know to be factual because I recall looking at the clock at least once every hour. Saint Nick was restless too, padding over my reclined body as if I were an uncomfortable couch he wished to return to the store.

Last night, Ryan informed me about the inspector's visit, and sure enough, when I checked my email account, there was a curt message requesting that I set a date for the evaluation within the next week.

I selected Monday for a few reasons. Reason One: It is still several days away but is not at the end of the period of time we were given. If I'd chosen the last day, it would have created the appearance that I'd done something wrong and was worried about being caught. Reason Two: Mondays are a day of transition, and I dislike them. Why ruin a day I enjoy? Reason Three: Most of my current guests are checking out on Sunday, and a few of the rooms will be empty until Thursday. Why displace people so the inspector can look at their rooms? Much better for most of the rooms to be unoccupied. Reason Four: Ryan and Jeremy Jacobs have offered to look over the building today, on Jeremy's day off, to try and get ahead of any possible problems. Admittedly, I have no idea how much experience Ryan and Jeremy Jacobs have in such things. I, obviously, have none.

I was tempted to text Weston and call him abominable names for doing this to me, but Cynthia, who came by after her shift to have dinner with Ryan and me, insisted it would be a bad idea to put anything in writing. So I haven't reached out to him. I've just been sending bleak thoughts his way, hoping he can feel them as he goes about his business.

If nothing else, I'm encouraged by something Ryan said—Weston will probably flinch every time he hears a trumpet, possibly for the rest of his life.

A couple of guests came by when we were eating in the dining room last night, and Ryan, who'd made much too much pasta for the three of us, invited them to join us. To my astonishment, they did. Within five minutes, we knew their names—Enoch and Grace; their dog's name—Udolpho; and what they do for a living—he's a brand manager, whatever that means, and she's an author. They're here to celebrate the release of her book.

It's fascinating to me, the way information gushes out of some people as if they've turned into hoses. I can't keep up, and most of the time I'm not tempted to try. So I didn't say much at first, but after they praised my holiday decorations, Ryan pointed out that I am knowledgeable about Christmas attractions in the area. And I actually enjoyed myself as I gave them information on what they can see and experience locally at this time of year.

You're getting too reliant on him, a voice in my head whispers.

It is an exceedingly correct voice, because Ryan has only been here for a few days, but I can barely remember what life was like before he showed up one day late. He's so good to me, to *everyone,* and the contrast between him and Weston is profound. It's impossible to comprehend how I willingly spent so much time with such a small-minded, exacting man, especially after what happened at the restaurant yesterday, followed by the inspector stopping by the house only five hours later.

I get dressed for the day while Saint Nick stalks me. While I would like nothing better than to stay up here and hide away from my problems by pouring myself into crafting, I can't abandon my guests or the B&B. I need to face my problems before they turn into a giant and swallow me up.

So I head downstairs to check in with Cynthia, who will have finished breakfast service but should probably still be here.

To my astonishment, the dining room is not empty when I come down. Enoch and Grace are still sitting in front of half-finished plates of pancakes, Ryan eating across from them, and Lauryn, the single mom who's staying in Room F, is talking animatedly to Cynthia while her son sketches in his book.

My heart grows in my chest. This room was always a hive of activity and fun when my grandmother was alive. She knew how to bring people together. I never have. Scenes like this—so happy and alive with joy—have always drawn me in, but I feel like a moth flirting with flames. If I went in there, the fun would probably die. People would leave. The room would be empty within five minutes.

So I stand by the door, frozen, until Ryan looks up. His eyes light up when he sees me. "There she is!"

Cynthia drops her fork and gets up. "Oh, thank Chr—" Her gaze drops to the little boy. "Thank goodness. You're always on time for breakfast, and today *Ryan* came down before you. I figured you'd taken a knock to the head or something."

"Sorry," I say, stepping inside the room. "I didn't sleep well."

Ryan gets to his feet too. "I'm going to go get you some coffee and breakfast. You eat pancakes, right? What am I talking about, everyone likes pancakes."

"He's making them in fun shapes," the little boy says, looking up with a shy smile. He and his mother have been here for four days, and it's the first time I've heard him speak. "I got a Santa hat."

Ryan lifts a finger dramatically to his lips. "He doesn't just know when you're sleeping, Ben. He also knows when you're telling people's secrets."

He winks and claps the little boy on the back as if they're best buddies, and even though what he said would have scared me silent when I was a kid, the boy beams at him—and then at *me*.

"What are you going to ask for, Miss Anabelle?" Ben asks.

"For Christmas or as a pancake?" I reply.

"For your pancake."

I glance at Ryan. His hair is wet from the shower, and the sleeves of his henley shirt are shoved to his elbows, showing off his muscular forearms. There's a finely detailed tattoo on one of them—a fox made of flames. My mouth goes dry.

"Uh. I want Rudolph."

Ryan grins at me, his eyes sunbursts of color. "Challenge accepted."

He heads out the door, cupping my shoulder with his hand as he passes me, and leaves me with the memory of his warm touch and his scent—pancakes and Old Spice.

Cynthia waves me over, and even though I'm still in a bit of a daze, I take two steps toward her before I stop.

My heart pounds fast in my chest as I regard the guests. I've decided to do something...unexpected...but it feels right. Okay, in this precise moment, it feels wrong. Surprisingly, though, I want to persist. So I clear my throat and say, "Uh, everyone, if I could have just a few seconds of your time."

Cynthia's eyes practically bug out, because I almost never speak directly with the guests unless it's check-in or checkout or one of them comes to me with a question.

I feel all of them looking at me, Enoch and Grace, Lauryn and her son.

I clear my throat again, then say, "I'm rebranding the B&B. It's going to be Christmas-themed."

"Like the pancakes!" the little boy says excitedly. "Mr. Ryan said I could have any Christmas shape I wanted. I was going to ask for a sleigh, but Mom said that would be rude, so I picked something simple."

I grin at him. "Like the pancakes. Except I think Mr. Ryan probably would have enjoyed the challenge. But I wanted to tell you all that I'd love it if you'd submit some ideas for a new name for the inn. I'm going to put a stocking up by the front desk after I finish breakfast, and I welcome you to put your ideas inside."

Grace says something encouraging that my brain doesn't fully process, Lauryn smiles at me, and the little boy shoves a huge bite of pancake into his mouth and speaks through it. "I'm going to put in ten ideas, Mom. I want her to pick mine."

I sit across from Cynthia, beside Enoch, my heart still beating as fast as a rabbit's.

"You know," Cynthia says, leaning toward me. She's speaking in an undertone that's probably not enough of an undertone. "You basically just invited everyone to stick a bunch of anonymous dick drawings into your stocking."

"You might have taken that as an invitation, but I doubt anyone else did."

In my peripheral vision, I can see Enoch laughing softly. Grace swats his arm and turns to smile at me. "We're going to go to that special sale you recommended, Anabelle. I can't wait."

I smile back. "Oh, you're going to love it, it's magical."

"And we'll give the name some thought. You know, Enoch is a brand manager."

"You'd already mentioned it," he says with a laugh. "I'm very generous with my bad ideas. My halfway decent ones will cost you in whiskey."

I feel a glow forming inside of me. Maybe I'm not inherently bad at this. Maybe Ryan's right, and the secret is to combine the things I think I'm bad at with the things I'm good at...

A throat is cleared in an attention-seeking way, and I look up to see Ryan carrying in a plate with great ceremony.

"Mr. Ryan," Ben says, "that doesn't look anything like Rudolph. It's just a big red circle."

Indeed it is. And I'm already laughing so hard tears are streaming down my face. "You...made...his...nose."

He grins at me, flashing his teeth. "A red velvet Rudolph nose for the lady," he says as he sets the plate down in front of me. I get another peek of his muscled, tattooed forearm as he sets the plate down in front of me.

Despite everything, I feel a gush of pure happiness. Of loving this moment. Of wanting to be nowhere else but here, with these people, in this place.

I try the pancake, and it is, of course, delicious.

"You're a *wonderful* cook," I tell him, holding his gaze. He's stopped in front of me, watching me as closely as if I were a *New York Times* restaurant reviewer rather than a woman who can barely cook noodles. I feel important when he looks at me like that.

His smile brightens. "I've got an interview on Saturday."

"At a restaurant?" I ask, excited.

"Nah." His smile falls a little. "But I applied to a few last night. I don't know if I'll hear back."

"Oh, they'll get back to you," Cynthia says. "No question. Every restaurant I know of is so hard up I'm surprised they're not scouring the nursing homes for the power walkers."

"Sorry," I say, glancing at Enoch and Grace. "She has a broken filter."

Enoch snorts. "It's not a bad idea, actually. They can have my father, if they want him."

Grace tries not to look amused. "Very funny. Let's go."

They do, but they don't appear to be fleeing, and Lauryn and her son are in no hurry to leave either.

They like it here. It's possible for people to like it here.

I take another bite of my delicious pancake, and Cynthia turns toward Ryan, who has claimed Enoch's chair. "Anabelle has decided she's moving forward with the Christmas rebrand. She's running a contest to see if anyone can come up with a new name for the inn. Now, this is the important part, so pay attention. She's going to hang up a stocking by her desk so the guests can put their ideas inside." Glancing at Ben, who's chatting away to his mother like a magpie, she lowers her voice. "How many dicks do you think she's going to get?"

"Five, and all from you," he says without missing a beat, and I laugh so hard I nearly choke on my bite of pancake.

After I swallow, I say, "That's what I told her."

He grins at me. "Great minds think alike."

But my mind isn't like other people's minds, and I know it, so I just smile back.

❄

A COUPLE OF HOURS LATER, I'm not smiling.

Jeremy Jacobs and Ryan have just come up from the basement, and Jeremy informed me that the pipes look like they've spent the last century at the bottom of the ocean with the Titanic.

He's not a plumber, but his uncle is, and he worked for him for a while.

"I can get you a good price," Jeremy says, accepting the drink Cynthia just poured for him and sitting on the loveseat next to the sofa.

She scowls at him and puts her hands on her hips. "Did you only offer to come over because you're trying to scrounge up business for your huckster uncle?"

He lifts his empty hand, palm outward. "What do you take me for, Cynth? I make an offer to help your friend, be a stand-up guy, and you accuse me of being shady?"

"Tell the truth, Jeremy. Do you still work for him?"

He wobbles his hand in the air. "Sometimes, when I need to make an extra buck."

She snatches the drink back from him. "You just lost your drink, Trumpet Boy."

"What gives?" he asks. I may not be a great judge of such things, but he looks genuinely hurt.

My gaze finds Ryan. I think Jeremy *is* telling the truth, but I want Ryan's take. "What do you think?"

"I'm no expert," he says, "but he's right. You probably need to get them replaced. You might need some rewiring too."

I slump back on the couch, trying to do the mental calculations. The inn is expensive. There are no mortgage payments, but the tax is exorbitant. Still, I have some money saved up from It's Christmas Again, and that money can go toward updating and rebranding the inn. "Do you think we can find someone to do it before Monday?"

Jeremy Jacobs gives Cynthia an accusatory look. "I can get my uncle to do the pipes tomorrow," he says, "because you're *friends*."

He says that last word acidly, and she rolls her eyes and hands back his drink.

"A thank-you wouldn't be out of line," he says, raising one eyebrow.

"Thank you, oh lord and master." She mimes bowing. "You know, you're letting your social media stardom go to your head."

"If it's only gonna last fifteen minutes, I might as well make the most of it. I got DMed five phone numbers last night."

Cynthia's nostrils flare. "Only five? I got seven numbers at the bar."

There's something strange going on with them, but I don't really care at the moment. I'll care later, because I love Cynthia, but right now, I just want to know if my B&B is going to survive this inspector's visit. "And the electrical?"

Ryan squeezes my shoulder, and some of the tension eases out of me. "I'll make some calls. I know enough to recognize if they're screwing us."

Us. The word makes me smile, even though I know it's not a promise.

"Thank you, Ryan."

Jeremy makes a sound of affront, so I turn to him and say, "And thank you, lord and master."

Cynthia laughs so hard, she bends over with it. I catch Jeremy watching her before he shakes his head and says, "And that's my cue." He downs the rest of his drink and rises, setting the cup on the coffee table, thoughtfully choosing to use one of the coasters. Then he nods at me. "I'll let you know what he says."

"Thank you," I say again, more emphatically. "I really appreciate your time, Jeremy."

"I'm glad someone does." His turns to Cynthia. "You need to report for your shift?"

"Yeah, soon."

"I'll walk with you."

She gives him a pointed look. "So you can sell me on your aunt's Mary Kay?"

He snorts and shakes his head. "You sure love giving me shit, Cynth."

"Someone needs to keep your head on straight." But she relents and smiles at him. "Come on. Maybe we'll see Weston, and you can serenade him again."

"Don't. Seriously, don't," I say. "A trumpet might be what got us here in the first place."

"Another reason for me to help you," Jeremy says with a nod. "I'm sorry if I caused you any trouble."

"Oh, it's not your fault," I say. "It's Weston who lacks a sense of humor."

I sense Ryan smiling at me. *He* certainly has a sense of humor.

Cynthia and Jeremy take their leave and walk out together, bickering under their breath.

"Sit with me a minute?" Ryan asks as the front door shuts behind them with a solid report.

"Gladly." I sigh, leaning back on the sofa, and pat the cushion next to me. He studies it for a second. "Don't worry," I say, "no Santas are hiding under the cushion."

"I'm going to take you at your word for that," he says with a crooked smile, then sits down next to me—a few inches away, but plenty close enough for me to feel every slight movement he makes. And Ryan Reynolds is not a man who knows how to sit still. The motion of him so close to me makes my blood warm.

I turn to face him, taking in his features, which are becoming so familiar, and it hits me that this man knows so much about me, but I know barely anything about him.

"Who *are* you?" I ask. After the words come out, I laugh, because it sounds ridiculous. We've spent the past four days together, and I'm only now asking. "I mean, who are you really, Ryan?"

"I can't tell you everything, but I'm not going to lie to you," he says, his fingers gripping the piping at the bottom of the couch's upholstery. "That doesn't sound terribly promising."

"You're right," he says, his smile returning, like he can't bear to let it go.

"So what else can you tell me about yourself?"

He pauses, as if giving this request actual consideration. "I told you a bit about my brother," he says at last. "He's my twin, and he's the most important person in my life. But I haven't talked to him for a year."

"What are you waiting for?" I ask, drawn in by him, by this story he's teasing. His sadness is heavy enough that I feel it.

"I've let him down too many times. I want to be able to tell him that I've changed. I can't...bring myself to talk to him before I can tell him that and mean it all the way. I'm close, but I'm not there yet. When I am, I think I'll feel it."

"And who were you before, Ryan?"

Emotion flickers through his eyes like a summer storm. "Someone who took more than he gave. My life was in a dark place for a long time, and I didn't know how to make things right. Your grandmother's the one who made me want to change. She was kind to me when I needed it."

Dark place.

What does that even mean? I want him to give me the diameters of it so I can fully take his measure. So I can know who it is I'm dealing with, and how much trouble I'm in. Because I'm attached to him being here, with all of his chaos and his cooking and his kindness. I'm getting used to seeing his handsome face every day. I can feel him carving away at a part of my heart, making me want to care about him.

"Have you ever killed anyone?" I ask.

"Oh, God no." He takes my hands and meets my gaze. "No. And I've never hit anyone who didn't deserve it."

I laugh again, half because I find it funny, and half because I'm scandalized. "And who decides that?"

"Me," he says, squeezing my hand. "Do you trust me?"

"More than I probably should," I admit. Because even though I know next to nothing about him, I do trust him. My grandmother trusted him, but that only provided the foundation for my trust. It's his actions this past week that have built it.

"I don't want it to be more than you should. I want to be worthy of it."

There's an intensity to his words, and I feel that warmth inside of me growing and reaching toward him. I maintain my grip on him, letting our clasped hands connect us like an electric cable.

"What else can you tell me?" I ask through parched lips. "I should warn you that I'd like to know everything."

His mouth twitches with a near smile. "I'm from New York City, born and raised, I'm allergic to peanuts, I've never had a relationship longer than a month, and I've never believed in Santa Claus, but I thought the Grinch was real until I was six."

My mouth drops open briefly before I can collect myself. "You told me your mother said your father was Santa Claus."

He huffs. "Of course you remember that. Well...she lied about everything else. I knew she was lying about that too."

"But how can you believe in the Grinch and not Santa Claus? What would he even steal if Santa hadn't brought Christmas?"

His eyes seem to twinkle with the reflected lights from the Christmas tree when he says, "Everyone knows the grown-ups give the gifts. Before I met you, I never much cared about Christmas, but I like the way it lights you up from the inside. Like you're full of Christmas lights. I could listen to you talk about Christmas for hours and not get bored."

I find myself leaning toward him, wanting to suck up his words as if I'm dry stone. The only person who's ever liked to listen to me monologue about Christmas is Jo. And no one has ever, ever told me I'm lit up from the inside. I've always just been Anabelle, the quiet girl. Or sometimes Anabelle, the girl who doesn't know how to shut up when she should. "Tell me more, Ryan. I want more."

He rubs his chin. "My brother and I are identical twins, and my mother left us when we were four. That's something else I can tell you. We had a few nice foster parents, but their Christmas decorations were for their real kids. We were lucky if they remembered to pick up a couple of discount stockings and write our names on them with glitter glue."

I feel that sadness blanket wrap around my shoulders again. It's like this for me sometimes—other people's emotions become my own. Especially when it's someone I care about. It can be easier for me to feel their emotions than to know what's going on within my own chest.

"I'm sorry," I say, wrapping my hand around his wrist, feeling the way the muscle cords around it. I find myself tracing his tattoo and snatch my hand back. Struggling to compose myself, I add, "That must have been hard."

"But I always had my brother." He sounds even sadder now, probably because he doesn't have him anymore. It must feel like a limb is missing. I wouldn't know, because I've never had a brother or sister. My parents couldn't have another child, much to their disappointment.

"You'll have him again," I insist. Wanting to move him away from his sadness, I continue, "And what did you do in New York?"

He brushes his mouth with his hand. "It's part of that dark place, Anabelle. I don't want you to judge me."

Emotion catches in my throat. "I don't want to judge you."

"But you might anyway, right?"

I consider this seriously and then nod before I respond. I want to be honest with him. He's not a murderer, so I wouldn't throw him out. I know him too well to wonder if he's a rapist or abuser. As for anything else...

I can forgive it, if it's in the past, but will I be able to not judge him? I can't say for sure.

I grew up believing in the rules—follow them and you're good, break them and you're bad. I've experienced enough of the world to know that metric is too simple for real life, but that doesn't mean it's easy to let go of it entirely.

"I...I don't know," I finally say, feeling a different kind of burn in my throat. "I'm sorry."

He brushes his fingers lightly over my cheekbone. "Don't be sorry. I like you exactly the way you are. Now, what do you say we go get that stocking you hung up earlier and see how many dick pics Cynthia stuffed into it?"

Seven. One of them is wearing a Santa hat. I can't hang it up behind my desk for obvious reasons, but it's definitely a keeper.

I wander through the rest of the day in a daze, fulfilling a few orders and checking the other guests' suggestions for the inn.

Santa's House.
The Red and Green Inn.
The Christmas Inn.
Santa's Helpers.

I text them to Jo, who writes back,

Jo-Ho-Ho: What about The Gingerbread House?

And my heart lights with a new glow, because that's the one. I can see the sign already in my mind's eye, welcoming people inside.

Ryan is the first person I tell. I admit that I'm worried about disappointing Ben, and he points out that Ben also submitted a very good suggestion about hiding some of my Santa Clauses around the inn and having a scavenger hunt for kids.

I go to bed with a heart that's both heavy and full. The Gingerbread House feels like it's coming together, but in order to make this place mine, I will have to transform it into something other than my grandmother's.

Life is always like this, a war between the past and the present, which the present always seems to win. Usually, I hate that. But tonight...

I'm excited for what the future might bring.

CHAPTER FOURTEEN

RYAN

The pipe repairs are *expensive*, but after Jeremy's uncle delivers his quote in the parlor, Jeremy takes me aside and says, "It's the best he can do, man. As it is, I had to agree to wear a sandwich board next spring and stand out on the side of the road shouting to people about cleaning their pipes. I'm probably going to get run over."

I smile at him and clap him on the back. "I'll be sure to tell Cynthia that, brother."

She's been gone all day, having driven to a casting call in Washington, D.C. Some Revolutionary War movie she should be a perfect fit for. Jeremy didn't get a call from them, which he's complained about half a dozen times.

He scowls at me and says, "What do I care if Cynthia knows?"

He's a better actor than I am, but he's still not going to win any awards.

We head back into the parlor and rejoin Anabelle and his uncle, who are talking stiffly about the weather. I can tell she's exhausted. She spent the whole time they were in the basement wandering around the parlor, picking out the Santas for the scavenger hunt. I nominated the one who's smoking a pipe, but she told me it was inappropriate. I was tempted to point out she's the one who'd bought it, but I did the rare thing and shut my mouth.

Maybe it's time to give her the sweetgum ornament.

She could sell it to cover the cost of the repairs she'll need to keep that dickweed away from the B&B and rebrand. Grace and Enoch are leaving tomorrow to spend a couple of days in Richmond, but he promised to let me ask him dozens of questions after they get back to the inn tonight. I'll record our conversation, obviously, because my memory's nothing like Anabelle's.

Still. I should probably give her the ornament.

I've been thinking about it a lot, though I worry if I give it to her, she might tell me to screw off—nicely, of course—and then I won't be able to help her with Hurricane Weston.

Besides, I don't think she'd sell the damn thing.

I did a Google image search for some of her Santas. Don't get any ideas—I didn't do it because I'm interested in stealing them. I wanted to know what resources she has available, and a few of them are worth good money.

But if she won't sell them, she probably won't sell the ornament.

So I'm holding out for now, because I don't trust Weston to play fair, and Anabelle's not a dirty fighter. I am.

The Jacobses say their goodbyes, and after they leave, Anabelle turns to look at me.

"I don't know what to do with myself," she says in a bewildered tone.

"Do you have to do anything?" I scratch my head, feeling helpless and out of sorts.

"I have a few things to ship," she says slowly.

"So let me help."

I expect her to say no—I brace myself for it—but she nods several times. "Yes, please."

There's a grin on my face as I follow her upstairs to her room. It's only when I walk inside that I realize I've made a dangerous offer. This is her space, with her *bed*. It smells like her and everything, from the little tree decorated in the corner to the worktable in the center of the space and small collection of her Franken-Santas sitting on top of the dresser, speaks of Anabelle.

"I've got to stand here for a minute just to soak it in," I tell her. "If I immerse myself too quickly, I may drown in the holiday spirit."

She gives me a bemused look. "We wouldn't want that. I would prefer not to explain myself to the authorities. Something tells me they won't believe me if I say the cause of death was Christmas."

I'm glad she's able to joke. I know all of this has settled heavily on her shoulders.

It's only when Anabelle shuts the door behind me that I hear a yowl and remember her cat.

"Uh...is he going to be okay with me being in here?" I ask, staying put.

"He'll need to learn to live with it," she says stubbornly, giving Saint Nick a hard look as he comes slinking out from the other side of the bed. Then she heads over to the worktable and grabs a plastic snack bag from one of the drawers before handing it to me.

I open it and am blasted with a meat smell.

I pop one of the little snacks into my mouth, and Anabelle gasps. "Spit it out."

She says it so emphatically that I do it without thinking, watching in horror as the glob of half-chewed jerky or whatever falls to the floor. "Shit, I'm sorry. What's wrong?"

"It was for the cat," she says, laughing now, gripping her stomach. "It's a cat treat. I should've said—"

She starts laughing harder as Saint Nick darts forward and eats the half-chewed cat treat. A wave of nausea blasts through me.

"Oh God," I say. "I need—"

Still laughing, she pulls a candy cane from a different desk drawer.

"Nope. Not going to eat it before I get verbal confirmation that it is a candy cane meant for human consumption and not a squeaky cat toy. There's only so much humiliation one man can take."

Laughing harder, she snorts, then her eyes widen. "I...snorted."

"I've been known to do that to a woman."

Something shifts in her gaze, turning hot and *aware*, and her laughter dries up. I'm again very conscious that we're alone together in her space, aside from the cat, who's currently chewing on my first-ever cat treat.

I clear my throat. "Is it a real candy cane?"

She snaps it into two, handing me the straight end, our fingers touching. "We'll test it together."

I'll be damned if it's not the sexiest thing a woman's ever said to me. Her gaze is holding mine, and I have to wonder—to hope— whether she feels it too. Then I watch, mesmerized, as she unwraps the candy and sucks on it.

Either the universe is suddenly being kind to me, or very cruel. Because all I can do is watch her, like one of those dipshits on a hypnotism show.

"Aren't you going to try your half?" she asks.

"Aren't you going to tell me what yours is like?"

She smiles at me. "That wasn't our bargain."

"You play dirty," I say, then unwrap my half and bite on the mint.

"Of course you bite your candy canes. You're too impatient to suck." Her tone is teasing, but damn, I don't think she realizes how she's affecting me with all this talk of sucking and biting in her bedroom.

The cat finishes the meaty treat and yowls for another. Anabelle nods encouragingly at the bag of doom. "Saint Nick loves those. Give him a few. Maybe he'll want to be friends."

I pop the rest of the candy cane in my mouth—earning myself an eye roll—and get down on my haunches and hold out a treat for him.

He stalks forward cautiously, sniffs the treat, and gobbles it. I stay down and try to pet him.

He stiffens at the first touch of my hand but then allows it.

I glance up at Anabelle, beaming. "It's a Christmas miracle. He doesn't want to murder me anymore!"

She's still sucking on the peppermint, but as she watches me, her eyes warm, and suddenly bites down on the candy cane and chews.

"Hey, that's not so bad," she says.

ANABELLE and I get her orders packaged up, and the cat who seemed to think I was the spawn of Satan a few days ago likes me so much now he humped my leg. Twice. Anabelle told me it's probably a dominance thing, which wasn't great for my ego. No one wants to think they're owned by a twenty-pound cat.

The electrician I found shows up a few hours later. Unfortunately, he delivers unpleasant news. Some rewiring is needed for safety, but it can't be done today. Anabelle makes an appointment with him, though, and at least we'll be able to tell the inspector the upgrades are in the works.

So I tell her to take a rest while I hold down the fort for Hot Chocolate Happy Hour. Again. I already know Enoch and Grace won't be back in time, and Lauryn and Ben are going on some candlelit tour, so I'm expecting a light crowd of no one.

I grab a drink, feeling the stress of the day in my neck, even though I was able to get in an early workout before breakfast, and settle back on the couch.

I text Javier, whom I haven't heard from in a while.

Any snow, man?

A few inches.

I bolt upright before his next text comes through.

On the ground, man.

[Photo of snow]

Got you good, didn't I?

My heart thumping in my ears, I write back:

You're a jackass.

Glad you noticed.

He's down for the count. Retired. I heard from a friend he just bought a property in the Caribbean. We're keeping an eye, though.

I don't forget the services of a friend.

Relief rolls over me. In the back of my mind, I've been worried Roark might still have some bite. I've also been worried about him.

Yeah, I know how that sounds. I don't like my old boss. He's a piece of shit who's used me and my brother since we were kids. He's a bad man who's taken his fortune from other people and paid the people he employs peanuts. But I used to look up to him and think of him as a father—the only parent I ever had. So a part of me wants him to sit down for the count, because I don't want Javier or anyone else to hurt him.

I'm glad.

I'm going into business for myself, Ryan.

I could use a guy with your talents, not gonna lie, but I'm not gonna ask.

He's not talking about my ability in the kitchen. He's referring to the only real talent I have—for picking locks and cracking safes.

I've only heard back from two of the dozens of places I've applied to so far—the colonial job, which was a big fat no, for previously discussed reasons, and a gig I'm interviewing for tomorrow. But it doesn't matter. Being here, with these people, I've started to feel like I can be a person of value. I also know my relationship with Jake will never improve unless I'm out of that life. So the answer to Javier's implied question can only be no.

> Thanks, man. I wish you nothing but the best.

I sit back, alternating between the high of remembering Anabelle eating that candy cane and the low of Javier hinting he'd like to hire me. Part of me still thinks breaking things will be the only thing I'm ever good at.

I've been sipping my whiskey for long enough to get a low, pleasant buzz when a young, out-of-shape guy wearing a fuzzy blue coat comes in from the front room. He has curly black hair, a five o'clock shadow that probably sets in ten minutes after he shaves, and big, dark brown eyes behind his wire-rimmed glasses.

I wasn't expecting anyone. Is this some other sort of inspector who didn't bother to knock? A spy sent by Weston?

I sit up so abruptly I drop the whiskey.

"Oh fu—" I try to correct myself midcourse, but I can't bring myself to say *fudge*, so I settle for not finishing the thought. It amuses me to realize I've done exactly what Anabelle did earlier this week, only the whiskey wound up on the floor instead of on my shirt. I grab an old-looking dish towel displayed on the credenza—Santa, baking cookies—to mop up the mess, but the stranger gasps.

"No! Drop that towel!" the guy says, waving his hands and taking several steps toward me. He's a good four inches shorter than me, thick but not muscular, but I get the feeling that if I don't do exactly what he says, he's going to come at me.

I'm not a person to shy away from a fight—even a fight I don't understand—but I told Anabelle I'd hold down the fort, and I have a feeling violence wasn't what she had in mind. So I drop the towel.

The guy in the coat stops short and takes a good look at me, his gaze lingering on my arms. His eyes go wide with alarm, and he pivots as if he's going to walk right back out of the room, the building, and maybe the whole town.

"Wait," I call out.

He turns and lifts his damn hands, as if I'm a cop who just asked him to put them over his head. "I'm sorry, man," he says, stumbling over his own words. "But that's a vintage Christmas tea towel. Anabelle found it at a tag sale, but it's worth at least three hundred bucks. You shouldn't be mopping up spills with it."

I'm tempted to ask him what I should be doing with a tea towel if not mopping up spills, especially a vintage tea towel that's hanging on a credenza, but he seems scared—whether of me or the possibility that I might ignore him and mop up bottom-shelf cinnamon whiskey with the tea towel, I couldn't say.

"Uh, thanks," I tell him. "Are you here for Hot Chocolate Happy Hour?"

He glances around at the room, empty of other people except for the Santa Clauses arranged on the shelves, the windowsills and every conceivable surface in the room. Anabelle chose the Santas for the scavenger hunt and plans on dispersing some of the others, but none of them have been moved yet.

I'm about to make some crack about *he knows where you've been sleeping*, but this guy doesn't seem put off by the Santas. He looks impressed. Hell, he looks awed—the way I felt the first time I visited Roark's New York City apartment, full of treasures, when I was a kid so poor I couldn't afford to use a gumball machine on my birthday.

This is the kind of guy we need more of at the inn.

His gaze returns to mine and he nods. "Yeah, I'm here to see Anabelle."

"I don't think she's coming down," I say, thinking about how pale she looked after the electrician left. "She's not feeling well, so she asked me to help out by running happy hour."

This guy looks like I just kicked him in the nuts.

He sure doesn't give off an inspector vibe. There are no hard edges to him, nothing that speaks of authority.

Is he another of Anabelle's admirers?

I can't say I blame him, but despite having immediately recognized the worth of that tea towel, he seems new to this space. I can tell by the way he's sizing it up.

Finally, his gaze rests back on me. "Are you Weston?"

He says it with the thread of contempt the man deserves, and surprised laughter gushes from me. "No. I'm just a guest here at the inn, but I was friendly with Grandma Edith. I'm Ryan."

"Ryan Reynolds?"

I laugh harder, because I'll be damned, word sure does get around. "Sure." I put out my hand, and he shakes it, his palm slightly damp.

"Joseph."

It's a familiar name, but I can't place it.

There's still something nervous about the guy, like he might turn around and run at the slightest sound or motion.

"How do you know Anabelle?" I ask.

"She's one of my best friends," he says, which sends my eyebrows up. Not because I don't believe men and women can be friends, but because he's clearly never met the man she dated for over a year. Anabelle and I have also spent a lot of time together this week—more time than I've spent with most of the women I dated for multiple weeks—and she never once mentioned a Joseph.

I clear my throat. "Uh...you're not some kind of stalker, are you?"

The look of offense on his face is real enough, but it doesn't mean he's innocent. I doubt anyone would be pleased at being called a stalker.

"Of course not." He tugs at the hem of his fluffy coat. "Anabelle and I...we met online."

"Like online dating?"

Jealousy throbs through me, making me crack my knuckles, but it doesn't track. I can't imagine her setting up an online dating profile, when she can barely bring herself to talk to strangers. Besides, she only broke up with Weston a few days ago, and his shitty behavior probably didn't make her want to rush back into dating.

Another thing I should remember.

But Joseph shakes his head, thank God. "Chat rooms." A sigh seeps out of him. "We're both..." He gestures around the room. "... collectors. She outbid me on that towel. That's how I know how much it's worth."

"Ah, so you have a weird room of Santa Clauses too."

He gives me a withering look. "Anabelle's collection has been written up in—"

"*House & Garden*, she told me. Look. She's not really in a good place right now. It's been a hard day. Do you want me to let her know you're here?"

He glances at the carpet-lined staircase, visible through the open doors, and then shakes his head. "Not if she's having a bad day. I don't want to give her more bad news."

I cock my head, curious. "Like what?"

He heaves a gusty sigh, his gaze floating back to the credenza. "You wouldn't care, man. Maybe she won't either. But I don't have anyone else."

His words latch onto something inside of me. I understand what he's feeling right now, and it's terrible. It's exactly the way I felt when I walked into this B&B less than a year ago. It makes me want to lend a helping hand. It doesn't hurt that this guy's apparently Anabelle's friend, and helping him will be like helping her.

"Sit down." I wave toward the couch. "I'm making you a drink."

His gaze weighs whether I'm serious, and when he decides I am, he lowers onto the sofa—only to promptly withdraw a cloth hand-kerchief and clean up the whiskey on the floor.

A snort escapes me as I make my way to the credenza and pour him hot chocolate, adding some cinnamon whiskey. "You always cleaning up other people's messes?"

"Yes," he says sadly as he regards the soiled handkerchief and then neatly folds it and sets it on the table.

I add more whiskey to his drink, fill my cup, and join him back on the couch. Handing it to him, I say, "Seems like you could use this. I might not know much, but I know how to listen."

He regards me doubtfully, so I shrug and tell him, "Last Christmas someone drew a dick on my face in permanent marker when I was passed-out drunk, and I didn't know how to get it off. I came here for the holidays, and Anabelle's grandmother had to wipe it off for me."

He starts laughing, so I keep going. "One time I got pissed off at my brother, like I was seeing red, but I couldn't bring myself to hit him. He's my brother. My twin. So I punched a tree and nearly broke my hand. Got an infection from all of the splinters."

He's relaxing, his shoulders loosening, and he takes a sip of the hot chocolate. So I go for gold. "And another time, this woman broke up with me because—" *I'm dumb*, is what I was going to say, but I swallow the words. "Because she realized I didn't know the differ-ence between 'your' and 'you're.' I tell you what, buddy. I've never fucked that up again."

He slides his glasses up the length of his nose. "You didn't know the difference between *your* and *you are*?"

Of course he latched onto that one...

"What can I say? Everyone tells you it's important to pay attention in school, and apparently they had a point. It was never any good for me, though. I couldn't sit still, and half of what they said went right over my head."

He settles back into the couch cushions. Something tells me *he* never had trouble paying attention in school. There's this air smart people have—an ownership of what they say and how they say it. Anabelle has it too. It's one of the first things I noticed about her.

Now I seem to notice everything about her—the way her hair is ten times messier at the end of the day than the start of it, because the wind seems to like her as much as I do. The way she always taps her fingers against her thumb when she's thinking. The curve her mouth makes when she wants to smile but isn't sure she should. All the little pieces that add up to make her the person she is.

He narrows his eyes at me, and I sense the test before it comes. "You look like the kids who made my life miserable in school."

"The only person whose life I made miserable in school was myself."

He sighs and sets his drink down on the table, careful to use a coaster. Then he unzips the furry blue jacket, revealing a Christmas sweater that makes me smile—Santa riding on Rudolph.

"Nice sweater."

He narrows his gaze, but I set my drink down and lift my hands up, palms out.

"Honest to God, I'm not making fun of you, my friend." I motion to all of the Santa Clauses positioned around the room. "I was a foster kid, so Santa was never a big deal for me. But it's cool that you and Anabelle are into it. My brother and I used to collect comic books and these pog things. Everybody should have a thing, you know?"

He takes another sip of his chocolate as if considering, then says, "I'm a reseller. Anabelle does some of that too, but she also makes her own stuff."

"I know. I've seen the Franken-Santas."

This seems to further relax him, and he lets out a long, slow sigh. "My boyfriend was cheating on me, and when I accused him of it and showed him evidence, he called me delusional and broke up with me. He said he's going to throw out all of my stock if it's not cleaned out by next Wednesday."

If I can do one thing, it's haul boxes. I can do that like a champ. "Where from and where to?"

He messes with his glasses, not looking at me. "Charlottesville."

A couple of hours away, but it's not a big deal if we have a few days.

"And where to?"

He sighs and dives both hands into his hair. "I don't know."

"You don't have anywhere to stay?"

He glances around. "I was hoping..."

Shit.

He doesn't have anywhere to go or anyone to help him. Again, I feel a wrenching sensation in my chest. That's how I felt last Christmas, and the kindness of a complete stranger changed my life. Sure, it took a while, but Grandma Edith planted the damn seeds, and this fall they sprouted.

Maybe it's time for me to pay it forward. Especially since this guy is Anabelle's friend.

I say, "Anabelle told me the inn's full tonight."

"Oh, sure." He adjusts his glasses even though they seemed in no danger of falling. "I can find another place to stay."

"I'm going to be here for a while. Kind of a...life sabbatical. You can bunk in my room until one of the others opens up. There are two double beds, but we'll need to talk to Anabelle about what to do with your stuff. There's a basement that seems to have space, and the water pipes just got fixed."

"But you don't even know me," he objects, his eyes rounding. "And I don't know you."

"I've got some pepper spray you can keep under your pillow if it'll make you feel better."

"You're not worried I—"

"Look," I say, waving my mug to make the point. "Not to be a dick, but I'm not concerned you'll try to kill me in the night. I may not be very smart, but I'm strong, and I have a hair-trigger startle reflex. You're not going to successfully sneak up on me."

He gulps from his drink and sets it down again. "No. I just... You know I'm gay, right? You're not worried I'm going to try to come on to you?"

I snort. "You know I'm straight, and I know you're gay. If you think I'm attractive, it would be a compliment, but I doubt you'd come on to someone you know isn't interested. Just like I don't go around hitting on hot married chicks."

He laughs. "So you think you're hot?"

"I know what I look like, and I wouldn't hold it against you if you've noticed. Plenty of other people do." Usually women who want a fling with the dumb musclehead for a few weeks.

He laughs again, smiling readily now, and I know I've set him at ease.

"Most straight guys don't think that way." He takes another sip of the drink before sitting back.

"Lucky for us, I'm not most guys. Let's go talk to our girl."

I've got no business calling her that, or thinking about her like that. She's a woman I've known a week. But I don't rush to correct myself.

Joseph throws back the rest of his drink as if he's steeling himself for something.

"What's wrong, Joseph?" I ask.

"If we're going to be friends, you can call me Joe." He looks into the bottom of his empty cup, as if hoping it will magically refill, before giving me his attention again. "Anabelle thinks I'm a woman."

I really must be an idiot, because I'm only now realizing I'm sitting with her friend "Jo."

CHAPTER FIFTEEN

ANABELLE

Friday, December 5, 20 days until Christmas

> *Inns in peril: 1, but at least the water pipes won't break*
> *Santas sold: 5*
> *Santas made: 2*
> *Number of times I've secretly worn Ryan's sweater: I'd prefer not to put it into writing.*
> *Number of times I fantasized about crunching into the other end of Ryan's candy cane so I could kiss him: That's between me and my broken brain.*

I didn't mean to put on Ryan's sweater. Again. In fact, I meant to return it days ago. It's just so comfortable. Wearing it, I feel more comfortable in my own skin. It's needed after this afternoon, when yet another stranger told me that my favorite place in the world was showing its wear.

I started working as soon as the electrician left, and the familiarity of crafting has sucked me in, bringing me to that creative space where I can make magic. Except I'm a Christmas witch who can only cast a single spell: making Franken-Santas.

I'm so lost in my work that I barely notice time has gone by or register the knocking on my door.

Saint Nick, who's been snoozing on a little patch of sunlight on my bed, complains. I glance at the clock and see that it's six.

I still feel lost to the world around me, but another knock lands on the door, and I remember that Ryan is hosting Hot Chocolate Happy Hour. Again.

It must be him.

A thread of self-recrimination gnaws at me, threatening to cut off my air supply. Part of me fears my father and Weston are right about me, and I'm just not cut out for inn-keeping. The last two days have gone surprisingly well, despite the visits from the plumber and the electrician, but that's because I've had so much help from Ryan and Cynthia.

I set down the Santa I'm working on and pad over to the door, followed by Saint Nick, who sits beside me when I stop to peer through the peephole.

I see Ryan, holding a mug of hot chocolate.

I find myself smiling as I open the door.

Saint Nick weaves around Ryan's legs and then sits down beside one of his shoes, so apparently their new truce still stands.

"Humping makes the heart grow fonder," he says with a laugh.

"I'll keep that in mind." The words slip out before I can capture them and tug them back, and my brain immediately zips into overdrive. "I mean—"

"I know what you meant," he says with a smile, capturing my hand for a moment. His eyes glide over me, clinging to the sweater, and his smile spreads wider. I feel a new awareness of the fabric engulfing me, its heat all around me.

"I'm sorry," I say again, self-conscious. "I know it's yours, and I still have every intention to give it back, but it's *very* comfortable. It's hard for me to find the perfect sweater."

"You don't have to be sorry. The sweater looks better on you. But you have a guest downstairs, and I thought maybe you'd want to see him—and also that you should drink this very alcoholic hot chocolate before you do."

I step back into my room, needing to burrow into its safety, and my little cat rises and joins me. "Is it Weston?'

"Not Weston," he says, catching my wrist again.

Usually I don't like being touched by strangers, but his grip is light, his touch surprisingly soothing—and as soon as I stop moving backward, he releases me.

He hands me the chocolate. "Now, bottoms up. I think you definitely need to drink that before we move on to Exhibit B."

"Exhibit B being the man who's waiting for me downstairs?" I say with a long exhale. "Is it Santa Claus? An elf?"

"Neither of those, I'm sorry to say, but I think you'll probably be happy to see him."

"So it's definitely not my father, then."

My father has texted a couple of times since the estate sale, but I haven't found it in me to message him back, particularly since neither of his texts contained an apology for A) saying I was a fool for not accepting Weston's proposal, or B) telling Ryan that I'm not normal. He was right, I suppose, but his comment was both cruel and ill-intended.

"No, I would have warned you," Ryan says.

"I don't care for surprises," I point out.

"And I usually like nothing better than ruining surprises, but in this particular situation, I don't think it's my place." He gestures to the cup of hot chocolate. "Why don't you take a good slug of that, though."

He's not wrong. I need it. So I take a gulp—cinnamon and chocolate, delicious—and then set the mug on the dresser.

"I'm as ready as I'll ever be," I announce, and Ryan grins at me encouragingly before nodding toward the stairs.

I shut my door behind me, because Saint Nick lost interest in our conversation a few minutes ago and has settled onto my bed as if he owns it. We walk down side by side, and I find myself giving Ryan a sidelong glance, taking in that little scar on his chin, the waves in his light-brown hair, and the powerful biceps hugged by his long-sleeved shirt. He's a surprise—a mystery—and I'd like to unfurl him too.

When we get to the parlor, Ryan gapes at the room beyond.

It's empty.

"Is the surprise that he's transparent?" I ask. "Because that *would* be impressive."

"Well, I'll be..." Ryan says, but then his gaze falls to the coffee table, mine following it.

There's a handwritten note:

*I'm a coward. Can you please tell her? I'll come back
for Hot Chocolate Happy Hour tomorrow.*

I give Ryan a quizzical glance.

"Why don't you sit?" he suggests.

"I'll stand." I'm tired of being a person who has to sit to absorb bad—or at least strange—news.

"So, it was your friend Jo who came by."

Excitement bursts through me. "She was *here*? She asked about meeting in person, but I thought we'd set a date."

Then I remember the note. The mystery man...

"Yes." His mouth hitches to the side, his eyes crinkling slightly at the corners, and I know he's amused. "But she is a he."

"*What?*"

He maintains a level gaze, his face impossible to read. "I'm surprised you two have never met before. He said you've been chatting online for a year and a half, about everything. Your boyfriends. Your businesses."

"It's easier for me to communicate in writing most of the time," I say, feeling completely thrown. Over the last couple of days, one surprise after another has materialized, like a set of Russian dolls. I don't care that Joe's a man and not a woman. It's his soul that matters to me. But the fact that we've been talking for this long and I didn't know, and he didn't tell me...it's stunning.

I don't like that he didn't trust me enough to tell me the truth.

"Joe realized you thought he was a woman, but by then you'd been talking for months, and he was worried you'd retreat. He didn't want to lose you, so he let the misunderstanding stand. But it sounds like his life just imploded in a big way and he might need our help."

"*Our* help?" I repeat, stunned anew.

It's not the first time Ryan has called us a "we," but this one really rattles me for some reason. In a good way, I think, but it also feels dangerous.

He meets my gaze, and his mouth curls again into that smirk, and something inside of me melts like chocolate yielding to a hot marshmallow. "Yeah. What do you know. I think he just became my friend too." He glances at my merry Santas. "He says he needs somewhere to stow his Christmas stuff. His ex-boyfriend is threatening to toss it all."

I gasp, promptly decide that I would like to sit after all, and plop down onto the sofa. Ryan's smile spreads wider as he sits next to me.

"It's not funny."

"Didn't say it was. It's just...cute, how into this you both are. He nearly snapped my head off when I almost used that tea towel on the credenza to wipe up a spill."

I chuckle, remembering. "Probably because that's how I met Joe. We both bid on it, and I won."

"Why didn't you sell it if it's worth that much dough? No offense, but it's nothing special to look at."

I glance at the tea towel, then at him. "I could have sold it. I had someone who wanted to buy it, but it was tied to how I met Joe, and I couldn't bring myself to give it up."

He watches me for a long moment, his throat bobbing up and down, like he's literally swallowing what I said.

I don't think any man has ever looked at me this way—like he likes what he's seeing. Like he wouldn't change a thing about me if given the chance. I've had men who have wanted me, and men who have used me, but never a man who valued me.

My hand reaches up without bothering to ask permission from my body, my fingers brushing the tiny scar under his lip. His mouth opens, and a hidden pervert who must have been dwelling inside of me my whole life suddenly comes out. I want to stick my finger in his mouth to see if he'd suck on it.

It's an intrusive thought, and I tug my hand back. But I don't move away from him.

"How'd you get that scar? I've been wondering."

"I did something stupid and got hit for it."

"What happened?" I ask, my heart hurting for him, because somehow I know it wasn't good, and it wasn't his fault.

He shrugs. "I was eighteen, maybe, and my boss asked me to do something a certain way. I thought I could do it better. He disagreed."

"So he punched you? What kind of work did you do?"

His smile feels half-hearted. "Dark work."

"So you said," I murmur numbly. Was he a wrestler? An underground boxer? Some kind of criminal? "Did you punch him back?"

He makes a snort of amusement. I feel myself edging a little closer to him, enough that our sides are lightly touching, and I'm so hyper-conscious of him that I can barely think.

"No, Anabelle, I didn't punch him back. He was... I looked up to him a lot back then. I figured I probably deserved it."

"No one ever deserves to get punched," I say fiercely, reaching up again to brush my fingers over his scar. He watches me as I do it. I can't read the look in his eyes, but it's warm.

"I've punched other people," he says. "Plenty. For saying my brother and me had fleas. For calling me stupid, even though it's mostly true—"

"It's not," I snap.

He smiles softly at me. "Thank you for that. But I got in lots of dumb fights in school. It's one of the reasons I dropped out. The other is that I couldn't focus."

I trace the scar again, trying to see him as the wild kid who got into fights. The lost kid who didn't get the help he needed.

"They failed you," I tell him, my hand still cupped around his face.

"You keep saying that." He shakes his head, the motion moving my hand. I'm struck by how little space exists between us right now, as if the world has shrunken to bring us closer together. He's still smiling at me, and I feel a painful awareness of him. At this moment we really do feel like an us. "And while I'm encouraged that you care enough to make excuses for me, you don't have to. I was a terror. They didn't know what to do with me."

"You're not like that anymore." My fingers trace the side of his face as if they don't know how to stop touching him. He shaved this morning, but I feel scruff under my fingers, everywhere except on that scar.

"I still am a bit. I can't tell you how much self-restraint it took for me not to punch Weston the other day. I still want to do it. Right this minute, I'd like to get up and track him down, just so I can punch his face the instant he opens the door."

"Oh, he'd never open the door if he saw your face through the peephole. I think he's afraid of you."

"He should be."

This time, my finger moves over the scar and then traces his bottom lip. His lips are softer than I expected them to be, and I feel my heart beating faster. Each breath I take feels harder to draw in. I'm dancing at the edge of a cliff, but I don't want to stop. This man is dangerous and full of secrets, and my parents would never, ever approve of him, but I've known him to be nothing but kind and thoughtful. Sweet.

"You didn't hit him, though," I say. "You're older. More capable of controlling yourself. You've learned."

"You're like a one-woman hype squad." He leans his face in a little closer, as if nuzzling my hand, and I'm so overcome by him it takes me a moment to form words.

"So are you. You make me feel..." Suddenly tears are forming behind my eyes. I brush my hand up and into his hair, weaving it around my fingers. "You make me feel like I'm capable."

"You are," he says intently, his brow furrowing, making me want to skate my fingers across that too. There's still a few inches between us on the sofa, but we're leaning into each other, our mouths so close that the air between us is shared. "I hope I also make you feel beautiful."

"You do," I say, that breathless feeling gripping me again.

"Because you're so beautiful to me, Anabelle." He leans in closer, his mouth a whisper away from mine, and I'm so enthralled by it, by him. Every bit of me is present and in need.

"And you're beautiful to me," I admit, to him and myself.

His mouth is still hovering over mine, so close I can almost feel his lips. But he doesn't span the distance between us, and he doesn't pull away. The tension between us is pulled taut like a caught thread. Maybe I'll always be hanging here, in the middle of something, because I'm not brave enough to take a chance.

That's the thought that finally does it, and I lean closer and press my lips to his. He sighs into me as he kisses me.

His mouth is soft on mine at first—a brush of the lips, almost like we were leaning in for a cheek kiss and someone got confused. My hand is still wrapped around his hair, though, and when I use it to bring him closer, his lips become more demanding. They move over mine as if he's as interested in learning me as I am in learning him. He sucks in my bottom lip and moves his tongue against mine, and everything inside of me is focused on him. I no longer hear the hiss of the radiator or notice the way the Christmas lights shine off the ornaments or hear the slight creaks of an old house filled with people. I only experience Ryan—the groan he makes in the back of his throat as he kisses me, the feeling of his lips and tongue, and the taste of his cinnamon whiskey. The way he keeps his eyes open, as if he wants to remember who it is he's kissing.

So do I. Kissing someone new for the first time after the end of a relationship should probably feel strange, but there's no awkwardness or regret. This is what kissing should be, I decide—so delicious and decadent you don't want to stop and maybe don't even know how.

Ryan is the one who pulls back, his hair mussed and his dark eyebrows arched as if in surprise. "Whoa," he says, tipping his forehead until it touches mine. Tingles of pleasure radiate through me.

"Whoa," I echo.

His hand reaches for mine, and I give it to him, only then feeling a brush of apprehension. Because there's an unreadable look in his eyes as he pulls his head from mine.

"God, I like you, Anabelle. I like you so damn much. But I don't know how long I'm going to stay."

"I know what indefinitely means," I say, my tone a little prickly, because uncertainty is starting to pulse back into my bloodstream.

"Of course you do." He smiles and traces my jaw, his fingers insistent on knowing me. "You probably know ninety-nine percent of the words in the dictionary."

I don't argue. I expect he's right. I just wait for him to get to whatever point he's inching his way toward, feeling dread in the pit of my stomach.

But he doesn't get to the point. He just peers at me, his eyes intense and full of a meaning I can't interpret, and finally I say, "You're trying to tell me this was a mistake."

He shakes his head, though his eyes are full of regret. Usually, it's hard for me to read other people's cues, but I can almost see it clustered around his pupils. "Not a mistake. A kiss like that could never be a mistake. But you're too important to me to..."

"Too important to kiss?" I ask in disbelief.

"Exactly," he says as if he agrees with that nonsensical remark. "I'm here to help you, and I can't let wanting to..." he clears his throat, "kiss you get in the way. Your grandmother asked me to help you with the inn, and that's what I intend to do."

It's as if he just broke the spell that had descended over us.

I get to my feet, suddenly furious with him, my grandmother, and every single person in my life. Even Joe, whom I've trusted with far too much personal information, has lied to and manipulated me. "That's what was in that letter?"

"Part of it."

"My grandmother asked a complete stranger to help me?"

He bows his head, his hair hanging in the front. "She meant a lot to me."

"She meant a lot to me too, Ryan. But *I* didn't ask you for help. And I don't need or want it, not if you're giving it to me out of some sort of obligation."

"I'm not," he says, getting up too. "I'm not. That's not—" He swears, sweeping his hands through his hair. "I'm no good at finding the right words, Anabelle. I'm not here because your grandmother asked me to get rid of Weston, I—"

"*What?*" I fume, my voice rising.

A groan rolls out of him. "Oh shit. That wasn't the right thing to say either."

The terse woman who's staying in Room C hurries past us and up the stairs.

"Have a pleasant day, Bea," Ryan calls after her.

Of course he knows her name. I do, too, but it's not because she and I have had any conversations. I dart an accusatory look at him.

Turning back toward me, he says, "I'm doing this all wrong."

He has the expression of a puppy dog who peed on the rug, but I can't worry about his feelings right now, while I'm being eaten alive by mine. There's anger, certainly, but beneath it is something rawer.

"You think? Why would I be happy to find out you only kissed me because my grandmother told you to *take care of me*, like I'm some kind of problem? I thought you believed in me." My throat gets tight. "I thought she did too."

"She *did*," he says, almost frantic. He reaches for my hand, but I tug it away. "So do I." His tone is firmer. "If you're wondering if I'm here because Grandma Edith asked me to come back, then yes. That's why I'm here. But I didn't have to stay. I wasn't going to mess with your life. I just wanted to stick around for long enough to make sure you were safe and everything was going well."

"And you saw what a mess my life really is. Fantastic." I fold my arms over my chest. "But I don't need you to fix me, Ryan. I don't need anyone to fix me."

Something like hurt passes over his face, but he nods. "Are you asking me to leave?"

I could.

I *should*.

The expression on his face suggests he'd listen.

But I still haven't unfurled his mysteries. If I don't, I'll always wonder. I'll wonder, too, if I sent him back into the darkness after he left this place.

So I shake my head.

"I'm your friend, Anabelle," he pleads. "I want to be your friend."

The part he leaves out—*I don't want to kiss you.*

He implied it was a good kiss, but maybe it wasn't. Maybe he's used to kissing fashion models who take kissing classes in Paris, and my lack of technique disgusted him. Or maybe I misread his signals and he didn't want to kiss me at all...

Anxiety pulses through me, springing back and forth between my muscles and skin.

"I have to go," I say.

"I'm sorry."

"I'm the one who should be apologizing it seems," I say primly. But I still can't bring myself to do it. "Good night."

I'm dying to tell someone about this, but Jo's...well, Joe...and that's something else I still haven't wrapped my head around. I could call Cynthia, but she's probably on her way back from D.C., and I don't want to be the reason she gets into an accident.

An hour later, there's a knock on my door, but when I peer out of the peephole, I don't see anyone.

I open the door and find a wrapped sandwich waiting for me.

He made it. I can tell by the layers of flavor and the perfect execution.

I eat it like a ravenous animal.

CHAPTER SIXTEEN

RYAN

I've screwed up with Anabelle, but at least she doesn't want me to leave the inn.

I'm never going to forget what it felt like to kiss her. It was pure bliss, easily better than anything else I've ever experienced in my whole life.

Kissing her was a bad idea, though. Grandma Edith wouldn't like it, for one thing. For another, Anabelle is the kind of woman who should only be pursued by a man who has something to offer. I don't have anything. I was rejected for a job shoveling horse shit, for Christ's sake, and while I do have an interview tomorrow, if I don't blow it off, the only other solid job prospect I have is to work for another criminal. Even though I have no intention of taking Javier up on his offer, that doesn't change the fact that it's sitting there on my phone—or that he's one of the few people I'd call a friend.

I'm no good for Anabelle, end of story. If I let myself think otherwise, I'm playing pretend, and no good can come of playing yourself for a fool.

Still, I can't stop thinking about the look in her eyes after I told her about her grandmother's note. She doesn't even know about the ornament or my criminal history, and she already thinks I betrayed her. What would she think if she knew everything?

Probably she'd feel like Jake.

She'd want me to leave.

Maybe the best thing to do would be to give her the sweetgum ornament and go. Hell, I don't even need to give it to her. I could hang it up on the tree, all nice and pretty, and disappear in the night.

I seriously consider doing just that. I even take the little box out of the closet, twice, but both times I put it back. I tell myself it's because one of Grandma Edith's dying wishes was for me to help Anabelle and the inn, and I'd be a dick to ignore it. But there's no denying I don't want to leave her. I can still feel her mouth against mine and her hand tracing over my scar as if she could erase everything that put it there.

I get only a few hours of sleep, but I wake up on Saturday morning with bouncy feet. I leave before breakfast and stop by the gym where I've been working out at all week. The owner gave me a good deal because business is slow in December, before the rush brought in by New Year's resolutions. Unfortunately, that also means he's not looking for any new employees right now.

While I work out, I think about Anabelle and The Gingerbread House and everything we can do to help it succeed once we get Weston to mind his own business. And I think about my interview, trying to decide whether or not I should even go. It's a ridiculous job. A temporary job. But I'm leaving, aren't I? So maybe a temporary job would be best.

It doesn't hurt that I know it's a job that would please Anabelle...

So after I shower and change into the clothes I brought for the interview, I head over to Curio. It's a huge toy store, and I'm not going to lie, I'm tempted to walk around and dance on the huge musical keyboard, play the handheld video games, and press every button in the place.

I can practically hear Jake calling me Arrested Development, but I don't know who he thinks he's kidding—he's always dived in right after me.

That's the problem, a voice in my head reminds me. *You've taken him to bad places, more than once. No wonder he wants nothing to do with you.*

I meant what I said to Anabelle yesterday. I don't want to be that person anymore. Maybe that's the real reason I pulled away from her. Obviously, I wanted to do so much more than kiss her. If I'd had my way, I would have carried her up to her room and lost myself in her, but then I wouldn't have been able to make myself leave. And there's a good chance I would have dragged her into my next bad decision with me.

I head to the front and tell an elderly woman at the cash register that I'm there to see the manager. She's wearing a pair of jeans paired with a button-up denim shirt and has bright-blue eyes and white hair cut into a short, shaggy style. Most of her wrinkles are around her mouth, so she either laughs a lot or frowns a lot.

She gives me a long look and blows an enormous bubble with her gum, which she lazily draws back into her mouth. The shop just opened, and the store's not too busy yet.

"And you are?" she says.

"I'm Ryan. I'm here to audition for Santa Claus."

She snorts. "I'm Ada. We spoke over email." She shifts and gives me an up-and-down look, her mouth pursed. "There's no jelly in your belly, kid. The last guy who came in here wanting the gig had at least a hundred pounds on you. That's what the kids expect. I'd be a fool to hire you over him."

"I can wear a pillow. One of my foster dads wore a pillow when he played Santa. Children believe what they see. Plus, I could pick up the reindeer." I lift my arm and flex. "Juggle some elves."

She studies me for a moment, looking unamused, then continues to chew her gum. "Foster kid, huh?" She chews aggressively for another few seconds before saying, "What would you say to a kid who asked you for a moped?"

"You'll shoot your eye out, kid," I say, referencing my favorite Christmas movie. Maybe the only Christmas movie I've ever seen from start to finish, owing to the fact that it used to play constantly on every network around Christmas.

She gives me a half smile. "Or you could convince them what they really need is in this store." She nods down an aisle. "We've got motorized scooters in aisle D."

"I like the way you think," I tell her with a grin. "I can handle that. I'll take a stroll around, familiarize myself with the goods. I'll be the best salesman Santa you ever had."

She pops another bubble, then slowly draws the gum back into her mouth. Through it all, her eyes never leave mine, like we're in a stare-off. Something tells me this broad would beat me, easy. "The pay's not good," she says after a moment. "Best I can offer you is fifteen bucks an hour. Four days a week, five-hour shifts."

Doesn't sound too bad to me. I could make a lot more as a bartender, but that lifestyle isn't good for me. Too many loud-mouthed jerks aiming for a fight and women wanting to go home with the bartender.

"All right. It's about what I'd expect for babysitting."

She gives a dry chuckle. "Okay. I'm an idiot not to go with the big guy, but I used to be a foster mom. I'm going to give you a shot. Get yourself a Santa suit and a pillow, and come back at three p.m. on Wednesday."

"Why Wednesday? Mustn't be many people passing through on Wednesday."

She pops her gum again, cackling. "Exactly. The days we have Santa are Wednesday, Friday, Saturday, and Sunday. I found someone more seasoned to fill in this weekend. We'll try you out nice and easy on Wednesday, see how you do. Don't forget the beard and wig."

"And where would you recommend that I find such things?"

She gives me a flat, unimpressed look. "If you can't find a Santa suit and a wig in December, you don't deserve to have a job anywhere, kid."

"That's fair," I say with a grin. Then, because she basically told me to, I do a walkaround of the store, pausing to play Jingle Bells on the step-activated piano. I'm about to head out and go on a Santa-suit-finding mission when something in the stuffed animal section catches my eye—a striped orange cat like Saint Nick, dressed in a Santa suit.

There's nothing for it. Anabelle has to have it. It's totally normal for friends to buy gifts for each other, right? Especially after one of them has royally messed up? I grab a shopping basket and stick the cat inside.

I look around some more and notice a Christmas coloring book. Huh. Maybe Hot Chocolate Happy Hour will be more successful if there's something for kids to do while their parents drink. The coloring book seems boring—or at least boring compared to drinking alcoholic hot chocolate—so I keep poking around until I find some colorforms and a Christmas-themed comic-book-creation kit. My brother's an artist, self-taught. He's the one who designed the tattoos we both have on our right forearms, and he's working on a graphic novel. Maybe he's finished it already. I feel a tug in my chest as I add both items to my basket.

I wish I could tell Jake what I'm up to. I definitely wish I could ask him for advice about Anabelle. But I'm not ready to talk to him yet. I figure I'll know when I'm ready, but it hasn't happened yet.

As I check out the other kids' crap, most of it plastic junk that'd offer an hour of enjoyment at most, I feel a growing sense of excitement for my new job.

I bring my basket to the front, and Ada takes one look at the cat and grins at me. "I understand the impulse of a bargain buy, but that won't fit you, you know."

I laugh with her. "No, but Santa needs a sidekick."

"You've got children of your own?" she asks shrewdly, looking up at me as she puts the cat in a shopping bag.

"Nah, the stuffed animal is for a friend who has a thing for cats and Santa suits. She runs a B&B, and I figured the kids who are visiting would appreciate some activities."

She huffs a croupy laugh that suggests she's adopted the gum habit to kick nicotine. Been there, done that. "This woman the reason you got a bee in your bonnet about playing Santa?"

Yes, dammit.

But it's not because I want to seduce her. I do, of course, and maybe I could have last night. But she's too important to seduce. The women I've seduced have never stuck around—because while I may know how to have fun, I don't know how to do much else. And because I don't trust most people.

I trust her, though. I don't think she'd ever lie to anyone, not about something important.

All the more reason not to give her anything to lie about. If we were together, I'd have to tell her everything, but she wouldn't be able to tell other people.

It would never work.

That said, I *do* want to please Anabelle. I sure as shit want to earn another of her smiles to erase the look she gave me before she went upstairs last night.

"Maybe," I admit. "What do you think my odds are?"

Ada makes a honking sound that passes for a laugh and winks at me. "You'd do better without the pillow. See you on Wednesday, stud."

And just like that I've got myself a chance.

CHAPTER SEVENTEEN

ANABELLE

Saturday, December 6, 19 days before Christmas

> *Inns in peril: 1*
> *Heart in peril: 1*
> *Santas ordered: I don't know. I haven't checked the*
> *website. I think I'm unwell.*

Text conversation with Weston

Are you dating that thug, Belle?

Your father said he saw you at an estate sale with him the other day.

Big mistake.

It's none of your business who I am or am not dating.

Ryan's done a few sweet things for me, sure, but last night he made it clear that his kindness stemmed from obligation. So as soon as I got back up to my room, I removed the sweater and folded it into a neat square. A wasted effort, to be sure, since I will have to get it dry-cleaned, but it felt like a message.

Not to Ryan, who won't see it, but to myself.

Do not get attached to this man. He doesn't want you.

I've had plenty of people be kind to me out of obligation, starting with my "best friend" in middle school, a girl who was forced by her mother to spend time with me because she thought it would be good for her to learn to be accepting of "differences."

It wasn't the first time someone spent time with me because I was a curiosity, an oddity they wished to observe up close. It probably won't be the last.

I want no part of it.

I come downstairs late, because I don't want to have to eat breakfast across from Ryan with his wet hair and the knowledge that he was just in the shower, *naked*. But he's not in the dining room, and I feel five seconds' relief, which fizzles into disappointment.

No one is in the dining room, actually, so I head into the kitchen and find Cynthia stooped over the dishwasher. Guilt dances across the small hairs at the bottom of my neck. I should be helping her with this. No, I should be doing it myself.

She looks up at me and drops the dish, but it's plastic and bounces. "Jesus. What happened? You look like you just saw the Ghost of Christmas Past."

I almost smile, but I don't have it in me. Instead, I pick up the plastic dish and fit it into the dishwasher. She rinses another dish and hands it to me, probably because she's aware having a task will help anchor me—and make it more likely she'll get information out of me.

"Yesterday was quite a day," I say, pausing as I look for the perfect placement for the spatula she handed me.

"Jeremy told me about the pipes. He was adamant that he got

you the best deal possible, but it's hard to tell with him. He's at least fifty percent bullshit." Her mouth scrunches to the side as she rinses a plate. "But he did call me up and ask me about my audition, so I guess that's something."

Oh snap. I forgot to ask her about the audition. More guilt dances at the bottom of my neck. "Cynthia," I say, taking the dish from her and setting it in the rack, "how was your audition? I'm sorry I didn't ask."

I'm guessing it didn't go well, because Cynthia would certainly have said something as soon as she saw me if it had. In fact, she probably would have offered a champagne toast to all of the guests, including six-year-old Ben, if she'd gotten a movie role.

"I'm too old," she says gruffly as she hands me a fork.

I drop the fork, caught off-guard, and then pick it up. "They didn't say that!"

"Actually, they did."

"Oh," I say, at a bit of a loss. All I can do is offer the truth, so that's what I give her. "You don't look old at all. Besides, life was brutal back then, and no one brushed their teeth. You probably look like a twenty-year-old from the 1600s would have."

She laughs, showing off her notably white teeth. "They still want everyone to be a perky blond teenager without any body hair. I almost bleached my hair last night, but Jeremy talked me out of it."

The way she says it ignites a suspicion that's been forming over the past few days.

"Do you like him?" I ask. "You know...*like* like?" Now, I feel like a teenager, but I'm not sure how else to ask.

She gives me an *Oh Anabelle* smile. It fades away, though, as she hands me the final fork from the sink. I stow it away and get the dishwater started.

When I look at her, she still has a far-off expression, but her eyes slowly focus on me. "He's only twenty-nine, you know."

"How old are you? I've never asked."

"Too old for him."

"That doesn't answer my question."

"Thirty-six." She arches her eyebrows. "I could have been his babysitter."

"Were you, though?"

"No."

"Good, because that probably would have been weird. But you weren't, so who cares if you couldn't have dated ten years ago. He's perfectly adult now. He's a year older than me, and you and I are friends."

I marvel over the ease with which I say it, and the conviction behind it, because it's perfectly true. We're friends. I value her, and she values me.

"You think he's mature?" She gives a harsh laugh and shakes her head. "He spends half his day on social media looking at that stupid video with his bulge."

Maybe this is where over-honesty will get me in trouble, but I like Cynthia, and I want her to be happy. I want her to be happy more than I don't want her to be upset with me. "I feel like you would also watch a viral video of yourself over and over again. Maybe that's something you two have in common."

"And would I brag about all of the women dropping me messages?"

I take a deep breath and hold her gaze. "I suspect most of them would be men, but I think you would, yes. I think the real question is whether he's messaged them back."

She looks taken aback, and it takes her a minute to respond. "Do you think he'd tell Ryan?"

My face must display a reaction to Ryan's name, because she gasps dramatically and grabs my arm. Her touch is slightly uncomfortable, but I don't want to jerk away. "Something happened between you and Ryan."

"Not really," I say, finally pulling away. But it hits me that

Cynthia might be better able to parse what happened than I am. She's dated a lot of men and kissed more of them. I have also dated several men, but my handful is smaller than her barrel. "I...well, I suppose I kissed him."

"Why, Anabelle Whitman," she says with excitement, her blue eyes fixed on me. "I didn't think you had it in you."

"I shouldn't have," I say forlornly.

She darts a furtive glance at the doorway. "Was it a bad kiss? Because I find that hard to believe."

"No, it was good...for me." My mouth puckers. "But it mustn't have been for him, because he apologized and told me that he only wants to be friends. Then he admitted that the only reason he's stayed around so long is because my grandmother asked him to help me take care of the inn. And she wanted him to get rid of Weston."

"We *all* wanted you to get rid of Weston," she says, shaking her head. "But he spoke just like men always do. Out of his ass. That boy is obsessed with you. I've been waiting for you to notice."

"He most definitely is not," I say stiffly. "He wants to take care of me as if I'm some stray dog. I don't need him to fix me. I'm perfectly fine on my own."

She smiles again, but it's a softer smile. "You may not need a man to fix you, and you may be perfectly fine on your own. But that doesn't mean the people who care about you won't want to support you."

Her words ripple through me, disrupting my thought patterns, but I firm myself against them. "He doesn't like me like that. He made it perfectly clear that he doesn't think we're suited for each other. Besides, I just broke up with Weston. I don't know what I was thinking."

"You weren't thinking, for once. You were feeling. And there's nothing wrong with that."

"Are you going to follow your own advice?" I ask her archly.

"Maybe I'll have a talk with Ryan."

"Don't!" I say, alarmed. The last thing I want is for her to make him think the kiss meant something to me. If he thinks that, he may realize that I'm starting to *like* like him. That would not be good, and...

"About Jeremy," she amends softly.

"Yes, you should probably do that," I agree with a relieved sigh. Then I remember Joe, who's probably somewhere in Williamsburg by her—himself. With no one to talk to. And from what Ryan said, there was a breakup with Craig...

Friends should support each other, exactly like Cynthia said.

"Anything else happen I need to know about?" she asks.

"My friend Joe is actually a man, and he's here in Williamsburg."

"Damn." She adjusts her bonnet. "This is what happens when you leave town for a day."

I smile at her, and she gives my arm a pat. "I have to go, hon, but you'll work it all out. And I mean it about Ryan. That boy has it bad. He's showing all the signs."

"What are the signs?" I ask in wonder.

"He doesn't look away from you. Everything he says is 'Anabelle this,' and 'Anabelle that,' and 'wouldn't Anabelle like this?' And don't even get me started on that red velvet pancake. Do you know he mixed a whole new batter to make that for you yesterday?"

"He doesn't seem like the kind of man who'd hold back if he wanted to kiss someone." No, he seems like a man who'd sweep a woman off her feet, kick the door open, and throw her onto the bed... Not that I've been thinking it.

"He wouldn't hold back if he didn't give a shit, probably. Which only means that he does give a shit."

"I don't know anything about him, though."

She sniffs. "All the better. The more you know, the less interesting they are. I'll see you later, sugar."

She turns and goes, leaving me in the kitchen with the whirring dishwasher. I take my phone out of my pocket and tap into it. I want to talk to Ryan, and I also don't, but I one hundred percent want to talk to Joe.

I open the chatroom messaging app.

Ana-bell: Ryan told me.

Ana-bell: I'd like to talk. Where are you?

Jo-Ho-Ho: I'm on my fourth gingerbread latte at Aromas. You know how I get with my comfort drinks, and I figured it was kind of an homage to The Gingerbread House.

Jo-Ho-Ho: I'm so sorry.

Jo-Ho-Ho: When my parents found out I was gay, they turned me out of the house.

Jo-Ho-Ho: I was worried you might feel differently about me once you knew.

Ana-bell: That's horrible, Joe.

Ana-bell: Wait. Is that how you spell your name?

Jo-Ho-Ho: Ugh. Yes. I'm sorry.

Ana-bell: Well. You know I would never turn someone away because of something like that.

Jo-Ho-Ho: Logically, I understood that. But tell that to my anxiety.

Ana-bell: I get it. Of course I get it.

Jo-Ho-Ho: I'm a mess. If you don't want to meet me, I totally understand.

I pause, my fingers poised over the keys. Aromas is just around the corner. I could be sitting across from Joe in five minutes. *Five minutes* after all this time.

I'm tempted to defer our meeting. To tell him that he can come to happy hour tonight, which will give me more time to process everything that's changed and changing, but Joe has been my number one confidant for a long time now. I *want* to meet him, even if he's not the person I'd envisioned him to be.

Besides, what good has waiting done for me lately?

I'd sensed something was off in my relationship with Weston for months, and I'd let it go because I was too upset over Grandma Edith to even think about making a change. If I'd been proactive then, neither of us would have needed to experience that awful proposal.

> Ana-bell: I'll be right there.

It's chilly outside, and as I walk down the cobbles, my head tucked, I feel butterflies and snakes uneasily coexisting in my stomach. I almost turn back twice, but I steel myself and continue on.

It's Saturday morning, and even though Colonial Williamsburg hasn't opened yet and most of the college students probably won't roll out of bed for hours, several people are still milling around, pointing to the red bows adorning gates, one of Williamsburg's notoriously bold squirrels, or a distant sheep in a pen. The air smells like winter—crisp and with an edge of cinnamon and campfire. I love the smell of winter air. It's something I yearn for in the middle of summer when Williamsburg is a swamp and everything smells like sweat and suntan lotion.

I try to soak it in now as I get closer to the coffee shop.

A few more steps, past a group of tourists with a small blonde child and a dog, around a college student so sucked into their phone they don't seem to notice the world around them. Then the door is in front of me. Then I'm opening it. The scents of the shop meld with the winter scent of the air, and I try to let that steady me.

It's only now, standing in the doorway of the coffee shop, that I realize I have no idea what Joe looks like. The snakes are starting to overpower the butterflies, but as my gaze sweeps around the shop, I see him.

I know it's him in my chest.

Not because of his dark hair and glasses or even because of his amazing Santa water-skiing sweater, but because he's Joe. He radiates Joe.

I take a deep breath, release it, and approach his table. He turns to look at me as I approach, his eyes rounding, and suddenly I feel tears pressing at my eyes. Joe's here, after all of this time, and it doesn't matter that he's a man or that I didn't have enough time to plan for this meeting. I'm happy he's here.

He gets to his feet, and I'm hugging him before he can even say anything. He starts laughing, and then we're both laughing, practically dancing on our feet.

"It's you," I say. "It's you."

"I got you a gingerbread spice latte," he says when he finally pulls away, taking his glasses off to wipe them on his sweater.

"Be honest, is it just your fifth latte?"

"No, it's really for you," he says, laughing. "When I ordered it, I could hardly believe that I was ordering a drink for you. That we were going to be here together."

"Me either. It's pretty spectacular."

I sit down across from him, happy that we were able to meet in this familiar place, which doesn't take up much of my bandwidth, so I can give more of it to him.

We smile at each other for a moment, and then my smile slips. "Ryan told me what happened with Craig, Joe. I'm so sorry. Does this mean he was cheating on you?"

He rubs his mouth wearily. "He says he broke up with me because I didn't trust him. But I found a string of texts between them. He said I was taking everything out of context, but one of the messages was about wanting to shove his dick in Dean's mouth, so I don't know how I could misinterpret that."

"That *jerk*," I say with a gasp. "And to think, I really believed he was a keeper." My mouth purses to the side. "Then again, I also thought you were a woman, so I've been making all kinds of mistakes lately."

"Tell me what happened with Weston," he says. "I want all of it."

I sigh and tell him about the proposal mishap, reliving the embarrassment and claustrophobia as if it were happening right this moment. I can practically feel eyes on me, enough that I look up midway through telling him the story—only to discover that the barista and two of the customers really are looking right at us. The snakes in my belly take the advantage once again, because surely this means they've seen the videos, but I finish telling the story.

"Oh, honey," Joe says, and I'm relieved by how natural it feels to be sitting here and talking to him. It feels ridiculous that we waited this long to meet in person.

"I could say the same to you," I tell him.

He pushes his glasses up. "You know what else Craig said? He wants to live, and what I do is the opposite of living. He told me I was dragging him down."

"How dare he!" I say, affronted on his behalf. Maybe on mine too, because how many times have I been accused of living too much in my head and missing the world around me?

Joe smiles sadly. "But he was right, wasn't he? You know how many hours I clocked on my laptop last week?"

"But that's your *job*. And we bring joy to people. How is managing a supermarket any more meaningful?"

Not just any supermarket, but one that always smells like rotten broccoli. Or at least the Williamsburg branch does.

His smile turns more genuine, but a feeling of sadness oozes off him. "He looks good in his uniform."

I find this doubtful—I don't think anyone truly looks good in a supermarket uniform—but I nod, trying to appear sympathetic. "Where did you stay last night?"

He plays with his coffee cup, which is probably empty. Joe isn't greatly affected by caffeine, so he drinks about five cups of coffee a day. Coffee makes me buzz, which feels good—until it doesn't.

"I stayed at Comfort Zone," he says.

"You didn't," I reply, making a face.

Weston's hotels are *awful*. Full of fluorescent lights, chemical smells, and sadness.

"It's fine," he says kindly.

"It's definitely not. I don't have any rooms tonight, but there's space starting Monday, presuming the inspector doesn't put me out of business. Until then, we can set up an air mattress for you on the floor of my room. We'll figure it out. And when a room opens, it's yours, for however long you want it."

I think of Ryan's room, right next to mine, and how perfect it would be if I could offer it to Joe. And yet...

The thought of Ryan leaving, of never seeing him again, makes my stomach drop.

I will never, ever forget what it felt like to kiss him and be his sole focus, if only for a minute. Ryan has a physicality unlike any other man I've ever dated—he's more present in his body. It makes me wonder what *other things* would be like with him.

I'm disappointed. Bitterly disappointed. But I'm not really angry at him anymore. I'm more upset with my grandmother. If she felt she had to recruit a stranger to help me, she didn't have much faith in me at all.

As if Joe is reading my mind, he says, "Actually, Ryan told me I could crash on his other bed for a while. Would you be okay with that?"

"He really said that?" I ask, shocked, feeling the butterflies within me steal the advantage from the snakes. It's such a kind offer.

Maybe Ryan only decided to stay because my grandmother asked him to help me, but I'm guessing she didn't ask him to also help Joe.

Just like she didn't ask him to buddy up with Jeremy Jacobs and Cynthia.

Joe nods. "He also told me he'd help me get my stuff from Craig's apartment, but I don't know where I'll put any of it. I don't know what to do in general, or where I should go. You know I only moved to Charlottesville to live with him."

Joe is from a small town in Southwest Virginia, but based on what he said to me earlier, he won't want to go back there.

"Here," I say firmly. "You're supposed to be here, with me. Don't you feel it?" The butterflies take flight, and I grip the edge of the table to ground myself before remembering it's probably been touched by hundreds of sticky fingers since its last cleaning. "Joe, we need to combine our online businesses. You can do all of the reselling, and I'll specialize in making Franken-Santas from what we can't save. And, if you want, we can work on rebranding The Gingerbread House together."

"Really?" he asks, already grinning at me. "You want to take over the Christmas world with me, sister?"

"Yes! And you'll stay with me, of course. You can live at the inn." My mind drifts to Ryan and lingers, recalling the solidity of him. I clear my throat. "You can stay with Ryan at first, and then we'll move you to one of the guest rooms after someone leaves."

There are five guest rooms, including Ryan's. Not including mine.

He gives me a lopsided smile. "I'm almost glad Craig left me."

He doesn't mean it, not yet, but I vow to myself that he will mean it. I'm not going to allow anyone to break my friend's spirit. Certainly not the manager of a subpar grocery store.

I don't mean to, but I find myself asking, "What do you think of Ryan?"

He watches me thoughtfully as I sip my latte. "My first thought was that he looked exactly like the kids who'd made me miserable in school. All that thick muscle. So good-looking, and doesn't he know it. But there's more to him than there appears to be. He's the good kind of surprise."

Part of me is certain he's wrong.

Part of me is terribly worried he's right.

I sigh heavily. "I like him too."

My phone buzzes, and I take it out to find a text from my father.

Anabelle, I need to speak with you. Please come over tonight at 5:30 for a talk. It's very important, honey. It's about your grandmother.

There he goes, saying the only thing that could possibly convince me to agree to see him right now.

With a huff, I tuck the phone away.

"More bad news?" Joe asks sympathetically.

"Yes," I say, "but I'm not going to let it bring me down this time. I'm sitting here with you, and we're going to make the inn fabulous, and I don't care what anyone else has to say about it."

CHAPTER EIGHTEEN

RYAN

I figured I'd see Anabelle at Hot Chocolate Happy Hour. She didn't ask me to take over today, and I happen to know that both Cynthia and Jeremy have a shift that ends right at five.

But when I come down at four fifty-five with the stuffed cat in the bag, the only person who's in the Santa parlor is Joe in his fuzzy blue coat, with a duffel bag about ten times bigger than mine.

He tracks my gaze and blushes. "I don't mean to presume, but are you still okay with me crashing on the other bed? I had coffee with Anabelle earlier. She said she was okay with it if you're okay with it, and Comfort Zone is really awful, and—"

I lift a hand. "Buddy, I'm the one who suggested it. It's really no problem. But where's our girl?"

There I go again, running my mouth.

Joe glances out the open parlor door, then says in an undertone, "She's with her parents."

A sinking feeling fills my gut. I wish I'd known. She probably wouldn't have wanted to bring me with her, after what happened last night, and also because her father probably wants to murder me. Still. I don't like the thought of her going there alone after what that man said about her. Sure, he may have brought her to a Christmas tree lighting a quarter of a century ago, but he obviously hasn't done much to prove himself since. His own mother thought he was worthless, and even though my mother obviously decided Jake and I were worthless when we were basically toddlers, she was a drug addict whose judgment is much more questionable than Grandma Edith's.

"Yeah, I don't like it either," Joe says. "They're obviously trying to shove her and Weston back together."

I groan. "You think they invited him over too?"

"Probably. I'll bet it's some parent trap setup."

"Fuck," I fume. "Do you think we should go over there?"

"You want to crash dinner with her parents?"

He doesn't sound like he'd object, so I nod. "Yeah, I really do. I don't like the thought of that guy being anywhere near her."

"I don't know where they live, or I'd tell you," he says. "You know, she tried to break up with Weston before. Six months ago. But somehow it ended with them going on this vacation together. To, like, Disney World. She hates crowds. He's got an uncanny way of convincing her to do things she doesn't want to do."

I don't like that one bit.

"What do we do?" I ask.

"She's not going to take him back this time, man. He threatened her." He peers at me through his big glasses and then smiles knowingly. "You've got a thing for Anabelle, huh?"

"No," I say quickly, but his gaze has already tracked to the stuffed cat I'm holding in the bag.

Grinning at me, he plucks it out and waves it in front of my face. "The Santa Cat is out of the bag."

"Oh, fuck you."

Looking very amused with himself, he sticks the cat back in the bag. "I'm not going to out you, man. But maybe you should out yourself, if you'll excuse the choice of words. I bet it'll cheer her up to know there's another option on the table."

"I'm not an option," I say, setting the bag down next to the credenza and pouring myself a stiff drink. Screw hot chocolate.

I can feel Joe staring at me, so I turn to look at him.

"Why aren't you an option?" He grins, obviously coming into himself. It hits me like a fist to the gut that Anabelle's friend trusts me. I've done barely anything to earn that trust, which makes me feel like an asshole even though I haven't acted like one. "Because you're in love with me?" he adds blithely.

"You got it in one."

"Seriously. Why aren't you an option?"

"She's not my type."

It's true that Anabelle is unlike the women I've dated, but it's a bald-faced lie to say she's not my type. She's lovely in a way I can't quite wrap my head around—a joining of soft curves and hard edges that's almost painfully perfect, from her upright posture to her soft, long hair and those big brown eyes. I've been thinking of her nearly constantly since I got here, and in truth, I'd also thought of her a few times over the last year, as I struggled to come back here. To do what I'd pledged to do.

Then she was a picture, an ideal.

Now, she's a woman whose wall adjoins with mine. Whom I can hear fussing about her room and occasionally singing softly to herself, her voice sweet and low.

Joe's smile drops, and he develops a look of contempt as he pours himself some hot chocolate, adding Baileys.

"Is this because she's on the spectrum?" he asks.

"What spectrum?"

The look on his face is comical, and he nearly drops his mug.

"Careful," I warn, "you might have no choice but to use the tea towel for its intended purpose."

He wags his head at me and sets the mug down on a coaster. "You knew her grandmother. I guess I thought you knew."

"What spectrum?" I repeat.

"Autism," he says. "I don't feel bad telling you because it's not a secret."

"I don't really know what that means," I admit. I've heard the word, of course. Everyone's heard the word, but I'd never paid it much attention. Then again, that's a common thread of my life—Ryan, not paying attention to anything.

I make a mental note to sit down and do some research.

"Her brain works differently," he says with a shrug. "It's why she shuts down sometimes and can't handle crowds. She can be sensitive to sound and touch."

I think this through and decide I've found another reason to dislike Weston and her father. My rage is a red fist, pounding on the inside of my brain.

"Weston knew all of this and he still proposed to her in front of a crowd, outside?"

Joe lifts his eyebrows. "I know, right?"

"And now he's coming for her B&B? We need to vanquish the asshole."

He laughs and takes his hot chocolate over to the couch. "And you say you don't have a thing for her."

I don't respond to that, because I have no real response. Instead, I join him on the couch. "Have you rented a truck?"

He glances at me. "Not yet. You're really going to help me move my stuff?"

"Sure," I say, "but an inspector's coming by the inn Monday morning, and I have somewhere to be on Wednesday afternoon. You'll want to be done by then, anyway, though."

"Tomorrow would be good. The sooner, the better. I don't like the thought of leaving my treasures around Craig when he's in a mood." He cocks his head. "What have you got going on this Wednesday? I thought you were here on some extended vacation."

I grin at him. I know he'll appreciate this. "I don't like sitting around much. I have a trial run for a temporary Santa Claus gig."

He gives me an up-and-down appraisal. "You're teasing me again, aren't you? There's no way someone's hiring *you* to play Santa."

"I don't need yet another person insulting my acting skills."

He still thinks I'm messing with him. I can see it in his face as he purses his lips and says, "Where's the trial run?"

"Are you going to try to steal my job, partner?"

He laughs and shrugs out of his fuzzy blue coat. "No, man. I don't want sticky children pulling my hair and shouting in my ear to get them presents. No, thanks."

"You love Christmas, but you don't like children." I shake my head, smiling at him. "Doesn't compute."

"I didn't say I dislike children. I said I don't want them tugging on my hair or shouting in my ear. Sugar is a powerful drug. Do you have a suit?"

"Yeah. I picked one up this afternoon. Will you help me practice? To be honest, I don't have any idea what I'm doing, and you and Anabelle are Christmas experts."

Grinning, he pushes his glasses up. "Uh, yeah. I definitely want to see you as Santa Claus."

"Hold that thought." I get onto my feet, leaving the shopping bag with the cat and the games.

Joe glances at his big duffel bag pointedly, and I laugh as I hoist it onto my shoulder. "Yes, Joe, I'd be thrilled to carry this upstairs for you."

"You know..." He beams at me. "You're already Santa Claus to me."

I whistle as I walk up the stairs, feeling pretty good, although I'd feel a lot better if Anabelle came back from her parents' place. Maybe Cynthia knows where it is? I could scope it out, see if I spot Weston through the window, and if he's there...

If he's there, there's no way I'm not getting her out.

When I step into my bedroom, I slap the bag down on the

empty bed and then get changed into my Santa suit, which is much too loose until I stuff a pillow into it. The wig and beard look ridiculous, but maybe Joe will be able to fix it or tell me where to get a more convincing getup.

I'm almost done when I hear footsteps on the stairs. I about trip over my own feet to get to the door, but when I open it I only see Lauryn and her son Ben, the guests in Room F.

"Mom," he says urgently, his little hand fisting around the fabric of her coat. "Is *Santa* staying at our hotel?"

Lauryn gives me a sheepish look, but I'm on cloud nine. I've said literally nothing, and I've already fooled this kid, who should be able to recognize me perfectly well behind the barely there beard. My job with Ada is in the bag.

Even so, I get down on my haunches so I'm level with him and say, "No, man. I'm not the Santa, but I'm one of his helpers. If you and your mom would like to join us, I'm going to be hanging out downstairs for a while with some cool games."

"Ryan?" he asks in a serious voice, then lifts my beard and gasps. "It's really you!"

I glance up at his exhausted-looking mom. This woman needs an alcoholic beverage. "There will be some drinks for the adults," I add. "We'd love it if you'd join us."

"Are you with Mrs. Claus?" Ben asks.

My grin stretches wider. "Nah, I'm with one of my jolly elves, and he *loves* children."

CHAPTER NINETEEN

ANABELLE

Parents I'd like to return to the store: 2

I return to the B&B with a pounding headache, glancing at my watch before I walk in through the front.

It's six thirty.

I'd told myself I'd only stay for fifteen minutes—a half hour, tops.

Problem One: People always have their own motivations in a social interaction, and it's impossible to prepare for every eventuality.

Problem Two: I find it very hard to consciously hurt someone. I unconsciously hurt people all the time. But doing it purposefully, knowingly, is different. It doesn't matter whether or not they've intentionally hurt me, the way my father did at the estate sale.

Problem Three: My father refused to tell me his "news" about Grandma Edith until I listened to his tirade about Ryan. It went on and on, but this was the gist of it:

What do you know about this man?

Very little. He stayed at the inn with Grandma Edith last Christmas, and she was fond of him. He's here on a sabbatical.

Is he a teacher?

I don't think so, but I guess it's possible. I don't know what he does for a living.

Isn't that strange?

No, I don't know what most of my guests do for a living.

Is he the person who's standing between you and Weston? Weston loves you. He's desperate to marry you.

It has become very apparent to me that the only person Weston loves is himself. Perhaps I would have realized it sooner if I hadn't been raised by someone who is similarly self-obsessed.

This, of course, led to an argument, which my mother had attempted to defuse by pouring drinks for everyone. She seemed disinterested in all of it, but then again, she is disinterested in most things related to our family. She's an attorney who spends so much time at her office she occasionally sleeps there, although when I said as much to Cynthia, she pretended to zip her lips. I, of course, asked what she was doing, and she said, "Your mother doesn't look like the kind of person who'd spend the night in her office chair."

She has a point.

So perhaps she's having an affair, or simply finds my father so insufferable she regularly pays for hotel rooms to keep away from him.

Eventually, my father got to the point, which is this—

After attending dozens of estate sales, Christmas pop-ups, and the like throughout the state for the past year, as well as trolling every corner of the internet, he's convinced that Grandma Edith didn't give her prize ornament away to another collector. He believes she hid it inside of the inn.

So he wants my permission to search for it.

Again, I have trouble consciously upsetting people, my father being one of them. He's my father. But I firmed my chin and said, "No. She left me the inn, so if it is hidden inside of the inn, then it's mine. And if I find it, I won't be selling it."

He went red in the face and started in on me, calling me ungrateful and spoiled, but before he got too far, my mother shocked both of us by saying, "Oh, for the love of God, shut up."

I doubt she said it to stand up for me, since she's never bothered. My guess is that she is legitimately tired of hearing about the ornament. But it felt good nevertheless.

Still, I'm absolutely exhausted when I arrive back at the B&B. I expect quiet, but there's a wave of laughter and conversation emanating from the parlor. I check my watch again. It's still 6:30. Well, 6:31. Hot Chocolate Happy Hour has *never* gone past 6.

I glance at the stairs, weighing my options. Part of me is desperate to collapse and let the stress seep away while I'm asleep. But Ryan and/or Joe must be in there doing something, and I need to know what.

So I turn toward the parlor, my heart thumping an uneasy beat, because this is unexpected, and so many things have been unexpected over the last few weeks.

But unexpected doesn't cover what I find when I peer around the corner into the parlor.

Santa is drinking from a snifter, laughing with Enoch, Grace, and Lauryn, while Ben draws pictures in a book on the coffee table.

The parlor is full of laughter and merriment for the first time since my grandmother died—the same way the dining room was on Thursday morning. It's only then that I realize what probably would have been incredibly obvious to anyone else. It's *Ryan* dressed in that Santa suit, with a ridiculous pillow in his shirt that does nothing to hide his solid build. Red's a good color on him. Ryan, with his rumbling laugh and easy ways and perfectly symmetrical eyebrows. Ryan, who has drawn these people to him and made them enjoy themselves.

A strange feeling tears through me. I'm happy that the B&B is a happy place again, and I'm jealous that it's not because of me. I got along with everyone well enough yesterday, but I'm carrying my mood with me today. If I walk into that room, they'll probably all scatter like bugs from an opened box. The fun will shrivel. Similar things have happened to me all my life. I want to be a part of something beautiful, and I ruin it just by being present. By not knowing what to say or when.

I turn to creep up the stairs.

Joe's probably up there, but I already know in my heart that I won't knock on the door to Room B. I'll go alone to my own space and stay there.

But I only make it up one stair before I hear Ryan say my name behind me. I turn, and he's standing in front of me. The beard is so fake-looking, he might as well have stuck cotton balls on himself, and a laugh erupts from me as I reach out to touch it without meaning to. It's coarse beneath my fingers.

"You never knew a man could grow a beard so quickly, did you?" he asks, smiling tentatively at me. "They were calling me sir in the fourth grade."

"It looks like a fourth grader's art project," I say, running my hand over the material before I remember myself and tug my fingers away. Leave it to me to throw myself at a man who made it clear he doesn't want to kiss me. He's just so touchable. My fingers have taken a liking to him, and they're slower to catch on than my brain.

"Does that mean you like or dislike it?" he asks softly.

"Both." I glance behind him, and see that the grown-ups are still talking and the little boy continues to draw in his book. My eyes seek Ryan out and settle on the bridge of his nose before sliding down to his scar. He's perplexing to me, and I like to study perplexing things, but I know that's not the reason I enjoy looking at him. Touching him. Being with him. "They're having fun," I observe.

His grin grows wider. "I was showing Joe my new Santa outfit, and Ben saw me on my way down. So I invited him and his mother to come down to happy hour. I'd already picked up some stuff for kids to do. I could never sit still when I was a kid—"

"You still can't."

One corner of his mouth lifts higher than the rest, and even though there's nothing symmetrical about this smile, I decide I like it best. "You're right. Anyway. Enoch and Grace came in because he wanted to run through The Gingerbread House concept with you, and he heard us laughing."

"And is there a reason for the Santa outfit?" I ask in wonder.

Did he wear it for me?

Part of me wants to believe it, like the little girl who tried to stay up all night on Christmas Eve, hoping to see a man in a red suit come down the nonoperational chimney. Because surely that would be a sign that there's real magic in the world.

He jostles his weight between his feet. "I told you I had that interview today."

He did, and I feel a pang of self-reproach for having forgotten, when I usually never forget anything. "You did." Then his meaning penetrates. "You interviewed to be Santa Claus?"

"It's for a toy store. It's just...something to do."

"I thought you weren't into this whole thing." I wave a hand to encompass my inn, my room of Santa Clauses, and perhaps the entire month of December.

He swallows, his gaze on me. "Maybe I want to understand you and Joe a little better."

My heart beats faster, because I don't hear that often. Most people want me to understand them better; they don't care to understand me.

"Thank you." My voice is shaky, so I clear it. "And I'm getting you a new suit and beard."

"Joe already threatened me, but I think I like this one. It leaves a lot to the imagination."

His voice is almost playful, but truthfully his outfit leaves nothing to the imagination. Everything he wears is strained by his broad shoulders and muscular arms and chest, even his oversized Santa suit.

I clear my throat. "Where *is* Joe?"

He smiles again, mischievously this time. "He went upstairs. Ben was on a bit of a sugar high from the hot chocolate, and Joe suddenly developed a headache. Who would have thought?" He pauses, his expression shifting. "How are you, Anabelle?"

"We're not going to talk about the kiss. It didn't happen."

His face completely serious now, he says in an undertone, "We don't have to talk about it, but it definitely happened."

I rub the back of my neck. "Well, you don't have to worry about it happening again. I'm mortified."

He reaches for my chin and turns it firmly toward him. "I'm taking a guess on what mortified means, but you've got no cause to be embarrassed by anything. You didn't kiss me. We kissed each other. I'd wanted to kiss you for days. But that doesn't mean we should do it again." He speaks softly, so we can't be overheard by the guests in the parlor, but every word is perfectly enunciated.

"You think I'm a naïve child," I say, feeling emotion tumble through my gut. "You're worried you're going to break my heart."

"Don't put words into my mouth," he chides. "And who says it's me who'd break *your* heart?"

I frown, taken aback. I've never thought myself capable of breaking anyone's heart, or even seriously wounding them. I'm used to other people meaning more to me than I do to them.

My lips open, although I have no idea what I intended to say, so I'm glad when he continues, "Look, I just...it's better if we stay friends. I want to be your friend. *Please* let me be your friend."

No one has ever spoken to me like this before. There's something so raw and honest about him. The unfortunate truth is that it makes me want to pull him to me by that ridiculous beard and kiss him. But I don't. I take a deep breath and let it out slowly. "I'm still upset about what you told me last night. But I think I'm more upset with my grandmother."

He considers this for a moment before nodding. Then he gestures toward the front of the house and my desk. "Do you want to go somewhere more private to talk for a minute?"

Not really, but also yes, really.

"Okay," I say, sensing Lauryn watching us. She might only be watching Ryan, actually, waiting for him to come back. Maybe she likes his soft hazel eyes too. She might want to invite him up to her room later.

Well, probably not, given that she's staying with her son, and Ryan's rooming with Joe, but the thought has thorns.

Ryan might not want to kiss me again, but I can tell he's kissed lots of women. He's not confident in his intelligence and skills, but he *is* physically confident. I can see it in his easiness on his feet and everything he does. He'd know what to do with a woman—a thought that makes me hot behind the ears.

He takes the first step, and I follow him, trying not to stare at the way his body moves beneath his clothes. When he reaches my desk, he stops and turns toward me, watching me from behind that ridiculous fake beard. If he thinks it's weird that I slide behind the desk, into my comfort zone, he has the grace not to say so.

"Grandma Edith didn't think I could do this on my own," I tell him, continuing our conversation as if he hadn't pressed pause on it. "No one does. Maybe I don't either, because I asked Joe to help me. And the guests." *And you.*

"I don't think it was about doubting you, Anabelle," he says, his eyes intent on my face. "She knew she was leaving you, and she didn't want to, so she did whatever she could to keep you safe and happy." He lowers his head, almost bashful. "Truth be told, I'm honored that she was so convinced I'd be coming back."

A wave of emotion tries to pull me off my feet. "Why do *you* think I need help? Did she..." Discomfort forms pretzels in my chest; anxiety eats them. "Did she tell you that I'm on the spectrum?"

"No," he says, reaching for my hand across the desk and then stopping himself. "No, but Joe told me this afternoon. I don't know too much about it, but I did some googling on my phone."

"Ugh, don't google. Every time I try to google something medical, the internet tells me I have bacterial meningitis or cancer."

He smiles at me. "I'm not a road scholar. Google is what I've got."

I think he means Rhodes, but the last thing I'd do right now is correct him. Even though a part of me is itching to do just that.

"You can ask me," I say. "And I'll tell you one thing for free, no asking required. I don't like it when people treat me like an invalid. I'm perfectly capable of doing things on my own."

"I know you are," he says seriously. "A hell of a lot more capable than most people. When were you diagnosed?"

I look away, remembering that time. Feeling the crush of it. "In my early twenties. I was…college was okay for me. The lecture halls were too loud, but no one else wanted to sit in the front row, so it usually worked out. But afterward, I had no idea what I wanted to do with my literature degree. So I took an admin job at an advertising company. It was awful. My job was in this office where there weren't any personal cubicles, just communal desks. It was supposed to make us all like each other more, or something, but it was so loud and overwhelming. I kept having panic attacks, and I went to see a psychologist. She was the one who suggested that I do the testing."

"You worked in advertising," he says with soft smile. "No wonder you hated it."

I fuss with the hem of my shirt. "It was so draining. I never felt like I had any energy, and my thoughts kept spiraling."

"Is it like that for you here?"

"Sometimes," I admit. "I'm not good with strangers."

"I was a stranger a few days ago, and you've always been 'good' with me."

"You knew Grandma Edith." But that's not the whole reason. He's good with people—even people like me, who usually struggle to respond to deceptively simple questions like *How are you?*

He nods. "Yeah, I get that. But is it any fun for you, working here? Don't you have your online business?"

"You sound like my father right now."

His expression darkens. "Was he trying to get you to sell to Weston? Was Weston at the dinner tonight?"

"Ew, no."

He laughs.

I poke his very solid chest. "Santa lesson one. Santa doesn't have a sexy laugh. He has a *jolly* laugh. You'll need to work on that."

"Should I be taking notes?"

"Probably. Take notes on this too. I might not be good at pandering to strangers, but I want to run the B&B," I say, a thread of anger weaving through the words. It's as I'm saying it that I realize how true this is. I'm not doing this because I'm rigid or stubborn, which my parents have accused me of being. I'm doing it because the thought of a world without this place pains me. I'm doing it because this is one of the only places I've ever felt at home.

I'm doing it because ever since I decided to embrace Ryan's idea about making it a Christmas inn, my heart has wrapped around and around the idea of The Gingerbread House until it formed a picture in my mind. And now, I can't bear to let go of it.

Ryan touches my hand for half a second, maybe a quarter, but the phantom of his hand lingers on my skin. "I know that, but you should be able to enjoy doing it. That's what I want to help you do. I think that's what all of your friends want for you. I'm hoping the rebranding will help. Because it'll be easier to deal with strangers if they want to talk about something you love."

I stare at him in shocked silence while he gives me a winning smile.

"I'm still upset," I say.

"As is your God-given right."

"But I suppose it's nice that you want to help me, even if it's just because my grandmother asked."

"It really isn't," he says, his voice a bit louder. Emphatic.

"Good."

I should have kept my mouth shut, but he doesn't throw back a quip. He just smiles, his eyes bright. "Will you come have a drink with us, oh Queen of Christmas? Enoch's got some good thoughts, and the little guy's a natural artist. I've been trying to think of not creepy ways to ask him to let me photograph his work."

"There aren't any."

I consider his offer for a long time. Maybe uncomfortably long. But I finally nod. I want to spend more time with my guests, and if Enoch really is a branding expert, I'd be a fool to miss out on the opportunity to talk to him. "I'll come, but not quite yet. I need a minute to myself."

"Of course," he says, and I can feel the smile behind his words. "Oh, before I forget, Joe and I are going to rescue his stuff tomorrow, if you'd like to come."

I feel those snakes roiling in my gut, the way they do prior to any adventure, minor or major. But I want to support Joe, to give Craig withering looks, and to spend the entire morning with Ryan.

"I will," I say. "But for now, I need..."

I trail off, but he nods, his eyes warm. "I know. You take what you need."

We walk toward the parlor together, and he gives me one final grin before stepping inside as if it's easy. I smile and wave at the guests, and to my surprise, they return the gesture.

"I'll be back down in a minute," I tell them, feeling my heart speed up with the words. It's hard to shake the old fears. *They prob-*

ably don't care where you're going or if you'll be back. It's better if you're alone.

I turn to go up to my room and make it to the bottom step before Ryan says my name softly by the stairs again. He's holding a shopping bag, and scratching the back of his head with his other hand.

"Déjà-vu."

"Sorry," he says, then shoves the bag at me. "I got this for you. Just a little something for your collection."

I glance inside and find a fuzzy little orange cat in a Santa suit. My heart quakes. "You got me a Santa cat."

I shuffle on my feet a little, feeling joy take the wheel. Sometimes it really is the little things. His thoughtful gift feels like proof that even if I don't mean as much to him as he's beginning to mean to me, I mean something. It shows his attentions toward me and the inn aren't only about my grandmother.

"The humping convinced me that Saint Nick might need a friend his own size."

I beam at him, delighted. "You're basically encouraging me to get Saint Nick a costume, *Santa*."

He grins back at me, his whole face alight with it. I feel a tugging sensation inside of me. "Well, if I could get you to believe, I figure I can definitely convince a bunch of impressionable children."

CHAPTER TWENTY

RYAN

Last night, Anabelle and I talked to Enoch for about an hour. I'm glad she was with us, because he gave what seemed to be solid advice about changing the branding for The Gingerbread House, and about eighty percent of it flew right over my head. I did volunteer to take over the scavenger hunt for the kids, though. I'm excited about that.

I didn't have any money when I was a kid, so I couldn't get Jake anything for Christmas. He'd always make me a drawing or one of his illustrated stories. So one year I figured out a way to pull my weight—I made him a scavenger hunt for things to find around our neighborhood. We nearly got into some deep shit, because one of the things on my list involved scaling the fence of a guy who kept a Doberman, but it was still fun.

I mean, obviously, I will not be sending these children off to play with Dobermans, but maybe I can work in a few fun surprises.

After I put in my daily workout, I head back to the inn and find a few people still hanging out in the breakfast room. Anabelle's sitting with Cynthia and Joe. She's wearing a red sweater dress, her hair down around her shoulders. She always wears it down, every day. It's like a gift she gives the world, because her hair is beautiful—thick and wavy and probably twenty shades of brown.

I can practically hear Jake saying, *You've got it bad, brother.*

I do.

But I'm going to keep my distance for her sake—and for mine. A lot of people have turned their backs on me, but I couldn't stand it if she did.

"There he is," Cynthia says with a grin.

"Can you already tell she's going to ask you for a favor?" Joe asks.

They must have met just this morning, but he's already giving her shit. That's the power of Cynthia, I guess. She's got one of those warm personalities that makes you feel you know her after all of five minutes. I've always gotten along well with people who are like that. In some ways, I *am* a person like that. But Anabelle's different. She's like a complicated lock. You've got to work hard to open it, and you don't stand a chance at succeeding unless you take the time to understand the way it's put together. But you know you're gonna find something good on the other side when you get it open.

"And what favor is that?" I ask, sitting down with them.

Anabelle gives me a sidelong look and immediately gets up. Shit. I figured we'd worked things out yesterday.

"Do I smell?" I ask before she can take more than a step away.

"You smell good," she says, turning. Her lips part, and something catches in my chest. "You took a shower after your workout. You always do."

I'm taken aback that she notices. I haven't even told her about going to the gym in the mornings.

"Christmas witch," I say.

She gives me a half-hearted smile. "I'm getting you some food. You must be hungry."

And again, there's that warm feeling spreading through my

chest. I watch her go, and when I turn to give my attention to Cynthia and Joe, they're both eyeing me with smug expressions.

I point at Joe. "You snore."

"I do," he agrees. "Just so you know, I told Cynthia about the Santa cat."

Meaning he told her that I have a thing for Anabelle. "What the fu—"

I cut myself off as I notice Ben is still present, working on his Christmas comic while he finishes his eggs and toast.

Returning my glare to Joe, I say, "What the fiddlesticks?"

Cynthia snorts. "You've been spending *much* too much time around him and Anabelle."

"Don't you have a day off?" I ask her.

"Tomorrow. But I'll still be around, obviously. Jeremy too. We're all going to follow this joker around while he does his inspection."

"A wall of intimidation. I like it."

"But you're not changing the subject. Joe didn't need to tell me you have a thing for Anabelle. It's probably obvious to the Martians studying us from space."

"If there were Martians, they'd have better things to do," I say with a sigh, tapping my fingers against the table. "Don't worry about me and Anabelle. We've settled things between us."

"You haven't," Cynthia says, glancing back at the doorway. "You made her think she's a bad kisser or something."

"You kissed her?" Joe repeats, much too loudly.

"Keep it down," I hiss. Turning to Cynthia, I say, "She said that to you? When?"

"Yesterday morning." Her tone is pissy now, like she's none too pleased with me.

"She knows that's not true. We talked about it last night."

"But did you talk about it in a guy way, or did you actually talk about it?"

"I don't know what that means," I admit. "But I do know that the three of us are done talking about it. Now what favor do you want?"

She darts another glance at the doorway, then says, "I want you to help me settle a bet. Can you find out whether Jeremy's been messaging back any of those girls who have texted him about the video? He's been acting too big for his britches, and I want to set him down a peg."

Something tells me that's not the real reason for her request, but I won't call her on it—even if she's made me feel like a dick with her questions about Anabelle.

Did I really make her question her kissing ability?

It's unthinkable, because that kiss meant more to me than all the other kisses in my life combined. I'll have to figure out a way to clear that shit up, quick, without it leading into another loss of willpower. I wouldn't put it past myself to try to rationalize sleeping with her to prove how much I want her.

Cynthia's still watching me, trying to pretend she doesn't care about how I answer her question even though she obviously cares a lot.

"Yeah," I say. "I'll ask him if he wants to grab a drink after we get back from Charlottesville. See what I can get for you."

"Thanks, Ryan. I told Anabelle I'd be on call today, so if anyone needs anything at the inn, I've got it covered." She says this as if I have some stake in the B&B too, and I can't deny I like the way it feels.

Hearing light footsteps, I look back over my shoulder. It's Anabelle, bringing me a plate of hot food. The warmth in my chest spreads. "You didn't have to do that."

"Obviously. But you've been bringing me food almost every day. It only seems fair."

She sits beside me as I fork up some eggs. And in that moment, with Anabelle beside me and our friends around us, I'm almost perfectly content.

Almost. Because Anabelle might still think she's a bad kisser, which is totally unacceptable. I'm not about to correct my mistake in front of Joe and Cynthia, though, so I promise myself to talk to her later.

I can't help but think there are a lot of things I've promised myself to do later but can't face yet.

NEITHER ANABELLE nor Joe have ever driven a big truck before, so I offer to drive the U-Haul. We stop at an office supply store to buy packing supplies for Joe's Christmas collection, which he'll be storing in Room C with him once it opens up this afternoon. That done, we hit the road. I sneak a sidelong look at Anabelle, who's riding in the middle between us in the front seat, and turn on the twenty-four-hour Christmas station. It gets me a smile that makes my chest feel sore.

Too much inner conflict will do that to a man. Part of me thinks I should leave Williamsburg after the inspection tomorrow morning, assuming it goes all right. I can give Anabelle the ornament and then go. Because the more time I spend with her, the more I want to be her man.

But if I blow town, I'll miss out on my Santa trial run, and I'll miss...

Well, shit.

I steal another glance at Anabelle, taking in the way she's rubbing her bottom lip. I've seen her do it half a dozen times. Maybe it's a stim.

Yeah, I googled "autistic spectrum disorders" last night while Joe was snoring in the bed next to mine. A lot of stupid shit came up, like Anabelle had warned me, but I learned some helpful stuff too. And I can understand why she got her back up about her grandma asking a complete stranger to help her out.

She'd probably be even more pissed if she knew what kind of stranger her grandmother had hit up for help.

Looking back, it blows my mind that Grandma Edith put so much faith in me—that she'd been certain enough that I'd come back to write a note for me, and certain enough of my basic okayness as a person that she'd write *that* note for me. She'd trusted me to be there for the person she loved most in the world.

I don't just mistrust other people; people usually mistrust me. Hell, my own brother doesn't believe in me anymore, and I've burned so many bridges I might as well be wearing explosive shoes. But Grandma Edith, the woman whose ornament I was sent to steal, trusted me above almost anyone.

The thought makes me feel like a chocolate lava cake exploded in my chest—and also like I want to drop my new friends off at a gas station and speed out of town, because no one should trust me like that.

I'm forcibly ejected from my thoughts when a new song comes on—"All I Want for Christmas." I groan, but I catch a spark lighting Anabelle's eye as she peers back at Joe. Suddenly, she's singing along with Mariah, Joe joining in, and even though this song normally makes me want to gouge my eyes out, I feel her excitement. Just like last night, when she pulled that stuffed cat out of the bag. She shuffled on her feet like she wanted to jump for joy, and over a little thing like that. It does something to me. It makes me want to gift wrap the whole world and set it at her feet.

So I give her another sidelong glance and join in, belting out the lyrics as I drive toward Charlottesville.

Her smile is more blinding than the sun.

We continue the sing-along until we get into town, Joe telling me the directions because "Google Maps always gets it wrong." I pull up in front of an apartment building that looks like any other—generic white, with windows with black shutters that probably don't shut.

"Home sweet home?" I ask, glancing at Joe in the rearview mirror as I park the U-Haul.

"It was for a while," he says, his tone dark.

"You have a better home now," Anabelle insists.

He has a key and his ex is supposed to be at work, so it should be quick—easy in, easy out. But when we get out of the car to approach the building, I can tell Joe's not feeling easy about any of it.

I've been there before. I may never have fallen in deep with a woman in the past, but it still doesn't feel great when someone grinds your nuts under their heel.

"Think about all the dank shit you hated about him," I say, patting him on the back as he leads the way to one of the entrances. There's one for every four units—two upstairs, two down.

Laughter gusts out of him, and Anabelle shoots me an approving glance as she falls in on the other side. She's still wearing that adorable red sweater dress. It's probably not the best choice for moving day, but she looks so damn sweet it's going to rot my teeth.

"Ryan's right," she says. "Craig's a liar and a cheat, and you're so much better off without him."

Joe heaves a sigh, his gaze on the unit, and says, "Thanks, guys. That helps. But let's get started. I don't want to be here when Craig gets back from his shift."

Except when we get to the apartment door, Joe's key doesn't work. He glances at the apartment number, as if a sudden inability to read is a more likely explanation than that the asshole changed the lock and decided not to say anything. Half a second later, an anemic-looking red-headed guy opens the door. There's a shit-eating smirk on his face, and judging from Joe's expression of horror, this is his ex. His look of horror becomes a hundred times worse when a balding guy with dark brown eyes and a green sweater steps in next to Craig and wraps an arm around his shoulders.

"Dean?" Joe squeaks. "Is that my sweater?"

Goddamn, what a vicious setup. This Craig guy obviously

invited his new boyfriend over so he could watch Joe carry his things out to the truck—like some extended and reversed walk of shame.

Joe's a nice, solid guy. No way does he deserve this.

My buddy looks like he'd like to change his name and relocate to another state where no one knows him; Anabelle looks like she's about to explode. And while I'd really, really like to see Anabelle put this guy in his place, I do what I do best—I act before I think.

I put my arm around Joe, who stiffens as if I'd just punched him in the kidneys.

"Oh, how embarrassing," I say. "Joe never would have brought me along if he knew you were home. He was worried about hurting your feelings, weren't you, honey? But I guess that's not a problem since you've both moved on."

CHAPTER TWENTY-ONE

ANABELLE

Sunday, December 7, 18 days until Christmas

Inappropriate crushes: 1

Ryan is magnificent.

There's no other word for it.

I have plenty of other words for Craig: scallywag. Putz. Pillock. Ninnyhammer. Unprincipled heel.

But now he's gaping at Joe, his attempted cruelty yanked out from under him like a thin rug, and it's a glorious moment.

Even Joe, who's clearly cut to the core by the sight of his ex-boyfriend of two years canoodling with his "just friends" co-worker, clearly feels the glow of it. A humiliation turned into a victory. Because Ryan is so clearly superior to both Craig and Dean that there can be no arguing as to who came out ahead in this breakup.

"And who, exactly, are you?" Craig finally asks, a sour expression on his face as he regards Ryan—taking in all of his Ryan-ness. He's wearing a black henley shirt, having left his coat in the car, and it hugs his muscles, providing a tantalizing peek of the ink at his wrist.

His gaze shifts to Joe before settling back on Ryan, who grins. "I'm Ryan. He hasn't told you about me yet?" He gives Joe a fond look. "You know, we were just friends up until the other day, when you threw him out. He was looking for some consolation, and I figured my moment had finally arrived. Thanks, man."

"But I've never heard of you before," Craig says, still standing in the doorway. Dean looks confused.

"Because I had feelings for him," Joe rebuts tightly. "I was fighting them, but then I figured, why keep fighting?" He nods at me. "And this is Anabelle."

"Anabelle, huh? I still don't think she exists. Did you hire these people to come help you?" Craig scoffs. "We both know you don't have any real friends."

Ryan spears him with a look. "And did *you* hire this dude to steal my boyfriend's sweater?"

"No," Dean says, coughing. "It was...uh...a mistake."

"You're damn right it was a mistake," Ryan says, shifting his glare to Craig. "And were you aware it's illegal to change the locks on someone who's on the lease? You're lucky we didn't show up with one of the boys in blue. I hope for your sake you didn't commit any other theft. My main man here keeps everything inventoried. If even one item is missing, you'll be answering for it."

Craig backs up abruptly, tripping over a Crocs shoe and nearly taking a tumble.

Joe steps forward and grabs the shoe. "That's mine."

Ryan pushes his way into the apartment, and I follow them inside. It opens into the living room, with an open kitchen on one side and a hallway across from the door, presumably leading to the two bedrooms and bathroom Joe has told me about. A six-foot Christmas tree presides over the living room, covered in garland, lights, and ornaments. The sight of it makes me gasp. Joe doesn't have any of his truly expensive ornaments displayed, but there are a few vintage glass ornaments I remember him buying at auction.

Craig and Dean are standing on the opposite side of the living room, facing off with us as if we're an insurgence, and they don't know whether to try to crush us or hoist the white flag.

"Where's the other Croc, Craig?" Ryan asks, a threat underlying his words. His gaze shifts to Dean. "And he'll take his sweater back too."

Dean immediately removes it. He's wearing an undershirt, thank goodness.

Craig clears his throat. "I don't know where the other Croc is."

"Then I'd suggest you find it, *friend*," Ryan warns.

I'm torn between a sense of wonder and unease. Ryan is legitimately menacing, but he's doing it in preservation of Joe, who absolutely cannot defend himself and agonized for a week after accidentally killing a spider in his bathroom. It reminds me of the way Ryan stood up for me that first day, when Weston tried to follow me into my bedroom.

A defender.

A knight.

Not a gallant knight, though—more like one dressed in leather and spewing swear words.

I feel a swell of cautious affection for him.

I feel a much less cautious swell of attraction. It was impossible not to notice Ryan before I kissed him, but now I can't stop. Every moment brings me more of him—his muscles, the way his face lights up when he laughs, and his magnificent eyebrows, which are three or four shades darker than his caramel-brown hair. His kindness. His *magnetism*—a quality that I'll never have even if I study it academically for four lifetimes.

Joe leads us to the second bedroom, from which he ran his business, and Ryan urges him to inventory his belongings before we carry them down. He reports that all is present and accounted for, and we start bringing boxes down to the truck—Ryan taking two or three, Joe and I one each. The first time we go down, we see Craig searching around the sink; the next, in the far-right corner of the apartment under the Christmas tree, while Dean buzzes through the bathroom. The third time, they're gone.

Joe looks around the apartment like a bloodhound, and once he's verified that they're really gone, he wraps his arms around Ryan and hugs him. My heart feels like it's on the verge of bursting, seeing these two men who mean so much to me hugging. "Thank you. Oh, my God. I almost burst out crying. Jesus, that would have been embarrassing. He's such an *asshole*, but you humiliated him. You...oh God, no one's ever done anything like that for me before. Ever."

Ryan pats him on the back. "I can still hit him for you, if you want. He did you dirty." He gestures to the tree. "But I say we take the tree and call it done."

Wonder threads through me, like tinsel twining with my soul. "You want to be the Grinch?"

He grins at me, his whole face taking part in the expression. "It *was* my favorite children's book. And that guy messed with Joe. He deserves to lose Christmas privileges for the year." He nods at Joe. "Besides. I'm guessing it's yours, isn't it?"

Joe nods, looking shell-shocked but not displeased.

Ryan turns his grin on me again. "It'll fit in the truck."

He's right. They only had the larger size available at U-Haul, so they upgraded us without upping the charge.

"I think we could use a second tree at the inn," he adds. "This one could go behind the reception desk. That way you could always be within sight of a tree, Anabelle."

In response, I take out my phone, plug in a quick search, and seconds later, "Mr. Grinch" is playing over my speaker. Ryan's laugh is full-bodied, and I find myself noticing him in a way I shouldn't. Wanting to lean into him and rub up against him the way Saint Nick does now.

I try telling myself I'm not interested in Ryan and that the kiss was a blip, a mistake, an uncharacteristic moment of putting impulse before logic.

I just broke up with my boyfriend, and if Weston and I were too different, than Ryan and I certainly are. He's also only here temporarily—and my heart has nothing temporary about it. It has such a hard time letting people go that I stayed with Weston six months longer than I should have.

All of that is true, but also...

Ryan is a person you can't help but notice. He gives out more light and heat than other people. He is more like the star on top of a tree than I will ever be.

Joe must be feeling it too, because he grins. "Let's do it."

Ryan reaches for the six-foot Christmas tree as if he's going to grab it by the stand and rip the lights free of their outlet, but I give an aghast sigh, echoed by Joe.

"Those ornaments need to be wrapped and boxed!" I object.

He gives me an indulgent smile. "Oh, all right, but it takes away from the dramatic gesture."

We get the ornaments boxed and loaded, then Ryan lifts the tree, still strung with lights and garland, by himself.

"Don't forget the stockings that were hung by the chimney with care," he says with a wicked grin. He's teasing us, which is nothing new—a person who has a special interest in Christmas is used to being mocked—but he's doing it as if we're all in on the joke.

"Should I take Craig's stocking too?" Joe asks, adjusting his glasses.

"Dean *was* wearing your sweater," I say.

"Agreed," Ryan says, still holding the tree. He's doing it one-handed, showing off, but I'm not annoyed by it. In fact, I'd like to take a photo of him like this—holding a tree one-handed—and frame it. I could hang it next to my grandmother's photo in the parlor.

"Wait!" I say, then get out my phone and snap the photo while he beams at me.

We're heading back to the car, Joe carrying the stockings in plain sight while Ryan strongarms the tree, when Craig and Dean return, a shopping bag slung over Craig's arm.

His eyes widen at the sight of the pilfered stockings and the tree. "Wha—"

"We got you a new pair of Crocs," Dean says, grabbing the bag from him and shoving it at Joe. "Your size and everything."

Ryan gives them a dark look before glancing at Joe. "Are you okay with that resolution, Joe? Or were you attached to the old pair?"

Joe takes a second to consider, then nods. "Let's get out of here."

"But...my aunt Bessie made us those stockings," Craig says, his tone plaintive.

I'm hoping Joe doesn't back down. I've realized it feels damn good not to back down, and I want that for him.

"She did," Joe says with a smile. "And it was so sweet of her. You'll say merry Christmas to her for me, won't you? Oh, never mind. Ryan and I will send her a card."

With that, we strut right past them with the tree and the stockings and finish loading up the truck.

CHAPTER TWENTY-TWO

RYAN

On the way back from Charlottesville, Anabelle, Joe, and I blast "Mr. Grinch" and sing along. People at red lights stare at us, which only makes me sing louder.

None of us mention the inspection, or Grandma Edith, or Weston.

Our good mood lasts all the way back to Williamsburg and continues as we set up the tree near the front desk, where the person-sized nutcracker used to stand. It's enormous for the space, and its branches will be dusting up against Anabelle's back, but she claims she doesn't care.

The unfriendly woman in Room C has already checked out online and left a shitty review complaining about the blinds, of all things, so we help Anabelle clean out the woman's room and then get Joe settled inside with his five hundred boxes.

"Is it weird that I'm happy?" he asks once we stack the final box. His room looks like a warehouse, but he and Anabelle are planning on setting up an office in the *other* first-floor parlor, formerly a smoking room, where old dudes hung out and puffed on cigars while they talked about politics or whatever.

"No," Anabelle says, braiding her thick hair at the base of her neck. It makes the slope of her neck look longer, and *very* kissable. Her temples are a little sweaty, and I wish I were one of those guys who carries around monographed handkerchiefs just so I could offer one to her. "You're here with your friends, and you're better off than you were with that man. He disrespected you, and lost your favorite shoes, and now you have a far superior boyfriend."

I grin at them. "Hey, maybe that's what I can do. I can offer people fake boyfriend services for the holidays."

"Don't you think people would catch on?" she asks, looking up at me, her eyes so big a man could easily get lost in them. "You'd become notorious in no time. It's not a very practical business plan."

"I'm not a very practical man."

Her gaze captures me, and I feel the glow of being appreciated by her.

"Thank goodness," she finally says, so sweetly that I feel like I just swallowed a handful of candy. My gaze drops to her mouth, taking in the curve of her lips, and I remember what they felt and tasted like the other night.

Like hot chocolate and heaven.

"Hey, can we pose for a Christmas photo before our inevitable breakup?" Joe asks, breaking the sudden tension.

"Only if you'll send it to Aunt Bessie and all of your Charlottesville friends," I tell him. "And I get to wear my Santa uniform. That's nonnegotiable."

"That's a good idea," Anabelle says, worrying at her lip. Turning to get a better look at Joe, she says, "We should also give Ryan some Santa Claus lessons before his first shift on Wednesday."

"I'm going to get lessons from the experts?" I ask, amused.

"You probably shouldn't get your expectations up," Anabelle says. "I'm a terrible teacher."

As if she could be terrible at anything.

"I don't believe you, valedictorian."

Laughter spurts out of her, escaping from her nose. "I wasn't the valedictorian."

"Don't crush my dream." I grin at her. "I liked thinking about you making a speech."

Her mouth drops open. "I hate public speaking."

"Still would have been cute. Besides, you love explaining things to people and showing them how to do things. You're a natural teacher."

"But I have no ability to make people listen."

"Now you have Ryan." Joe says, waggling his eyebrows at her. "He can stand behind you and look menacing. People will run around and buy you new shoes."

"Damn straight, they will." I wink at Anabelle and then leave the room, their laughter streaming up behind me.

Upstairs, I change into my Santa costume, putting on the beard that Anabelle says looks like something rats would use for nesting, and meet them down in the parlor.

Anabelle takes some photos of Joe and me in front of the tree, hamming it up for the camera, and then she moves an armchair in front of the fireplace and declares it's time for my Santa lessons.

I've barely lowered into the chair when Joe says, "You're too jacked. You need a pillow."

He grabs one from the couch and throws it at me.

I stuff my new bowlful of jelly under my Santa jacket. "Better?"

"Say something as Santa," Anabelle says, propping a hand on her hip. She's still wearing the task-inappropriate red sweater dress, although there are a few smudges of dust across it from moving the boxes. Her hair has escaped the braid she didn't bind with an elastic, and is now running wild across her neck.

I want to run my hands through it and feel the weight of it in my fingers again.

"Well?" she says expectantly.

"Have you been a good girl?" I ask, the words coming out a little more sultry than they should. A blush heats up her cheeks, and damn, she's adorable. "Should you come sit on my knee?"

She looks away, her cheeks flaming. "You're an abominable flirt, and it's unspeakable for you to do it in front of your boyfriend. Now ask Joe what he wants for Christmas."

I force myself to look away from her, my gaze landing on Joe, who mouths something that looks suspiciously like *Santa cat.*

I roll my eyes. "And what would *you* like for Christmas?"

They tell me my voice doesn't sound very Santa-like, which isn't a big surprise given the way I bombed the Colonial Williamsburg interview. I try again, dropping my voice an octave. *Too menacing.* And again, trying to sound singsongy, like someone talking to a baby. *Just no*, although both of them laugh.

Anabelle's brow furrows, but she's not a woman who gives up easily. "Maybe we should try going back to the beginning," she says.

"Should I climb up the chimney?" I ask.

Joe coughs a laugh. "I'd like to see that."

"So would I," Anabelle says. "But no, I was thinking we should practice *ho ho ho.*"

She looks dead serious, so I rest a hand on my pillow stomach and give it my best. "*Ho ho ho.*"

Joe makes a doubtful face at Anabelle. "It's not supposed to sound sexy."

"You're right," she says thoughtfully, observing me in a way that makes me feel hot behind the ears. "Try not to make it sound sexy, Ryan."

Hearing her say sexy and my name in the same sentence is hardly putting me in a chaste mindset, but I clear my throat and try again. "Ho ho ho."

They exchange another look, and Anabelle says, "You know, it's not necessarily a bad thing. All of the mothers will want to come see him."

"Hot Santa," Joe agrees with a nod.

"Hot Santa," she repeats, taking me in. I'm suddenly uncomfortably turned on...and very thankful for the pillow gut.

"Can I go change now?"

Anabelle meets my gaze, and more blood pulses down south. "If you must."

WE SPEND the rest of Sunday night pretending to relax before the inspection. I suggest a Christmas movie, which turns into us airing *A Christmas Story* in the main parlor. Anabelle has the guests' phone numbers from check-in, so I text them an invitation to join us. Two of them actually come. They settle onto the love seat that sits catty-corner to the main sofa, where Joe, Anabelle, and I lounge together, me in the middle. About half an hour in, I notice that Anabelle's eyes are getting heavy.

Fifteen minutes later, she's fast asleep and leaning on my shoulder. I'm tempted to sit like that for the rest of the movie, because it feels damn good, but I can tell how exhausted she is. Each time the dad in the movie shouts, her eyes flutter open and she glances at the screen for half a second before they close again.

So I gather her up in my arms and bring her up the stairs, making a point of avoiding eye contact with Joe.

When I get to Anabelle's room, I open the door and then push it inward with my foot. Saint Nick scurries out before following me back inside, his whiskers twitching as I lower Anabelle onto her bed.

I pull back the covers and sheets, smiling at the pattern of candy canes, and then adjust her so she's covered. I turn to leave, but her hand wraps around my wrist.

"I'm scared, Ryan."

My heart lodges in my throat, and I get down on my knees beside the bed. Her eyes are glassy, and her hair is loose around her face. She's so impossibly beautiful.

"You've got nothing to be scared of." I let myself smooth the hair out of her face. "You heard Joe. I'm going to be there. That guy tries to mess with you, and I'm going to make him buy you some new boots. Nice ones."

Her smile is barely there, but at least it's a smile. "He better watch out."

"Damn straight," I agree. "Because you have friends. Lots of friends. And we're not going to let anyone hurt you. I'm not going to let anyone hurt you."

She smiles at me, then brushes her hand over my stubbled cheek. "I believe you. Goodnight, Ryan."

"Goodnight, sweetheart," I say.

Then I lean in and press my lips to her forehead before I go.

CHAPTER TWENTY-THREE

Monday, December 8, 17 days until Christmas

Intimacy dreams about Ryan: 2
Near panic attacks: 4

"I'm unwell," I say to Cynthia. We're in the kitchen, attending to the dishes, while Ryan, Jeremy, and Joe hang out in the breakfast room. Cynthia suggested it was rather sexist for the men to relax while we attended to the work, but I insisted. Not because I believe women should do the dishes; rather, I need the normalcy of our daily routine to ground me. Even if everything is already topsy-turvy since Monday is Cynthia's usual day off.

"You should eat. Jeremy's already had three cinnamon rolls, and he's not even a guest here." She doesn't sound annoyed about it, though.

"It was nice of him to come," I say tentatively.

"Yeah, he has his moments," she concedes, handing me a plate, which I position in the dishwasher.

We continue in silence, both of us lost in our thoughts. Mine are mostly bleak. The inspector will come. He'll find a colony of rats living in the walls, and then the building will need to be knocked down. I'll have to stand by and watch, consumed by the knowledge that I've failed my grandmother.

Or maybe he'll tell us that there's black mold, or—

Cynthia wraps her damp hands around my shoulders, pulling me out of my spiral. "Stop. Whatever you're thinking right now, stop."

"How did you know?" I ask in shock.

"The look on your face."

"Can you also tell by the look on my face that I don't like it when my shirt's damp?" I say it with a smile, though, because I love Cynthia, and she laughs and pulls them away.

"Now, step back from the dishwasher. I'm going to finish up here. Make sure you think happy thoughts. Why don't you go pull Ryan into an empty room and make out with him? That would make anyone feel better."

"It would make me feel more anxious, which is something I definitely don't need right now."

"Then go take a shot of whiskey from the parlor."

"I don't think the inspector will have an agreeable impression of me if I answer the door smelling of whiskey first thing in the morning."

She plants a hand on her curvy hip. "Anabelle Whitman. There's a reason they invented mouthwash."

I'm fairly certain the reason wasn't so people could go around drinking whiskey whenever they feel like it. But I leave the kitchen and drift toward the dining room. I stop a few steps form the doorway. Ryan's sitting with Joe and Jeremy, who's eating what must be his fourth cinnamon roll over a napkin that is inadequate for the job. Taking it all in, I decide I can't be in there right now. Most of the time, I'm not bothered by the sound of people eating, but I'm too keyed up to handle it.

Ryan catches sight of me. I expect him to motion me in. If he does, I'll have to join them. It would be incredibly rude not to, given they're all here to support me. But instead he gets to his feet, says something to the other guys, and then leaves the room.

"Are you okay?" he asks as he reaches me. "You look a little pale. Maybe you should take a shot of whiskey before the inspector gets here."

"Goodness. You and Cynthia give the same bad advice."

He grins. "Maybe that means it's actually good advice."

"Or you'll both lead me into depravity."

Something flashes in his eyes, and he swallows, my eyes tracking his Adam's apple as it bobs in his throat.

"It would be my pleasure," he says with a smirk.

He's teasing me. Or at least I think he's teasing. He made it very clear the other day that he didn't think we should kiss again, and if kissing is off the table, then I'm guessing depravity certainly is.

The bell over the front door rings, and I gasp. But the next instant, Ryan's hand weaves around mine, and the feeling of his strength joining with mine bolsters my ability to walk to the door with him and open it.

The inspector is an unpleasant-looking man with a fierce expression, a full beard, and a work cap. He's carrying a clipboard and a red pen. Goodness, does it have to be red?

He looks like a man who dislikes children and small animals.

"Hello, and welcome to The Gingerbread House," I say cheerfully.

He gives me an unimpressed look. "Says The Crooked Quill over the door."

"It does, yes. We haven't had a chance to change the sign yet."

He grunts. "You'll have to update it on the paperwork."

Oh, dear. This is already falling apart like a poorly constructed gingerbread house.

"We're in the process of doing that," Ryan lies fluidly. I hear footsteps approaching us from behind, followed by a friendly feeling presence behind us. The cavalry has arrived.

The inspector, Sam, glances at them. "Are these your guests, ma'am?"

"No," I say proudly. "They're my friends, and they're all involved in the B&B in some way. We want to support the inspection, because if there's a problem, we're going to resolve it."

He grunts again, still standing outside on the doorstep. Looking past him, I can see tourists wandering the street. It's cold out today and blustery enough that the red ribbons decorating the street posts and fences are fluttering in the breeze.

The inspector finally steps inside and shuts the door after him. "You don't need to accompany me. You can go about your business."

"Yes, but we're still going to," Ryan says pleasantly. "Like my associate said, we want to make sure there aren't any problems."

We'd discussed the wisdom of telling him up front about the electrician's upcoming visit, but Ryan had argued it would be best to save it. If he thinks we're unaware of the electrical problem, perhaps he won't make a point of finding other issues.

As Sam makes his rounds of the house, pausing to test that the windows aren't painted shut—a common problem in old homes— and that all the utilities are functional, we trail after him in a silent parade. My pulse is racing; my breath is coming in fast puffs. I'm embarrassed by how afraid I am of this stranger with the beard and the clipboard. But Ryan has not released my hand. Every now and then, he smooths his thumb across my knuckles as if to reassure me that I'm not alone. Warmth spirals through me from those touches.

I'm tempted to climb into his arms and ask him to carry me, but I'm also determined to push through and do this normal thing. If I'm going to be a dual business owner, for both It's Christmas Again and the inn, I will have to learn to face my discomfort in situations like this.

Sam the Inspector spends an *especially* long time in the basement, and my earlier worries about mold reassert themselves. I keep a large dehumidifier down here, but what if it stopped working? What if I've unintentionally been poisoning my guests?

The inspector doesn't say a single word, but after what feels like an eternity in the basement, which is somehow both damp and dusty, he heads back up the stairs and brings us into the parlor.

"You'll need to move those," he says, pointing to a few of my Santas perched on the window ledges. I'll have to let go of Ryan to do it, something I haven't done since Sam arrived—even walking down the stairs, we went together. I glance at him, and he squeezes my hand and releases me.

After I move the Santas, Ryan immediately reclaims my hand, thank goodness. Sam checks the windows—which creak but open— and then peers into the chimney.

"Looking for Santa Claus?" Jeremy quips, earning a shove from Cynthia.

Then, with great ceremony, Sam pronounces he has finished his inspection.

"What happens now?" I ask nervously. Ryan steps a little closer, his side pressing against me, offering his body's warmth and hard strength. I feel a surge of gratitude and affection. He was Joe's protector yesterday, and today he's mine.

"Yeah," he says, "what happens now?"

"Now, I go write my report," says Sam.

I lick my dry lips, worry thrumming inside of me. "Is there—

"Nothing poses an immediate threat," he says.

Relief washes through me, so sweet and soothing I almost laugh. "Oh, that's great. So great. Would you like a cup of hot chocolate before you go?"

He gives me that *I hate puppies* look but then clears his throat. "Do you have marshmallows?"

I release Ryan's hand and then bear the indignity of being

stared at by everyone as I prepare a to-go hot chocolate for the inspector, doubling up on the mini marshmallows.

He takes it from me and immediately makes his way toward the front door.

Ryan watches him, his jaw flexing, and then calls, "You're welcome."

He doesn't reply.

We trail Sam to the front of the inn, and Jeremy gives his back the middle finger as he walks out the door and heads down the front steps. I give Jeremy an admonishing look, but I don't really mind. It's a profound relief that the man is gone. For now.

I shut the door and turn to look at my friends. My gaze settles on Ryan, possibly because I can still feel the impression of his hand in mine.

"Well, that went okay, didn't it?" I ask.

"I don't like it," Ryan says, his voice soft but his words extremely unwelcome.

"Oh." Something inside of me sags.

Ryan shifts on his feet. "We know they have bad intentions, so why did he just walk out of here without doing anything?"

"It may be a scathing report," Joe puts in. "Some people are better at being mean in writing."

"I could use a drink," Jeremy says. "Anyone else want a drink?"

Cynthia gives him a pointed look. "We have an afternoon shift. You should have had one when Anabelle took her shot of whiskey this morning."

"I didn't do that!" I protest, my voice coming out louder than intended.

Ryan smiles, but it's a blip of an expression, there and then gone in an instant.

Jeremy groans dramatically. "Oh, come on. That was brutal."

"I'll grab a drink with you tonight," Ryan tells him.

"I can't tonight." He grimaces. "I promised my uncle I'd babysit.

His little girls are a nightmare. They always try to braid my hair. Anyone want to come?"

He delivers this part hopefully, but no one volunteers.

"We can get that drink tomorrow night?" Ryan suggests with a half grin.

"Sure, I'm gonna need it."

"Anyone else want to come?" Ryan asks. His looks directly at me, and I feel another gush of affection for him. But not enough that I want to spend tomorrow evening in a loud, probably dirty bar. I'll probably still feel depleted from the inspector's visit, and Joe and I have a lot of work to do on our office.

"No," I say. "I'll probably stay in."

"So you can worry about getting a strongly worded email from Sam the Shithead?" he asks in a teasing tone.

"That'll definitely be part of the evening's plans," I admit, then gesture to Joe. "But we also have business to discuss. I'm guessing it will take several nights."

Like how to change the B&B's name legally and what kind of role Joe wants to have at the inn while we partner up our Christmas businesses.

"All work and no play will put Anabelle on the naughty list," Cynthia singsongs.

"I didn't hear *you* say you're going to the bar," I point out. "Or babysitting tonight."

She shrugs. "Because babysitting is a thankless task, *especially* if the kids are related to Jeremy, and I have plans tomorrow night."

Jeremy flinches. "Oh? What are you doing?"

"Wouldn't you like to know," she says with a sassy grin.

I can tell that he would, indeed, like to know. They're playing a game with each other, that's for certain, and I can't make out what it means.

My gaze lands on Ryan.

I'm playing a game, too, I think, and I'm in over my head.

CHAPTER TWENTY-FOUR

RYAN

I'm in trouble.

Anabelle held my hand during the entire inspection as if I were her lifeline, and I didn't want to let go. Hell, I wish I were still holding her hand.

I haven't done more than kiss her, but I've never felt like this with a woman before. It's overwhelming and exhausting and incredibly sexually frustrating, to be honest. Because she's always there, within touching distance, but I've told myself I can't touch her.

Everyone's tired on Monday night, and the evening passes in a blur. Tuesday's another blur—I spend an extra-long morning at the gym, and when I get back Cynthia is already gone and Anabelle and Joe are setting up their office. They confirm that no one has heard from the inspector yet.

There's nothing obvious for me to do, so I drive around and look for restaurants that have Help Wanted signs posted. There are a couple, but the chefs are looking for experienced help, which I'm not.

In the back of my head, a voice tells me it's time to go. It insists that my usefulness is wearing out, and it's time for me to pony up the ornament and then man up and visit Jake.

The thoughts are like an itch at the back of my brain—I can't get rid of them, they're annoying, and I also can't bring myself to give in to them. The thought of hanging the ornament on the tree or leaving it at Anabelle's door and simply walking out leaves a sour taste in my mouth.

So I'm more than ready for a distraction by the time I meet up with Jeremy at the Green Leafe Café. I arranged to get a drink with him for a few reasons, one of them being that Cynthia asked me to. Another being that I like Jeremy, so I think it'll be a good time.

Despite its name, the place has a bar atmosphere, with a long wooden bar at the rear of the room, along with some booths to the left and group seating at a large rectangular table next to the bar. There are a few mounted TVs that add to the atmosphere.

Jeremy's already waiting when I get there, wearing his street clothes—a green William & Mary hoodie and jeans.

"Fuck me," he says with a grin as I approach the bar where he's waiting on a stool. "It's the Grinch himself."

"In the flesh."

"Thought you'd be greener." He slides his full pint glass around in a circle, then nods to the bartender, who comes over and asks me what I'd like as I settle onto one of the stools. I order a local red ale on tap.

"This is on me," I tell Jeremy with a nod. "I did some research. I know how much of a deal you and your uncle cut us."

More than twenty percent.

He angles his head. "I don't like what that guy is pulling on Anabelle."

"Neither do I," I agree as the bartender brings me my brew. "I expect more trouble from the inspector. There was something dodgy about him." I can't put my finger on what, exactly, other than that Weston obviously sent him. But my gut was screaming at me the whole time he poked around the inn.

"I don't disagree," Jeremy says, "but we'll all be around to keep an eye on her."

I feel a swell of gratitude. I haven't known a lot of people who'd bend over backward for someone they're not bound to by duty or law. Maybe because all the people who were like that lived in Williamsburg, VA, for some damn reason. "Thank you, man. I appreciate it."

We shoot the shit for a while. He tells me about his troubles. There's not a lot of steady work as a trumpet player that doesn't involve playing the same song multiple times a day, every day, until he's bored of himself. I share a bit about mine, keeping things vague, for obvious reasons.

"Sorry, man," he says after I tell him about falling out with my brother.

"So am I."

We've been sitting at the bar for about forty-five minutes when a pretty blonde woman approaches Jeremy with a big grin on her face. "You're the one from that video," she says, then glances back at a table of four other women who are giggling. They look old enough to be drinking here, but barely. Seniors in college maybe, or grad students. It's miserable outside, so cold your breath is foggy even before it leaves your nose, but there's only maybe three sleeves among them.

"Sure am," Jeremy says with plenty of swagger, his gaze tracking to the table and back.

"Do you care to settle a bet for me and my friends?" she asks.

"Anything to help a lady."

She looks like she's holding back laughter as she asks, "Do they give you a codpiece as part of your uniform?"

"No." He waggles his eyebrows. "They absolutely do not. That was one hundred percent natural."

She gushes laughter, then says, "Why don't you two come join us at our table? We'd love a little company."

I have no interest in sitting around with a bunch of barely legal women when there's a chance that I could go home and possibly find Anabelle still in the parlor. I still think I should stay away from her, for her sake and also Grandma Edith's, but she's the woman I want. There's no changing that. No substituting her with anyone else.

So I'm about to excuse myself, but Jeremy speaks first. "Sorry, sweetheart. I'm here with my friend. But you do me a favor and share that video."

Interesting. Cynthia's question may have just been answered for me.

The blonde pushes her bottom lip out, probably hoping she can still convince him, but he says, "You have a good night now," and she steps away from us.

He gives me a self-conscious shrug. "If that video goes viral... well, you never know. Maybe some brass band will want me."

"Not into blondes?" I ask, raising my eyebrows.

He swears under his breath. "Did Cynthia say something about me keeping her from dyeing her hair? Because, I swear to Christ, she doesn't know how to do half of the things she thinks she's an expert at. She'd probably fry her hair off. Besides, they'd fire her if it's an obvious dye job. People didn't peroxide their hair in the 1600s."

I grin at him, knowing this means I have something good to tell Anabelle. I don't know fuck all about Cynthia's plans for her hair, but Jeremy just confirmed that he likes her enough to listen to her talk about them.

"Cynthia? No, man. *I* have no knowledge about Cynthia and her hair."

He smirks. "No, you're too busy drooling over Anabelle to notice."

"The good things in life don't come easy," I say, not bothering to argue with him. We can both see right through each other, and even though I don't know why he's holding back with Cynthia, and he doesn't know why I'm holding back with Anabelle, that's okay. At this particular moment, we share an understanding.

"I like you, man," I say as I lift my glass to his.

"I like you too. Now, we gotta find you a job other than shoveling horse shit and seasonal work so you can stick around."

Sticking around isn't part of my plan, but for some reason I don't correct him.

✳

WHEN I RETURN to the B&B, I'm disappointed to find the parlor empty.

It's unchanged from this morning, not that I expected otherwise. We haven't started the Great Santa Moveout yet, but I've already amused myself by thinking of where I'm going to hide the little fuckers for the scavenger hunt. Hanging from the vents. Peeking up from storage containers. Hiding behind plants. Of course, I'm not allowed to play with any of the valuable ones, but it's open season for the ones on Anabelle's list. I think adults might enjoy the scavenger hunt too.

I peer up at Grandma Edith's photo.

I'm sorry, I want to tell her. *I didn't mean to fall for her, but I'm doing my best not to mess everything up. I'm trying here.*

Sighing, I head upstairs, my mind a mess. I'm thinking of that ornament, nestled in its box in the top of my closet. I'm thinking about Weston and his grudge against Anabelle and how far he might be willing to go. And, dear God, I'm thinking about Anabelle —her wavy hair and her little sighs. The dreamy expression on her face when she's happy. The way her lips felt against mine, so soft and sweet, tentative but needy...

I need to tell her she's a good kisser.

I need to tell her that I haven't thought about anything else but her since it happened.

To do that, I have to talk to her privately. It could wait until tomorrow, to be sure, but she'll want to know what happened with Jeremy, right? It wouldn't be right to keep her in suspense.

My mind slides back to the ornament.

That's another thing I've screwed up. I should have given it to her that first night, and I should *definitely* give it to her now. But if I do, she might tell me to go, and the thought of leaving now, before we even know what Weston has planned, is suddenly unacceptable.

I pause at the top of the stairs, my gaze sliding from my door to hers and back. My fingers itching with indecision.

Bracing myself, I step toward her door and knock.

A few seconds later, she opens the door wearing an old-fashioned, floor-length white nightgown. It looks like the kind of thing someone in the seventeenth century might have worn. Somehow it's also the sexiest outfit I've ever seen, especially since she's not wearing a bra, and I can see her nipples pressing against the fabric as if they're desperate for someone to let them out. Now, *that's* a job I'd be good at.

Saint Nick has joined her and is sitting at her feet, but he and I seem to have reached a new truce now that he's humped me. We've established that I'm his bitch, basically.

"Ryan?" she says, her voice a little husky. Her eyes are heavy-lidded.

"I'm sorry. Did I wake you?"

"I must have dozed off," she says and then yawns. "Would you like to come in?"

Fuck, yes, I would. But I can tell she asked it innocently, without having any idea of the effect she's having on me. If I were to enter that room, I'd feel like a wolf invited in by Red Riding Hood.

I shift on my feet. "I...shouldn't. It's just...I thought you'd like to hear about what happened tonight. I'm pretty sure Jeremy has a thing for Cynthia. A bunch of attractive women invited us over to their table, and he didn't want to go. He would have gone over if he was unattached."

The sleepiness has faded from her face, her eyes becoming sharper and more alert. "And did *you* go over?"

I swallow, fighting the urge to back her into that room and lower my mouth to the thin, slightly translucent fabric of her nightgown and run my tongue over her nipple.

"Uh, no." I pause, knowing I should get the hell out of there, but first I need to clear up the kiss misunderstanding. Because there's no way I want her thinking she's anything but the most desirable woman in the world. "I had no interest in those women. I suppose I'm still thinking about...well. Just so you know, our kiss was the most memorable kiss of my life."

"Because it was bad?"

I can tell from the look in her eyes that she doesn't really believe it, thankfully, but that doesn't stop me from taking a step toward her. Saint Nick comes out and circles my legs, rubbing against my calf.

"Because it was *you*. I like you, Anabelle. I didn't come here meaning to like you, but you're so damn likeable, I could barely help it."

Her hand lifts to her throat, moving over all the places I'd like to kiss her.

"Now, I know *that's* not true," she says with a soft, self-conscious laugh.

"Did Weston make you think that? Your father?" I take another step closer, pulled in by my need to be near her warmth.

"Life made me think it, Ryan." Sadness passes through her eyes and she takes a step back. "Look, I'm glad you're here. You don't need to make me feel better about the kiss. I understand why you don't want it to happen again. You're probably right."

I can tell she doesn't understand. It might be better, for her sake, if she assumes I brushed her off because I don't have feelings for her. I'm a man who messes things up. An asshole who hurts people even though I don't mean to. A man who has nothing to offer to a woman but his body. But I can't let her think that. I *can't*.

"I *like* you," I say again, firmly. "I like you because you're beautiful, and kind, and funny, and smart. Your father was only right about one thing in his whole life, because you *are* the star on every tree. The most noticeable part. The brightest. No one is like you, and I'm happy no one else is like you, because it makes it more special to know you. But I also think the world would be a better place if everyone was like you."

Her lips part, but she doesn't say anything at first. She just reaches for my hand, and I give it to her.

"Come in and shut the door," she says.

When she tugs me inside, it feels like she's saving me from something, even though it's only myself.

I close the door, feeling numb but hopeful. Feeling *everything*.

When I turn, she's right in front of me. Saint Nick is nearby, but he's keeping a respectful distance, like he's giving us the chance to figure out our shit. There's a future treat with his name written all over it.

"I know you think you can't stay," she says slowly.

"You won't want me to stay once you know everything about me." I run my hands through my hair, frustrated.

"Why don't you tell me, and allow me to decide?"

"I don't want you to tell me to leave before we figure out what Weston and the inspector are planning."

"What could be so awful?" she asks, her eyes wide. "You said you didn't murder anyone, and I know better than to think you're some kind of sexual deviant."

I scoff. "I wouldn't be so sure. Your nightgown is giving me *thoughts*."

"This nightgown?" she asks, baffled. "This belonged to my grandmother."

I laugh into my hand. "You know. You think that'd put me off, but it doesn't. You don't look like anyone's grandmother in it. I can see your nipples."

She crosses her arms over her chest.

I place my fingers on her arm, tentative. "Don't. It's the best fucking thing I've ever seen in my life. Besides, there's nothing you could do to cure my mind. It's never been clean in this room."

"Even when you were eating cat treats?" she teases, her voice breathy.

"Five minutes later, you were sucking on a candy cane. What do you think?"

Heat flares through me. I'm painfully aware of her as she stands there in that innocent little nightgown, so tempting my hands are shaking with the need to touch her.

"I'm not some untouched virgin, Ryan," she says, a touch of schoolmarm in her voice. "I've had plenty of sex."

"I don't want to think about *him* touching you." It makes me want to stalk over to Weston's house and break in just so I can beat the shit out of him.

"He's not the only person I've slept with. I'm twenty-eight."

"I don't want to think about anyone else touching you."

She licks her bottom lip. If she were any other woman, I'd wonder if she were doing it on purpose to make me feel overcome, but I know better. This is just Anabelle—and by being herself, she is effortlessly the sexiest woman I've ever met.

"I don't want to think about other women touching you, either. I'm positive there have been quite a few more of them."

I hang my head, feeling like an asshole again.

"There've been a lot," I admit. It takes me a few beats before I find it in me to look her in the eye again. "I'm not smart like you are.

But I've always been good on my feet and liked working out. That's all women have ever wanted me for."

"Your body," she says softly.

"Yeah." I swallow, feeling self-conscious. I've felt this way before, but I sure as shit haven't told anyone. For one thing, any guy who complains about all the women he gets with isn't going to get a pat on the back and a lollipop. For another, saying this shit makes me feel raw, like my skin has been peeled off.

I wait to see if she's going to pour on the salt.

"I appreciate your body. Anyone would." Anabelle runs her fingers gently over my bicep and down my arm to my hand, which she squeezes. Then she lifts her hand to my face, running her fingertips over my cheek and my lips, each stroke filling me with need. They stop on my scar, which she rubs softly before lowering her hand. "But not as much as your heart."

"I don't have anything to give you." It's a lie. I have the ornament right next door, in my closet. But if I give it to her now, she may ask me to leave.

My heart speeds up, and sweat beads across my brow.

I don't want to leave her. But I'm stuck between two choices, and only one of them makes me an asshole.

The other might save me.

"Actually, there is something I need to give you," I say. "Right now. Can you wait right here?"

CHAPTER TWENTY-FIVE

ANABELLE

Tuesday, December 9, 16 days until Christmas

State of mind: Confused and very turned on

Is Ryan getting a condom?

Do I *want* him to get a condom?

I want to kiss him, and yes, to do *more* with him, but I'm not sure I'm ready for that yet. I can tell that sex with Ryan would change everything, and so much is already in flux. Impossible to predict. Different. *Terrifying*.

I start pacing, Saint Nick mewling and then following me, but I don't make it more than a few back-and-forth steps around my worktable before Ryan comes back in holding a square black box, about six inches by six inches.

What's in the box? A whole collection of condoms? Will he let me choose?

No, from the look on his face, it's something different. Weston's severed hand?

I've been reading too many novels. Even though Ryan's

punched people before, I can't see him willfully hurting someone, especially in the studied, committed way sawing off a limb would require.

"What is it?" I ask, my voice strange to my ears. I'm tired. Over-stimulated. Overwrought. I should be in bed now, sleeping, but I'm tired of sleeping my life away. I'll pay for it tomorrow, but right now this is where I want to be.

He holds the box between his hands, looking at me with that same expression. *Worried*, I decide.

"I can't tell you why, not yet, but your grandmother gave this to me to keep safe."

"Ryan, let me see the box." My heart is beating fast. I'm pretty sure I know exactly what's in there—the missing ornament. My father's not the only one who has been looking for it: he wants it for selfish reasons; I want it because it was hers.

Ryan hands the box over, and I flip it open. My heart bursts when I see the ornament's spindly spikes glowing in the dim light from my lamp. I gasp and carefully tug it out, letting it dangle in a full circle so my eyes can drink in every angle.

Saint Nick stalks up to me, probably with poor intentions, but Ryan scoops him up into his arms without hesitating—and my cat lets him.

Once I'm certain the ornament is as it should be, completely undamaged, I tuck it back into its box and glance at Ryan over the lid. "You're the person she gave the ornament to."

He nods and steps over to my bed, letting Saint Nick down. My cat bats at his hand, then starts weaving in ever-shrinking circles until he plops down, letting his body collapse. "Last Christmas Eve. She gave it to me before I left the B&B."

I swallow, considering the implications. This ornament meant a lot to my grandmother. She would only have given it to him if she trusted him *deeply, implicitly,* and *without reserve.* And yet, he's held onto it for a week since returning to the B&B.

I turn my back to him and bring the ornament into the closet, where I stow it in a spot I know it will be safe and hidden. Once I'm done, I stand in the closet for a few seconds, trying to gather the scattered bits of myself and focus on this moment, this place, this man.

Then I turn back toward him and find him watching me with eyes like a chastened puppy's. "Were you going to keep it?" I ask. "It's worth a lot of money, and none of us knew you had it."

"I never even considered it. I was always going to give it to you," he says hoarsely. "It was only a matter of when." He scratches the back of his ear in a self-conscious gesture. "I came here to give it back to *her*."

"You're asking me to believe a lot." I'm already halfway toward believing him, but I'm aware of my own inclination to believe in the people I care about. I want them to have good intentions, so in the past I've been guilty of not being suspicious enough.

He sighs and rubs his heel against the floor. "I wouldn't believe me if I were you. But it's true. I came here to bring it back. And I held onto it because I felt like I was running out of reasons to stay. You dropped Weston, and you and Joe have the inn about covered, so if I gave it to you..."

"You want to stay?"

"I want to stay because of you."

I want to press him for more details. To find out exactly what happened between him and my grandmother a year ago, and what comprised that dark period of his life. But he asked me the other day whether I would be able to withstand judging him, and I still can't say no with a clear heart.

It must have been criminal, whatever he was mixed up in.

But Grandma Edith trusted him.

Insofar as I can, I trust him too. But I don't have a clue what I'm going to do now. I don't think I can process anything else after the day I've had. I need time for everything to be sorted into the proper portion of my gray matter.

I press my fingers to my thumb, trying to ground myself. "So you came here to stay with my grandmother, you told her your story, and she gave you this ornament for safekeeping. But why did you come *here*, of all places? Was it...was this the place your mother left you?"

"No."

He obviously doesn't intend to expand upon that. I could either accept that or throw him out.

I'm not ready to throw him out.

"You know, my father's been looking for that ornament," I say, nodding toward the closet.

"I expect he has."

"The other night, he told me he thinks it's hidden somewhere in the house," I say, my voice quavering as I consider what that might mean. "Do you think that's why Weston wants the inn? Is that what the inspector guy was hoping to find? Although...no, that wouldn't make sense."

For one thing, Weston is wealthy. No one would be unhappy to fall into a couple hundred thousand dollars, but he certainly doesn't require it, and indeed, it wouldn't make buying the B&B worthwhile to him.

I say as much out loud, and Ryan shakes his head, his lips a firm line. "Maybe. Financial value isn't the only reason why people want to own something. He might want it just because he doesn't want *you* to have it. I wouldn't put it past Weston."

Nor would I.

"I won't let him take it from you," Ryan adds, his voice gruff.

"*I* won't let him take it," I correct. "I'm a grown woman perfectly capable of looking after myself."

"Do you want me to leave?" he asks, rubbing the back of his ear again. "I can clear out my stuff. It won't take long."

He came in with a duffel bag. I know he's from New York, but does he have an apartment there? A house?

"Is that all you have?" I blurt.

He tries to smile. "Grandma Edith didn't give me any other precious Christmas antiques, if that's what you're asking."

"No, the duffel bag," I say through the squeezing sensation in my throat. "Is that all you have? Or do you have an apartment or a house waiting for you?"

"No. I was gone for a month or so, and my roommate assumed I wasn't coming back. He got rid of my shit." He looks away. "I've got some money tucked away, though. Plenty to pay for my room. I'm not a charity case."

"I didn't think you were," I murmur, "but that's so *sad*." My voice wobbles on the word.

I think about all the stuff I have, tucked into the nooks and crannies of this house. Ornaments and trees and Santa Clauses. Furniture and Tupperware and dishes. Clothes. Everything Ryan has right now fits into a bag.

My stomach is a pit, a black hole.

"I don't want you to feel sorry for me."

"I don't," I tell him. "But I care about you, and if you're sad, then I'm sad."

His expression becomes less severe. "I'm not sad right now."

"I don't want you to give me anything. I only want to spend time with you."

His eyes change. One moment all the darker colors are taking prominence—deep greens and browns—and the next they're all gold. He takes a step toward me, his powerful body tensing with the simple movement. "*Anabelle*."

"I like the way you say my name."

"One of us is going to get hurt," he says, reaching up to cup my cheek, his fingertips playing with my hair. Each touch sends an electric sensation across my scalp. "It would be better if we were just friends."

"But we're *not* just friends," I say. "I don't want to kiss any of my friends."

"And you want to kiss me?"

"*Yes*. I'd like to spend all night kissing you."

"I don't know what it can mean," he says, shoving his hands so aggressively into his pockets I'm surprised they don't come off.

"Neither do I. There's so much I still don't know about you."

And yet...I think he's probably told me more than he tells most people. That makes me almost as sad as knowing that duffel bag contains all of his earthly belongings.

"I'm trying to be someone worth knowing," he says. "In the past, I wasn't."

"Then you've already succeeded. Because you are a man worth knowing. You've only been here a week, and you've changed so much for the better. Not just for me, but for Joe, and even for Jeremy and Cynthia. You're a better man than you're letting yourself believe."

He swears under his breath, and then he gives in, thank goodness, weaving his hand into the back of my hair. He leans into me, his mouth hovering millimeters over mine again. But this time he's the one who presses forward. His kisses are hard and soft, as if he wants to be the one to break me and put me back together. His hand tightens around my hair, and his lips travel from my mouth to my neck, where he kisses me softly and then sucks in my flesh in a place that makes my knees want to buckle.

Usually, the world is a place of too-loud or too-soft voices, buzzing lights and machines and hundreds of unwanted sensations —too hot, too cold, too hard, too soft, too much—but at this moment, he's captivating all of my attention. Every bit of me is focused on the feeling of his mouth brushing over me while he holds me close, pressing my body against him. He touches me like I'm something precious, and also like I'm a dessert he wants to gorge himself on, and I can't get enough of it.

As our lips move together, he runs his hands over my body, always moving. They glide over my back and my butt, through my hair and around to the side of my breasts. My hands are touching him everywhere too, running over the hard muscles of his arms and chests, tracing his tattoo, lifting up his sweater so I can feel his hard back. They travel everywhere except for one place. The thought of touching him there still makes me embarrassed and jittery and hot. But I can feel the hard press of him against me.

I know how much he wants me.

I'm overwhelmed by him. I'm humbled by him. And yet...

This is happening fast after all of the slow dancing we've done over the past week. I'm tumbling into him, and I don't know when or how my fall will be broken. There's a part of me that doesn't care —and that scares me most of all.

He pulls away, looking down at me, his lips pinker from kissing me. "I want you, Anabelle. You can probably feel how much I want you."

"I can," I admit, feeling a spike of worry again. I've never slept with a man so quickly before. Will I regret it if I do it now? Or if I don't? I know there's a chance he's leaving, and if I don't get to be with him at least once, I'll always regret that.

He smooths a hand over my hair and then tucks it beneath the heavy mass, pressing his palm flat against my back. "I'm only going to kiss you tonight. Do you have any rules about where I can kiss you?"

CHAPTER TWENTY-SIX

ANABELLE

Oh dear.

"What do you mean by *where*?" I hedge.

"I want to make you feel good, sweetheart," he says, his thumb caressing my back beneath my hair, his other hand finding my hip. "I want to make you come with my mouth. But if you're not ready for that, that's okay."

"You want to kiss me *down there*?" I ask, instantly ashamed of myself. Because I sound like a virgin. But the truth is, no one has ever done that for me before. I'm worried I won't like it. I'm more worried that he won't like it, and I'll taste bad and make embarrassing sounds.

"I'm dying to kiss you down there." He rubs his hand over my hip, his fingers brushing perilously close to where my body wants them. "I want to bury my face in you."

My face is in flames. "You might not like it."

"Oh, I'm going to fucking like it, Anabelle. I'm going to love it."

"*I* might not like it."

"If you don't like it, I'll stop." Something flickers in his eyes. "No one's ever done that for you before?"

"No," I say, feeling awkward but also excited. I want to explore this side of myself with Ryan. I trust him with it.

He swears under his breath, his hand leaving my hip to brush against my cheek, my lips. "I'm glad I get to be the first. You don't know how much that turns me on."

"Really?" I ask, bewildered. Then I feel the need to add, "I'm not very good at...you know, reciprocating. I've been told I'm not very good at it, anyway."

A different kind of fire fills his eyes, and he swears again, dropping his hand from my face. "I want to kill him."

I grip his hand. "He's probably right. I'm not very...it can be hard for me to be in the moment."

"You don't have to reciprocate. I don't want you to tonight. I want to make you feel comfortable and relaxed, and I want you to come against my mouth. But if you ever want to do that for me in the future, I'd be nothing but grateful that you want to make me feel good."

He sounds pissed off, but I know he's pissed off for me, not at me. A wave of powerful emotion passes through me, leaving my eyes hot. "Oh, Ryan."

He leans in and kisses me hard, his tongue finding mine, and gathers my hair in his fist. That wave of emotion ripples through me again and again as his lips move with mine and then trail down my neck. In between kisses, he whispers, "You're so beautiful, Anabelle." And, "I want you so bad."

I believe him. For now, I can see myself through his eyes, not as an awkward woman who turns people off but as a sexy Christmas witch who makes men mad with desire.

He looks up at me, as if asking permission, and then lowers his head enough to stroke his tongue over the fabric of my nightgown, passing over my nipple, and the dual sensation of his warm tongue and the fabric sends desire quaking through me.

He does it again on the other side, and then he gently backs me toward the bed. I sit down on it, my heart racing, and then lie down.

"You look like you're waiting for dental surgery," he says with a smile that spills into his eyes. "We don't need to do this. We don't need to do anything. I only want you to feel good."

"But I really, really want you to do it." I'm almost on the verge of tears again, because I do want this, so badly, and I'm also afraid. "I'm anxious, is all."

"What can I do to make you comfortable?"

"Just be close to me. It makes me feel better when you're close to me," I say, reaching for him. He pauses to take off his shoes and then climbs into the bed beside me.

His eyes are so soft and warm and reassuring as he glides his hands over me and presses soft kisses to my face and neck. I don't know how much time passes, maybe five minutes, maybe fifty, but I feel a building pressure between my legs desperate for a release.

"Now," I say, my voice shaking, although not with nerves anymore.

He contemplates me for a second, as if making sure, and then starts kissing his way down my body again. My heart is pounding as he pauses to place a kiss over my belly before continuing downward. Then his head disappears beneath the hem of the billowy nightgown, which hides almost all of him from view. But I can feel him. He kisses my thigh, his hair brushing against the flesh with a tickle that makes me laugh, and then slides my underwear down my legs and throws them.

His breath flutters against me, sending hot shivers through my body, and then he does exactly what he said he would and buries his face between my legs, his mouth sucking and licking. The shock of it almost makes me cross my legs, but then a bolt of pleasure rocks through me and escapes from my lips in a breathy, wordless sigh.

He shifts the hem of my nightgown and looks up at me, his hair a mess and his mouth glistening slightly. I'm embarrassed. And I'm hot everywhere. And I *need* him to continue.

"Do you like it?" he asks.

"You know I do," I say, my face burning. "Do you?"

"Oh, I could do this all night, sweetheart. I will if you'll let me."

He lowers his face back down, spreading my legs wider for himself. I'm still embarrassed and full of a hundred different things, but I watch him. And I find myself lifting my hips to meet his mouth as the feelings he's unleashing furl and unfurl through my limbs, making them move of their own accord.

I didn't know it could feel like this.

I didn't know *anything* could feel like this.

I lower my hand to his hair, needing something to anchor onto, and weave my fingers through his loose curls. They feel so good against my hand, and he's still licking and sucking me as if he really could do it all night.

But am I taking too long? I don't want him to stop, but what if his mouth gets tired? What if—

He does something with his tongue that makes pleasure arc through my body, and a strangled sound passes my lips. It's almost too good, too intense. Maybe I should tell him to stop. It's enough for me to have experienced this much...

He lifts his head again, checking in on me. "Everything okay?"

"You can stop," I tell him. "You've been down there for a while."

"I'm going to be down here all night unless you tell me to stop. Do you want me to stop, or are you just informing me that I can stop?"

"I..." I weight the options and then say, "The latter."

"I don't know what that means."

"Don't stop."

He grins at me and lowers his head again, placing a soft kiss before he starts up again.

I realize he means it. He really will continue doing this all night if I want him to. Moreover, he clearly wants to. And somehow that allows me to relax into the moment, folding into it like warm butter into cinnamon roll dough.

It's a few minutes later that it happens. Another bolt of pleasure hits, only this time it webs throughout my body, engulfing every muscle, limb, and hair follicle. My whole being trembles with it, and as it subsides, leaving my body languid, Ryan slides up next to me.

His shirt is on, which is unacceptable.

"Thank you," I say, pressing a kiss to his cheek. "Take your shirt off."

He laughs and pulls it off over his head, and the beauty of his body is breathtaking. His chest and arms are covered in sculpted muscle, and for the first time, I can see the entirety of the tattoo on his forearm.

"You're beautiful," I say with a happy sigh.

"You're fucking breathtaking," he tells me, tracing down my cheek to my breast. "But I'm not going to ask you to take that off. I only have so much self-control."

"Will you stay with me tonight?"

He kisses me, and I'm stunned but not repelled by the taste of me on his lips. "It would be my honor."

CHAPTER TWENTY-SEVEN

RYAN

Obviously, I don't sleep.

How could I with Anabelle curled up next to me, her head resting on my arm, her hair draped over me like a blanket? The taste of her is still in my mouth, and my dick is so hard that I pull out my phone after she's asleep so I can google whether anyone's ever died from a hard-on.

Undetermined, but it definitely doesn't help me sleep.

I'm in deep with her, and I only want to go deeper. I can't tell whether that's because I'm self-destructive or because I'm finally on the right path. My judgment is no good when it comes to my own life. Never has been.

I want to talk to my brother about all of this, but I can't reach out to him asking for a favor after everything. When I reach out to him, it has to be man to man.

Joe's too close to Anabelle for me to talk to him about her, but maybe I can level with Jeremy.

I need to level with someone.

When the digital clock on her nightstand reads 6 a.m., Saint Nick jumps up onto the bed and, no shit, settles right on top of my face. So either he still dislikes me or he *really* likes me. I'm not sure which I prefer, but I'm not in the mood to get pink eye from a cat, so I get up and maneuver his furry body next to Anabelle, who sighs and curls herself around him.

She looks at peace, her hair sprawled out around her and her long eyelashes resting against her cheek. Even the cat looks cute, so I give in to impulse and snap a photo of them. Hopefully that's not weird.

I don't want her to wake up and find me gone, like a thief in the night—hardy har har. So I put on my shirt, then find some sticky notes and scrawl *Went downstairs for coffee* on one and place it on the second pillow.

I usually start the day with a workout, but I don't want to miss her when she comes down. That feels important today. Maybe I can make her a special breakfast.

I shut the door behind me and head down the stairs humming. When I get to the kitchen to see about the coffee, Cynthia's already in there. She's wearing street clothes, and oh shit, she clearly went with the peroxide plan because her brown curls are a stiff, unnatural blond. A beat later, she turns to greet me, and—

"Oh!" I say, taken aback by the full effect. "Wow."

"You look like shit too," she says with a sigh. "You didn't sleep? Me neither. I made about ten gallons of coffee."

"Your hair's not bad," I lie.

"It's horrible. I stayed up crying half the night. I have to fix it, but I can't bring myself to dye over it yet. I had to call in sick to work. They can't see me like this."

I think about what Jeremy said last night. He had a point, but it would be dickish of me to tell her that I agree with him now, after she's already done it. I know plenty about doing impulsive things and having to sit with the consequences. Punching that tree when I was a kid. Trying to pickpocket Roark. Hopefully, going down on Anabelle won't end up on that list someday.

"Uh, why don't you go to a salon?"

She plants a hand on her hip. "Ryan, do you have any idea how long it takes to get into a good salon?"

"No offense," I say, finding a mug and pouring myself some coffee. I lift the mug toward her. "But even a bad salon might be better at doing hair than you are."

She looks like she's about to bite my head off and swallow, but she takes a breath, releases it through her teeth, then says, "You may have a point."

"Maybe Jeremy knows someone who can help." I have no idea if he does, but might as well throw my buddy an in.

"What, because he has five thousand women sending him DMs?"

"He may be hearing from five thousand women, but I think he's only interested in responding to one," I tell her, grabbing some half-n-half from the fridge and doctoring my coffee.

Her hand lifts to her fried hair, and for the first time since I met her, she looks like she might cry. Shit. I wouldn't know what to do if Cynthia, of all people, started crying.

"He wouldn't look at me twice now," she says. "I'm hideous."

I set down the coffee cup and look at her. She's dressed in a sweatshirt and yoga pants, and there are circles under her eyes, but her inner beauty shines through. "You're not hideous. You're lovely. Your hair is hideous, but that's a problem we can fix."

She barks out a laugh. "I can't tell whether to be insulted or flattered."

"Choose flattered. It'll go easier on both of us. Now, what does Anabelle like best for breakfast?"

She gives me a shrewd look. "You're wearing the same clothes as yesterday."

"I need to do laundry."

"And I need good news, Ryan," she says. "Tell me you at least kissed her."

I take a sip of my coffee. "Anabelle can tell you whatever she'd like, but you won't hear anything from me."

She wags her eyebrows up and down. "That sounds an awful lot like a yes. We're making more of those red velvet pancakes, by the way. Suit up, sous chef."

She seems like she's in a better mood now, and we work well together, shooting the shit about anything but hair. About twenty minutes later, Anabelle enters the room, dressed in a white sweater with a high neck cinched by a red ribbon. Maybe she's wearing it because she has a hickey. I'm probably a dick for hoping so.

She blushes when she walks in, and I grin at her, feeling like a king among men for making her come last night. She might not think I'm a deviant yet, but I want to strip that ribbon from her sweater and tie her hands with it. I'd like—

"Something definitely happened between you two," Cynthia accuses. "I have eyes."

"Cynthia!" Anabelle says, her eyes widening as she gets a good look at our friend.

She pats her hair. "Gorgeous, isn't it?"

Anabelle's horrified face nearly makes me laugh, but I want to put her out of her misery, so I say, "Cynthia thinks it was a mistake, but we're going to figure out a way to fix it."

"Oh, thank God."

Cynthia laughs, shaking her head. "At least I know you'll never lie to me. Which brings me to my next question...what happened with Ryan last night?"

Anabelle blushes adorably.

"And that's my cue to leave." I pour my girl a cup of coffee and then kiss her forehead before I give it to her. "We made you more Rudolph pancakes."

Her brow furrows. "You don't look like you slept."

"I got something better than sleep," I say in an undertone. "I got to look at you."

Then I leave and head into the breakfast room.

Cynthia has watched and listened to our entire interaction, of course, but I don't care if she knows. If I'm being truthful, I want everyone to know. Weston is first on the list.

Text conversation with Jeremy

> 911. Cynthia dyed her hair.

Fuck.

> Excuse me for saying so, but this is your chance, bud.

Uh, what do you mean?

> You're interested in her, right?

It's that obvious?

> To me, yes. Cynthia is more hardheaded.

So what do I do?

> Fix the hair situation.

I've got to go to work, and I don't know dick about hair.

> Develop a cold.

> Use the internet.

If I mess this up, she'll never forgive me.

> Yeah, but think about what happens if you fix it.

I decided to do something about Anabelle, and now I think this is your time, brother.

JEREMY SHOWS UP AFTER BREAKFAST. The guests have left, but Cynthia, Anabelle, and I are sitting in the breakfast room drinking coffee. Joe hasn't come down yet.

I've got to hand it to Jeremy. He's a much better actor than I am, because he doesn't react at all to Cynthia's terrible dye job.

"What are you doing here?" she says, self-consciously lifting a hand toward her hair before she shoots me an accusatory look.

I grin and wave at her from across the table.

Anabelle doesn't say anything, but I can feel her watching me. My grin gets so big it's in danger of swallowing my face.

"I heard you called in sick," Jeremy says. "But here you are, playing hooky."

Cynthia glowers at him. "And here you are, doing the same."

"You know what, you're right," he says, patting his chest with the flat of his hand, which he then holds it out to her. "Come with me, Cynth."

"To where, exactly?" she asks, still sitting.

"Richmond," he says, then pulls out his phone to check the time. "And we'd better leave now in case there's traffic."

"What's in Richmond? If you're trying to sell me into sex trafficking, Ryan and Anabelle are both here as witnesses."

"My cousin's best friend's girlfriend is in Richmond. And she works in a five-star hair salon."

Cynthia darts a quick look at me before turning back to him. "Ryan told you."

Jeremy's lips twitch. "Sure, but I have eyes. I was going to find out. I took the day off so I could take you."

Anabelle is on the other side of the table, but her hand finds mine under the surface. She links our fingers together and squeezes, her face exuding happiness, and I feel like I've done right. I didn't do it just for her, but I definitely wanted to please her.

"I don't know," Cynthia says, drawing our attention. She turns to us with a quizzical glance. "I said I'd go to the toy store with you guys this afternoon to pretend to hit on Ryan."

"That's okay," Anabelle says, squeezing my hand again. "I'll hit on him enough for both of us."

Cynthia nods and finally gets up. "Thank you, Jeremy." She releases a sigh. "This is definitely going to bite me in the ass, but I'll admit to you once, and only once, that you were right."

He gives her a smug grin. "This is the best day of my life. You both heard it," he says, pointing at Anabelle and then at me. "I have witnesses."

"Witnesses to you being a jackass, yeah," Cynthia says, but she's smiling softly at him, and I have no doubt my buddy is going to get himself a date.

They leave together, Anabelle and me watching them. The moment they disappear from view, she leans forward and kisses me across the table.

I grin at her. "What'd I do to earn that?"

"You helped Cynthia. You made my friend very happy." She leans forward again, kissing me more thoroughly before sitting back.

"And that time?"

She smiles at me. "That one was for me. You make *me* very happy, Ryan. Do you want to go practice your *ho ho ho* for a while before Joe wakes up?"

"Yes, Anabelle. Yes, I do."

"Because I have something for you. Wait right here."

"Can I move an inch or two? Or do you want me to sit in exactly this spot?"

She smiles and gives an *Oh Ryan* shake of her head. "Exactly that spot."

So I stay put, but my foot pats the floor and my fingers tap the table. What's she doing? Is it too much to hope she's going to come down in a negligee? Probably. And I also don't want the two guests who are here to see her like that.

Finally, she steps through the door with a big gift bag tucked behind her back.

"That's for me?" I ask, feeling even more jittery. Excited, but also...the last woman who gave me a gift, that sweater Anabelle likes so much, dumped me right afterward.

"It's for you." She hands it over, and I get right to it, opening it up and pulling out a Santa costume far superior to the one I bought on discount.

I glance up at her, pleased as hell. "You didn't have to do that."

"I know, I wanted to."

I tug on one end of the red ribbon at her neck, and she's smiling as she leans in to kiss me. She gasps into my mouth when I pull her onto my lap, her legs straddling my thigh. "I think I'd like it if you were on the naughty list," I say.

I don't know what sight is better—Anabelle gasping with pleasure or Anabelle bashful and sweet. I'd rather not choose, because I'd like them both. I want all of the Anabelles.

"I *feel* like a naughty girl," she says, grinding against me just enough to drive me nuts.

"Tell the truth, did you wear that shirt because I gave you a hickey?"

"Yes," she says, and then delights the hell out of me by pulling down the neck of her sweater. "And I think it's past time for you to give me another one."

CHAPTER TWENTY-EIGHT

ANABELLE

Wednesday, December 10, 15 days until Christmas

Lovestruck fools: several
Work completed: minimal
Happiness achieved: great

We have a quiet day at the B&B, with no word from the building inspector. I'm trying not to worry, and I'm mostly succeeding, because my mind is full of Ryan. His hands, which I can hardly look at now without having a dirty thought—even if he's just eating or packing up a box. His lips, which are extraordinarily talented. And especially his heart.

He's helped all of my friends now.

Cynthia and Jeremy, who needed a push.

Joe, who is ecstatic, because Craig sent him a frankly scandalous text about missing his...well...

My friend is much too wise to seek a reconciliation, but it's better to be missed than to be forgotten. Or so he says. I would rather be forgotten by Weston. He's the source of the sense of foreboding that lurks beneath my happiness. Because Ryan is right: Weston is not a man who gives up. He wouldn't have sent an inspector to the inn and then failed to follow up. He has a plan, and he will pursue it.

But Ryan insists it's time for what he calls "The Great Santa Moveout." Joe and I photograph the Santas that will be used for the scavenger hunt and release them into Ryan's custody. Even though he barely slept last night, he's practically bouncing on his heels as he spirits them away to hide them throughout the inn's common spaces.

He is, in a word, adorable.

Joe and I sit at the computer in our new office, the retired smoking room, and he eyes me as we put together the form for the scavenger hunt, our computer chairs pressed close together. It's still stunning to me that a few days ago I thought Joe was a woman. If I hadn't taken a chance and agreed to meet him in person, then he wouldn't be sitting here with me right now. He wouldn't be my real-life friend and business partner.

I'm so much less alone than I was two weeks ago.

"So you're kissing Ryan now?" he asks point-blank.

Ryan kissed me on the cheek before he gathered up the Santas for his project.

I could claim it was a friendly cheek kiss, but I'd like Joe's advice. "I am."

He grins. "Look at you, stealing my boyfriend twenty-four hours after we went Facebook official."

"That's me. I'm a ho-ho-ho." But I give it more thought and frown. "Are you worried about people finding out?"

Laughing, he says, "You're not even on Facebook, Anabelle."

I'm not. There's a page for the B&B, which will need to be updated with our new theme, but I'm nearly as negligent as my grandmother was at maintaining the inn's online presence. Perhaps Joe or Ryan will be willing to take over.

"No," I say. "But if it'll cause trouble for you—"

He turns in his chair to face me. "I'm not going to give you any excuse not to be with that fine man. He may throw his dirty socks on the floor and work out more than any sensible person should, but he's a good one, Anabelle. You deserve that."

I glance at the door, my pulse thrumming. "I suspect he's done bad things, Joe. Criminal things. He won't talk about his past, but he basically told me as much."

"Like what?" he asks, his eyes widening. "Did he kill someone?"

"I asked, and he said no."

"So drugs?"

"I don't know," I say, wringing my hands together. I've thought about this a lot, of course—if he didn't kill anyone, and he's not an actual sexual deviant, what's left? Drugs, theft, and white-collar crime. Based on everything he's told me, he was *not* a white-collar criminal...

"Oh, this is bad, isn't it?"

"But he says he's not involved in whatever it was anymore?"

"That's what he says," I start, then add more firmly, "and I believe him."

Joe grabs a candy cane from the old pencil cup behind my laptop and starts to unwrap it.

"I wouldn't eat that one if I were you," I say. "It was in here when I moved into the room, and Grandma Edith used to store candy canes with her other Christmas decorations. For all we know, it could be several years old."

"I don't care, this conversation calls for sugar." He sticks it in his mouth and makes a face. "Okay, maybe I care. It tastes like a frankincense and myrrh candle smells."

The candy cane goes into the trash.

Joe pushes out his lips, then says, "I still like Ryan."

I sigh. "I do too. A lot. I've *never* liked a man this much."

"Good to know," he says with a glimmer of dry humor.

I give his shoulder a gentle shove. "You know what I mean."

"I do. And I don't think you should let his past hold you back. You know, we all have our faults. I used to watch *Full House* reruns as an adult."

"Well...it was wholesome, I guess."

"It made me cry."

"Oh, Joe," I say, thinking of his family, who threw him out because they couldn't accept him. How awful that must have been. My parents have never really accepted me, but they didn't throw me out or disown me, and I always had my grandmother to give me the warmth they never offered. "You have a family here. We'll be your family."

He pulls me into a hug, and I feel tears pressing the backs of my eyes. "Maybe Ryan needs a family too," he says.

I think of his twin brother. Of his parents, who abandoned him, and his boss, who left him with a scar and made him do things he's ashamed of.

Some of the tears start falling, and I say, "I think maybe you're right."

THAT AFTERNOON, I drive Ryan to the toy shop. Joe tags along and the two of us do our best to build him up, even though he doesn't seem nearly as nervous as we are for him. He's wearing the Santa costume I bought him, and seeing him in it makes me feel... possessive. I like that he's dressed in something I got for him. I like that I placed a mark on his neck too. It's hidden, thankfully, by the collar of his Santa suit, but *I* know it's there.

About halfway there, Ryan, who is the front passenger, since I mistakenly thought he'd be the anxious one and thus should not drive, looks out the back window and says, "Is that car following us?"

Okay, so maybe he's more nervous than he's letting on.

"Which one?" I ask, checking my mirrors. There's a large white van that promises whiter smiles from The Dental Warehouse, followed by a black Kia and then a little silver Honda Fit.

"The Fit."

"I don't know," I say. "Maybe they're just going the same way."

He grunts, but his gaze doesn't stray from the window until we take a turn and the Fit doesn't follow us.

"I can tell you're nervous," I say. "But you're going to do great. Word will spread far and wide about Hot Santa."

"Will you be jealous?" he asks, giving me a sidelong look.

"Horribly."

When we arrive, we are greeted by the toy shop owner, Ada, who doesn't look at all like I'd imagined her. She has a harsh voice, an all-denim pantsuit, and is chewing an enormous wad of bubble gum. There is a clapboard sign set up outside of the shop reading: *Santa visit, 3 p.m.*

"You brought adult friends," she says. "Fantastic. Do you have any children in your lives?"

I don't know whether she's being sarcastic and actually wants us to leave or is just teasing. Either way, I'm sticking around.

"No," I say. "But a lot of people think I'm childlike, so there's every possibility I'll want to buy something."

"Nothing better than being young at heart," she says, then blows a bright-pink bubble and winks at me. I'm so taken aback, I nearly trip. "Well, come in, come in. No point in getting frozen."

As soon as the four of us step inside, children start clustering around Ryan, so Ada herds him into the back of the shop to give him instructions.

Joe and I wander around the shelves until we find a plastic throne set up at the rear, in a nook created in the middle of three long, low bookshelves. It's decorated with fake pine garlands and tiny ornaments. Seeing it makes me overly warm, as I'm certain Ryan is going to look *incredibly* sexy in that chair.

Joe gives me a wry look. "Do you feel like we just dropped our kid off for his first day of school?"

"No," I say with a sigh. "That's not what I feel like at all, but I *am* worried. He hasn't been getting a lot of callbacks, and I think it'll shake his confidence if this doesn't work out."

A sigh gusts out of him. "I don't think anything could shake his confidence."

I can understand why he thinks so—Ryan oozes confidence in everything he does. He wears his clothes confidently, works out confidently, cooks confidently, and talks confidently. But that doesn't mean he's never anxious. His anxiety is buried deep inside.

Children crowd around the throne as the time approaches, a few parents gathered behind them, and then Christmas music starts playing over the shop's loudspeakers. Anticipation tingles in my fingers and toes. I'm excited and nervous, and it's all a bit much. I'll probably need to go upstairs and reset after we get home, even though it'll only be early evening.

"This is it," Joe whispers to me, reaching for my hand and pressing it lightly before releasing it. "It's the big show."

Ryan emerges from around a corner, and a little girl calls out, "That's Santa!"

I beam at him, because he looks impossibly handsome, even though I can tell Ada shoved another pillow under his shirt. This costume is much better than the other, the beard fuller, and although it's obvious he's no old man, he will at least not be in danger of ruining anyone's childhood today.

Ryan grins back at me and then winks, and again, the butterflies in my stomach best the snakes. Then he launches into a spirited, "Ho ho ho!"

"Still sexy," Joe mutters beside me, and he is entirely correct.

But the children don't seem to care. They're so eager to get to Ryan, they're practically tripping over each other's feet.

Even though I'm overwhelmed, I sense a chance to restore order, so I help the kids line up as the first child approaches Ryan. Then I step back and watch him while children whisper their heart's wishes to him and their mothers eagerly take his photograph. My heart grows several sizes in my chest.

He's *good* at this.

He may not look like Santa or act like Santa, but he's effortlessly charming, so very Ryan, and I start to think the afternoon is going well enough that he will certainly be given the job.

Until a little boy rips off his beard and screams.

CHAPTER TWENTY-NINE

RYAN

Well, shit. My face stings from the ripped adhesive.

"You're not Santa," the little boy shouts, holding my torn-off beard up in the air and waving it around. "You sit on a throne of lies."

"Yeah, kid, we've all seen *Elf*." All of the kids are staring at me, and half of them are pointing and crying. I'm guessing I should do something about that. It took Ada, who is surprisingly good on her feet, about five seconds to get on the scene. But she stopped a few feet away from me. She has her arms crossed over her chest, which I take to mean she's letting me handle this.

Another test.

Anabelle and Joe are watching too, Anabelle wearing her scared-deer look. I want to pass Ada's test if only for her. I'm going to feel like a real chump if she sees me blow this opportunity, same as I blew my interview for shoveling horse shit the other day.

The boy who assaulted my fake beard throws it at the crowd, and a little girl screams as if she's being murdered when it lands on her.

"Santa's beard is stuck to me. Santa's beard is stuck to me!"

A middle-aged woman with a high bun runs forward to intercept her, and the other kids look like they're about to riot. One of them, a little boy, charges forward and rubs his sticky, peppermint-scented palm all over my face. "He has scratchy brown hair on his chin like my dad," he shouts to the others, backing away with a look of horror. "And he's only kinda old, not really old like he should be. I think it's a wig too."

"It is!" shouts the boy who yanked my beard. "I saw the stitches!"

"I know a future stampede when I see one," Joe shouts. "Run away from those kids, Ryan! Run while you still can." He's backing up, and he bumps into a shelf of baby dolls. One of them drops and starts wailing, and he swears and takes off, leaving Anabelle behind. She's still standing there, staring at me with those big eyes, when a little girl calls out, "Ryan? Who's Ryan?"

Shit. This is spiraling quickly. Anabelle's eyes still on me, she gives me an encouraging nod, and purpose rolls through me.

She believes I can fix this.

Joe clearly doesn't. I don't. But Anabelle does.

So I stand up and clear my throat. "Kids, I'm not the real Santa Claus."

"No shit," a little boy calls out, and a woman hurries forward to cover his mouth, two seconds too late.

"Because it's December eleventh," I continue, "the real Santa is up in the North Pole, busy as hell—"

I cut myself off as the mother whose little kid just swore in public frowns at me, and start again.

"He's busy, kids. Busy getting your presents ready and checking that list twice. Do you know how many kids there are in the world?"

I have no idea, actually, but I'm not surprised when Anabelle calls out in a small voice, "Approximately 2.4 billion."

"That's a lot," I say dramatically. "So my man Santa is busy. He needs helpers like me to visit with you and find out what you want for Christmas. There are a lot of us."

One of the kids in the back raises her hand.

"Yeah?" I ask, pointing at her.

"But why couldn't he find someone with a real beard? There are lots of men with real beards. My daddy has a beard down to his chest, and Momma says she's going to shave it off when he's sleeping."

It's hard not to laugh at that, especially since there's a big, sleepy-eyed dude with a long braided beard standing at the back of the group, and he looks like someone just took a boot to his balls.

I clear my throat. "Well, Santa is an equal opportunity employer. He wouldn't tell me I can't help him just because I don't have a beard. That's not the kind of guy he is."

"So you really know him?" asks the kid with the sticky hand.

"I do," I say, nodding emphatically. "And he is one hell of a guy."

Oops. The woman with the swearing kid gives me a dirty look and tries to hustle her child away from the crowd, but he makes his body go limp. Faced with the choice between bodily carrying him out and pretending she meant to stay, she decides to pretend.

Being a parent is no joke. No wonder Joe is terrified of kids.

"How do we know you're not lying?" a girl calls out.

"You don't," I tell her. "But if you ask me, Christmas is all about the power of belief. I believe in Santa. That's why I wanted to be one of his helpers. Do you believe in him too?"

The girl crosses her arms over her chest, looking like a little Ada. "Of course I do. But if you really believe in Santa, then why did you pretend to *be* him?"

"Don't you ever dress up like people you admire?"

She pauses before nodding. "I was Duo Lipa for Halloween."

I have no idea who that is, but I give her a knowing nod. "See? Now, who has my beard?"

Someone throws it to me, but it's covered in dirt and what looks like animal hair, so I shove it into the pocket of my Santa coat. Only

I do it too hard and the extra pillow Ada shoved in there, which didn't get tucked in well enough, tumbles out.

"What else is a lie?" cries out the little boy who snatched my beard.

Damn, might as well put it all out there. So I pull out the other pillow while the kids gape at me. Ada watches with those folded arms and an expression that would do a statue proud, and Anabelle regards me nervously. Then I tug off the wig and stand before them: Ryan, in a Santa suit that now sags. "Any more questions, kids?"

A hand lifts in the air, and I call on the kid whose daddy has a huge-ass beard. "Can we still tell you what we want for Christmas?"

"Yes," I say, rubbing my hands together. "That's what I'm here for, kids. Memory like a steel trap."

Thankfully for me, the kids who've already visited with me are long gone, so no one will be able to test me on that.

The little girl lifts her hand again, waving it around more confidently.

"Yes?" I say.

"Can you put the pillow and beard back on? You look kind of scary without it."

The beard is still gross, but I'm not going to get hired for this poorly paid seasonal job if I don't do it, so I don't hesitate. "Sure, kid. Like I said, I like dressing up like my hero too."

And, I'll be goddammed, Ada smiles before she walks away. I work for another hour, after which Joe finally comes back with a couple of hot chocolates and an embarrassed expression. Which becomes downright terrified when Ada comes over and tells him there's no outside food and beverages in the shop.

I've never seen a man run to the trash can more quickly.

Despite his humiliation, Joe stays at the store with Anabelle. They're still there after another half hour. I don't like that Anabelle's been standing so long, so I tell the kids that even Santa's special helpers have to take a leak.

"How long will that take?" one kids asks.

"Fifteen minutes."

"Sounds more like a number two."

"That's between me and the toilet," I tell him, and then I walk up to Anabelle and Joe.

"I'm so sorry, man," Joe says. He glances at the line of children, many of whom are openly staring at us. "There's a lot of kids here. They're all excitable. It felt like a situation that could end poorly."

"One of them patted candy-cane hands all over my face. Does that count?"

His look of horror is classic, but I look past him at Anabelle.

"You handled that so well," she says. "I would have frozen, but you did exactly the right thing. I'm so proud of you."

I beam at her, feeling pretty proud of myself right then too. But she's still standing—has been for hours—and I don't like it.

"I need to get a chair for you."

"Oh, I'm okay. I'm good at standing." She sighs and shakes her head at herself. "Sometimes I don't know how stupid something sounds until it comes out of my mouth."

"You *are* good at standing," I say, tucking a lock of hair behind her ear, not because it needs to be tucked, but because I want to touch her, and we're in a room full of children staring at us. "But if you want to stay, I'd feel better if you were sitting."

I talk to Ada, and she tells me that she has no issue with temporarily donating a couple of inflatable chairs to them so long as they tell everyone who asks how comfortable they are. So Anabelle spends the rest of my shift sitting in a unicorn chair, while Joe is in what could either be a bear or a dog, who knows.

"Why do they get chairs?" one kid asks her dad.

"Because that's Santa's girlfriend," replies a little girl who obviously missed everything that happened earlier. It's a good thing these kids aren't on social media yet.

Seeking out Anabelle's gaze, I say, "That's right."

Maybe I'm a dick for wanting to declare it for everyone to hear, but it feels good. Especially when Anabelle blushes and smiles.

The rest of the evening goes pretty smoothly, and by the time Ada comes around and says that Santa needs to leave, the line has already thinned out. Another shout from Ada is enough to clear out the store entirely.

She asks me to stick around for a minute, and Anabelle squeezes my hand and leaves with Joe, who has acquired a candy cane from somewhere.

My nerves are buzzing a bit as I watch them walk out. The evening ended well, but it sure didn't start out that way, and Ada's a no-bullshit, no-drama kind of person. She might not appreciate how I handled the situation.

After the door closes behind Anabelle and Joe, she turns to me. "We had some complaints about you swearing."

"Shit, I'm sorry."

She gives me a level look, and for half a second, I think she's going to kick me out on my ass. And then she laughs hoarsely. "You handled those kids' questions well. You're hired. Provisionally. Clean up your mouth."

"I'm hired?" I ask excitedly, because I'd mostly expected this was a one-and-done situation.

"Wednesdays, Fridays, Saturdays, and Sundays. Three p.m. until closing." She pauses, chewing her gum with a thoughtful look on her face. "That kid who pulled off your beard...his mother brought him over before they left."

"Did you rap his knuckles with a ruler?" I ask, mostly because that was the favorite punishment of one of my foster mothers.

She ignores the question and says, "He let on that some guy came up to him. Gave him twenty bucks to pull off your beard. Maybe it was just one of those schmucks who like to cause trouble for the fun of it, maybe not. I figured you should know, either way."

"Did he say what the guy looked like?" I ask. One summer, I got it into my head that I wanted to get the honey out of a bee colony I found at the park. But when I knocked it over, hundreds of bees flew up around me. This moment feels a little like that, except the bees are caught inside my skull.

There was someone following us earlier, I'm sure of it.

What if it was Roark, and he's decided to be a problem after all?

But he wouldn't have given a kid cash to pull off my beard. He'd have told me to get my head out of my ass and then pushed me into the back of an unmarked car.

So it must be...

Weston.

All the anxiety I had fifteen seconds ago is burned away by rage. Weston has been watching us. I'm guessing he hired someone to do it, because the car that was following us earlier wasn't his. Anabelle would have recognized it if it had been. Besides, the guy driving it was too good at trailing us.

She lifts a shoulder carelessly and chuckles. "He said it was some blond guy who looked like a pencil."

Weston himself. That tracks. A private investigator would follow a couple of people, but he wouldn't give a kid a twenty to pull off a store Santa's beard.

I'd laugh if I weren't so pissed off. I'm not going to let Ole Westie get away with this. I'm going to go have a talk with him.

"So...you want the job?" she asks, popping her gum.

"Yes."

I head for the door, and my hand is on the handle when she asks, "What do you really want to do, kid? We both know this won't hold you for long."

"Maybe I don't want to be held for long," I lie.

She holds my gaze, her face completely no-nonsense even though there's a piece of bubble gum on her cheek.

I tap my cheek, showing her where it got stuck, and she shakes her head. "Don't care much about that. You get to be my age, you don't worry about your appearance anymore. Not like you, stud. But you've got a pretty girlfriend, and it seems to me that you're a man who's trying to turn his life around. So what do you want to do?"

I release the door handle, shocked. Why would a stranger care this much about my failure to plan properly?

"I think I might like to work at a restaurant. I like to cook."

She sniffs. "Restaurant work will cure you of that dream quick enough."

"Did working here cure you of liking kids?"

"No," she says with a smile. "I'll always like the little delinquents. You know, one of my old foster kids runs a restaurant about fifteen, twenty minutes away. I don't think he needs anyone right now, but I'll talk to him."

"Why?"

I didn't mean for it to sound so raw, but a million different emotions are rolling around inside of me.

"I like you, kid. I sense you could use a break. Everyone needs a break sometimes. But no more swearing. The last thing I need is a parade of parents showing up at dawn. The kids, I like. The parents, I could do without."

"Thank you, Ada," I say, feeling choked up. "I'll be here Friday."

CHAPTER THIRTY

ANABELLE

Santa Claus boyfriends: 1

I'm so exhausted I can barely keep my eyes open.

"He did good, didn't he?" Joe asks. "She'll have to hire him. It isn't his fault kids have poor boundary issues and sticky fingers." We're sitting in the car, waiting with the heater on full blast, and Joe has been nervously monologuing for at least two minutes.

"He did fantastic," I say, my heart full of pride. He did. He was glorious, just like he was at Joe's old apartment. Just like he was last night, with his head buried between my legs. Just as he is *always*. I lift my fingers to my lip, remembering how he feels there too. "It was sweet of him to get us chairs."

"It felt like sitting on a pool floaty, but I'd rather sit on a pool floaty than against a shelf of screaming dolls. Why were they screaming? In what world would a child want their doll to scream? I didn't want a screaming doll when I was a kid."

"No, neither did I," I say, paying only half attention to him because my mind is fuzzy with fatigue. "My mother got me a crying baby doll, and I tried to hide it in the back of a drawer. She said I lacked a maternal instinct."

He snorts a laugh.

Movement at the front of the store catches my eye, and I straighten when I see Ryan coming toward us. He looks...upset.

Oh no, oh no, oh no. Did she not give him the job? I don't want him to feel lesser for having been rejected from two positions he's more than capable of doing. I know I'd feel downtrodden.

"He doesn't look happy," I say, pulling on the side of my lip nervously. "What should we do?"

Joe releases a gusty breath. "I just ran and left you and Ryan to a stampede of children, so I don't think I'm a good person to ask for advice."

Ryan comes around to the driver's side of the car and raps gently on the window with his knuckles. He's removed the Santa beard, wig, and hat, and is holding a plastic shopping bag. I roll the window down.

"Why don't you get in the back, sweetheart? It was a lot in there, and I can tell you're tired. I'll drive."

Affection for him swells inside of me. He understands my needs and doesn't make me feel lesser for having them.

I get out of the car, but as I pass him, I lift up to brush a kiss on his lips. He makes a surprised sound but then presses a hand to my back to pull me closer. My heart is thumping fast when he lets me go. "It's okay if you didn't get this job," I say. "We'll find something else for you."

He gives me a smile that feels hollow. "I got the job."

"Oh, then..."

"I'll tell you in the car."

He opens the door for me, and when I climb into the back, he pulls the remaining pillow out from under his shirt. "Here you go."

"No, thank you," I say. "I have a thing about having someone's sweaty chest pillow next to my head. Even yours."

He grins at me, a more Ryan grin, and says, "At least I got an 'even yours.'"

"I'll take it," Joe offers from the front. "I have a crick in my elbow. It got hit by the falling baby doll."

Ryan's grin stretches wider, and he shuts the door for me before getting into the driver's seat and handing Joe the pillow.

"What happened?" I ask, fighting impatience.

He glances around, looking in all of the mirrors. His vigilance reminds me of the way I get when I'm feeling unsafe. "Weston was having someone follow us. He paid that kid twenty bucks to pull off my beard."

My mouth drops open. "He *didn't*."

"It's okay," he says, darting a reassuring look at me. "I'm going to go have a little talk with him."

"No, Ryan. That's not a good idea. It won't make him back off. He—"

"I don't care if it's a good idea," he says firmly, his jaw flexing. "I'm not going to let him have you followed. That's bullshit. Have you heard from that inspector?"

"No, not yet."

"Email him in the morning. Something's off. It doesn't make sense that he'd look at everything and not comment on the wiring. I think we need to start locking the front door. We can give all the guests a key." He pauses. "And the windows. That dude took a real big interest in the windows. We need new locks for them."

"Okay." My heart is thumping faster now. I don't like thinking about the inspector, but I'm more afraid for Ryan. I don't want him to go talk to Weston. Weston could hurt him or get him arrested or—

"*Please* don't go talk to Weston," I say, my voice coming out tinny and strange. "*Please.*"

I can see him working his jaw again in the mirror.

"Don't you think that's what he wants?" I ask. "He must know we've been...spending time together, and he wants to make you angry. He's hoping you'll react physically so he can have you arrested."

"I don't care," he says again. "I can't let—"

"Go with Jeremy. Or Joe. *Please* don't go alone."

"I'll go with you," Joe says. "It's the least I can do after running from the stampede."

Ryan is quiet for a moment, and then he reaches into the back seat and takes my hand. "Okay. I'm sorry. Let's get you home."

We're quiet for the rest of the drive, but Ryan turns on the 24–7 Christmas station, saying he needs to live, eat, and breathe the role of Santa to prepare for the weekend crush at the store.

I barely manage a smile, and Joe's quiet too, all of us consumed by worry.

When we get home, Joe heads upstairs, saying he has a lot of reflection to do as to why he let fear overpower him. I'm guessing he's going up to play *Animal Crossing*, but I need quiet time too, so I don't call him on it.

Ryan and I walk into the parlor in silent agreement. The tree's brightly colored lights soothe something inside of me. Everything looks as it should. Nothing here has been broken, though my sense of safety has been shaken like a snow globe.

"I won't let him hurt you," he says.

I look up at him, holding his eyes—the darker flecks rising to prominence today. "Then you know exactly how I feel."

He stops walking in front of my grandmother's photo, and I study it with him, feeling a swell of grief, of missing her in a visceral way. I want to peer into her bright, happy eyes and hug her. I want to tell her so many things. I'll only ever see her in my memories or photos and recorded videos, though. It seems deeply unfair, but at least I have some scattered pieces of her left. I have this building too, which always felt like ours.

Ryan heaves a weary sigh. "I feel like I did her dirty. She wanted you to get out of a bad relationship."

"And I did." I take his hand.

"That doesn't mean I get to have you myself."

"Why not?" I say. "My grandmother must have trusted you *implicitly* if she gave you that ornament. She must have seen the good man you are. And I wouldn't be so sure that it didn't occur to her that you and I might get along. She wanted me to find someone who cares about me, someone who sees me as I am, and you do."

He gathers me up in his arms, his hand finding my hair. "I don't know what to do."

A sad laugh escapes me. "Neither do I, Ryan."

"I'm desperate for you."

The moment feels surreal. No one's ever been desperate for me before. I peer up into his warm, beautiful eyes. "Show me."

He kisses me then—a deep, needy kiss—and I return it in kind, wanting to sink into the way he makes me feel without worrying where it will lead or whether I'm chasing something that will break my heart.

Breaking the kiss, he pulls back and searches my face. "You're exhausted, and I'm not helping. You probably need some time alone. I'll bring dinner up for you."

I lift a hand to trace his lips, fascinated by his face. By my new ability to touch it whenever I'd like—which is so often it will probably shock and possibly repel him. "Will you eat with me?"

"If you want me to."

"I want you to."

He needs to change out of his Santa things, so he walks upstairs with me and kisses me once more before I enter my room.

True to his word, he makes us spaghetti. He also prepares a special dinner for Saint Nick, which smells atrocious but is devoured in such large and eager gulps it must be delicious to him. I'm so enraptured by Ryan that I do something truly brave.

After we're done eating, I get down on my knees and unfasten the button on his jeans.

His eyes are full of warmth as he watches me. "You don't have to do that."

"I know," I say, my pulse hammering. There's a voice in my head telling me that I don't know what to do and it won't be pleasurable for him, but it's overpowered by my need to show him how much he's starting to mean to me. "I want to make you feel good. Help me make you feel good."

He runs his hands over my hair. "You already do that, sweetheart."

I unzip his jeans and take him out. Then, after looking up at him to reassure myself I'm doing it right, I wrap my mouth around him and suck.

If it's not very good for him, I certainly can't tell, because he moans and buries his hand in my hair and tells me that I'm definitely not on the naughty list, because I'm a *very* good girl. Honestly, I feel like it.

THE NEXT MORNING, I wake up early, feeling refreshed. I get up, leaving Ryan on my bed with Saint Nick. My heart feels like it's made of sweet chocolate when I look at them. Ryan seems so innocent when he's asleep, his hair in soft curls and his lips slightly parted, his legs curled beneath him. I'm humming as I walk down the steps, and I allow myself to skip into the kitchen.

It's only when I see Cynthia, her hair restored to its usual brown—albeit a couple of shades lighter—and tucked prettily into her costume's bonnet, that I remember I never texted her last night.

Remorse floods me. I forgot to text Cynthia about her trip to Richmond. How could I have forgotten? A good friend would certainly have texted, perhaps several times.

"Oh dear," I say as she turns toward me. "Your hair looks fantastic, but I forgot to check in with you. I feel like a horrible friend."

She lifts her eyebrows. "I didn't text you either. Did Ryan get the job?"

"He did," I say, "and there are some other developments I should tell you about, but I'm not going to be able to focus on anything else until you tell me what happened with Jeremy."

A satisfied smile stretches across her face. "Good, because I was going to talk about him anyway." She lifts her hands to one of her curls and tugs on it as she says, "He took me out to dinner, and he told me that I drive him crazy."

"I hope that's not the only thing he said."

"The good kind of crazy," she says smugly. "He said I'm all he can think about lately, and he showed me his Instagram inbox. There are, no shit, like five hundred messages in there from super-hot women, and he didn't answer any of them."

"I didn't think he had," I say, feeling a swell of fondness for Jeremy. "And what happened next?"

Her eyes glimmer, and she glances furtively behind me before continuing. "We stayed at a hotel halfway between Richmond and Williamsburg."

"You did?" I gasp.

"We did. And I figured the least I could do after he helped me with my hair and bought me dinner was to suck his dick."

"You did that too?" I ask, my mouth agape.

"You also sucked Jeremy's dick?" She's obviously teasing me, and I find myself laughing even as heat floods my face.

"You know what I mean."

"I do, and I'm delighted." Laughing, she pulls me into a hug. "I hope Ryan's enough of a gentleman to reciprocate."

"Oh, he already did that," I say.

Can a person's cheeks actually catch on fire?

"Oh my God, Anabelle. I can't believe it. Look at us." She squeezes me harder before releasing me. "Jeremy wants to try this with me. We're together. I still have two dead-end jobs, no offense, but I'm so happy. I didn't know I could be this happy. And it's all because of you and Ryan. I'm glad you're giving him a chance."

"I didn't do anything," I protest, surprised.

"You did," she says. "You were a good friend. You *are* a good friend."

I open my mouth to object, because I have failed to meet my personal list of what a friend should do: I forget to call or text, and most of the time I need to remind myself to ask people about their interests. But then I stop myself; the truth is, I'm starting to feel like a good friend. Maybe all this time it wasn't me that was the problem. Maybe I was trying to form relationships with the wrong people.

CHAPTER THIRTY-ONE

RYAN

"If you warn him off, he'll know you're onto him, and he'll do something less stupid," Jeremy says. "You want him to keep being a dumbass so we can catch him in something illegal and have *him* arrested instead of you."

We're at the Green Leafe Café again. When I told Jeremy I needed his help with something, he insisted on buying me a drink, saying, *I think I'll have to keep buying you drinks for the rest of my life.*

The trip to Richmond went well, and now he and Cynthia are a thing. I'm happy for the guy. It's a hell of a feeling when the woman you're falling for wants you too.

Anabelle and Joe spent most of the morning working on their online store, although Anabelle also filed online to change the B&B's name and ordered a new sign.

I picked up locks for the windows at the home improvement store, plus a deadbolt for the front door. If Westie is still having us followed, installing new locks is likely to be noticed. Maybe he'll see it as evidence that we have the ornament, if that's what he's after. But fuck it. I'll feel like Anabelle's a hell of a lot safer with the locks.

The supposed building inspector has yet to answer her email, and my suspicions about him are getting stronger, like a stomach virus that sets in with indigestion and then has you puking your guts out over a toilet for ten hours.

I'm consumed with the painful need to keep Anabelle safe. The way she got down on her knees for me last night broke something inside of me—and then healed it. She's my Christmas witch. I'm not going to let any harm come to her, from anyone. I *will* protect her at all costs.

Jeremy, Joe, and Cynthia have all volunteered to help with the locks, but only Jeremy has any experience with home improvement projects. So Cynthia said she'd help Joe and Anabelle disperse the non-scavenger-hunt Santas and also finish writing new ad copy for the inn.

"I don't like that you're right," I say, finally responding to Jeremy.

"I can't agree with you there." He grins as he touches his glass to mine. "I always like being right. But if it makes you feel better, I can recruit some of my buddies to serenade him the next time we see him on DoG Street."

I grin at that thought, then shake my head. "Nah, it would be funny as hell, but you're right. I don't want to get him any more riled up."

He laughs. "True." He takes another sip of his beer, then asks, "You have any interest in plumbing? My uncle's losing one of his guys in January, and he could use another helper who's good with his hands."

"Seriously?" I ask in disbelief. "I don't have any experience."

He shrugs. "Even he uses YouTube to figure shit out. I'll be perfectly honest with you, though, I hated working with him. He's a loudmouth, and half of the job is clearing out people's toilets after they flush down all manner of things. You literally don't want to know. But there's some cool shit, and the pay's not bad. Definitely better money than playing trumpet or pretending to be Santa Claus."

"I'll take that under consideration," I say, feeling like my words have dried up. It's hard to believe two people have gone out of their way to try to find me work in as many days.

He claps me on the back. "We gotta keep you around, man."

"Is that Cynthia talking, or you?"

He gives me a slow grin and taps the bar. "You know what? I feel confident that I'm talking for all of us, man. Anabelle and her buddy too."

ON SATURDAY, we get the locks on the windows and front door installed. At one point, I see someone watching us from the street— a bald guy in a nondescript black coat, jeans, and generic tennis shoes. I don't know if he's the private investigator, but I do know what it looks like when a guy dresses to avoid getting noticed. I've done it myself often enough. So I salute him.

He flinches and immediately walks off, which doesn't mean anything, but I'm left with a feeling that we're being watched by shitty-sneakers guy.

"Weston will give up eventually," Anabelle tells me, but I'm not banking on it. He didn't just lose his woman—if he's having me followed, he knows by now that he lost her to *me*. He'll have guessed that I'm in her bed almost every night, that I'm kissing and holding her and making her moan. I haven't fully made love to her yet, but he doesn't know that. It must drive him crazy thinking that I have what he was stupid enough to lose.

I'm worried Weston will try screwing up my weekend shifts at the toy shop, but Ada put up some signs saying, "Parking lot is under surveillance." I don't see any cameras, and I doubt she went to the trouble of actually installing any, but Weston doesn't seem like a guy who'd know what a security camera looks like. He's a man who pays other people to do things for him and has never learned to do them himself.

I told Anabelle she didn't need to come back to the shop with me, being that it can't be fun to watch me pretend to be Santa Claus for several hours in a row, but she said that I "greatly underestimated" how hot I looked in my Santa suit.

She comes both days, although she brings noise-cancelling ear protection and a book.

It fills my fucking cup to have her there.

Cynthia gets her a Mrs. Claus costume as a gag, and she actually wears it to the shop on Sunday. The kids pay her more attention than she'd probably like, and I'm worried that she'll be worn out by it. After my shift, though, she insists it was fun—and I insist that she keep her costume on while I get down on my knees beside the bed and tuck her legs over my shoulders so I can lose myself in heaven.

Monday passes, and there's still no word from the building inspector. I call the number on his card, and it bounces straight to a voicemail service. The message sounds like it's on the up and up, but my gut insists he was casing the place. So when he doesn't respond by Tuesday, I look up the office online and call the general service line.

They've never heard of the guy.

I share the news with everyone over lunch at The Bread Shop, holding Anabelle's hands for my own sake as much as hers, and Jeremy suggests calling the police.

My first thought is *hell no*. But this guy is slinging some murky shit. In the past, a paper trail was my enemy, but this time we need one. Someone in a position of authority has to know that Weston has been going after Anabelle and is escalating.

"Ryan?" Anabelle says, her voice heavy with concern. I know what she's thinking... I haven't told her anything else about my job for Roark, but she's too smart not to have realized I've done illegal shit before.

"You should call them," I say. "They need to know that guy was planning something."

So she does, and although the officer she speaks to is receptive, he can't do anything. We don't have any direct evidence that Weston sent the guy, any photos of the "inspector," or anything other than the fake business card. He tells Anabelle to keep her eye open for scam artists, promises to look into the matter, and that's that.

For them.

I'm on guard.

It feels like I'm in a silent war, and I wish again for my brother. Jake's smarter than me, and he'd know how to handle this.

I start wearing the watch I got at the estate sale, which bolsters me in a strange way and reminds me that I've decided to be a new man.

On Wednesday, the new sign for the inn arrives, and Jeremy and I install it over his lunch break. It looks damn good, and Anabelle has tears in her eyes as she takes it in.

"Your grandmother would be so proud of you, sweetheart," I tell her, letting my hand settle on the small of her back. I know it's true. Grandma Edith was a woman who owned her shit, and she would have loved to see that her granddaughter had inherited the same backbone. Hell, the thought puts tears in my eyes, and I'm not ashamed to admit it.

She gives me a sidelong look, leaning into my hand, and says, "She would have been proud of you too. I know it."

I want to believe it. I want to believe I'm not being a selfish prick for sticking around, especially since Weston must be driven crazy by the knowledge that I'm still here, still with Anabelle. He's the one who broke his relationship with her, but to his mind, I'm the thief who took his woman and the B&B he wanted for his portfolio.

What wouldn't a man like that do?

I ask myself that every day as I go about my business, pausing to look out the windows and search the street.

I ask myself that as I kiss my girl until my lips are raw, and as I make her come with my mouth and my hand. But I still haven't let myself have her all the way, even though she's hinted she's ready.

By the time the weekend rolls around again without any developments, I'm so past ready to sink into her that my dick's sending me hate mail.

It's just...

I'm in love with her. It would be impossible to feel any other way. But she doesn't know everything, and some broken bit of logic in my brain tells me it's not fair to make love to her without telling her who's been sharing her bed.

So even though I'm happy in a way I've never been, it's incomplete. Because I can feel trouble at my back, just two steps away, and I can't relax or take comfort in her the way I'd like. But I try to hold back my worry, not wanting to infect her, or Cynthia and Jeremy, who act like every day is their honeymoon despite bickering as much as ever, or Joe, who's already worried enough about everything.

The inn looks great, and the guests are crazy about the Santa scavenger hunt—a reporter even got in touch with Anabelle about doing a national story about it. The thought of taking the interview gave her hives, so she responded that she'd "get back to them," but still, it's cool as hell that they're interested.

The Gingerbread House has been full for days, and it'll be full until after New Year's.

It's a lot for Anabelle, but Cynthia, Joe, and I work together to make sure she doesn't get burned out—which seems entirely possible given that she and Joe are like Christmas elves in their office, sending out dozens of packages a day.

Christmas is coming, and I want to be excited about it. I want to think it's all going to be okay. But that nagging worry just won't go away.

CHAPTER THIRTY-TWO

ANABELLE

Saturday, December 22, 3 days before Christmas

*Presents purchased for my nice list and stowed in my
super secret hiding place that only Ryan knows about: 15*

It's Saturday morning, three days before Christmas, and my whole body feels like it's buzzing. This is *always* my favorite time of the year, and this year it's so much better and bigger, because Ryan, Joe, Cynthia, Jeremy, and I will be spending Christmas together! Cynthia and Jeremy both have family in town, but Jeremy's parents are divorced and fighting, so he says he has the perfect excuse to avoid them. Cynthia told me privately that while her mother is over-joyed that she "finally" has a serious boyfriend, her father isn't that pleased that it's a "doofus who plays the trumpet in a marching band." So she's going to be with us too.

My parents asked me to join them for Christmas dinner, but my father made a point of saying that Ryan is not welcome...and also that I should really hear Weston out. They've been talking, and he's certain Weston still cares about both me and the inn, and wouldn't it be much better to date a man who has a thriving career rather than a deadbeat who plays Santa on the weekends? I assured him that it wouldn't be and brought the conversation to a quick end.

I wasn't disappointed, because I hadn't really expected any different. My father clearly sees Weston as the son he never had, whereas I'm the daughter he'll never understand. On the plus side, his attitude made me feel much less guilty about my decision not to come home for Christmas.

Another upside: Ryan is cooking for everyone!

We're even doing a Secret Santa gift exchange, in addition to the presents I have of course purchased for everyone. I drew Joe for the exchange, and I'm going to give him the tea towel that he once yelled at Ryan not to use. It has a lovely circular feeling to it.

In addition, everything is going *very* well at the B&B. One couple *did* cancel because "Christmas is a commercial and oversaturated holiday," but their room was instantly snapped up by a delightful man named Stanley, who has already done the scavenger hunt twice. Ryan pointed out that his second hunt was pointless since we only move the Santas when he gets bored and wants to change things up, but I admire Stanley's enthusiasm.

At Ryan's suggestion, we've started offering a daily activity in addition to Hot Chocolate Happy Hour. A mounted whiteboard by the front door advertises the day's activity and Hot Chocolate Happy Hour, and there's a box of flyers directly underneath it containing the information and rules for the Santa Scavenger Hunt. Anyone who completes it successfully gets a chocolate bar.

Yesterday, Ryan led a cookie baking session, and the previous day, Jeremy and Cynthia talked about working as historical interpreters and gave everyone a tour. Today, Joe and I are going to bring a few guests to an estate sale—with Ryan, of course, both because he's basically indispensable to me at this point and he's much better at reading a crowd than either of us.

Admittedly, most people likely wouldn't call a group of five guests a crowd, but it can certainly feel that way.

On the whole, life is looking pretty bright right now. But there's something that's been on my mind, and I'm in the kitchen with Cynthia while she prepares waffles, trying to figure out a way to talk to her about it.

"So..." I say, watching her cut some unseasonable and dry-looking strawberries.

She shakes her head and smiles. "I've tried, really I have. But I still can't read your mind, Anabelle."

More's the pity.

Sighing, I fuss with the little wreath tea rack I ordered a week ago. I've been slowly replacing some of Grandma Edith's old things. Each time I feel a pang of guilt, but I can't deny that it feels good to take ownership of the inn. Ryan keeps telling me that's exactly what she wanted—for me to be strong and independent and *happy*—and I'm starting to believe him.

"Well?" Cynthia prompts, pulling me back to the present.

"I was just wondering how...you know...how you let Jeremy know you were ready to take the next step."

I know that they have. She came in the morning afterward looking like she'd just been given a million-dollar lottery ticket and told me, speaking much too loudly, that it might be harder to go down on a big-dicked man, but it sure made it worthwhile when you were...well...sleeping with him.

"You mean anal?" she asks now.

"No!"

Oops, that came out too loud. I check the door for eavesdroppers and then whisper, "No, I mean...just...you know, regular sex."

Her eyes go wide and she drops the knife. "You haven't had sex with Ryan yet? He spends almost every night in your room. I've been wondering when you're going to have him move in so you're not wasting a perfectly good room that could go to a paying guest."

I blush furiously and check the door again. There's no sign of Ryan or anyone else, thank goodness.

"We have..." I glance at the door again, "done things."

Cynthia rolls her eyes but smiles.

"A *lot* of things," I continue.

"Yes, I'm well aware that you've sucked his dick."

I wrinkle my nose. "But he doesn't seem to understand that I'm ready for . . ." I wave my hand in circles.

"A hot dick injection."

I groan. "You delight in embarrassing me."

She gives me a fond smile. "Absolutely." Then she turns from the counter to face me and picks up her coffee, taking a big sip. "So he's not giving you the dick. Do you have any idea why?"

I'm still embarrassed, but I would also like to get to the bottom of this. "Not really. He seems to...he definitely would like to. I can... you know...tell, and he's been making his workouts even longer in the morning. The internet tells me that's a sign of sexual frustration. But there's something holding him back from taking things further."

"He's worried about Weston," she says thoughtfully.

My mouth puckers at the mention of his name. Now that I'm with Ryan, who treats me like I matter and listens to me and touches me like he's the luckiest man on earth because I want him to, I realize that Weston never cared about me. I, most certainly, never cared about him. The only thing he liked about me was his ability to talk me into doing and saying what suited him. The only thing I liked about him was his disinterest in involving himself in my hobbies.

I want to believe that Weston no longer cares about me or the B&B. I actually saw him from a distance the other day when I was at the grocery store. He didn't attempt to approach me, even though I was alone. Surely that's a sign that he no longer cares...

"Yes," I agree. "And Ryan still hasn't told me everything about his past. I think he's worried I'll judge him or throw him out."

I would *never* do that. I know Ryan's a good man, no matter what he did or was involved in. He's shown it to me, my friends, my guests, and even my cat every single day he's been here. He's taken over my heart so thoroughly, there's no piece of it left that doesn't contain an echo of him.

"So maybe tell him you won't judge him," she says. "Or you can also give him a big, wrapped box of condoms. That would work too."

I smile at her, feeling a deep fondness. My friendship with Cynthia has evolved so much over the past month. And with Joe too. Ryan was the catalyst. I don't think he realizes how much he's brought us all together.

So tell him, a voice in my head insists.

"I want it to happen tonight," I say, my voice quavering slightly.

She gives me an unimpressed look.

"It's going to happen tonight," I try.

"That's the spirit." Cynthia pulls me into a hug. "And I'm going to take you lingerie shopping after my shift later, because there's no way you're going to get your seduction on in one of your grandmother's old nightgowns."

Little does she know...

THE DAY PASSES QUICKLY. The estate sale is a huge success, and afterward Cynthia picks me up to go lingerie shopping.

"Are you getting another Mrs. Claus costume?" Ryan asks me before he leaves for work, wagging his eyebrows up and down.

"Something like that," I say cryptically and give him a very thorough kiss before he goes.

I *do* choose something like that—a scandalous red satin nightgown edged with lace. Or at least I think it's scandalous until I see what Cynthia picked out for herself—an outfit that's made solely of purple straps but covers nothing important.

"What's the point of wearing anything at all?" I ask when she holds it up for display.

This makes her laugh and give me one of her fond looks, and then we make our purchases. I have run out of time to launder the outfit before wearing it tonight, but at least it came in a sealed package.

It's six o'clock—a couple of hours before Ryan gets off work—so Cynthia drops me off at the Curio parking lot. It's stuffed with cars, just like last weekend, and there are still parents coming by with their kids.

I head inside, and Ada nods at me from her position at one of the front registers. She has another two cashiers tonight, and they each have a line of customers to serve.

"Our boy's doing well," she tells me, which makes me grin at her, even though she's already returned her attention to the woman in front of her.

When I get to the back, my usual unicorn blow-up chair is waiting for me, and I smile when I see the little cardboard sign sitting on top of it: *Reserved for Ms. Claus.*

Ryan sees me sitting down and blows me a kiss, and I feel a swell of emotion inside of me that makes me realize what should probably have been obvious to me already.

I love him.

I love him, and I want all of him.

Tonight.

CHAPTER THIRTY-THREE

RYAN

"Santa, why do you keep looking over there? I don't want a *baby* doll. I want a Rainbow High doll. But it has to be the one with the colorful hair, and not the little one, because her eyelashes are painted on."

"Uh, noted," I tell the seven-year-old girl named Frances. Her middle name is Margaret, but she would have preferred something like Rose or Hyacinth. She probably would have told me her parents' social security numbers too if she knew them. "And I'm looking at *her*." I point to Anabelle, who has her head bent over a book, her hair falling around it in sexy waves. "She's my girlfriend. Isn't she beautiful?"

Her mouth falls open. "You're cheating on Mrs. Claus?"

"Five minutes," Ada announces over the loudspeaker.

Thank Christ. I've got a headache, and I need a shot of whiskey and at least an hour alone with Anabelle.

"Rainbow High doll with rainbow hair," I say, loudly enough for her parents to hear, hopefully. Then I add, "Aisle 5," for good measure. Doesn't hurt to be helpful.

Frances gets up but stomps her foot. "What about Mrs. Claus?"

I'm tempted to say something like *what she doesn't know won't hurt her*, but I have a job to do, so I draw in a deep breath and say, "She *is* Mrs. Claus. She's in disguise." Then I lift my finger to my lips, and she makes the lip-zipping motion in response.

It's cute enough to lift my mood, and I listen to one other kid's capitalist wishes before Ada puts an end to the evening.

I get up, give 'em one last *ho ho ho*, and go to Anabelle. "You didn't have to come, sweetheart. I thought you were going shopping with Cynthia."

It's a bit unusual for her and Cynthia to go clothes shopping together—Anabelle usually buys her clothes online, and almost always from the same stores because she knows how the fabric feels —but I figured maybe she was going Christmas shopping and didn't want to say so. I've already bought her a couple of Christmas gifts, although I second-guess myself at least five times a day.

"I wanted to come," she says, kissing the side of my face.

"Ooooooh," says a young boy who hasn't cleared out of the store yet. "That lady's kissing Santa Claus."

Ada actually *smiles* at me on my way out. "Good job, kid. You don't have to put any dollars in the bucket today."

We have an agreement that I need to put a dollar in her donation bucket every time I swear—which apparently includes saying hell and damn around kids. It's helped me clean up my act. The money goes to a fund for foster kids, though, and I'm going to make a donation on purpose as my Christmas present to Ada.

My head still aches, but I feel good as I open the car door for Anabelle and then walk around and climb in. Maybe the ache in my head is from the stress of carrying around the feeling that the other shoe is about to drop...

Every day it doesn't drop, I know it's getting lower and lower.

"Are you okay?" she asks, giving me a worried look.

"Yeah, fine."

"Would you like to see what I got with Cynthia?" she asks.

"Sure."

She pulls a slinky red silk teddy out of the bag.

"Jesus Christ." I tug it from her, my eyes on her. "You bought this, Anabelle?"

"Do you like it?"

"Yeah," I say, my throat feeling raw and my dick suddenly rock-hard. "Yeah, I like it. Does this mean...?"

She looks me dead in the eye and says, "I want you to make love to me, Ryan."

Damn.

"Are you trying to get me to speed?" I ask.

She smiles at me, then returns the teddy to the bag, which she sets primly in her lap, and somehow that only makes me more eager for her.

I lean in and kiss her hard, and she opens her mouth and invites me in without hesitation.

I'd told myself I wouldn't do this until we have a conversation about my past, but I've put that off. And put it off some more. And put it off further.

Because if she sends me packing, it's going to break me.

But maybe we don't need to have that conversation first. Maybe—

We're still in the toy store parking lot, and someone honks their horn at us. I pull away from Anabelle and wave at the scandalized-looking woman behind the wheel of a minivan, hoping like hell she doesn't give Ada a call later.

I glance at Anabelle, grinning, suddenly feeling on top of the world. "Let's go home."

It's not until I'm almost there, going fast but not fast enough to get pulled over for speeding, that I realize what I said.

Home.

I've been here less than a month, but it *feels* like home. Anabelle feels like home. I love her, and I love her bed and breakfast, and I love all of her friends. I even love her cat. And although the Santas and I didn't begin on such a great note, I've gotten to like those crazy bastards too. Hiding them in new places for the scavenger hunt is one of my favorite things to do, because Anabelle and Joe always do a test run to see if they can find them. They're funny as hell about it —super competitive—and I enjoy watching them.

I'm thinking about all of this, my heart so full it hurts, as I park the car. Grinning at Anabelle, I grab the bag with the teddy and stuff it into the pocket of my Santa coat. It's only as we get out and walk toward the inn that I spot the police cruiser parked outside, where no cars are supposed to go.

She shoots a look at me, her eyes full of horror. "Joe."

I grab her hand, and we run toward the entrance, but when we get to the steps leading up to the front door, she shakes her head so hard I'm worried she'll hurt herself. "I can't go in there, Ryan. I'm frozen. I can't go in there."

I can feel it in her grip. I'm dying to go inside to see what the fuck is going on, but my priority is Anabelle. I wrap her up in my arms and hold her, whispering to her promises I don't know if I can keep—*it's going to be okay, I'm going to make it be okay*—and one promise I will keep, no matter what—*I won't let anyone hurt you.*

She lets me guide her to sitting on the cold step, and it's then that Joe hurries out of the B&B, a police officer trailing behind him. His eyes are red, which isn't very promising, but at least he's alive and uninjured. This is about something else.

"You're okay," she says. "You're okay. You're okay."

"I'm fine," Joe assures her.

I help her up and then nod toward the door. "Let's get her inside. It's too cold out here."

"Not yet." Joe bites his bottom lip.

"Cynthia?" Anabelle croaks.

I wrap my arm around her, holding her up. I'm not too worried about Cynthia. If something had happened to Cynthia, the police wouldn't be here. She wouldn't have had any reason to come back to the inn after dropping Anabelle off at Curio.

"I'm so sorry, Anabelle," Joe says, tears leaking down his cheeks. "I'm so sorry."

"What happened?" I ask, looking from him to the officer, who's rocking on his heels. He's a big guy with a crew cut and the beginnings of a beer gut. Maybe thirty-five, maybe fifty.

"There's been a robbery," he says.

And there it is: the other shoe dropping.

Anabelle and I exchange a knowing look. The ornament must be gone.

Only...

Joe doesn't even know about the ornament, so why would he have called the police?

"I don't know how this happened," Joe says, tears streaming down his face. "I was here the whole time, and we changed the locks. Ryan even put those locks on the windows himself."

"No one broke in," the officer says, squaring his jaw. His gaze tracks from Joe to me. He smirks when he notices my Santa suit.

"The guests all have keys," I say, my mind working at the puzzle. "Maybe it was one of them, or someone lost one. What did they take?" I ask, holding Anabelle close. Her body is stiff, but I feel small tremors working through her.

"They took the ornaments and all of the Santas," Joe says, crying harder now. "Do you think it was Craig retaliating? I don't think it could have been because he's been posting vague Instagram stories every thirty minutes, and they're all from the stockroom at the grocery store, but I don't know. I can't think clearly. I can't make sense of any of it."

Anabelle is silent and pale, her eyes far away, and my protectiveness takes over. I don't want her to see this. I think maybe she can't see this right now, so I turn to the officer. "She's in shock. I'm going to bring her upstairs."

"I'll need to talk to her if she's the owner," he says.

"Of course. But she needs time to process this."

He rolls on his feet again, and I decide he's a douchebag. His next words hammer the impression home: "I don't have a lot of time to spare, son. A collection of dolls and a few craft projects isn't exactly a pressing problem in the scheme of things."

"Her collection was written up in *House & Garden* magazine," I snap. "It's worth money. And someone clearly knew it. She also has an ornament that was on *Antiques Roadshow*. It's worth hundreds of thousands of dollars. If that's gone, it's a big deal."

He seems more interested by this, but he just nods. "Okay. Your little buddy here has filled me in. You come on down to talk to me, and I can interview her later."

Now, I'm *positive* I don't fucking like him. "My *little buddy* is an expert with antiques, so I'm sure he can tell you exactly what was stolen. He and Anabelle are in business together."

"Insurance fraud is a felony," he says, giving us hard looks.

"Insurance fraud? We haven't been here for hours!"

"What about the little guy?" He nods at Joe. "You got those stolen Santas hidden in your room, buddy?"

Joe looks horrified. "Of...of course not. I'm the one who called you. And I told you about Craig."

"We'll look into it," he says dismissively. I'm guessing Craig won't get a single phone call. Not that I think he did it. I got Craig to buy Joe replacement Crocs just by frowning at him—I'm guessing he didn't grow a pair of balls big enough to turn around and do this. He's the kind of man who might enjoy being a petty prick, but he's not very good at it.

No, this is the work of a master.

"I need to sit down," Anabelle says in a tiny voice, and worry for her swallows the need to take action, which would likely involve doing or saying something stupid that would result in me being arrested.

I swear under my breath and then gather her up in my arms and carry her inside and straight up the stairs, not stopping or pausing or otherwise allowing her to see the parlor.

She's crying softly now, and I want to hold her forever. I also want to murder whoever did this to her.

Let's be real. I want to murder *Weston*. Because there's no way he's not behind this.

Saint Nick meows and hurries toward us as I tear off the blankets with one hand and then lower her into the bed and tuck her in. The cat curls up next to her, and I give him a pat, feeling like we're on the same team.

I know I should head down right away, but my God, look at her. I run my hand over her hair. She's still scarily silent, and I feel like a bottle rocket ready to blow, because I hate seeing her like this.

I hurry over to inspect her super secret hiding place in the closet, which is not super secret to me given how much time I spend in here. It does look like someone might have rummaged through the closet, but the ornament is still in its spot. I return to her and kiss her forehead. "The ornament's still there. No one took it."

I can tell it's no comfort at all. The ornament might be worth more than the whole Santa collection, but she doesn't love it the same way. It's not important to her. Even the decorations stolen off the trees on the first floor are probably more important.

Anger lashes through my veins, making the blood hotter. Weston knows that, which is the only reason he took all of it. Sure, he was probably hoping his guy would find the sweetgum ornament, but he was content to ruin her Christmas. She didn't give him what he wanted, when he wanted it, and now he wants to break her.

"I love you," I say. "I love you, Anabelle. It's going to be okay. I promise."

This wasn't how I'd planned to tell her, but I need her to know. Before I turn to leave, she reaches for my hand. "I love you too," she says, tears spilling down her face. "Please don't do anything dangerous. *Please.*"

"I won't," I say as I trace away her tears with my fingertips. "We just need to figure this out. It's all going to be okay, sweetheart."

But I don't really believe it. That other shoe just dropped on my neck.

Sure enough, when I go back downstairs, Weston himself is in the front room, chatting with the shitty officer as if they're the very best of buddies. Joe is sitting behind the desk, his chair shoved so far away from them it's practically buried in the Christmas tree we "freed" from his old apartment. It has lights and garland still but no ornaments. He looks terrified, not that I blame him.

Weston turns and looks at me, a smug smile on his face.

"What the fuck are you doing here?" I say, feeling the rage pumping harder, faster.

"I saw the police cruiser. I was worried about Anabelle, obviously. We may not be together anymore, but I'm still concerned for her safety. And the safety of the guests, of course. This kind of thing can leave a stain on a hospitality business. People want to believe they're safe."

"You think we don't know you're behind this?" I hiss through clenched teeth. He looks so damn pleased with himself, and I guess he should be. He's probably going to get away with it. Rich, self-important assholes almost always do.

He smirks at me, his eyes a pale blue—like they've sat in the sun so long the color's washed out. "I'm rich, Ryan. What would I want with a bunch of tag sale trash?"

From the way he says it—with his sneer and taunting tone—I know he's not just talking about Anabelle's precious belongings.

He's talking about the love of my life. So I don't think. I just lunge forward and punch him in the face. Exactly the way he wanted me to.

Five minutes later, Officer Asshole is dragging me out of the B&B and cuffing me, in full view of dozens of tourists.

Here I go again, creating a mess, when all I wanted to do was avoid one.

CHAPTER THIRTY-FOUR

ANABELLE

"He did what?" I squeak, sitting up in the bed. Saint Nick yowls, and I gather him up in my arms, needing the reassurance of his soft orange fur.

Joe must have called Cynthia, because she's standing by the bed with him. She's wearing a too-big sweatshirt that has to be Jeremy's, and her hair is a mass of messy curls. I have no idea what time it is, or about anything but the emotions throbbing inside me —so many of them, I can't hope to untangle them. The overall feeling is a sense of deep unease. Of everything being horribly wrong and so messy there's not a broom in existence that could clean it up.

Cynthia shoves a glass tumbler at me, and I don't question her— I grab it and slug down a mouthful, cringing a little at the earthy bite of the whiskey. But it pools needed warmth in my stomach. She takes the glass back from me, her expression pinched.

Joe rubs his face nervously. "I'm trying to think of a nice way to say this, Anabelle."

I'm brought back to the beginning of the month, when I said much the same thing to Ryan about my grandmother. I often take pleasure and reassurance in echoes, but I don't feel that way at the moment as I repeat Ryan's line back to Joe: "There probably is no nice way."

He furrows his brow. "Yeah...I guess not. So...I don't think Craig was behind this at all."

"No one believed Craig was behind it," I mutter numbly.

"Weston made an appearance, and he was a dick. It was super obvious he'd arranged the theft, so Ryan punched him in the face. It was awesome actually. I mean, damn, Ryan is really strong. I think he broke Weston's nose. But he did it in front of the cop, and the cop put him in handcuffs, arrested him, and dragged him off in his squad car."

"Oh my God," I say, new fear engulfing me like a cocoon. First, I thought I might have lost Joe, just like I lost Grandma Edith a few months ago, and then I found out someone had taken the collection I'd spent years piecing together, not to mention every last ornament except the one that we'd hidden. But losing Ryan...that's unthinkable. Even worse to imagine him in some jail cell by himself. Three days before Christmas.

I've never truly hated anyone before now, but I hate Weston. I *hate* him. The memory of having ever touched him with anything but the intent to injure is so completely repulsive to me.

Tears run down my face, and in this moment, I hate myself too. If I hadn't melted down earlier, then Ryan wouldn't have gone downstairs alone. I could have held him back. I could have kept him from playing Weston's stupid games, the way I had in the past.

"It's okay," Cynthia says, leaning in and rubbing my shoulder. She probably means to do it gently, but I suspect Cynthia doesn't know how to do anything gently. "My dad's a defense lawyer, and he brought Jeremy with him as his assistant. They're down at the police station working to get Ryan out on bail."

"Your dad went with Jeremy?"

It's a stupid detail to latch onto, but she smiles. "Yeah, so we're all screwed, I guess."

I smile for half a second, which is all I have in me. "I'll cover whatever it costs, of course."

I don't have a lot of money in my bank account, especially after replacing the pipes and wiring, but it doesn't matter. I'll sell the ornament if I have to. I'll strip the inn of any antique that's worth more than a few bucks. I'm going to get Ryan out, and I will not, under any circumstances, allow Weston to win.

"We'll all chip in," Cynthia says firmly, rubbing my shoulder again. It's still uncomfortable, but I appreciate the sentiment behind it too much to tell her to stop. "Ryan's important to all of us."

A rush of warmth fills me as Joe nods in agreement. I can tell they mean it—and I know how much it will mean to him to realize he's so loved by all of us.

Joe blurts out, "There's more, Anabelle."

"More?" I ask, my voice coming out weakly.

"Someone was outside taking photos of Ryan being walked out. It was a total setup, and photos are already circulating online." He gulps air. "There are kids reposting them, telling the police department to *free Santa*. Someone tagged Curio."

More emotion blasts through me. Ada loves Ryan, but I suspect she'll have no choice but to fire him. Even if he's released in time for his shift tomorrow. No parent will want to send their kid to sit on the lap of a Santa who spent the night in lockup.

"I *hate* Weston," I seethe.

"Oh, you're preaching to the choir," Cynthia says, "but don't you worry. We're not going to let ole Westie ruin Christmas for everyone. My dad will get Ryan out. Weston's not permanently injured. Simple assault is a misdemeanor. And once we prove Weston's behind the theft, he's the one who'll be wearing the orange jumpsuit."

Fresh tears flood my eyes at the thought of Ryan behind bars. He hates being cooped up. He'll go crazy.

She glances at the clock on the wall. "Why don't you try to get some sleep, honey? I've got Xanax."

"I won't go back to sleep until he's home. I need to see him with my own eyes."

"That may not be until tomorrow," Cynthia says gently.

"So I'll stay awake until tomorrow." I swallow, realizing I've been neglecting my job on top of everything. I've been lying up here, frozen, for hours. Doing nothing. Fixing nothing. I bury my hand in Saint Nick's fur, needing it. "I forgot all about the guests."

"Of course you did," Cynthia says, stroking my hair with the same rough affection she gave my shoulder. "You had a shock. A couple of them checked out online after the kerfuffle. Stanley and that couple that smells like beets."

Horror rips through me as the pieces join together to form a picture.

Stanley was behind this.

Stanley, who checked in at the last minute.

Stanley, who was so interested in my Santa collection he did the scavenger hunt twice.

Stanley, who seemed like such a sweet and charming man.

The "inspector" was sent to find the easiest way in, which was why he spent so much time testing all of the windows. But when we redid all the locks, Weston had to pivot.

So he sent someone inside...

Stanley did this for Weston.

My gaze shoots to Joe. "Stanley took that room at the last minute."

He gapes at me, his face full of the same betrayal I feel. I don't need to take a moment to interpret his expression—I feel it down to my bones. "He pretended he was so interested in Christmas," he says scathingly. "Ugh, yeah...it had to be him. He had a key, and he knew where all the scavenger hunt Santas were hidden. All he'd have to do was walk around and throw everything into a box."

"Oh goodness," I say, petting Saint Nick again, "let's pretend he tucked the Santas in gently. I'm anxious enough."

"You're right." His gaze falls on the little cup of candy canes on my desk, and he hurries over and grabs one, practically stuffing it in his mouth before he unwraps it. Apparently, he's so overcome he no longer minds the flavor of frankincense and myrrh. "Anyone else?"

"I prefer alcohol," Cynthia says.

"Candy canes make me think of Ryan," I confess. Although, truthfully, everything in this inn, even my two dear friends, makes me think of him. He's only been here a month, but he's become infused into everything.

I swallow and try to bolster myself, because Ryan needs me to be strong. I pick at the problem from different directions, and recall the couple who cancelled their room reservation at the last minute after learning about the rebranding of the B&B.

I gasp. "The couple who cancelled...do you think...could Weston have found out they had a reservation and paid them to cancel? Their note was strange, don't you think?"

"Send them a message," Cynthia says.

I set down Saint Nick and grab my phone from my pocket. The first thing I notice is that it's just after eleven p.m. What are the odds that Ryan will be released tonight? Or that the Capitalist Christmas couple will be fussed to answer my email?

The second thing I notice is a message from Weston:

I'll drop the charges if you sell me the B&B.

My fingers curl so tightly around the phone, the edges hurt, and I shove it toward Cynthia, not able to speak yet.

"Oh, that jerk. He all but admitted to setting this up."

"It's not enough," I say softly, my voice gruff.

She pouts at the phone. "No, I guess not. Can we tell him to fuck off?"

"You'd better not," Joe says, glimpsing the message. "We don't want to play our cards too early."

He's right, unfortunately, so I reclaim my phone and search for the couple's message. I quickly draft a note to them, my heart beating fast as I press send.

I will them to answer quickly. Because if they don't, I'm going to have to do something unthinkable in the morning and call them on the phone.

"This is good," Cynthia tells me, helping me up off the bed. "We're putting the pieces together, Sherlock Holmesing this shit, and it's definitely to our benefit tonight that my father is an asshole. He'll take care of business. I'm going to call him and tell him about that Stanley guy. Maybe they can send a police officer to find him. Do you have the information he used to check in and out?"

"A credit card and name," I confirm. "It's on my computer downstairs."

"That's not nothing. I'll send the information to my dad."

"We need to work with a different police officer," Joe says, sucking on his second candy cane. "That cop knew Weston. They were talking like old friends."

"This was all a setup." I shake my head, feeling hopeless, but also pissed off enough to do something about it. If Weston had done something awful to me, I might have let him get away with it to avoid an uncomfortable conflict. But this is different. He went after someone I love and stole my most precious belongings. He needs to be stopped.

"I'm not going to sleep until Ryan comes home either," Joe declares.

Cynthia sighs. "Same."

"Let's go watch Christmas movies in the parlor and drink," I tell them as I finally get up from the bed. I reach into the closet and pull on a sweater. It's freezing in here, suddenly, as if someone ripped a hole in the outer wall.

"Honey, I don't know if you should go down there," Cynthia says. "It's not the same."

We've moved around my Christmas collection, but the nexus was still the parlor. Bracing myself, I step toward the door. "I can do it if you and Joe are with me."

It does hurt to see the parlor, empty of my little, red-suited men, and the tree, glowing but devoid of ornaments. Still, it doesn't hurt as much as missing *my* Santa.

I send Cynthia the information I have about Stanley, and then I settle in to do my least favorite thing.

I wait.

CHAPTER THIRTY-FIVE

Texts from Ada

Just got this in my inbox

[Photo of "Free Santa" post]

I'm disappointed in you, kid

Maybe this is my new lowest moment. Sitting in the back seat of Cynthia's dad's car with a bag of frozen peas wrapped around my bruised knuckles at three in the morning, listening to Christmas carols while Jeremy keeps hopping over land mines planted for him by his girlfriend's father.

Yes, I really do intend to continue making a living by playing the trumpet. I know, it's wild.

No, I'm not very interested in making money. If I were, I'd probably have a different job.

Yes, Cynthia does deserve the best. That's why she's with me.

I'd be impressed if I weren't so miserable.

I wanted to save Christmas for Anabelle. I promised her I'd

never let anyone hurt her. But her inn was robbed, I got myself arrested, and here's a cherry to top off the shit sundae...

After the police discharged me, they handed me a plastic bag containing everything that had been in the pockets of my Santa suit prior to my arrest. Including that red teddy Anabelle's probably never going to wear now.

It's like every mistake I've ever made in my life has been rolled down a hill of snow, growing bigger and bigger until it's the size of a boulder before it crashes down on me.

I'm too impulsive.

I'm too hotheaded.

I don't pay attention.

I don't listen.

I thought I was being careful. I thought I'd learned from my mistakes, but I didn't, because here I am.

They've got me on an assault charge that Weston is most definitely not going to drop, especially since I felt his nose crunch under my fist. And Anabelle's prized personal Santa collection, written up in *House & Garden*, is gone, along with all of her ornaments other than the sweetgum one. Maybe Weston destroyed everything. I wouldn't put it past that prick to throw someone else's favorite things into a fire.

The car stops, and I look up to see Cynthia's dad has pulled over close to the inn. He glances back at me. He has a gruff face, a square jaw, and thick, curly salt-and-pepper hair. "You did something dumb."

"Yeah," I agree, feeling it more intensely than the pain in my fist.

"But I'm guessing most guys would do the same. If some prick was stalking my wife—" He looks pointedly at Jeremy. "Or my daughter, I'd deck him in the face too. Only next time don't do it in front of a police officer. We'll get you off, though. The publicity's going to be a bitch for that guy once it comes out that he stole from

Anabelle."

"If it comes out," I say numbly, feeling defeated. Because Weston is definitely fucking smarter than I am. If it comes to a battle of wits, he wins. The only satisfaction I have in this situation might be the feeling of his nose cracking under my fist. I'm not going to lie and say I didn't enjoy it, but it was definitely not worth it.

Jeremy nods at me as he unlatches his seat belt. "Come on, buddy, let's go inside."

Cynthia's dad, who introduced himself as Mr. Matthews even though we're all adults, frowns at him. "Don't you need a ride back home?"

"Nope," he says with an easy grin as he gets out of the car. "I'll be going home with your daughter, sir. Have a good night."

Damn. Maybe I *am* impressed.

I half-expect Mr. Matthews to come out swinging, but he actually chuckles before saying, "I'll be in touch. Don't go anywhere, and don't do anything stupid."

"I won't," I say as I get out of the car behind Jeremy, feeling miserable in my Santa suit.

Part of me feels like I should just take off. Get in my car and leave and never come back. Maybe it would be better that way for everyone. If I'm gone, I can't fail Anabelle anymore—and she and her friends can't realize what everyone else has. That I'm a man who causes trouble but can't fix it.

"Oh, would you stop it?" Jeremy says, grabbing my shoulder. It's only then that I realize I'm still holding the peas. I don't really want to anymore, but if I drop them in the middle of the street, it will make me feel like more of an asshole.

"Stop what?"

"Getting down on yourself. Cynth's dad is not a man who gives a shit about preserving people's feelings, and he told you he would have done the same thing. I would have too." He glances down at his hands. "Well, I would have kicked him. Can't play the trumpet with a bum hand. My point is that you got set up, and it sucks. No one's going to tell you it doesn't suck. But you can't just roll over and let that guy win. That's not like you."

I kick at a stone in the pavement, not able to look at him. "How would you know?"

He grabs my shoulder again. "Because you're Ryan Fucking Reynolds."

My mouth tips up. "You know my last name is really Langston."

At least, he does now.

I didn't come to Williamsburg to do any harm, so I figured there was no reason to lie or use a false ID. I also didn't have one. While I'd had papers for Ryan Reynolds last year, I'd disposed of them after returning to New York. Roark was the one who took care of setting that shit up. I wouldn't have the first idea how to go about acquiring that kind of thing.

Up until now, I haven't shared my real last name with anyone. Ada hired me under the table, and Grandma Edith arranged for me to pay for my room in cash. But the police wanted to see my ID, and obviously I had to give it to them.

I probably should have told everyone sooner, but it felt like that name was attached to a different Ryan—the one I didn't want to be anymore.

Jeremy exhales loudly through his nose, probably trying not to laugh. "Ryan Reynolds sounds cooler, no offense. My point is that you've been fighting the good fight for all of us over the last month. Why stop now? Why give up? We're all ready to fight with you, Ryan. We want to."

I feel like he just gave me a shot of the hard stuff and a pat on the back, but the warm feeling fades after a second. "None of you know who I really am. I've kept it from you."

He lifts his eyebrows. "I couldn't give a shit if your last name is Langston or Reynolds, or what you used to do or where you used to live. I know you, just like you know me. And I'm happy to call you my friend."

"I'm not smart enough to beat him."

"You think I am? We're goddamn lucky we're with two of the smartest ladies out there."

I smile at that, because he's obviously right. But still...

"What if she's not willing to let my past stay in the past?" I say, not even able to look at the inn yet, or to focus on any of the dozens of other questions charging through my head. What if she's hurt? What if whoever did this for Weston came back? What if *Weston* came back?

"There's only one way to find out." He claps me on the back then, and I nod, feeling a burning sensation behind my eyes, and start walking toward the inn with a greater sense of purpose.

But the good feelings inside of me only last as far as the door to the B&B. It takes all the energy I have left in me to unlock the door and step inside.

"They're here, they're here!" Cynthia yells from the parlor, probably waking up any guests who decided to stick around after the theft, followed by my very public arrest, and she comes charging around the corner. Jeremy grins and catches her as she jumps into his arms.

"Oh, thank God, he didn't kill you," she says.

I chuckle at that, but my focus shifts as soon as Anabelle comes into view. Her face is pale, but she's okay. *She's okay.* Joe is with her, but he just gives me a barely there smile and hangs back.

My eyes begin to well as I step forward and wrap my arms around Anabelle. The feeling of being unworthy takes hold of me, tightening like a plastic bag around my neck, threatening to cut off the air I need to survive.

"Come upstairs with me," she says.

I couldn't deny her anything. I nod in acknowledgment to the others, and then let her lead me upstairs and into her room, the door clicking shut behind us.

Saint Nick meows and twitches his tail but doesn't get off the bed. I'm still clutching the damn peas. I lift the bag up and admit, "I don't know what to do with this."

She takes it from me and throws it into the trash can, then lifts my scraped and swollen knuckles to her lips as if she can kiss it better.

"I messed up," I confess. "I don't know how to make it better. I... there are some things I need to tell you." My mouth tries to smile and fails. "To start, my name. Jeremy knows now, so it only feels right to tell you. It's Langston, not Reynolds."

"None of us really believed your name was Ryan Reynolds," she says softly, and you don't have to tell me anything you don't want to." She looks up at me, with her hair loose around her shoulders, her mouth in a firm, determined line. Staring at her is like staring at the sun.

"I do. I want to." It's part lie, part truth. I want her to know everything, because I want her to accept me as I am. I don't want her to know everything, because I'm terrified she'll turn me away.

"So tell me. Tell me everything. I'm ready to listen."

I slump down onto the bed and prop my head in my hands, and she leans down and presses a kiss onto my brow.

"I love you, Ryan. Nothing is going to change that. I don't expect you to be perfect. I'm not perfect. When we got here this evening, I was worried something had happened to Joe, and instead of charging into the B&B to make sure he was okay, I sat down on the steps. That's awful."

"You shut down," I say. "That's just the way your brain works. It's not your fault. This is...this is my fault."

She kisses my brow again, her lips soft and sweet—a blessing I probably don't deserve. Then she surprises me by climbing into my lap, facing me, her legs wrapped around me. She's wearing her clothes from earlier, and even though I have that new teddy of hers in my pocket, I don't wish she was wearing something different. This is my Anabelle—naturally sweet and sexy. My girl, for at least for another fifteen minutes.

She wraps her arms around me, resting her head on my shoulder. "I used to have a lot of trouble looking people in the eye when I was a kid. It felt strange to me. I'm mostly used to it now, but when I have to tell someone something that's hard, it's still easier if I don't have to look at them. Maybe it'll be easier for you to tell me like this."

"I don't deserve you," I say, finally letting the thought out.

"Don't be one of those foolish men who says that and then runs away."

"I'm not going to run. I'm not strong enough. I don't think I could bring myself to leave you."

She runs her hands over my back and kisses my neck. "Good, but don't tell yourself you're not strong." She pulls away enough to look at me, then leans in and kisses my scar. "You're strong, Ryan. You're kind. And you've spent the last month changing our lives for the better. Not just me, but also Cynthia, Jeremy, and Joe. We're all in this together, sweetheart."

Hearing her call me my nickname for her warms me up from the inside. I bury my face in her hair, taking in her scent and the feeling of her wrapped around me. I feel like I really am at home.

I'm still scared she'll come to her senses and realize that I'm all liability, no reward. But I owe it to her to tell her everything and let her decide.

I wrap my arms around her and then loosen them—so she can pull away if she wants to.

"I used to be a thief, Anabelle."

CHAPTER THIRTY-SIX

ANABELLE

Life-shaking revelations: 1

I'd expected something like this. I'd decided it was either theft or drugs. I always assume people are watching me for a reaction I don't know how to give, but this time I *know* Ryan's waiting for me to react. And he obviously thinks I'm going to react poorly or pull away from him, so I keep rubbing his back softly, my face pressed to his neck.

His clothes smell stale, but he still smells like Ryan.

When I don't try to leave, he continues, "I...I was a dumb kid, and I wanted to get my brother and me out of our foster home, so I started pickpocketing people when I was thirteen. I wanted to get enough cash for us to find our own place. It was stupid. But I tried stealing from the wrong guy, and after he roughed me up, he offered to teach me how to properly rob people. He hired Jake and me. I was dumb in school, and I'd never been good at much of anything besides getting into trouble, so it felt good to have someone take an interest. It took me a long time to realize that it wasn't because he liked us and wanted to help us. It was because—"

"Because you were twins," I say, my heart hurting for him and his brother. I remember what it was to be thirteen and misunderstood. My middle school was so much bigger than my elementary school, full of people I didn't know, and so loud and smelly and overwhelming that I used to fake stomachaches in the hopes my parents wouldn't make me go in. They always did.

"He was using you," I add, hating this man I've never met.

"He was," Ryan agrees, speaking the words into my hair. "I was an idiot."

"Stop calling yourself that." I pull back enough to look at him, because he needs to know how serious I am about this. How unwilling I am to listen to anyone call him names, even if it's himself. "You're not an idiot. You're not dumb. You're not any of those things."

"You may change your mind about that."

"I won't," I insist, wrapping my hands more tightly around him and burrowing my face into his neck. I can feel his pulse beating fast, and I press a kiss to the pulse point.

"I was good at picking locks," he says after a moment. "It's the only real talent I've ever had."

"That's not true," I insist, speaking into his neck. "You're a wonderful cook and a better friend. And you're very good at...pleasuring me."

"Anabelle," he says, his voice low and husky. "God..." I can feel his body responding to the feeling of me wrapped around him. "I..."

I want him. I want him so badly, but I sense he'll never fully be mine if he doesn't tell me his story. "I didn't mean to get us off track. Tell me more."

He pauses a beat, composing himself, then says, "I wanted to believe it was okay, what we were doing for him, because we were only taking things from rich people. They would hardly miss them, and it was steady work, even if he only paid us a fraction of what he paid himself. And he was..." His pulse is racing along faster, and I know whatever he's going to say next will hurt him. I rub his back and kiss him once, twice, five times, and finally he breathes out and says, "I fooled myself into thinking he was...you know...my dad. That he cared about me and was proud of me. I told myself it was no different than helping out with a family business."

I kiss his brow and run my hands through his hair, needing the softness to anchor me as much as I want to give him comfort. I've spent the last month wondering what his story is and dreading it, but now that he's finally telling me, my greatest concern is making him feel loved. What he's sharing isn't any worse than what my anxious whirlwind of an imagination has already conjured.

"It was his watch you got rid of," I realize, having pieced together the clues. "Your boss's."

He nods against me.

"And what happened with your brother?"

He's quiet for so long that I wonder if he's talked himself out. I do that all the time and wouldn't hold it against him. But finally he says, "Last year, Roark asked my brother to steal an antique watch from someone. Jake got cold feet. He liked the guy who owned it too much, and it had sentimental value for the man. But we didn't have the kind of job you could just walk away from. So I took the watch for Jake, and my brother couldn't forgive me for it. He cut me off and quit the business."

I shift in his lap, earning a groan from him before he flexes his hand against my shirt and then slips it under. His palm presses to my skin.

"I'd treasured that dumb watch my boss had given me," he continues. "It had seemed like proof that he gave a shit, you know? But he obviously didn't. So I tried to give it back to Roark out of spite, but he told me he didn't want it. That he'd never liked it, and if I didn't want it either, I could throw it away. So I did."

I can tell the memory's a bitter one, so I continue my ministrations, rubbing his back, pressing kisses to him.

He sighs and says, "By then, I wanted to quit too. I finally saw our boss for the man he really was. But he said he'd only leave Jake alone if I did exactly as he ordered."

He's shaking slightly, his breath quickening, and I know what he's about to say. I've considered this too.

"He sent you here to steal my grandmother's ornament," I say softly, my hands still caressing him—his hair, his back, his firm chest through his clothes—while my legs encircle his waist.

"Anabelle," he says, pulling away enough to look me in the eye. "How'd you..."

I smile at him. "Why else would you have come to The Crooked Quill by yourself under an assumed name?"

He gives me a half-hearted smile. "Right. You're smarter than me."

"Is it a problem that you were arrested? Will the police know it's a fake ID?"

"I had my real ID on me. Roark always had us destroy our fake IDs after sending us somewhere."

"So all I had to do was look in your wallet to learn your real last name?"

He shrugs, looking remorseful. "I should have told you. I was... ashamed. I wanted to leave the past behind, but you were right when you told me that's impossible. I might not want to be Ryan Langston anymore, but he'll always be a part of me."

"Good. Because I love him too. I love all of the parts of you."

"God, I really don't deserve you."

"We're going to add that to the list of things you should stop staying."

He holds my gaze. "I need you to know I didn't steal the ornament. I couldn't. I got to talking to your grandmother, and she told me about you and the inn and your parents. Hell, she told me the whole story of the ornament I'd been sent to take. She also told me she was dying. I decided I was going to leave in the night and face the music with Roark, but I went in to look at the ornament one last time. You know, one last look at the thing that was going to screw me. She caught me in there and knew I was up to something. I found myself telling her everything, Anabelle, and she…"

A couple of tears fall down his cheeks, and my whole heart belongs to him. To this man who only knew my grandmother for a day but loved her. To the boy he was, so lost and lonely and in need of human kindness that he let himself be taken in by a horrible man.

I lean in and kiss the tears away, tasting their salt, and look up into his golden eyes. "She gave it to you, didn't she?"

Fresh tears fall from his eyes, and I squeeze my legs around him and hug him. "She did," he says. "And I promised her I'd come back on December 1st."

"You did."

"No," he says, pulling back to smile sheepishly at me. "I was tardy."

I smile too, loving this symmetry between us. But I have one question left for him, perhaps the most important. "How'd you get away from that awful man, Ryan?"

"It's a long story, but it comes down to this. He wasn't going to let me leave. One of his enforcers, Javier, and I were good friends, and I got to know his other guy, Mike, too. I convinced them there was no reason we should keep getting paid peanuts when we were the ones who did all the work and took all the risks. So I helped them empty his stockroom full of stolen goods. I took the ornament and the antique watch that cost me my brother, which Roark hadn't sold yet, and they kept everything else. I returned the watch to its rightful owner for Jake before I came here."

"Are you sure Roark isn't going to come after you?" I ask, instantly imagining the worst. A criminal, showing up at the B&B to kidnap Ryan.

"Yeah," he says. "His operation had gotten a lot smaller by then. Javier and Mike were the only muscle he had left. Without them, without me and Jake, he's just an old man without any respect for the law. Javier's been keeping an eye on him, and it looks like he's buying a place in the Caribbean."

"He's getting away with it," I say with an aggrieved sniff. "That hardly seems fair."

He nods. "But if he doesn't get away with it, then neither do I. Or Jake. Or Javier. Maybe I don't deserve to. I can make excuses for myself all I like, but I was a criminal, Anabelle." He rubs his nose, looking so obviously miserable that I don't need to ask him how he's feeling. "And even though Cynthia's dad seems like he's a great lawyer, there's a chance he won't get me off. I got arrested a couple of times as a kid. I don't know if the police have seen that yet. I wasn't sure how much to tell Mr. Matthews."

"Say anything you want to Cynth's father, and then only share what he tells you it's okay to say. Aren't juvenile records sealed?"

"I don't know anything about that. Or anything in general, it feels like."

"We'll figure it out."

"We?" he asks, giving me a look that's half puppy dog.

"*We*," I insist firmly. "Now, as much as I love this Santa costume, let's get you out of it and into the shower. You smell like a jail cell."

"Oh shit, sorry." He gently lifts me off to the side and then takes off his socks and shoes and gets up. The sight of his bare feet on my carpet makes me feel grounded, and I nearly laugh. I'm relieved, I realize. Relieved that it wasn't worse, and that I, at least, find his past excusable. I have no doubt that a judge and a jury would feel differently, but I have no intention of letting him face a judge and a jury anytime soon.

I get up too and unfasten his Santa coat, running both of my hands up his powerful chest until I get to his thick arms. One push, and the oversized jacket falls to the ground, revealing more of him to me. But not enough.

"There's my hot Santa," I say, pressing my palms to him and

looking up at him with a smile. Needing him to know that I'm still here, still all in. "Now, while I love that you wanted to protect me, I'm going to need you to keep your hands to yourself in the future. When it comes to defending my honor, that is. I definitely don't want you to keep your hands to yourself when you're alone with me."

"I'm a mess," he says, almost like he wants me to turn him out. Or maybe he's just so certain it's going to happen sometime that he wants to get ahead of it.

"So am I."

"And I think I lost my job. Ada's disappointed in me."

"You'll make it up to her."

I unbutton his pants. Unzip them. He lets me undress him while I stay clothed. When I'm finished, he stands before me completely naked, his arousal jutting up toward me. But he doesn't touch it, or me, or even himself. He's just watching me. Waiting. *Trusting* me.

"You don't want to touch me?" I ask.

His Adam's apple bobs with his gulp. "I don't trust myself to touch you right now."

"*I* trust you."

"If you threw me out bare-ass naked in the cold, it would be no more than I deserve."

"For defending my honor and being good to me and my friends? I hope you think better of me than that."

He opens his mouth, then closes it, before saying quietly, "I think better of you than anyone else in the world. I'm damn lucky just to know you, and I would have felt that way even if you'd thrown me out."

I take his hand, weaving my fingers through his rougher ones, and lead him into the en suite bathroom. Then I turn the shower on, letting it get warm, and remove my clothes, all while he watches me with as much interest as if I'd been wearing the red teddy instead of an old sweater.

Still, he doesn't reach for me.

I test the water and find it warm, so I take a fresh cloth from the storage cabinet by the door and lead him into the updated shower stall with me. He's overcome, which is something I understand all too well.

I don't say anything in the shower. I just wet the cloth and lather it up and start to clean his body, leaning in to run my lips over his chest, his arms, and then lower down to trace his hardness with my tongue after I finish with the cloth.

His eyes are full of warm emotion as he lifts me to my feet and kisses my wet lips. "I don't care that you're too good for me. Does that mean I'm still an asshole?"

I don't know if he's talking to me or himself, but I decide to answer. "No. You're not an asshole. You're the man I love."

I kiss him again and again, moaning into his mouth a little when his hand reaches between my legs, and moaning more loudly when he leans down to suck and kiss my breasts while his hand continues to caress me. His fingers dip inside, and suddenly it's not at all enough.

"I want you to make love to me, Ryan. Now."

He already knows I'm on birth control to help manage my cramps. He's seen the packs in my room. I don't want any more barriers between us, and I hope he feels the same way.

His eyes darken with desire, and he presses me against the wet wall of the shower. "Thank God."

CHAPTER THIRTY-SEVEN

RYAN

I'm a man who's exercised tremendous self-restraint for almost a month, but I need to be inside her now. I need it more than air.

"Does it feel good to be in the shower, sweetheart? Do you like the way the water feels against your skin when I touch you?"

"I do," she says, her lips parting as I move my fingers inside her. She's so gorgeous, so generous, and I know I'm going to last all of five seconds once I'm finally inside her. But I'll have all night to make up for it. I'll have her here first, and then in the bed, and then against the door and in the five dozen other spots I've been dreaming about.

I kiss her, capturing her moans and swallowing them down like they're the only food I need to survive. It feels like maybe giving this woman pleasure is the most important thing I could do in life, second only to protecting and supporting her.

It's funny to think that asshole Roark gave me the best thing in my life when he decided to punish me last year. If he hadn't sent me to The Crooked Quill, I never would have met Anabelle. I wouldn't be here with her right now. I wouldn't have learned what it is to love and be loved by Anabelle Whitman.

I wouldn't be the man I'm becoming, who's so much better than the man that I was.

I kiss her harder as the water pounds against us, the contrast between the hot water and the cold air in the bathroom making every sensation stronger. Then she wraps her hand around my dick, and I can't wait any longer, not when she's already so ready for me.

I tip my forehead to touch hers. "I don't know how long I can last the first time."

"I don't care," she says, looking up at me through wet eyelashes, her hair in wet heaps around her shoulders. "I want you inside of me. I've wanted it for days."

Hell. When the girl you love says that, it's not something you say no to.

"I'm going to pick you up and press your back to the wall. If it doesn't feel good, tell me."

"It's going to feel good," she declares, and I smile at her, reminded of the first time I tasted her. The first of many times, because I can't get enough. If I could get away with spending all day with my head beneath her dresses, I would.

I pick her up, my hands hugging her ass, and press her to the wall. She wraps her legs around my waist, the pressure adding to the sensations building up inside of me, making my dick feel like it's going to burst before it even gets to where it wants to go.

"You're so strong, Ryan," she says, as if I needed to be any more turned on.

"I could hold you up all day, sweetheart."

I lean in and kiss her and then hold her up with one arm while I use the other to line myself up. I'm trembling, every bit of me humbled by this woman. By my love for her. I didn't think I could love anyone like this. I didn't think I wanted to. But she's proven me wrong every step of the way, and I'm not sorry for it.

I push in slightly, and the sound she makes floods me with need even more than the insanely good sensation of being inside her. So blissful, I'm nearly done for. I kiss her more desperately, my tongue seeking out hers as I push in further.

It takes a great force of will not to come immediately, especially since she tightens her legs around me, trying to pull me in deeper.

"Oh, Ryan," she says as soon as I pull my mouth from hers, still buried deep and not ready to move yet, because if I do, it might be over. I'm nearly crazy with need. Her mouth feels otherworldly around my dick, but this is better. This experience of being with her, of taking our pleasure together, is beyond anything else I've ever experienced.

"You're everything to me," I say as I pull out and drive back into her. Getting even deeper this time. Taking in the way her eyes hood with pleasure when I thrust in and pull out. Her legs pull me in closer each time, and I want to memorize the little throaty sounds she makes and the way her hair looks against the tiles as she leans her head back. I feast on her neck and her perfect nipples and her mouth, taking all of her that I can. I'm driven by a wild need to possess her—and to accept that she forgives me for the man I've been and wants to stand by the man I'm becoming.

When I look into her eyes, I can almost see myself the way she sees me. I don't feel so much like an asshole anymore.

Her hips arc into me, and I feel her tightening around me—and thank God, because I need her to come before I do, and willpower will only bring a man so far.

"You feel so good around me," I whisper into her lips. "So beautiful. I've never wanted anything as much as I want you."

She captures my mouth in a deep kiss as I drive in again, and again, and then I feel her falling apart around me, her mouth still pressed to mine. And even though so much is still wrong, the world feels right.

❋

I WAKE up to Anabelle's gasp. I'm disoriented and tired after staying up half the night, but the light flooding in from the window tells me it's late morning. Meaning that we only got a few hours of sleep. Groaning, I pull a pillow over my face.

Anabelle removes it, smiling down at me, and even though I liked the light-blocking abilities of the pillow, it's impossible not to smile back. "Are you thinking about my dick?"

She bats me with the pillow and then waves her phone at me. "Something more important."

"Doubtful," I mutter but take the phone.

She launches into a story about Stanley, the dick, and the couple who gave up their room for him as I scan the message.

Oh my goodness! I'm so sorry. Yes, a man contacted us about giving up the room. He paid us double what it would have cost, and we didn't think we were doing anything wrong because he said he was going to surprise his girlfriend. He told us his name was Ryan.

I glance up at her. "Nothing gives me greater pleasure than seeing you excited, Anabelle, but I don't see how this clears my name."

"Weston was trying to set you up," she says. "But you obviously didn't email them. It'll have come from a junk account, and someone who knows what they're doing might be able to track down the source."

"It's not a smoking gun. I don't know what I'm doing, and I still know how to use a VPN," I say with a sigh, pulling her on top of me.

Then it hits me. I don't know what I'm doing when it comes to computers, but I *do* have certain skills, and I haven't been using them. "We have to find out where he put the Santas and ornaments."

"No," she says, her voice sadder than she probably realizes. "I think he probably destroyed them."

I can tell she's already given them up for lost, but I refuse to accept that for her.

"He wouldn't do that. He'd keep them as leverage. Or tokens. But I'm guessing he would keep them close. He wouldn't want anyone knowing what he's done."

Hope sparks in her eyes, followed by a *what the heck, Ryan?* look of horror. "You are *not* breaking into his house. He has an alarm system."

I hesitate, not wanting to remind her of the way I used to live my life, before I admit, "That won't be a problem."

"But it *will* be a problem if he catches you."

I grit my teeth, not liking this next part of my plan but recognizing it's the best way to keep Weston busy. "Tell him you want to discuss selling the inn. Cynthia can go with you, and you can text me before he leaves."

She considers this for only half a second before shaking her head, her hair brushing my chest. "I'm not going to risk you. If you get found in there, you'll be in much bigger trouble. Besides, what would you do if you found them?"

"Steal them back," I say with a harsh laugh. "How's he going to report us for taking something he supposedly doesn't have?"

"So he can try something like this again?" she challenges.

She has a point. Ole Westie would be as pissed off as a wet hornet. But...

"Let me find out if he has them and where. Then we can figure out what to do next. Maybe we can call in an anonymous tip. Convince the police to do a search."

"Ryan," she says with a sigh. "Don't you think there's a very good chance they'll do a routine search anyway? Weston would never keep them somewhere they could so easily be found. I don't think they're at his place."

Shit, she's right.

"Then where would he keep them?"

A little crease cuts between her eyebrows. I run my finger over it. Her lips part but not in pleasure. "I'm afraid I might know the answer to that," she says after a moment, "and I don't like it one bit."

"I probably won't either, then."

She tells me, and I was right—I *don't* like it one bit. I'm also not terribly surprised.

"So how do we handle this?" I ask.

She sits straight up, her legs on either side of my waist. I can tell from the unconscious way she does it that she has no idea straddling me with her tempting bare chest on display could make me forget Weston even exists.

"I have an idea."

"So do I," I say, thrusting my hips up, and her smile is the best reward a man could claim. Okay, the second best. "Can your idea wait five minutes?"

"Oh, I think this will take longer than that."

God help me, this woman is going to be the life and death of me.

CHAPTER THIRTY-EIGHT

ANABELLE

Sunday, December 23, 2 days until Christmas

Terrifying plans: 1

"I've changed my mind," I say. "I don't think it's a good idea anymore. It may be a horrible idea."

"Too late." Ryan traces his hand down my hair. "No take-backsies."

We're sitting in the parlor with Cynthia, Jeremy, and Joe. Ryan and I are on the sofa with Joe, while Cynthia and Jeremy are on the love seat. It's their lunch break, and we're discussing Operation Save Christmas.

Unprincipled though he is, Stanley the Serpent at least left our trees. They're frightfully bare, though, and I long for my little men in red. Even Ryan said he was surprised by how much he misses "the little suckers." Of course, he didn't say suckers.

"I like the plan," Jeremy says.

Cynthia shoves his shoulder. "Yeah, because you don't have to have a sit-down with Weston."

He chuckles, sweetly running a lock of her hair between his fingers. "Nice try. I know you're looking forward to it. I'm guessing he'll walk away with one less nut."

She smiles primly at him, looking pleased, before she shoves his shoulder again. I glance at Ryan, wanting to say, *you did this.* In a positive way, of course, not accusatory. He winks at me and pulls me closer.

"What do you want me to do while you're..." Joe waves his hand to encompass the breaking and entering part of the plan.

"The most important job of all, buddy," Ryan tells him. "Hold down the fort. We shouldn't leave the B&B empty right now. The guests might need something, and there's plenty of other shit here that we don't want stolen."

"Oh, thank God," Joe says, then clears his throat and adds, "I mean, I'll do it if you need me to, of course."

"You'll be great," I tell him.

It's unnecessary to do dangerous acts to be a hero. I would be horrible in dangerous situations, and I suspect Joe wouldn't fare much better, given the way he ran from those children and the falling baby doll. But that's not to say there are no roles for us.

I still hate the thought of Ryan putting himself in harm's way, but he's convinced me the risk isn't great, and I can tell he still feels the need to prove himself. Not to me or any of our friends, but to his brother.

Maybe, if we succeed in making Weston pay and saving my Santas, Ryan will finally feel like it's time to reach out to Jake.

The plan starts out like this...

I'm going to get in touch with the woman who was interested in writing an article about our scavenger hunts. This late in the year, it's unlikely she'll still be interested in our story, but Cynthia says people who make bold asks get big returns.

There's a chance that Weston will dump the Santas to avoid making it onto the news as the Santa Stealer. But we agreed it's still important to shift the spotlight onto him. If he was worried about what a failed proposal might do for his business, he's bound to care about people knowing he's a stalker who "allegedly" stole his ex-girl-friend's prized Christmas collection.

Which might give us more leverage in squashing Ryan's assault charge.

The next step will be for me to go to the police station to follow up on the reported theft. Luckily, I already spoke with an officer about the "inspector," so the case already has a home other than with the odious officer who arrested Ryan.

When I speak with him, I'll submit an itemized list of every-thing that has been lost. I will also provide him with all of the infor-mation we have on Stanley the Serpent, including his credit card number, the photo that Joe clandestinely took of him doing the scav-enger hunt for the second time, and the information that he checked out of the B&B online immediately after the theft occurred. I will also put the officer in touch with the guests who were paid not to come, as well as with Ada, who can tell him about the grown man—meeting Weston's description—who paid a child to pull off Santa's beard.

Then, this afternoon, Cynthia and I will ask Weston to meet for hot chocolate to discuss selling the B&B. We'll suggest that we need a show of good faith before we enter into negotiations with him. Mainly, we need him to allow the police to search his house.

While we're meeting with him, Ryan and Jeremy will be hard at work on *their* part of the plan.

It's a little...well, audacious. Perhaps a little immoral. But even though I feel plenty of anxiety about it, I feel no guilt.

Ryan squeezes my hip, his touch reassuring and always so, so good. "It's going to work."

"It has to," I say.

Because I took to google while he was getting freshened up in the bathroom earlier, and even simple assault can lead to jail time and outlandish fines. Maybe that's what Weston was counting on—that I'd have to sell the inn to him in order to pay Ryan's legal fees.

I still don't understand why he'd go to such lengths to ruin us. It can't be the inn itself, or even the starburst ornament. I say so, and Cynthia says, "Honey, no one's ever said no to him before. He's one of those men who'll do anything to make a *no* into a *yes*. And it can't feel good to see you with such a hot piece seconds after you broke up with him. Between you and Jeremy, his ego's full of pinpricks."

I suppose she's right, which means the only way for us to stop him is to make him stop.

THE REPORTER RESPONDS MORE QUICKLY than I would have thought possible and speaks with Ryan, Joe, and me.

"I can't promise anything," she says, "but this is Christmas gold."

"At least my problems are entertaining."

She's embarrassed by my response, which I didn't intend for her to be. But she ends our call with the promise to let us know if and/or when the story will be running.

After we get off the phone with her, I text Weston. He's quick to agree to a meeting, and Cynthia and I decide it would be best to have it at the inn—our home field. Joe agrees to join us, which will make us three to one.

That arranged, I head to the police station. The visit is beyond exhausting—everything in the building, from the humming fluorescent lights to the serviceable, uncomfortable chairs, saps my energy. But I'm driven by the need for justice, and it helps that the officer I speak to, Officer Daniels, seems interested in what I'm saying. He agrees to have a talk with Weston.

On the way back to the inn, I steel myself and make a different call. To Ada.

She answers on the second ring. "This is Ada."

Oh dear. I didn't practice what I was going to say, and for half a second, I forget every word in the English language. I can sense she's on the verge of hanging up, though, so I say quickly, "Don't hang up. This is Anabelle. Ryan's Anabelle. You know, the Ryan who—"

"Got arrested last night after promising me he was going to keep his nose clean. Yeah, I remember Ryan. I'm going to be remembering him real well when I've got no Santa here this afternoon and the kids are pounding down the door."

"It wasn't his fault," I blurt, and then add, "And there's someone who can take his place. He wanted to make sure of that."

Oh, dear. Joe is going to kill me. It'll have to be him, since Jeremy is helping Ryan.

I can swear I hear a bubble pop on the other end of the line. "Go on."

I rush through the whole story, starting from Weston paying that boy to pull down Ryan's beard and then sending the fake inspector to the inn.

She listens, asking a few questions, and finally says, "Okay, Mrs. Claus. You can send in your Santa replacement, and tell Ryan I'm sorry. I'll be talking to him."

I thank her at least three times and then park the car and walk to the inn, trying to figure out how to break the news to Joe.

It's easier than expected, which is a refreshing change.

When I arrive at the door, my friend opens it before I can take out my key. His hair is frizzier than usual, like he's been combing his hands through it every five minutes, and he's wearing a Christmas sweater that says *Ugly Christmas Sweater* on it in pom-poms.

"Oh, thank God you're back," he says. "Ryan and Jeremy left half an hour ago. I was worried the police were going to arrest you too, and we only know one lawyer. I've been going out of my mind trying to focus on something else, but I've packed up all the orders and brought them to the post office, and Cynthia won't let me help her make cookies. She said something about my 'nervous energy.'"

"I have something you can do. Something that will be incredibly helpful to Ryan. I know he'll be so grateful."

I walk in and close the door behind me.

Joe looks around with a cautious expression. "Is it dangerous?"

"Not in the least bit. We need you to take over his shift at the toy store. I have his other Santa costume you can wear."

Joe gapes at me. "You tricked me."

I don't deny it; I can't deny it. "You *did* let me think you were a woman for over a year."

"You know how I feel about children."

I do. He thinks they're cute in theory but terrifying in practice. "I know, but this is your chance to be Ryan's hero, Joe. I believe you can do it."

He rubs his cheek and takes stock of the Christmas tree behind the front desk, which Ryan carried single-handedly from Joe's old apartment. His ornaments were stolen too.

"I'll do it," he says with the bravery of a man about to drive off a cliff.

"That's the spirit!"

"I expect you to sympathetically listen to my stories when I get back, even if it only sounds like I'm complaining."

"I'll let you complain as much as you want."

He sighs dramatically. "Take me to the Santa suit."

"I love you."

"I love you too." Smiling, he nudges his shoulder against mine. "Even though you stole my boyfriend."

AFTER JOE LEAVES for the toy store, I find Cynthia in the kitchen. Sure enough, she's making cookies, and they smell divine. I go to take one of them off the cooling rack, and she raps my knuckles. "Those are for the guests."

"We only have two people staying with us right now," I point out.

"No, I meant Weston." She gives me a wicked smile. "It's a special recipe."

"Cynthia Matthews, we are *not* poisoning him."

"It's not poison. Just a little Ex-Lax. Don't you think he deserves to publicly shit his pants after everything he's put you through?"

"We already have plans for him," I say, propping a hand on my hip, Cynthia's signature move, and look her in the eye for half a second before shifting my gaze to her nose. Right now, my system is overloading, everything a bit too much, but I have to get through the day. I *have* to. Gusting out a big puff of air, I say, "The last thing I need is for you to get in trouble for a juvenile prank."

"What if we leave them out and tell him they're only for the guests, and he eats one anyway? That would be his own prickery biting him in the ass. "

I consider her argument for a moment before admitting, "There's some poetic justice to that, and we may need the extra delay, but we'll have to throw out the rest so none of the guests eat them."

She beams at me. "Ryan's a good influence on you."

"You know, I may actually be a bad influence on him," I say, thinking again about my plan. Fretting. I'll probably do it constantly until he comes home to me. That's what matters; I care less about whether we get the Santas and ornaments back or force Weston to pay for what he's done.

"Oh, good influence, bad influence." She waves her hand. "We're all fabulous, and that's what matters."

She certainly is.

I pull her into a spontaneous hug, and she hugs me back before saying, "Are you drunk? No judgment, but you're usually not a random hugger."

"Not yet, but I think I'd like to be. After Weston leaves."

Weston knocks on the door fifteen minutes early, but if he meant to make us flustered, he failed, because Cynthia and I have been waiting in the parlor, the plate of forbidden cookies out on the coffee table.

I open the door, gasping when I catch sight of him. He has two black eyes he's tried to cover up with concealer—ineffectually—and he has some kind of tape over his nose, which is swollen and red.

"Yeah, you see what your thug boyfriend did to me," he says.

I don't feel sorry for him.

For one thing, he clearly intended for Ryan to hit him. He had people waiting out front to get a good photograph of him being handcuffed. Weston stalked us, tried to get Ryan fired, sent two strangers into my home to steal from me, and if I'm right about where the stolen ornaments and army of red-suited men are right now, he did me another unforgivable wrong.

So, if anyone can be said to deserve a broken nose, it's my ex-boyfriend.

"Allegedly," I say, stepping aside so he can enter.

He gives me a disbelieving look. "Who have you become?"

"Someone I like. Come in if you'd like to talk. Ryan's not here."

He enters as slowly as possible, probably to maximize my inconvenience and make me cold from the open door. Fine. The longer he takes, the longer Ryan and Jeremy will have.

By now, Cynthia will have already texted them *Gingerbread o'clock*, our agreed-upon signal for *It's go time*.

"I hope you've thrown him out," Weston says, grabbing my shoulder to stall me. I recoil, my skin revolting from his flesh coming anywhere close to mine, even through layers of fabric.

"For defending me?" I ask, raising my eyebrows.

"For being a violent animal. He's lucky they didn't put him down like a rabid dog."

Any possible remorse over my plan dries up on the spot. He deserves it. He deserves whatever is coming to him.

"Right this way," I say, and as soon as I lead him into the parlor, I ask, "Would you like a cookie? Cynthia just made them fresh."

CHAPTER THIRTY-NINE

RYAN

Group text

Cynthia: Krampus has left the North Pole.

Cynthia: I repeat, Krampus has left the North Pole.

Jeremy: You don't need to do that unless you're on a radio, Cynth.

Cynthia: You're no fun.

Jeremy: Not what you said this morning.

Ryan: What happened this morning?

Ryan: Also, when do you think he's going to the station?

Cynthia: Krampus has gone to the ranger station.

Cynthia: Repeat, Krampus has gone to the ranger station.

Jeremy and I are drinking coffee in a park across from Weston's house, both of us wearing dark colors and plenty of layers to keep from being noticed. We're too far away to be heard and probably too far for anyone without perfect vision to identify.

Westie just walked in with two police officers, the three of them shooting the shit as if they're bros headed out for a drink.

At least he's not with the guy who arrested me last night.

"You think they'll find it?" Jeremy asks nervously.

"Hell if I know," I say, tossing my empty coffee cup into the trash a foot away from our bench so I can run my hands through my hair. I'm working on a few hours of sleep and starting to feel it. We took a chance, and if it doesn't pan out, we may have just given the man who wants to ruin Anabelle and me exactly what he wants. I can't stop fidgeting. It's like I've been body-swapped back into my middle school self.

We sit around for fifteen minutes. Twenty.

"Is it always boring like this?" Jeremy asks, swinging his legs as he glances at the house, where nothing appears to be happening. It's a modern house with small, slit windows and grey siding. Inside, there's an open floor plan and minimalist furniture, which should take less time to search.

I fidget some more. "Yeah, mostly."

It's not totally true—the adrenaline's addictive—but I don't want to do my friend a disservice and lead him into a life of crime. This needs to be a one-and-done experience for Jeremy Jacobs. And my last act of breaking and entering.

Five minutes later, Jeremy leans forward, as if he can squint his way into seeing through the funky windows. "What are they doing in there? Watching home videos of the first time he ate spinach as a baby?"

"Is that what you do when you have people over?" I ask, amused.

"I'll have everyone over after Christmas. You're in for a treat."

I laugh, but everything inside of me is still on alert.

"They're gonna find it," I mutter to myself.

Our mission went something like this...

Anabelle figured Weston would never leave the Santas lying around his house, knowing there was a chance the cops might ask to search it.

So we couldn't break in and steal them back.

But we could break in and plant the expensive-ass ornament he'd hoped to steal from her, which she'd reported missing this morning, along with the other treasures that had actually been stolen.

And that's exactly what Jeremy and I just did.

Once we got inside, which was much easier than he'd believed it would be, we argued for ten minutes about what to do with the ornament. I'd wanted to go for the bedroom closet, but Jeremy had pointed out there were already ten other black boxes in there, and if the cops did a quick search, they might not check them all.

Which was when it hit me.

Why take chances when we could hide it in plain sight?

Weston had a Christmas tree up, decorated like it had come right out of a box, with silver ornaments and white lights.

So we hung the little sweet gum ornament up in the middle.

It had felt right, doing that, as if Grandma Edith were guiding my hand. And, sure, maybe spirits don't help people set up their fellow man, but he pushed us into it.

Now, it just needs to work its magic.

The ornament had looked obvious to us, but we also knew it was there. Most people aren't fixated on Christmas the way my girlfriend is, so maybe they haven't been trained to take a look at every Christmas tree and gingerbread man they come across.

"I'm getting nervous," I admit.

Because if the officers don't find it, and Weston does, he'll have everything he wants.

Well, nearly everything. He won't have Anabelle. He'll never have her.

"Don't get nervous," Jeremy says. "Should we play Go Fish?"

"You've got a pack of cards?"

He shrugs a shoulder. "I took one from the house. I figured we might need something to do."

My lips twitch up. "I've created a monster. Sure, I like a good game of Go Fish."

We try to play, but both of us have forgotten the rules, and neither of us cares enough to google it.

It's another twenty minutes before it happens.

The door bangs open, and then Weston is marched down the front steps. No one has handcuffed him, but it's obvious he's not happy.

"Oh, it's going down," Jeremy mutters, grabbing out his phone and taking a snap.

Relief fills my cup. Until this moment, I wasn't sure it was going to work. I mutter as much to Jeremy, who says, "It was Anabelle's plan."

He has a point, but it still relied on us to carry it out.

Jeremy sticks his phone back into his pocket and grins at me. "Come on, can I do it, man?"

I grin back at him and wave at a huge hemlock tree. "Let's get behind that first."

So we sidle up behind the big trunk, and Jeremy pulls his trumpet out of its case just before the car door closes behind Weston.

Moments later, Weston is driven away to the tune of "I'll be Home for Christmas."

When the car drives out of sight, Jeremy holds his fist out for a bump, and I give it to him.

"Let's go home to our girls," I say.

❄

ON THE WAY to the inn, I stop at a discount store so I can pick up some replacement ornaments for the trees. Anabelle hasn't said so, but I know it makes her sad to see them bare, especially this close to Christmas.

I haven't given up on getting her things back, but if I can make her happier now, I'm not going to wait.

When we return to the inn, Anabelle swings the door open for us before we even clear the top of the porch steps. She's so gorgeous, and as soon as she sees us smiling, she smiles back and gets even more gorgeous. Cynthia is right behind her, giving Jeremy a wicked grin, and we both try to enter at the same time, nearly getting jammed in the doorway before Jeremy laughs and pushes me inside.

I set the bag of ornaments down on the front desk, sweep Anabelle up into my arms, and twirl her through the air, the skirt of her green dress billowing out.

I kiss her joyfully, because I spent the last few hours worrying about the future, and now it's feeling pretty okay.

Besides, she needs to be kissed. Everything inside of me demands it. Her lips open for me, and she wraps her arms around my neck, burying her fingers into my hair. Maybe she feels the need to reassure herself like I do, because it's several seconds before she pulls back.

"It worked?" she asks in an undertone, her face inches from mine.

"We saw them take him away, and he looked none too pleased."

I feel the air from outside cut off, signaling that Jeremy has closed the door, and my buddy says, "I serenaded him as they drove him away. It felt only right."

"We don't know what took them so long to come out," I say, tucking a few strands of hair behind Anabelle's ear.

Cynthia erupts into hysterical laughter, and Anabelle starts laughing with her.

"Come on," my girl says through it. "Come into the parlor."

As the others file down the hallway, I pause to grab the ornaments from the desk before joining them. Anabelle and I sit down on the sofa, and I pull her into my lap. Jeremy and Cynthia settle in beside us in much the same way, and he asks her, "So what'd you do this time, Trouble?"

"I made some Ex-Lax cookies, and Anabelle offered them to him. He took two. I'm guessing the effects kicked in by the time he got back to the house with the police officers."

"Brutal," Jeremy says, kissing her nose.

I hug Anabelle close to me. "How wicked of you."

She snuggles in, and a feeling of deep contentment fills me. "Where's Joe?"

She smiles at me. "I convinced him to take your shift at Curio."

Holy smokes. He took off after one baby doll bumped into him, and now he's going to hang out at the toy store for hours?

"He's a good friend," I say, feeling choked up again. Doubly choked up, because Anabelle's not someone who asks for favors easily.

"He's family." She gives me a brave smile. "We're all family."

I know why she's saying it, and my heart hurts for her. I kiss the side of her face. "We are."

"There's something else we have to tell you," Cynthia says, sounding reluctant to share her news. "The reporter says she can't run the story."

Not ideal, but what I care about most is that Weston is, temporarily, behind bars. He'll get out on bail, of course, but maybe the scare will be enough to get him to act right. He's never been in a holding cell before, I'm betting, and I have a feeling he won't like it.

Anabelle was hoping we could get the charges against me dropped, but I doubt it. I hit him in front of a cop. Not smart. And if you do not-smart things, you sometimes pay for them.

What I care about is convincing Weston that he'll get nothing but pain from hurting Anabelle.

"We need the publicity," Jeremy says firmly.

Cynthia turns in his lap, her eyes bright, and places her hands on either side of his face. "You're going to do it, you big, handsome lug."

"Excuse me?"

"Didn't you get tagged in like five thousand reposts of your dick video? We can use that to our advantage."

"You want my dick to make a video about the missing Santa Clauses?"

"No. I want the stardom of your dick to spread the word far and wide for us."

He grins at her and then at us. "Joe's not the only one who can take one for the team."

Cynthia leans in and kisses him. "I'm the one who's going to have to tell off another five thousand women in your DMs."

"I'm not going to pretend that doesn't make me hot."

"Our thanks to all three of you," I tell Jeremy with a grin, and he reaches out for a fist bump.

I give it to him, of course, and then we all get to work, making a big batch of videos for social media. We keep it about the stolen Santas and the sweetgum ornament without making any accusations that could bury us in deeper trouble. Then we spend the rest of the evening watching the views grow.

Slowly. *Very* slowly.

"That's it," Jeremy says, slapping his phone onto the parlor table. "I've had my fifteen minutes of fame. I say we get drunk."

"And I say we redecorate first," I say.

Anabelle tips her head in my direction as I grab the bag I brought in earlier. "We're gonna get your ornaments back, sweetheart, but in the meantime, I figured we didn't need to keep looking at a couple of bare trees.

Her lips part a second before she says, "You really bought me ornaments, Ryan?"

"I'm learning to speak your love language," I say through a grin.

"You *are* my love language." She kisses me quickly and then takes the bag from me. Each time she pulls something out, she exclaims over it as if it's the best thing she's ever seen and not a crappy discount-store find.

She's adorable, even if the ornaments aren't, and we soon join her in decorating, finding the best places for the ugly ornaments.

We've been at it for a few minutes when we hear the front door open. We exchange looks, and I quickly survey the room for potential weapons on the off chance it's someone who isn't supposed to be here. But then Joe shuffles into view wearing my original Santa suit. The beard is light pink, and as he gets closer, we get a whiff of curdled milk.

"What happened to you?" Anabelle cries, getting up and going to him.

"Don't touch me," he says. "I'm disgusting. A girl threw her strawberry yogurt smoothie on me after I told her it was unrealistic to expect a real, live unicorn for Christmas. Her father told her to apologize...to him, for wasting the drink."

I get to my feet and join Anabelle, clapping Joe on the back. "Thank you, man. I can't tell you how much this means to me."

He pulls a card out of his pocket and hands it to me. "It's from the lady with the bubble gum fixation."

"Thanks," I say, my heart beating a little faster as I take it. Those texts Ada sent me have been added to my memory loop of other people telling me I was a disappointment.

"I want you to know I didn't fill in for you just because you did me a big favor," Joe says seriously. "I did it because I'm probably the best friend anyone's ever had."

I grin at him. "You are." Emotion fills me up until I feel like a balloon about to burst as I turn and look at each of them, ending with my Anabelle. "You all are."

"Is it time to get drunk yet?" Jeremy asks.

"Yes, it is," I declare.

We don't actually get drunk, but we make Christmas-themed cocktails and light a fire in the hearth and talk and laugh and play Go Fish, because of course Anabelle remembers all the rules. Through it all, I can feel Grandma Edith looking down on us. I hope like hell she approves.

There's a nagging thought in the back of my mind, a feeling of unfinished business, but tonight is just for Anabelle and our friends —as it should be. And when Anabelle yawns so hard her jaw cracks, I usher her upstairs.

I want to make love to her. I want to make love to her every single minute of every single day. She clearly needs sleep, though, so I gather her in my arms and wonder at the miracle I've been given. She knows everything about me, and she still loves me.

When she shifts and rolls onto her stomach, I let myself take out Ada's card. Maybe she wanted me to open it on Christmas, but that's the kind of rule I still can't be bothered to follow. I open it and read:

To Hot Santa (yes, I have ears):

Sorry for misjudging you, kid. We all make mistakes, me more than anyone. Merry Christmas. I'll be in touch.

In the morning, we wake up to another miracle.

One of Jeremy's videos has over a million views, and there's a message from the reporter saying she's running our story at noon.

CHAPTER FORTY

ANABELLE

Monday, December 24, Christmas Eve

It happens quickly after that.

Early this afternoon, Stanley turned himself into the police and confessed to having stolen the Santas and my ornaments. He was hired by Weston, who instructed him to deliver his ill-gotten gains to the house where I grew up. Officer Daniels asked my father for permission to search the house, and my father turned himself in for his part in the burglary.

I know this because my dad used his one phone call to call me. I'm on the phone with him now, listening to him make excuses for himself.

When the phone rang, I was sitting in the parlor with Ryan, Joe, and our two guests, who seem surprisingly delighted by all of the drama that's unfolded. After I figured out who was calling—and where he was—I left the room and made my way to my desk chair in the front lobby, where I sit now. Ryan and I redecorated this tree too, but the bulb ornaments are no replacement for Joe's collection, and it's hard to feel forgiving while I'm sitting here looking at them.

"I did it for your own good," my father says after he's explained all the ways he betrayed me.

I know he's lying. He did it to get his own way. My father had wanted the ornament, and Grandma Edith had refused to give it to him. Then I'd refused to let him search the property for it. So when Weston had approached him and claimed he wanted to "save" me by getting rid of Ryan, and hey, maybe they'd find the ornament, too, he'd been quick to agree.

My father is adamant that he didn't know the Santas would be taken too until they were stuffed into his garage. But by then it had been impossible to backtrack.

That may be true. Certainly Weston had more motivation to hurt me. Regardless, my father hadn't cared enough to return them or the ornaments to me.

"Will you call my lawyer?" my father asks when I don't respond to his non-apology. "I used my one phone call to talk to you."

"I didn't ask you to do that, but yes."

"Will you tell the reporters to leave this mess alone? This is bad for business. For all of us."

He's mistaken. It is bad for his business, most assuredly, and worse for Weston's. It is not, however, bad for The Gingerbread House. We've had dozens of bookings since noon, and Ryan insists he's going to move out of Room B to make it available for guests. I'm inclined to move him directly into Room A with me and Saint Nick, but it would be too much change, too quickly. He agrees, so he's going to temporarily share an apartment with Jeremy. He's also decided to take a job with Jeremy's uncle until he can find something more fitting. It must be said that Ryan also tried to pay me, in cash, for all of the time he's spent at the inn. I refused but have conceded that he can continue to buy supplies for the inn as needed.

"No," I say to my father. "No, I will not. Weston has been trying to hurt me, and someone needs to hold him accountable. The only thing he cares about is public opinion, so I'm doing what I need to do."

"Weston made a mistake, but he—"

"This is the last time you and I will be talking for a while."

Maybe forever, but it's hard to commit forever to words when the forever is going to part you from the people you've tried to love as best as you can.

Tears form in my eyes as I think of the way he lifted me onto his shoulders all those years ago and pointed to the star. *That's you, Anabelle. You're my star.*

But Ryan was right. He hadn't made me feel that way in years. And my mother barely seems to remember I exist most of the time.

"You'd abandon your own father for a man?" my father huffs.

Ryan steps out of the parlor, his brow puckered as he walks toward the desk. I'm getting better at reading him and can tell without asking that he's worried. He doesn't say anything, just circles around my chair, probably crushing himself between it and the tree, and rubs my shoulders. Each pass of his hands seems to pour strength and determination into me.

"No," I say into the phone. "You're the one who abandoned me. He never would."

I hang up, my whole body shaking, and turn the chair toward Ryan. He looks down at me with eyes full of love. "It was your dad."

I nod, feeling the tremors everywhere—my fingers, my toes. My whole being is buzzing with the feelings I can't process.

"I'm so sorry," he says. "Can I touch you now, or is it too much?"

"I don't know," I tell him, my voice small and desperate.

He gently reaches down and takes my hand—and it's good, it's needed. "More," I say. "I need more pressure."

Without missing a beat, he tugs me up from the chair and puts his arms around me, hugging me tightly to his body. It feels so good, so comforting, and tears begin tracking down my cheeks.

"Oh, Anabelle," he murmurs, holding me tighter.

"It's okay," I say, wanting to mean it.

"It's going to be okay," he whispers into my ear, and that's so much closer to being true. He kisses the top of my head, and I feel it everywhere. "Will they give you back your Santas?" he asks.

"They're evidence, I guess. We'll get everything back, but not before Christmas."

"We'll have a party to welcome them home." He must see the aghast look on my face because he smiles softly and adds, "A private party. I'll make cookies."

"Just don't let Cynthia help." I smile at him, but I can feel it slipping from my face as sadness floods me. "It hurts, Ryan," I say, gripping his shirt and feeling the hard, reassuringly strong chest beneath. "It hurts so much. It sounds stupid, but I hate to think of my Santas being alone on Christmas, in some police station evidence locker. It's not right."

"It doesn't sound stupid at all." He glances at the front door. "Let's go."

"Go?" I ask, thrown. It's late afternoon on Christmas Eve. I wasn't planning on *going* anywhere. We may only have two guests, but they said they were definitely going to be at Hot Chocolate Happy Hour.

I tell him as much.

"Cynthia and Jeremy said they'd host Hot Chocolate Happy Hour. We have somewhere to be."

"I don't think I can bear any more surprises right now," I warn him, feeling a tremor at the thought. "I have to call my father's lawyer for him. I won't bail him out—my mother can do that—but I will do this."

"Okay," he says, his brow furrowed. "And then we're going to go see your grandmother."

❄

I HAVEN'T BEEN to the graveyard for a few weeks, and tears pool in my eyes when I see there's a small potted Christmas tree next to the last, frozen bouquet I brought.

"You've been here," I say, glancing at Ryan in wonder. He's never once mentioned it.

He squeezes my hand. "I found out where she was buried from the funeral notice. Some mornings I stop by after going to the gym. I never had a grandmother, so I like to borrow yours sometimes."

"Do you talk to her?" I ask.

"I do. I tell her about you, mostly." He tucks my hair behind my ears. "I know she'd be so proud of you. Not so much of your dad, but she already told me she thought he was stupid."

"She didn't," I gasp, delighted despite myself.

"She did. And she told me that her granddaughter was smart and beautiful, and much too good for her deadbeat boyfriend. I've got to say I agree with her. About Weston *and* about me."

I nudge his shoulder. "Weston's not a deadbeat. He's rich and successful."

He grins. "There you are, with your truth bombs."

"But his soul is rotten. Yours is beautiful. You may not have the job you want right now, but you're going to find it, because that special light in you creates light in other people. However rich and successful Weston becomes, he will never have that. Ever." I brace myself, preparing to say something I'm not sure how he'll receive. "You know, I hope you're going to reach out to your brother soon, because I don't have any brothers or sisters, and I might want to borrow yours sometimes."

He traces the side of my face, his gaze distant. "You might like him better than me. He's less scattered."

"It would be impossible for me to like anyone better than you. I like everything about you."

"Even my lack of order?"

"It allows me to impose my own order."

He smiles at me and leans in to brush his forehead against mine. "I'll reach out to him. After Christmas."

"You don't need a fancy job to impress him, either."

"I know...and I'm going to call him. I even wrote it into that planner you gave me last week. I just have to think about what to say."

I'm not going to push him harder, not tonight.

Swallowing through a tight throat, I look down at my grandmother's grave and try to remember her as the titan from my childhood, not the woman with bones so brittle it felt like you could snap them by shaking her hand. "I love you, Grandma Edith. Thank you for bringing Ryan to me."

He pulls me into his side. "Thanks, Grandma Edith," he says. "I have trouble believing you wanted us together, but I'll be damned if I'm not grateful. I...if you wouldn't mind too much, I'd love it if you could give us a sign that you're with us." His eyes dart to me before he continues. "And that you approve."

My lips part, fresh wonder unfurling inside of me. "Ryan, I love you."

He draws me in for a soft kiss, his lips cold but his mouth so warm I don't want it to ever end. When he pulls away, he's smiling, but I can feel his uncertainty—about my grandmother, about Jake. About not being good enough. I'll spend the rest of my life wiping that away if I have to.

I glance down at my grandmother's grave. The remains buried beneath the stone are not my grandmother in any real sense, but this place still feels important. "Please, Grandma. Give us a sign."

Once we get into the car, Ryan turns toward me, his hands fussing with the wheel. "I thought maybe we'd go see the Christmas tree in Market Square. What do you say?"

It may be crowded, and I'm not sure I can stomach a crowd right now, but I don't want to disappoint Ryan. He has such a sweet look on his face, and his hair, which was in need of a trim when he arrived, is now always messy—in a tempting way that makes me want to bury my hands in it.

"Okay," I say.

On the way there, he turns on Christmas carols, and it's impossible not to smile when he starts singing along. I join him, and by the time we park the car and get out, the holiday spirit is reasserting itself inside of me.

"Now, the first order of business is to get you hot chocolate."

"I think I drink too much hot chocolate."

"No such thing."

He swings our joined hands back and forth, and giddiness fills my chest. We're together, Ryan's staying in Williamsburg *indefinitely*, and in a few hours it'll be Christmas.

A few minutes later, we're standing with a dozen other people around the tree. Carolers stroll past, and lanterns have been set out, and it feels incredibly merry.

"Can you put your hot chocolate down for a second?" Ryan asks, giving me a sidelong glance.

"Why?"

"Because you're getting on my shoulders."

"What?" I ask, half-laughing, even as my heart lurches in my chest.

"We're making new memories, Anabelle. I'm going to lift you onto my shoulders every year so you can see the star, because you deserve it every year."

"Ryan, I can see it anyway," I object, laughing harder even though my eyes are suddenly hot. "I'm more than three feet tall now."

"I don't care." He swears under his breath and looks around, taking in the presence of other people. "Or...if you don't want to, it's okay. I wasn't really thinking. I—"

"I do want to," I say, and he gets down for me.

Someone gasps and says, "Look, that man's proposing," in a whisper that can probably be heard in the North Pole.

I feel a prickling of awareness and discomfort, but Ryan says, "Nah, that's next year. I don't want to freak her out. I'm just giving her a better view."

"Ryan?" I ask, my heart pounding. *Next year.* "You're really staying forever?"

He's already told me so. Assured me of it. Whispered it to me while kissing his way up and down my body. But I don't think I can hear it enough. And this...

I stoop down to kiss his mouth and the side of his nose and his eyebrows, and he laughs and tells me to hurry up and get onto his shoulders. The people around us probably think we're nuts, but I do just that, and he lifts me up. With the wind tousling my hair and Ryan supporting me with his powerful shoulders and arms, the star seems almost reachable.

I really do feel like a Christmas witch.

"You're my star," he says, lifting an arm back to touch me.

The very instant he says it, the golden star winks out and comes back a glowing green. A gasp escapes me and Ryan at the same time, and even though I know it was almost certainly an intended effect, it feels like Grandma Edith heard us and gave Ryan his sign.

"Ryan," I say, my voice breaking, and he lowers me down, turning me to face him. "It was Grandma Edith."

"I think maybe you're right," he says with a smile and then leans in to kiss me right there, in front of the tree.

We stay for another hour or two, walking up and down DoG street. Ryan checks his phone a few times, probably for updates from the B&B, but I don't ask about it. It feels good to take time off with him. After a while, the pedestrians on the street thin out, everyone heading home so they can lie snug in their beds, and we stroll back toward the B&B. Part of me dreads going inside. The safety of my home has been taken away from me, and by a person who was supposed to protect me. But I also want to celebrate the holiday with Ryan and our friends.

Ryan seems a little agitated, and when I ask him what's wrong, he pulls me to a stop outside the front door.

"I know you don't like surprises, sweetheart, so I'm warning you, there's a surprise in there."

"Is it a good one?" I ask, lifting my hand to my throat.

"I hope so, and either way, I owe Cynthia and Jeremy big. Do you want me to tell you what it is?"

I consider the offer and his earnest expression. Once again, the butterflies in my stomach overpower the snakes. They're getting stronger. "No, let's go in."

So I open the door, and gasp.

At least fifty Santa Clauses have been arranged all around the foyer.

"Ta-da!" Cynthia says as she finishes arranging two of them on my desk. They're in an unspeakable position, which is so Cynthia I almost laugh. I would if my emotions weren't crushing me from the inside.

"Oh, goodness," I say, stopping in my tracks. Jeremy's next to Cynthia, and Joe, my sweet Joe, has already stepped in to fix Cynthia's Santa scene.

They're not my Santas, but a few of them are antiques—similar to the ones who are sitting in an evidence locker.

"You all..." My gaze finds Ryan. "How?"

He nods to Jeremy. "There were lots of comments about It's Christmas Again on Jeremy's video. People wanted to see your Franken-Santas, and a bunch of them volunteered to donate their old Christmas stuff to you. It's amazing how much of it stays in boxes." He must see my expression, because his face softens. "And by amazing, I meant heartbreaking. So we did the humane thing and took some of that shit off their hands. We've been messaging people all day, and Cynthia and Jeremy did some pickups while we were gone."

"We found a few of these guys at secondhand stores," she says, pointing to a resin Santa smoking what looks like a blunt. Not exactly an antique, but I know I'm going to treasure it forever. Because it will always remind me of this.

"And I held down the fort," Joe says. "It was very important. Hank and Rachel came downstairs twice, and both times, I asked them if they needed anything."

I grin at him, and suddenly I don't feel so heavy anymore. My Santas may be in lockup, but the one Santa that really matters is here with me, doing everything within his power to ensure I have a good Christmas. And I *am*. I can already feel it changing.

"Thank you, everyone. This is…I'm speechless."

I take a few steps inside, holding Ryan's hand as if it's my life-line. Part of me fears it's all going to disappear if I blink enough times. Ryan. Our friends. The Santa Clauses. When I reach the desk, I run my finger over a stuffed Santa that looks like it's from the 1970s, then pick up a wooden one with a worn belly. My gaze meets Ryan's, and I know we're both thinking about the estate sale we went to together and my nail-polish-makeover Santa.

He settles his hand on my lower back. "You'll get the other ones back, and when you do, they'll have more friends."

It feels like someone just stuffed a stocking into my throat. "I don't know how you managed to do all of this without me realizing it."

"Your tunnel vision occasionally works to our advantage," Cynthia says with a smile. "We'd do a whole lot more for you, you know." She nods behind me. "And for Ryan."

This is the real magic of Christmas. It can bring out the best in us. It's a reminder that we're meant to appreciate and love each other. And right now, standing in the lobby of the B&B I had no idea how to run when it became mine, I feel peaceful and whole in a way I never have before.

"Thank you," I tell my friends. Then I turn to Ryan. "*Thank you.*"

"I know your Santas are still in jail, but I can tell you from experience that jail's not so bad if a guy gets to come home to you."

"*Oh, Ryan.*"

I kiss him, in front of all of our friends, and they don't seem to mind terribly much. We laugh and position and re-position the Santas, and then we watch *Die Hard*, Jeremy's favorite Christmas movie, in the parlor.

It is not a true Christmas movie, but I won't be telling him that tonight.

It's late, we're all tipsy, and the only guests in the inn are currently Hank and Rachel, who declined to watch *Die Hard*, opting instead to go upstairs and have intercourse that made the floor creak. Cynthia and Jeremy have agreed to stay the night, and we all go to bed in our respective rooms, although I grab Ryan by the bottom of his shirt and lead him into mine.

"Seeing all those red bows around town has given me ideas," he says, giving me a wicked look.

I like that look, when it comes from him. It makes me feel a little wicked too, and wanton. "Would you like me to tie your hair up in a bow?" I ask as he shuts the door and backs me into the wall, the proximity to him making my whole body hum from pleasure.

He gathers my hands in his, easily encircling my wrists, and says, "I had a different idea."

"Show me."

And he does, thoroughly, making me come twice, the second time as the hour turns over at midnight—a fact confirmed by my digital clock on the bedside table.

"It's Christmas," I say, once I'm able to form words again. Using his teeth, he grabs the end of the bow he used to tie my hands to the headboard and pulls it loose.

"That could have come off at any time."

"I may have exaggerated about being a good boy scout. I just…I really want you to open one of your presents."

"You didn't need to get me more presents! You got me fifty-two Santas."

He waves a hand, giving me a flash of his tattoo. "That came later. I'd already finished my shopping. Come on. This is one you have to open now."

He opens my closet, then grabs a present wrapped in green paper from behind the hanging dresses.

"You hid it behind my clothes?"

"If we have kids, you'll obviously be in charge of hiding the presents. Your super secret place is much better."

I smile at him, imagining a little Ryan. "Deal."

He brings the wrapped present over to the bed, and I run my fingers over it, then shake it, all while he watches me, practically bouncing on his feet.

I open the wrapping paper, smiling to myself, and find a beautiful green sweater. When I run my fingers across the fabric, I know.

"You found one that has the same fiber blend as your blue sweater," I say through that same stocking-in-throat feeling. No one's ever taken such notice of my sensory preferences.

"I washed it so you can put it on now, if you'd like to," he says, his eyes flashing with excitement.

I do, then go to the closet and pull on a pair of underwear and my favorite snowflake pajama pants.

"Are you ready?" he asks.

"For what?"

"I assume you're about to play Santa Claus, and I figured maybe you'd let a former Grinch be your sidekick. I got something for everyone too."

"Even Hank and Rachel?"

"It would have been rude not to," he says, pulling on his clothes. I'm still in the closet, so I throw him his Santa jacket, now laundered.

He grins at me and tugs it on. "You ready?"

I glance at him as I pop the hidden button in the closet, and the secret compartment, built by an ancestor who didn't think much of Prohibition, pops open. I'm grateful for their love of alcohol, because this space is what saved the sunburst ornament, allowing it to be used in my plan. "Absolutely."

He steps close, his bare feet padding against the wooden floor. Saint Nick, who left the bed in a huff earlier, when we decided we'd like to use it, follows him, his tail twitching.

Ryan crouches to peer inside of the secret compartment and then stands up straight and grins at me. "Can we take them down in a big red sack?"

"Oh, absolutely not," I say. "It would look impressive, certainly, but we don't want to damage the presents."

Then he kisses me as if I'd just said something sexy. "How about we do it my way next Christmas?"

I'd rather not, and yet….he's promising that we'll be together next Christmas. "Only if we get to do it my way again the following year."

"We'll probably both agree your way is best by then," he says, grinning at me. "So the fourth year, we can just call it *our* way."

I only have so much self-restraint, so I kiss him. I have a feeling that will be happening a lot as we put the presents under the tree and hang the stockings by the chimney with care.

And even though it's not a very orderly way to carry on, I'm much too happy to care.

EPILOGUE
RYAN

"They must almost be here," I say, glancing at the clock. *Eight p.m.* I'm finishing the last of the appetizers—deviled eggs with cut bell peppers forming Santa hats.

Since we're going to be a year-round Christmas B&B, Cynthia and I have been experimenting with Christmassy recipes, trying to one-up each other. We'd probably be doing it tonight if she and Jeremy weren't at his mother's "famous" New Year's party, which he claims is only famous because it's so boring everyone always gets shit-faced before nine.

"But we're not going to," he told me before they left, waving his trumpet case at me. Apparently his mother always makes him play in front of the guests, and has since he was ten years old. "We're going to stay sober at this incredibly boring party so we can leave early and meet your brother."

"You just want to convince him to pull pranks with me."

"I do want that," he said with a laugh. "But I mostly want to meet the man who had the misfortune of sharing a womb with such a scene-stealer."

I've been living with Jeremy, technically, although I spend most of my time at the inn. So does he. His apartment is a perfectly fine two-bedroom with a view of the parking lot, but the B&B is something different. It's home.

I was also going to work with Jeremy's uncle—everything was settled for me to start in January—but Ada got in touch with me yesterday and said she'd talked to her "kid," and he could use a reliable line cook at a Greek restaurant that's a ten-minute drive from the inn. No experience necessary as long as I didn't think I was above hard work.

If I didn't think I was above shoveling shit or unclogging it from toilets, I definitely don't feel like I'm above washing plates. So I'll be doing that instead. The hours aren't great, but it'll give me plenty of time to help out at the inn during the day and to work out in the morning.

Cynthia's father thinks he can get me out of the assault charges given the "interesting" nature of the case, in exchange for doing community service. And Ada told me about a program that supports foster kids. I'm gonna help with that whether the judge orders me to or not. Anabelle keeps telling me that things might have been different for Jake and me if we'd had someone on our side, and I think maybe she's right. If I can be that someone for a kid, I'd be taking another step in the right direction. Making myself worthier.

As for Weston and Mr. Whitman...

They're both out on bail, surprise, surprise, but Anabelle was able to get an emergency restraining order against Weston. All the same, I don't think he'll be coming around anytime soon. He cares about his public perception, and right now it's not very fucking good. It didn't take the internet long to put the pieces together—that he and Anabelle's father were the ones who'd stolen the Santas and the ornaments, and Jeremy says he saw on social media that someone had spray-painted a Grinch on Weston's car.

It wasn't me.

It felt weird not to tell Jake about my new job and Anabelle and all of our friends. Especially Anabelle. That was what finally pushed me to make the call this morning, which just so happens to be New Year's Eve.

Anabelle, who has spent the last hour trying to keep me sane, furrows her brow. "What if Jake doesn't like me? I can't believe I didn't think of that before now."

"Impossible," I say, setting down the last deviled egg so I can grab her by the waist. She's wearing a long-sleeved red dress with a tempting little skirt that seems like it was designed to be flipped up from behind. Imagining it is a good distraction from my own nerves. "My brother's going to love you, and if he doesn't, I'll be the one who disowns him."

Jake is coming *today*, even though he had plans and the drive from Asheville is seven hours. That's a good sign, right? Most people wouldn't drive that far just to tell someone who'd pissed them off to go fuck themselves.

When he answered the phone early this morning, and I said *hey*, he was quiet for a second, before he said, "Jesus Christ, is it really you?"

"Is that a bad Jesus Christ or a good one?"

"Do you know how worried I've been?"

"No," I said honestly. "I figured you still might not want to see me."

"Well, you figured wrong. I've been emailing you practically every day for months. Ever since you and the guys turned the tables on Roark. Where are you?"

Five minutes later, after I'd told him about Anabelle and the inn and he'd told me about his girl, Lainey, he said he had to go, but I'd better not fucking leave the inn all day, because he was coming. And he was bringing his girl.

Again, all of that sounds pretty good. But my body is jumping around inside my skin, and it won't settle until I see him.

It's been so long. So damn long. I hate that he hasn't met Anabelle yet, and also that I don't know his girlfriend. He says she's the one.

I'm happy for him. Beyond happy. I know from experience that the love of a good woman can be the making of a man. But I don't have to be the smart twin to realize what it means—he's happy there, and I'm happy here. There's no way I'm leaving Anabelle, and there's no way *she's* leaving Williamsburg. Which means Jake and I are not going to live in the same place anymore. You'd think not seeing each other for a whole year would have gotten me used to that idea, but it hasn't.

Anabelle kisses me and then breaks away and leaves the room.

"Hey, isn't it my turn to freak out?" I call after her.

But she's back a few seconds later with a tumbler of whiskey for me and one for herself.

"Joe's making a playlist," she says with a soft smile.

There's a full house at the inn this week—all four "free" rooms, including my former room, are occupied, but there's space for Jake and Lainey because Joe has kindly offered to give up his room for the night.

I have a feeling Joe's playlist probably isn't going to be to my brother's taste, or mine, but I'll be damned if I don't feel supported.

"You're all too good for me," I say.

"I guess that makes you a lucky man," she replies, lifting her glass to clink with mine.

We carry the appetizer trays into the parlor, where Joe's wearing the fuzzy Grinch sweater I got him for Christmas.

"Will I be able to tell you apart?" he asks nervously, glancing out the front window before shrugging. "I can't see anything out there. The only thing I see is a reflection of myself. Speaking of which...I don't like that I might not be able to tell you apart."

"I've seen photos," Anabelle tells him in an encouraging tone.

"His brother doesn't have a scar on his chin, and he's not so..." She touches her shoulder and then expands her hands outward.

"Am I the Hulk?" I ask, laughing.

"Close enough," Joe says.

That's when the doorbell rings.

We all flinch. If Saint Nick were down here, I'm guessing he'd flinch too.

My gaze finds Anabelle, and she reaches for me, weaving her hand in mine. Thank God. We walk to the door together, and I open it, half-expecting it's not going to be Jake at all, but the close talkers staying in Room C.

But when the door cracks open, I find myself looking at....well... almost at myself.

Jake grins at me and then punches me in the arm—only to immediately shake out his fist. "Goddamn, why have you been working out so much? You're gonna make me look bad."

I pull him in out of the cold, wrapping my arms around him, everything inside of me quaking. Because, fuck, I missed him. It was like I was missing a piece of myself, all this time, and now Anabelle can finally know all of me.

I squeeze him so hard, he laughs and nudges me further inside. "Come on, buddy. We've got to get Lainey inside."

I finally register the person standing just behind him—a pretty woman with dark-brown hair, almost black, and bright-red lipstick. I let go of him and hug her next, because she loves my brother, which means I love her too.

"Come in," I say, ushering them inside. "I want you to meet Anabelle."

Anabelle's standing by the desk, looking a little unsure of herself, so I hurry to her side and wrap my arm around her. "This is the love of my life." I nod to Jake and his girl. "Meet Twin One, Anabelle."

Jake laughs, the corners of his eyes crinkling, and shakes his head. "Look at you, making me look bad. If I introduce Lainey as the love of my life now, it's gonna seem like I'm trying to one-up you."

"But it's still true," Lainey says with a smile. She looks around the foyer, grinning. "This place is amazing."

Jake lifts his eyebrows, and I know what he's thinking. I used to think it too.

We've rearranged the Santas, but there are still a dozen in this room alone. People kept on sending them after Christmas, from all around the country, and each time a package arrives, Anabelle says it's like Christmas. We still haven't been able to collect her old Santas, and won't until Weston and her father take a plea deal or go to trial, but we certainly have enough.

"You get used to all of the staring eyes," I say. "It helps when you give them names."

He grins at me, shaking his head. "Who are you, and what have you done with my brother?"

Anabelle leans her head against me and wraps her arms around me. "This, Jake Langston, is Hot Santa."

And, you know what? I like that title a lot more than "asshole." I think I'm going to keep it.

There are a lot of details to work out, and I have a lot of making up to do with my brother. A lot of the past to go over and get over. But right now, right here, I have my brother and my girl, and I am truly, deeply happy. I'm in love with my life, and this new year is going to be the best one ever.

I have Anabelle in my arms, and with her, I can do anything. Even help save Christmas.

ABOUT THE AUTHOR

ANGELA CASELLA is a romcom fanatic. Writing them, reading them, watching them—she's greedy, and she does it all. In addition to her solo releases, she was lucky enough to collaborate with Denise Grover Swank on three complete series, with more co-written projects to come.

She lives in Asheville, NC. Her hobbies include herding her daughter toward less dangerous activities, the aforementioned romcom addiction, and dreaming of having someone else clean her house.

Visit her website at www.angelacasella.com or Angela and Denise's shared website at www.arcdgs.com.